INSPERATUS

An unrelenting love. An undeniable destiny.

kelly varesio

Library of Congress Number: 2009920527
13 digit ISBN 978-1-58385-289-7
10 digit ISBN 1-58385-289-1

Printed in USA

Cover Photos:
©iStockphoto.com

First Edition: January 2009
10 9 8 7 6 5 4 3 2 1

To my parents (and little brother)—you're the best.

"And this is the condemnation, that light is come into the world, and men loved darkness rather than light, because their deeds were evil. For everyone that doeth evil hateth light, neither cometh to the light, lest his deeds should be reproved. But he that doeth truth cometh to the light, that his deeds may be manifest, that they are wrought in God."

— *John 3: 19-21*

INSPERATUS

prologue

the men's drunken laughter and endless taunting filled the frigid air as a lantern was lit from around a darkened, stone corner. The shadowed guard moved back further into a bend by the dungeon cell, watching the flickering light of the lone lantern grow brighter, the smell of beer filling his nostrils. The light finally exposed the two inebriated sentries shoving a bloodied and shackled prisoner through the dungeon's narrow hallway. The prisoner was a young man, perhaps in his early twenties, and his body was battered and bruised. As the lantern swung side to side, a swollen and bleeding bite mark could be seen on his neck.

The two sentinels staggered, each one holding onto an arm of the dragging prisoner. As they approached the last cell, by the shadowed man in the bend, the young prisoner was unceremoniously tossed into the iron-barred maw, collapsing upon impact. Locking the cell, they stumbled away, still laughing, and the lantern's light faded off behind the corner.

The only form of light was that of the crimson-outlined moon filtering through a dusty, barred opening at the height of the cell. The young man, wet with sweat, moved to his knees and stared at his ghostly white hands. The guard felt faint as he watched the prisoner suddenly hunch over and grab his stomach. The writhing man in the cell was wincing and panting. The guard could tell he was trying to bear up despite having been battered by the soldiers. With blood dripping down his neck, the prisoner looked up into the dim light of the cell and let out a stabbing cry. Four of his teeth speared into a point, appearing lengthened and sharp. He felt them inside his mouth, hands shaking hard, a look of shock surfacing on his face. He was changing, and with each change came horrible agony. His pain was evident in his posture; he was bent and twisted. His light brown hair streaked darker.

The guard could see through filtered light that the prisoner's once unobtrusive eye color was now a brilliant shade of red. The prisoner pulled himself to the other side of his cell where a dusty shard of a worn mirror was hung. His curiosity, despite his terror, was all that could have driven him to search his exterior, and the guard suddenly realized why he had been ordered by his own chancellor to place the mirror there.

Using the last bit of strength he had, the prisoner pulled himself up and looked into the mirror, but he shrank back with fear as he witnessed his strange appearance. As he brought up his hand to feel the mirror, he realized that his reflection was slowly vanishing; soon, there was no reflection at all. He had only a moment to see himself as a strange apparition. He was now a pale and gruesome sight.

The guard could not help but feel pity for the man. The prisoner's expression had gone from fear to something strangely numb. The captive slid his trembling hands over his stomach, to his chest, and stopped. His breathing—his panting—ceased. His hands rested there until he panicked; he could feel nothing, his heart was not beating. He turned with revulsion and eyes cold as ice toward the watching sentry. The guard watched in abhorrence, with knowledge that the boy saw the guard's own fear and antipathy within him. He dropped his spear at the sight of the young man and ran off behind the corner.

The prisoner's eyes had glared at him so questioningly. The sentry heard the man still: panting heavily, cursing whoever heard, and yelling for answers.

But neither the guard, nor anyone else ever answered his echoing screams.

chapter 01

the town was filled with the common bustling and busyness of life. Ladies held umbrellas high to shade their delicate skin from a blistering sun, and gentlemen walked with them, their suits fashioned to please. It was a rather common-man town, but it was a wealthy one nonetheless. The houses were quaint and lovely; gates were swung open and carriages were stationed elegantly along the roads; fields stretched across the plains with horses running blithely among the moss. In the midst of the town activity, the town's surgeon ran the hospital, the bank was flourishing, the grocer and baker's shop were eventful, the wine house and auction barn had its customers. There was even a learning institution near Sherwood Street called Barnard that was thriving.

It was May of 1843, and just past the boarding school, across the railroad tracks, Rein Pierson bent over to brush the dust from her dress. She stood straight, looking up at the sky and squinting. The weather in Teesdale was warm and the sky was clear, but it was dreadfully windy, and she had no umbrella or hat to shade her. She did not mind the sun, however, or darkening her skin in it. The weather was too gorgeous to hide from.

Despite enjoying the sun, the wind was so frustratingly fierce that it stirred the dirt from the road high into the air, making her cough. Her hair had been pulled back in a chignon, but she realized she had not made it tight enough. All she could see were the black, wavy wisps of her hair pulled from their placement as they tangled and blew into her eyes. Pushing them behind her ears, she lifted her dress above her ankles to walk across the wide, dirt road.

Opening a large iron gate, she saw old Jonathan Kendrick tip his hat to her. He was hunched over and sweating while raking his yard, as he did every day, around his prized flowers and small trees. He chose to do it himself over his servants.

"Good day, Rein," he said to her as he propped his arm on the rake, wiping his tanned forearm across his face.

She smiled back in greeting. "Afternoon, Mr. Kendrick. How are you today?"

He glanced up at the beaming sunlight, his heavily wrinkled eyes bunching up. He laughed looking back at her. "Ah, I'm well, dear girl, not granting the sun being hotter today than it should be, but I can see you do not mind it." Rein smiled as he took another break of laughter. "Is it Saria you're looking for?"

"Yes," she replied, shading her eyes with her hand. "Is she home?"

"She's most likely waiting for you, dear girl! Check around by the garden. She spends all day in that garden of hers behind the estate."

Rein smiled at him again and thanked him with a nod. She let go of her dress, letting it fall and drag in the dirt, and walked around the back of the estate into the garden.

Saria, a small, thin girl, sat in the garden with her head tilted to the side. She was almost hidden between the ivy and the different sorts of flowers she was watching from the bench. Her parasol was high and her bonnet large, shading her well from the sun. Her dark, braided hair was neatly tied in a ribbon, and she was in a most elaborate dress. She motioned for Rein to come near, but as she approached Saria's face grew grim with shock.

"Rein!" she called with frantic distress, sitting tall and slapping her hands on her thighs. "Dear Rein! What are you doing to your dress?"

Rein looked down at herself and laughed a little. "It is an old dress, Saria."

"An old dress especially! It is much too beautiful and antique to be dragging in the garden! Look at the bottom of it—already filthy!"

Rein blinked a few times as her hair blew into her eyes again. "Why do you worry so about my dress?" she asked, taking a seat next to Saria on the garden bench.

"Oh, please do not make me say it!" Saria huffed with intolerance.

Rein smiled. "I merely came to ask you if you've spoken with your father yet."

"About what?"

"Oh, please, Saria, the trip! Have you spoken to him about the trip?"

Saria looked bemused for a moment, but then sighed with a giggle. "I did, I did, yes. Have you written to your own father?"

"I don't need to write to him," Rein answered impatiently. "He is still in France, and I'm sure he won't respond. He hasn't for fourteen years."

Saria looked sad for a moment. "You want this much to leave?" she asked with a sigh. "America is beautiful, I am sure, but I do not think your idea of leaving England for it is suitable enough for my parents."

Rein stared down at her feet. "It isn't that I want to go to America. I just want to see the ocean, on a ship. Visit a place far from here—"

"Oh, Rein! Can you not give up these dreams of yours? We're meant to be here! We are barely even allowed to travel around the *town*, let alone to another country!" She sighed. "Rein, it's hard to have a serious conversation with you when you are so careless and obstinate about your attire! Look at you; you're dustier than an ox! Your beautiful face is filthy and your *dress*—"

"Is dress all you can think about?" Rein asked with a moan. Her smile won Saria over. "I've looked into it," she continued on, forgetting Saria's distaste. "I've spoken to Mr. Harold, the baker, and he said he's been there. It's wonderful. He said there is a port as close as Easington."

"But we have no reason to go," Saria replied, her green eyes looking hopeless. "Can I do nothing to change your mind?"

"Saria, it's only a trip. Only for a little while. Imagine seeing the ocean on a steamboat! Wouldn't it be wonderful?" Rein looked at Saria's father on the front lawn. "I have no one to stop me from going. My father has no choice. I have been out of Barnard long enough to do what I please. I have the money."

"You know that my parents tried very hard to get you out of that boarding school to live with us, but your father—" Saria cleared her throat, and then she smiled. "And I must agree, Rein, that I would enjoy a trip away from here." Her smile became mischievous. "And I *am* going with you…I'm just trying to persuade you to stay."

"Persuade me to stay?" Rein repeated, still pushing the lingering thought of Barnard from her mind. "Why persuade me?"

She slid her hand across her head to make sure her hair was in place. "I don't know. I just think it's an insensible notion. I *do* want to go with you, though." With a bite of her bottom lip and a teasing smile she pulled three pieces of paper from her hand purse.

"I've even made arrangements," she said slyly.

Rein's eyes widened and she smiled with overjoyed delight. "*Tickets*? You have *tickets*? You *rag*, Saria! You love to torment me, don't you? Well when? When are we going?"

"Tomorrow! I've talked to my father and he'll take us. Well, to the ship, anyway. Edgar, one of our senior butlers, is going to come with us. But knowing him, he'll leave us plenty be, and—"

"Saria, that's so wonderful!" Rein said, hopping off the bench and throwing her arms around Saria. "You already have tickets—my goodness!"

"Apparently it's one of the finest ships there are," Saria said, pulling away. She looked down and brushed off her bodice. "Oh, Rein! Look what you've done, hugging me like that! My dress is nearly covered in dirt!"

"I don't have a bit of dirt on me," Rein said with frustration. "I don't understand why you pester me so much!"

Saria sighed and then giggled, throwing her arms around Rein despite the dirt. "Oh, I love you just as you are, Rein! You beautiful piece of God's creation! You should just learn to work *with* your beauty instead of working against it. If only we were blood sisters, perhaps I'd have a slight chance of having as much beauty as you!"

"Don't say such a silly thing, ever. You're perfectly handsome! And tomorrow will be fine—*great*!" she said with a laugh, turning and making her way toward the front of the house. "We'll have so much fun together! It will be worth it, I promise."

"I am sure it will be."

"My! I have to pack!" Rein burst with excitement. "You will enjoy it, won't you?" she called, turning around to face her friend.

"Yes, of course I will. It just isn't common for women to leave home. We have everything we need. I'm not yet nineteen and you're barely twenty. We've still time to find nice gentlemen, marry, have children—" Saria stopped abruptly. "Oh, my! Nice gentlemen will be absolutely abundant on a steamship, won't they?" She clapped her hands together. "And any on a steamship ought to be rich, too, you know."

Rein shook her head with a grin. "Sometimes your intentions worry me."

Saria laughed. "Well then I shall meet you at your gate a little after noontime with my father. Is that all right? Then we can have lunch before we go."

"That's perfect," she returned. With a wave of her hand, Rein turned and exited through the iron gate, full of excitement for the next morning.

chapter 02

⚕

the sky was black with night, and the combination of the ocean mist and the downpour was freezing on Rein's face. There was a beautiful full moon that lit the ocean's surface enough to see the boat's reflection in the water. But a thick fog made it hard to see any farther than a yard or two. Despite the chilling downpour, the waves were rather calm. She shivered; her skin was crawling with chills. She was on the small boat with only Saria, Mr. Kendrick, Edgar, a skipper, and a small rowing crew. Despite the terrible weather, Rein did not complain about having to ride on a dinghy for a few miles to the new steamship that would eventually take her to America.

They'd arrived at Easington port late, and it was mainly because of Mr. Kendrick's slow going. The *Olde Mary*, their ship, had already taken off. Fortunately a skipper had approached them and, for an extra pound, said he would ride them to their ship on his dinghy—he said the *Olde Mary* had only been absent port twenty minutes or so. As absurd as the skipper's notion sounded, they accepted the offer, and were told that the *Olde Mary* was a most beautiful and high-class ship.

Reviewing what happened, Rein hoped it was not an illegitimate deal. The skipper was talking to Mr. Kendrick as they rode, and Saria was holding an umbrella above her head, but both she and Rein could see that it wasn't doing much good. Rein had brought only a small suitcase filled with a few dresses and belongings she thought would be needed for the voyage, but Saria had two large bags, full to the buckle. Edgar was holding them for her.

Rein pulled her cloak closer, and although it was wet, it stopped some of the chill. She continued gazing ahead. Any moment. They had been on the sea long enough...

Rein leaned forward, straining to see through the fog. There it was; her heart skipped a beat when she saw the ship suddenly appear through the fog. Her eyes widened at the sight of it, for it was massive in size;

bigger than any she had ever seen or heard of. Two large sails were blowing high above the smoke stacks, and it was tall and dark.

No wake was left in its path. This relieved Rein since it affirmed that the ship wasn't moving, and she was reassured that the deal she had made was, indeed, honest. The ship seemed to have seen them arriving behind.

The skipper moved aside and opened a drop on the side of his small boat. It was directly next to a step that led to a long stairway on the side of the massive ship.

"Yeh must go," he said loudly, over the rain and beating water. "We mustn't be much of an hindrance to em. Tisn't often ships stop and accept more passengers like this."

Saria turned and held her father. "I'll return soon. This is a wonderful chance for Rein, and I've always been so curious." She moved her umbrella up and threw her arm around him, kissing him before her departure.

"Have a wonderful trip, dears," he said. "Please take care! Watch them well, now, Edgar!"

The butler smiled from beside them, his arms full with only Saria's belongings. "Aye, Master Kendrick, of course!"

Saria's bony, old father waved one more time and held up his cap until he and the dinghy disappeared into the murkiness.

Rein looked around at the deck after climbing the stairwell, and just when she had gotten truly drenched, the downpour slowed into a slight drizzle. Through the mist, lit by the moon, a figure came into her view.

He was a hunched ghost of a man who was hardly visible, even in the moonlight. He wore an old commander's uniform, faded and frosted as if it hadn't been touched or washed for years. Two epaulets hung on his shoulders, a begrimed color of gold. His faded cap was torn in three spots, and though the brim was black and metallic, it was dull. But it was his eyes that made it hard for Rein to swallow; they were entirely white.

She heard Edgar murmur, "Oh dear," as she turned to Saria. He had caught sight of the eyes, too. Saria appeared a little shocked at the sight of them.

The old man's grin was twisted and snarled, and he opened what seemed to be a black door made of some sort of metal. It shrieked as he opened it.

"We saw the dinghy following us," the man said as to charm. "We're happy to have more passengers. I apologize for not being in port. Welcome to the *Olde Mary*."

Saria returned a cautious smile and Rein thanked him timidly. They followed him into the ship, a dank smell of salt filtering from the deck.

Rein brushed the water off her cloak and followed quietly after the man. He walked unhurriedly and with a limp, holding a candle he had taken from a sconce. His features were sunken in his face, and white hair curled out in a frizzy mass under his captain's hat.

When Rein reached the hallway, the salty, mildewed smell of the deck transformed into the more pleasant smell of cedar. She tried not to think about her upset stomach as she continued to follow the man. It felt like it was blistering with the unintentionally ingested rainwater she had partly consumed outside.

At that exact moment, Rein felt her breath escape her. She was treading on unexplored territory. There was only a butler whom she did not know with them. Saria's father was much too old to attend such a trip, and her two brothers were already married and had families of their own. Rein had no family as far as she knew, except her father: the man who left her when she was little. She had no brothers, sisters, cousins…

She wiped a wet tangle of hair from her face as if to push away her thoughts. Their eerie greeter led them through another door into a large, dim atrium.

"It is very odd that a dinghy would follow us for passage," he murmured from pursed, wrinkled lips. "Were you that desperate for a ride?"

"Not at all," Saria answered. "But we had just missed you, and that skipper had given us an excellent review of your vessel." She looked around at the intricate woodwork of the foyer. "I see he was not wrong."

Saria looked at Rein and smiled, and Edgar trailed behind them quietly, his top hat crooked from the wind. He was a portly man, and rather short. His face had all the joy of the world portrayed within it, but he stayed as quiet as a church mouse unless spoken to.

Rein returned Saria's smile, but her wary nature was still in full stride. Why did she feel the need to be so cautious? She laughed to shake off her apprehension. Saria did too, then.

She finally took in the beauty of the ship's interior. There were old chess tables that stood around the lobby, their games only half finished, pawns sitting undisturbed. Antique chairs and sofas were around the lobby with tables between them, and a lit fireplace stretched to the right of them, tall and made of stone. Suitcases, top hats, and canes were propped up against it. Two rocking chairs sat in front of the fireplace, slightly creaking back and forth, yet no one was sitting in them. The lighting there was very soft.

There were passengers sitting on couches reading torn books, staring coldly at them, but conversation was going on nonetheless. The cedar smell faded off as Rein, Saria, and Edgar left the hallway behind them. A chill struck Rein. For a 'spectacular ship,' the interior seemed years old.

She then realized the man with white eyes was no longer leading them but was pointing in the direction of the front desk. As she looked toward his hand, she did spot the desk, but behind it she saw a small date engraved on a stone block in a wall. It read 1702.

She stared with curiosity. Brand new smoke stacks; just the sheer size alone… no ship more than one hundred years old would be fashioned like that. A ship that old wouldn't even be around any longer. This was a steamboat, besides, and a bigger one than she had ever seen.

"Part of the décor," the man said from beside her. "We've built it around the date engraved, for show purposes."

She smiled. "That is amazing," she gasped. "It is so well fashioned."

He grinned back at her, bowing slightly for her to pass. She quickly approached Saria and Edgar, who already stood at the counter. The woman behind it was tall and pale, wearing an old, light blue dress that fit snuggly on her tall yet waifish body. She stiffly bent her hand beneath the desk, looking at Saria, and handed her an iron key to her sleeping quarters. Her long, bony finger pointed toward the left-hand hallway. Rein saw Saria gleaming with brisk cheer. Saria was more excited than she was, it seemed.

After Edgar took a key, Rein nearly went to follow Saria when the stewardess said, "Wait, miss." She approached the counter and the woman gave her a key, pointing to the right; the opposite direction of Saria's room.

"What?" Saria whispered.

As she looked down the dark hallway, Rein asked, "Sorry, but why is my room not *with* my friend?"

The woman's expression grew vague. "Hmm? Oh, your friend. I do believe that you are going to belong down *that* hall." The woman spoke in a deepened voice, her finger still pointing in the wrong direction.

"But why wouldn't I have the same sleeping quarters as she?" Rein questioned her again, a bit more assertively.

"Don't worry," was all the stewardess said in response and looked down at her desk.

Rein sighed mannerly, walking toward Saria. The woman, though puzzling, seemed a good enough and respectable person. She didn't want to cause any commotion; she hated causing disruption or conflict. She preferred to keep her thoughts and concerns to herself most of the time anyway. In spite of the fact that she had grown up without parents, which forced independence upon her at an early age, Rein tried to stay far away from being aggressive.

Rein looked down at her key. It had a room number engraved in it, and she glanced and saw Saria's key did as well. Their room numbers were significantly different.

Rein looked up gravely, but Saria was smiling with contentment. "This is odd," Saria said, giggling. "But, then again, so are *you*."

Rein cocked her head in disagreement.

"Remarkable detail," Saria said. "Making this ship look like it is from the previous century is amazing, isn't it?"

"Yes, remarkable," Rein replied, shaking her head. "Let's just explore and settle into our staterooms, and we'll meet out here afterward."

Saria laughed and bit her finger, nodding, but then giggled when she looked down at the umbrella under her arm. "Oh!" she said. "Here, let us trade, dear Edgar. Take my umbrella, and I'll take my other bag back."

The quaint man nodded and did as she asked, smiling the entire time. After Saria had taken her large bag, now holding both, the man was able to hold his own small one comfortably.

"Did you want me to see you to your room before we go? See, I'm down Saria's hall as well." Edgar began meekly.

"Oh, no thank you," Rein said, slightly dazed. "So odd…well, if I have a problem I will request another room."

"See you, then, in a bit," he said, smiling with his little mouth.

Rein relaxed at both his and Saria's jovial manner, but as she glanced up at the hallway frames, she noticed that they were marked strangely, which, thus, reinstated her anxiety.

Above Saria's hall and on the frame, M-Wing was engraved. She turned around the atrium and saw that above her designated corridor the frame read V-Wing. The other two halls were the B- and C-Wing.

After thinking a moment about what they all stood for, Rein walked over to the lounge area to greet a few of the other passengers before she went to her chamber. She noticed three people seated on a sofa talking, and she approached with the notion that she could perhaps take part in their conversation. Hoping that no one would have ill feelings toward her, she took a seat near a few people talking lowly.

"Good evening," she said pleasantly.

The two women looked up and stared at her. One cocked her head and replied, "Good evening."

The other said nothing, and the man sat there motionless, eyeing her up and down, staring with contempt. "Pouring out, is it?"

Rein blinked a few times in humiliation and looked down at herself. She was soaking wet and her dress was dripping onto the wooden floor.

"Oh," she muttered. "I'm sorry."

The man groaned back to her in reply.

"I'm Rein Pierson," she said again, hoping to crawl out of the ditch he had thrown her into.

The girl who had previously answered her said nothing, staring, and the man did not respond at all. With mounting frustration, Rein stood, picked up her parcel, and walked back toward the V-Wing. She was more than slightly confused as to why no one seemed to want to greet or introduce themselves to her, but left the thoughts behind on her way.

She glanced once more around the room and noticed that there was a small dining hall in the farthest corner of the atrium, and beyond that, two of the hallways, the M- and the C-Wing, were stretched out and fading off into darkness.

Piano music began to fill the air, and Rein turned to see a young woman playing a tune. Changing her mind again, she yawned and took a seat in a grand chair that was isolated from the others. She had a headache from the ride to the ship, and she thought if she sat and closed her eyes a moment and listened to the piano, she would relax. It was an unfamiliar, melancholy tune, but she was enthralled by it. She planned to retire to her chamber, down the West hallway that was marked V, as soon as the song ended.

chapter 03

t he young man opened the porthole in his chamber. He had seen something moving on the deck out of the corner of his eye; he stared through the mist, and saw, in shock, that there were two girls being spoken to by the captain. After they exchanged a few words, the captain led them into the ship, and they disappeared from sight.

He stood back in his room, closing the porthole tight. His mouth was open in shock. There was never any noise there. It was always quiet and calm, and new passengers were more than rare. Turning and pacing to his front door, he opened it and walked silently into a dark corridor.

When he reached the edge of the hall, he stared out into the atrium. The captain was already in the lobby with the two women. The man ducked back into the shadows of the hall and continued to watch. One of the women caught his eye instantly.

She was standing very quietly in the foyer, clothed in a dark, tight dress, holding a dripping wet cloak over her arm. She was the taller of the two, long and slender, yet voluptuous. He felt tightened at such a Junoesque appearance. Her black hair was wet and draped against her face from the rain, despite its pinned up style.

He stepped back into the hall as she walked a little closer. He was still examining her when she began walking nearer to the stewardess at the desk. She approached a candle, and under its glow he was able to see her face in a good light.

She was incredibly beautiful; the prettiest woman he had ever seen. She had bright blue eyes and flawless lips. Her face was perfectly symmetrical and thin. She was wearing a cravat tucked into her bodice with a netted brace across her bosom, and below she wore a long, dark underdress that draped to the floor and made her body impenetrable. Long sleeves hung down smoothly, and at the wrists the sleeves were tied together and frilled. She was dressed formally, but simply still. Her figure was so striking, and her manner of speech, from what he could hear as she conversed with the stewardess, had all the elegance that any man could want.

He glanced at the other girl. She was plain, but well dressed—too extravagantly for his taste—and was shorter in stature than the other girl. Her green eyes were less elegant, and she was talking without end, giggling and beaming with gaiety. As polished a girl as she was, his eyes continued to stray toward the other. For some reason, a strange feeling kneaded at him when he looked at her.

She flashed a glance in his direction, and he withdrew back into the hallway; so far back he couldn't see the foyer anymore. She hadn't seen him, and he didn't want her to.

Perhaps she would make it somewhere, wherever she thought this ship was headed. Or she might be another victim snared by the captain. He tried to think nothing of her as he turned back down the hallway and re-entered his stateroom. She was probably a typical first class woman who wanted nothing of...

An immediate knock on the door startled him, and as soon as he pushed his thoughts aside, he apprehensively answered it.

"Hello, Romanoff," the young man said as he opened the door from inside, regaining all composure.

"I felt her!" Romanoff, a thin, sharp-featured man said in exasperation.

"What the devil are you talking about?"

"The Mistress! I felt her in my head. I think something terribly good is going to happen! Can't you feel it?"

The man inside the door sighed. "No."

"Well I know you saw those women as well," the man stated blankly from the hall. "Why didn't you greet either of them? Perhaps that is what Mistress—"

"Are you bloody mad? What do you mean, 'Why didn't I greet any of them?'"

Romanoff laughed, his French nature prominent. "No I'm not mad; how dare you! I'm entirely serious!"

The young man huffed, cocked his head toward the Frenchman, and closed the door on him. Sighing and faltering deeper into his bedroom hollow, he collapsed onto the end of his bed; his elbows leant on his knees. He ran his fingers through his hair in contemplation.

He could not meet the girl he had instantly been attracted to. He felt so strange about it. He had never once seen a woman like her, and she seemed to hold more meaning for him than he could understand. *Did she have anything to do with…?*

Shifting his mystified eyes forward, he noticed a few books on his dresser that were not his. They belonged to Carden Romanoff, the man who had just been there. He sighed and stood again, picking the books up and walking back into his foyer. He left his room for the hall to find Romanoff and give him back his books, and he did so without a second thought of the women, because he knew he would see neither of them. Those ladies would *not* have been assigned a chamber down the West hallway.

chapter 04

☿

Rein still sat in the lobby, her wet cloak now around her arm, and bag in hand. The piano piece had ended, so she stood to go down to her chamber.

As she entered the V-Wing, her eyes couldn't help but wander up and down, carefully studying portraits lining the corridor walls. There were portraits of families, couples, children, and single persons. *Strange*...there were no portraits in any of the other halls she had seen. Also, the expressions and positions of the people were alarming, and she felt her heart beginning to beat wildly. She shifted her glance to straight ahead of her, right down the hall. The sconces' candlelight began to appear dimmer and dimmer as she walked, as if the hall was supposed to be closed off. With a shake of her head and an uncertain smile, she cleared her throat and searched for her room number. Why was she feeling so peculiar?

Just as her heart had begun to calm, she noticed a shadow drawing near to her out of the dimness. She heard footsteps clicking on the wooden floorboards, and she stopped cold when she realized that the dark figure was walking in her direction, slowly becoming more visible as it neared. Her heart swelled and hammered ferociously, and her mind began to exaggerate things.

But then the deep pounding of her heart relaxed into a light, unnoticeable beat. It was an oblivious gentleman approaching from the darkness with a few books in his hands, and a regretful feeling overwhelmed her for her senseless panic. What harm—? Her thoughts suddenly stopped as fast as her footsteps did. She could see the man more clearly under the sconces as he neared, and she lost her breath when she got a better look.

His muscular physique clung to her eyes from the distance. His hair was longer: it was about three quarters down his neck, somewhat long in the front as well, and a bit shaggy. It was very dark in color, but the terrible lighting made it difficult to tell whether it was black or brown.

He wore no hat, either, to her surprise. It was the custom for men to wear hats, usually without exception, but it was no bother to her. She could see already that he was tall and very broad-shouldered, and his waist was thin, which enhanced his build even further. He strode toward her with a walk most precise, like a trained soldier from the military. There wasn't the slightest sign of a slouch in his posture, yet his neck was not held tight or high by the stiff collar men generally wore. In fact, he wore only a loose white shirt—the sleeves thin but full to the wrists where they buttoned—under a waistcoat with a small and simple white cravat. His boots were displayed above his dark trousers.

She waited for him to notice her as she stood motionless in the corridor. He was still looking down, organizing his reading in his strapping arms, and when he came within a few feet of her, she felt captivated by his entire presence.

She could see clearly that he was young and extraordinarily handsome, but very pale. A shadow of bristles covered his chin and jaw, and after reviewing the fact that he was unshaven, wore no hat, and had on only a simple, loose shirt, she surmised that he was probably a rugged type of character. Though he gazed downward, his eyes unseen, and despite being unshaven, his features were perfect: his face was chiseled immaculately, and his nose and chin were very well-balanced. He had a strong jaw, short sideburns growing down his face, and flawless eyebrows. But then she noticed there were lifted scars on his face—very thin, but long. They were almost unnoticeable; almost.

He glanced up while she was in the middle of studying him. There was a sudden change in his previously calm expression; he was startled.

Then one of the sconce candles caught his eyes, and her insides wrenched. She stared at him speechlessly, her captivated feeling beginning to twist. His eyes were as unfeasible as the first man's were. Although this man had pupils, full and dark, his surrounding irises were a fiery red.

He closed his eyes in a long blink and opened them just as slowly, altering his stare hard past her, to the atrium, and then back into her eyes.

She bit her lip quickly in frustration at herself for wearing such a shocked mask. He probably thought her an arrogant woman for making such an astonished face toward him. But as she stared, she realized that despite their alarming color, his eyes were gentle.

"I'm sorry," she had to say, giving up any chance of an elegant greeting. She looked down and then changed her expression to a more formal one as her head rose. "I didn't mean to stare, sir."

He looked grave in his stillness, and she could've sworn he muttered something to himself grimly. But although he returned her stare, his manner seemed reluctant. He stumbled to reply.

"Don't…don't apologize," he said as if he was only talking to cover up thought. "It's happened before."

She began to notice the smell of fresh, pleasing cologne coming from him, and the scent made her heart flutter. Although his burning red eyes were tense, he was charming, and she already felt pity for him because of his subtle facial scars and unique eye color. He had a heavy British accent, one that was elegant yet masculine and appealing. It seemed antiquated. As she memorized his appearance, all of his attributes began to seem alluring. Especially his eyes.

"I'm sorry," she repeated, pulling her head out of that daze. "There was no reason…it's just your eyes are such a bright…*red*." She quickly tried to correct herself. "But they are rather stunning."

He looked genuinely shocked, as if he hadn't heard a description like that before about himself. He looked at his books. "Stunning is an…an uncommon way of describing them," he stuttered. "There was a laboratory accident I was in…where I am employed." He looked at her small bag and then at her. "I live on this ship. Travel with it, working."

Rein hesitated as his eyes met hers, piercing any veil by which she was covered. She laughed with refinement. "It's odd, because you aren't the first person with…" she stopped. She was ruining the conversation, and all chances of having another one with him.

"I understand," he said quietly.

"It's just that…for a moment, your eyes make you almost seem—"

"Blind?"

She huffed in anger of herself. That was exactly what she was going to say, but she tried to continue speaking more elegantly, returning the wrong answer. "I wasn't going to say…You don't look…"

He stifled a laugh and cleared his throat a second time. "It's all right. People tell me that often as well, and I am, in a fashion—"

"Oh, I'm sorry," she murmured.

He clenched his teeth with his head down, as if he were hiding as much of his face as he could in shadow. Perhaps it was that he hated the fact that he was blind. Was that it? Or those subtle scars? But he had to be capable of seeing slightly because he had met her eyes.

Hoping that she would make him regain his composed bearing, she introduced herself. "I am Rein Pierson," she said with delicacy. "I've just boarded—"

"I know," he replied quietly, his masculine, smoky voice deepened.

She paused at his quick words, but continued respectfully. "I'm from Teesdale, England. I cannot explain to you how much I've wanted to travel on a ship," she said. "To the U.S.—"

He cut her short again, but this time he was perturbed. "T-to America? Who told you that?"

She felt a sudden chill engulf her. "I was told by two different men."

He appeared to be pondering her words for a moment. "But…God. How long were you on the deck?"

"Only for a short time." She felt her eyebrows dip in question. "You saw me on the deck?"

He stammered in reply. "I saw…yes, and the small vessel you traveled on. But you're also soaked, which is indication enough."

She smiled kindly, nodding in acknowledgment. "I know; it's raining ridiculously," she said, looking down and holding out a heavy part of her dress and then dropping it with a squish. "And I am glad I found someone on this ship that is pleasant about my being drenched."

He sighed, and she thought for a moment he didn't like her remark. But she soon understood that he was partially ignoring her when she said that. He was thinking about something else.

"The man who let you in," he said gravely, looking at the floor to the side of him. "He's wearing a white coat, queer eyes I understand you've noticed." She spotted him pulling up his shirt collar closer to his neck as he was talking. "You mentioned I was not the only one you saw with an uncanny eye color."

"Yes," she replied. "He led my friend and I into the ship from the deck, but—"

"Did he give you anything?"

"No, I only met him briefly on the way in."

His temperament was becoming severe. "Please try to stay away from him. He does things…well, he isn't a *well* man."

"Oh, I see." Rein met his intense eyes as he looked up with his mouth firmly closed and then down again. "I don't think I quite understand," she said on a different subject. "If you are, in a fashion, blind, how did you…?"

He seemed to realize she wasn't paying full attention to what he had been saying and sighed. "I am not really, *truly* blind," he said with another puff of breath. "My vision is much different than your own. It isn't…normal."

Rein looked down as he spoke those last words. He wasn't blind, but he saw differently? She wondered what he meant exactly but didn't want to make him any more uncomfortable than he already was.

"Sir? May I ask; what is your name?"

He stood still and gazed at her hesitantly. "Traith. Traith Harker."

She smiled. "It is nice to meet you, Mr. Harker," she said with a delayed formal greeting. "You are not…ill, are you?" she asked with a casual gentleness, hoping that there was a reason for his extreme pallor.

"No," he said with a puzzled expression.

"Then why are you so tense?" she asked with good intent. "Something must be the matter. If I can help in any way—"

"I'm fine," he hastily returned. "Thank you." He glanced down at the key she had in her hand. "May I?" he asked with his voiced toned down and his manner again grave. His eyes were intently focused on the key, so she handed it to him without question. "Why are you down this corridor?" He asked almost inaudibly, nearly so that she thought he was speaking to himself. "Your key could not…" He suddenly stopped talking, and his eyes grew wide as he read the tiny number imprinted on the metal.

"It does belong down here," she replied, holding her parcel up a bit. "The woman at the front desk gave me a key for this hall specifically. Though I'm not sure why." She looked down at the key he was holding. "She said I would need that chamber. It's strange though, because I came with a friend, and we were not placed near one another."

"Who have you come with, Miss Pierson?" he questioned, standing still.

"I am traveling with my friend, Saria Kendrick."

"You've not come with a male escort?"

"Yes. My friend brought a butler from home to escort us," she said. "He is escorting us both, but mainly her. I have no living relatives to assign me my own escort, other than my father, but he's been away in the Queen's service."

"Oh," he said in a breath. "The...the *Queen*. Right."

She knew she had made a curious expression at his words. "Yes," she said, smiling. "Is there something odd about that?"

He shook his head and chuckled very lightly. "Forgive me," he said, clearing his throat. "Never mind. What I said—"

"But it is odd, isn't it?" she asked, reverting back to the previous topic. "Odd that I am not with my friend?"

He didn't reply, then, but continued to stare at her key.

"What is it?" she finally asked with wonder about his reluctance to reply. "Am I not supposed to be down here?"

"No...no, that isn't it." He handed her back the key. "My own chamber is—" he stopped himself quickly. "Your quarters are a few doors that way, to your left."

He walked right past her without another word, the books in his hand no longer the target of his stare.

She turned and gazed at his back, but she couldn't let him go. "Will I see you again?"

He stopped a moment, turning only his head. "Miss Pierson, I must warn you, if you don't get to your room and change, you'll catch a bloody chill in this hall. Do not linger, please."

He smiled a bit more than he had all the other times. For a moment, his eyes were constant, and he was looking directly at her. By the time she had gotten a quick glimpse of his white teeth from his smile, he turned away. That smile, she remembered because it was friendlier than those she had yet seen from him. To her dismay, he was too far for her to see him well. He soon faded into the hall from which she had come initially.

Rein leant back on the wall of the corridor, raising and holding her parcel, cloak, and umbrella in her arms. She had just met a man like no other. Traith Harker. He seemed kind, unselfish...despite his wary looks and undecided manner. She felt like she could trust him, and she had no earthly explanation as to why. She had just met him, but a fluttering feeling tickled her when she thought of his face. Did she like him? She did. She knew she did, because for some unknown reason she felt different, even in that few minutes she was near him. Even at the age of twenty, she had not yet had a relationship with a man. She'd been avoiding them, perhaps, but even still…she had never seen a man that controlled her thoughts so. It was like he was trying to keep her safe, and she felt thawed in the cold corridor.

She still heard him walking, the sound of his footsteps clicking against the wooden floor. But then they stopped a moment. They hadn't just faded; he had stopped. Was he going to come back? Then they began again.

She did wonder why he had stopped, but she had to stop thinking about him for the time being. It was late, and she was very tired. She turned and walked a few doors down until she came to her chamber: room 1237. She placed the key in the lock, turned it, and opened the door.

chapter 05

as the door creaked inward, light from the chamber instantly lit up the gloomy hall. Rein walked forward in awe of the candlelit room. Someone had made it ready for a passenger, for her. It was not at all small, as she had thought, but very vast. There was a large bed in a long hollow in the wall to the left side. Black lace was layered below the mattress, and the sheets were black satin. The walls were painted a beautiful shade of red. It seemed as though the room, shrouded in dark décor, was meant for something sinister. Rein chuckled to herself in astonishment of the chamber, but something scratched at her; something struck her as unusual.

The peculiarity of the chamber made her think about it all: the man with no pupils, the eerie presence that seemed to linger on the ship, the dimness, the coldness of it…the sheer, colossal size of it. So far as she had seen, the only deck of the ship was located in the front where she and Saria had come in, leaving much space unaccounted for. The atrium was large, and so was her stateroom, but even if most of the other rooms were equally grand, there would still be space unaccounted for. Something else had to be taking up space in the vessel for it to be so enormous. It all seemed an impossible feat of building. She would have heard of the building of this ship somewhere, due to its amazing complexity of design and enormity. On top of it all, the luxurious ship was run on coal, with smoke stacks, which was barely fathomable.

She walked forward and, with a sigh, sat quietly at the foyer table. Despite the oddity of both the ship and its passengers, she found herself smiling. Security. She felt it, but she shook her head in disbelief. She knew better than to trust those feelings. She had felt secure with her father for a long time, but that proved to be wrong. What's to say she wasn't wrong about it this time?

She jumped quickly off of the chair when she remembered how wet she still was. Laying her cloak and bag on the wood beneath her, she bent over and untied her thin boots, slipping them off and setting them next to her on the floor. She undressed, sliding off her frozen gown and then her still-soaking, skin-sticking undergarments. With an unending shiver she was naked, and she quickly pulled out a chemise from her bag and threw it over her head, letting it fall down her body.

Her eyes went to the door as she reached for another gown from her suitcase. She had first seen him walking past that door, past the room she was in now.

His eyes; piercing, red eyes…

A most peculiar man, but so dashing! Not wearing modern attire, and, though he had to be close in age to her, his manner of speech and behavior seemed so old-fashioned. He was so pale, but so deeply intriguing! It was as if she needed to just watch him, just to absorb his motions and his speech. She wanted to see if he was always dressed in such an informal way. She wanted to see if he had any deeper emotions, as he seemed to conceal as many as he could.

She was so confused—she was never a girl to fall for someone. In fact, she had up until then doubted the feeling of love was real. Although she wasn't *in love*, a sudden feeling warmed her like a winter coat—one that was completely novel to her. Without even knowing that man, she yearned to, and that had never happened to her in her life.

But she tried to forget about him and her feelings because she knew he was one of many passengers on board, and the chances of anything forming were slim to none. Even still, with all her expectations, she was ecstatic. It was merely the beginning of a fairly long voyage; one she'd been dying to go on.

After taking a few minutes to hang her dresses up in the chamber wardrobe, Rein walked to the huge featherbed and fell upon it, breathing deep. Relaxing her tense and weary body, she ran her fingers through the silky covers. She felt safe; somehow, for some reason, with their only meeting having been a particularly odd one, she knew that the man she had just met would watch over her. Somehow his eyes would always be straying toward her on this ship, wherever she was.

She laughed at her instantaneous and inexplicable feelings. He was a complete stranger. She didn't know who he was, where he came from, or what he was like, yet she trusted him.

She felt herself sinking deeper and deeper into the feather mattress, and her eyes slowly closed. In no more than a few minutes, she had drifted off into a much needed sleep.

chapter 06

⚕

the moment Rein opened her eyes, she realized it was no longer night, but the next morning. Rays of sun were filtering through the porthole next to her bed, lighting up the dust particles that floated in the air. She was comfortably sunk into the luxurious bed. Yawning, she sat up, and then stood up sleepily to stretch, the swaying of the ship causing her to totter. She turned lethargically and looked at the large bed she had fallen asleep on. It was so comfortable that she nearly wanted to lie back down on it and sleep the day away.

But then the recall of last evening's events shocked her to a complete awakening. She realized she had forgotten all about meeting Saria after unpacking. She had even managed to momentarily forget that she was on a ship, on the trip she had wanted to be on for so long.

Perhaps she would run into that man again as well; ask him further why he had been so concerned. She really did want to see him again, and her reasoning didn't even seem liable enough to *her*. But she wanted to concentrate on the way she had felt last night, all of a sudden—see if it was a truly genuine feeling. She liked it. She wanted to feel the butterflies again.

Looking down at herself, she realized she was still only in a chemise. She felt the pillows and noticed they were wet from her previously soaking hair. She stumbled over to her bag and pulled out a petticoat and then a dress, tying the corset from the front as tight as she could. Once she was dressed decently enough, she slipped on her shoes. They had mostly dried overnight, to her relief. She tied them quickly and took a glance in the vanity mirror at her side. Her hair was stringy but still in a bun. She knew Saria would be distraught at the sight of her, but she ran out the door anyway, locking it behind her.

As she walked into the tall, dome-shaped lobby, she became acutely aware of her hunger; she hadn't eaten since earlier the day before. She glanced around, hoping to find Saria and have breakfast with her.

She breathed a sigh of relief when she recognized her friend sitting on a stool in what appeared to be a beverage lounge, looking unworried; but then again, she usually was. Edgar was sitting there as well, a little farther away. He seemed to have found someone to converse with.

Rein paused in her steps a moment when she noticed who was at the entrance door that they had come through last night. The gentleman with the white eyes stood there still. Rein had a sudden, fanciful notion that he never left that post, but waited there, ready to devour anyone who dared run toward that door.

Then she knew she was being ridiculous. He was just an old man with a terribly ugly look about him. Why was she so alarmed? Because the handsome man she had met last night had told her he was unwell. She believed that stranger.

She looked back over at Saria and headed for her, pacing quickly past the staring eyes of those around her. Saria stood up and encouraged her to come over to where she was sitting. As Rein followed her order, she noticed the troubled expression on Saria's face.

"Rein, you left me alone last night after you proposed to meet me," she said, replacing for her concerned expression a cheery one. "What happened to you? I almost went to find you, but I was so caught up in my unpacking and settling in that I fell asleep!" She sighed with a smirk. "Odd, isn't it?"

Rein sat down on a wooden stool next to her. "I fell asleep, too," she sighed. "I didn't mean to, but so much happened to me after you left, and I was quite tense."

"What ever for? What happened?"

"On my way to my chamber, I met a peculiar gentleman named Traith Harker. He seemed worried about me being here, and he specifically said I should stay away from the man who let us in last night."

"The man with no eye color?"

"Yes, him. And while we're on the subject of strange eyes—" Rein choked a moment before she could speak. "Mr. Harker's were…"

Saria sighed at her hesitance. "They were what?"

"Vibrant *red*."

Saria's head lifted, and she snorted a laugh. "Vibrant red? Rein, I—"

"Yes, as if they were on fire!" Rein stared at her with intensity, but

Saria's eyes returned an incredulous gaze. "He said he was in a laboratory accident. Something hit his eyes or…it was terrible enough that it affected his eyes… and vision. I felt so awful because I pointed out—"

"He's *blind*? And you asked him about it? My, Rein! Lord!"

"Well, I didn't exactly. He isn't stone blind. He said there was something different about his sight, though, like something wrong. Oh, but Saria!"

"You *liked* him! Rein, you *like* someone? My! Was he very handsome?"

"Incredibly!" Rein laughed, sitting straighter. "He was incredibly handsome, but very, very odd."

"You *must* show him to me! He sounds like your type."

Rein smirked.

Saria squealed in delayed excitement. "Oh, Rein, what if he's the one? Your first man, dearest! Oh, my heart is so happy for you! And I should like to think that he was immediately charmed with you, too, seeing as your beauty could never be surpassed!"

"Thank you." Rein had to laugh at Saria's excitement for her. "I do appreciate your comments, Saria, but please, let's not get ahead of ourselves. The next time I see him I will be sure to point him out." She was biting her lip to hold back more laughter. "I'm sure this is nothing anyway."

"Always thinking like that! It very well could be something, if your pursue it! Well then," Saria asked after a laugh and a sip of her drink, "what did this most charming man you found warn you about, regarding the man who greeted us?"

"He said he wasn't well, and to not deliberately be near him."

Rein flicked her sight over to the white-eyed man. He curled his shriveled mouth her way, and a chill ran down her neck when she felt his eyes lock onto her. He turned with a nod to her and crept out the door he was guarding.

"Rein, he seems quite all right to me," Saria said. "Quiet and sweet, but his eyes are terribly uncommon. Something's definitely wrong with him, but it isn't serious." Saria giggled without noticing Rein's eyes straying away toward the door. "Or maybe it was that he was in the same laboratory accident your Traith Harker was in. Well, in any case, the captain came up and offered me this warm, spiced tea, here…"

"The man with the white eyes is the *captain*?" Rein asked swiftly.

"Yes, didn't you know? He told me himself." Rein sat in thought as Saria continued. "This drink is so palatable! Oh yes, and I have to admit, my room is beautiful."

"How can a madman be a captain of a ship?" Rein asked, more hysterical. "How does he have time to offer you drinks, when—?"

"Rein!" Saria blundered. "Why are you going to take a stranger's word about another stranger? For all you know Mr. Harker could be a terrible and nasty person and the captain could be a kind and unselfish one. You mustn't be so judgmental! He probably has a man to assume navigation when he needs a break! He cannot possibly be steering this ship *all* the time."

Rein sighed quickly in frustration, because Saria was right. "I don't know," she finally answered. "When I met Mr. Harker last night, he strictly told me to keep away from that man. He seemed so trustworthy."

Saria laughed again in the middle of her speech. "Yes, men can do that. My dearest Rein, you need relax yourself! And as far as trust goes, the captain seemed as trustworthy as could be when he conversed with me." She took a long breath. "So anyway," she blathered, "My chamber kept me ever so busy! I ate the delectable foods I found in the icebox. There were pretty blue walls and wooden flooring. Small bed, but the sitting room was spacious enough." She tilted her head in wonder and stopped her rambling. "What is it? What's the matter with you, Rein?"

Rein looked down and shook her head side to side. "My chamber was large, dark, and decorated as if centuries old." She paused a second and could feel Saria scanning her. "It was strange."

"By God, Rein," she stated with a groan. "Your hair is more dishev-eled than your clothes! Haven't you thought of doing your hair over?"

Rein glared disturbingly at Saria and her composure. "Is that all you think about? You cannot possibly focus on anything else for very long, can you?" Saria laughed, but Rein knew that was her nature. "I'll go back to my chamber and fix my hair, if it irritates you that much," Rein said, stiffening.

"Oh, don't be sarcastic, I'll manage to be seen with you," Saria said, holding in another laugh, and her long, dark hair fell onto her cheeks with a movement of her head. "It's funny; this ship and its chambers may seem rather chilling, but it's all a façade; part of the décor that makes it hallmark."

"You seem quite free from care," Rein replied. "I assume you must have spoken to the people around, as well."

"Of course," Saria replied. "I've talked to a few of the passengers, yes, and although they weren't very conversational, they weren't ignorant."

That didn't mean anything. Saria was probably talking so much that she didn't notice that no one was paying attention to her. Rein wanted to speak again, but Saria's attention was elsewhere.

"Do you see that man over there?" Saria asked, changing the subject. "Look! He's looking at us!"

Rein gave an irritated smile when Saria bit her lip with excitement. "You like him, do you?" Rein asked, void of enthusiasm. "You've probably been staring at him for awhile, hmm?"

"Yes, I do admit I have. He's quite handsome, and he's been talking to others all morning, but I've been trying to get his attention."

"Then shouldn't you go over there and greet him with a curtsy or something of the sort?"

"No! I couldn't possibly! He's with so many others right now."

"That has never stopped you before."

"Look! Look again! He's coming this way!"

chapter 07

the man Saria had been watching was tall and slim, slimmer even than Traith Harker. The two were probably the same height, but Harker had much broader shoulders than he. It was amusing to be able to so quickly perceive the differences in those two men, and the difference between her and Saria's choice of them.

The gentleman Saria was staring at appeared rather pretentious and rich, his features were sharp and cold. But he was dressed well enough that it made him much more attractive. Traith Harker had features so flawless he seemed unreal. His face was naturally handsome, but she had to look underneath the thin layer of scars and bristles, past simple and casual attire, and through his blunt mannerisms, which she had roughly seen the night before, to see his allure. That was something Saria was unable to do.

And there she went again, thinking on about the man she didn't know.

The man approaching was smiling to others and dipping his head to them. He was incredibly fashionable, as if royalty, and he had long brown hair that was tied back and large, dark brown eyes that matched his large eyebrows and high, stiff-collared suit. His face was slightly aged, but it was decently handsome; it was pointed, but prestigious. He came up to the lounge and asked for a hot drink, and as he leant over the side, Saria leaned back and turned around her seat to view him. Saria's back was now to Rein and she was facing the man with a smile, which must have made him speak.

"Bonjour, Mademoiselles," he said in French.

Rein could tell by his voice that he was a charmer. She had looked down in the process of his walking over but she glanced up now in respect.

"I am Carden Romanoff," the Frenchman said enchantingly. "It is a pleasure to meet you both."

"It is a pleasure to meet *you*," Saria replied with excited animation.

"Who, may I inquire, are you two? I have failed to *parlez avec vous* before. You boarded last night, *je crois?*"

"We did. My name is Sara Kendrick, but no one ever calls me Sara; they change it to Sar*i*a. I'm not sure how it ever came about."

"And you?" he asked with a large smile.

Rein laughed kindly to him. "Rein Pierson."

"I heard you, Miss Pierson, speak earlier of Traith Harker. You have met him?"

"You heard us speaking of him from all the way over there?" Saria asked with masked marvel, her mood changing to a frivolous one to gain his attention. "As you were talking?"

"I did. My hearing is quite remarkable."

"Yes, I met him last night," Rein answered. "He's a very hand—" She stopped and cleared her throat. To her embarrassment, she had already said it. "He is a very handsome,"—she said it quickly and through a single breath—"but a very odd gentleman."

Romanoff laughed at her. "I must agree he is a tremendously dashing man, but he would tell you no such thing." He turned and looked behind him, as if he thought Harker was there. Suddenly his manner changed to a more amused one, and he smiled to them as if Harker was behind him. "He can be unusual as well, without doubt. I am a good friend of his. He is a nice man; it would do you good to get to know him."

Rein was confused when he kept looking behind him and smiling with a laugh. But he seemed interested in the two of them, as if he knew them, or was trying to. Saria must have liked that, because her posture was far from relaxed and she moved directly in front of Rein's line of vision, twirling the loose ends of her perfectly pinned-up hair in gaiety. She was trying to get his attention and was adamant about staring straight upon him.

"Are you married, Mr. Romanoff?" she asked louder. "Have you a companion?"

"No, I am most definitely not," he said with a rumbling laugh. "Nor do I have a companion. Have either of *you* come with a man?"

"Just him, over there," Saria answered. "His name is Edgar Johan. He keeps his distance, though. It's so very kind of him to give us room."

Rein closed her eyes and shook her head. How much more blunt could she have been, asking in a second question if he was married?

Then Rein saw, out of the corner of her eye, a lady jump backward as if she was hit by something. Her insulted shout made both Rein and Saria turn completely. The woman had her hands out by her sides with steam nearly coming out her ears.

"Traith Harker!" the lady screamed, frustrated. "Run into me one more time!"

Rein flinched in surprise.

Traith Harker was nowhere in sight.

"Isn't that the man you were talking about?" Saria asked. "What did he do? Point him out!"

"He…he isn't there," Rein murmured.

Saria looked shocked with a laugh. "What? That lady must be silly and yelled out the wrong name or something, then."

Rein turned and looked at Romanoff, who was shaking his head with a grin. As Saria turned back to face the Frenchman in conversation, Rein found herself still trying to figure out why the woman had yelled Harker's name as if he actually had run into her. Concerned, and with her head partially down, Rein noticed how Romanoff was looking at Saria with a most tender expression.

"Interesting," he said. "Well neither of you know of a woman called—" He suddenly coughed and jerked in his seat. Looking over his shoulder again with a shocked chuckle, he shook his head and quieted. "N-never mind."

Rein's heart sank when she saw something more in Romanoff's large smile. Two of his upper teeth were very strange; they were actually pointed.

"I'll be right back," Rein spoke very clearly but softly, thinking, hoping that it was just a coincidence. But that accident? What about the accident Mr. Harker had mentioned? That excuse was wearing out, although Mr. Romanoff's eyes were brown, the first set that weren't odd in color.

"Where are you planning on going, Rein?" Saria asked.

"I have a question for the woman at the desk. About my chamber."

Romanoff had begun to say something as she stood to leave when suddenly he stumbled up and stopped his slur of a word. He closed his mouth quickly. She thought for a moment that he stood to her leave, but it looked more as if he had been pushed out of his seat. His head swung around, but still, no one was there. He said something under his breath as if he was talking to someone else.

Rein watched him with puzzlement and a sigh but left with a nod of her head. He was too busy mingling with the invisible person behind him.

As she walked away, she heard him clear his throat and begin talking with Saria again, a bit more intimately. She was obviously trying to win him over. She did that with most garish men. That being known, there was no need to stay and chat. She was terribly hungry, and she knew now that Saria was going to be preoccupied, so she didn't even bother asking her to eat. But her desire to find Harker was becoming fiercer. She knew he knew more about this ship than met the eye, and she had a right to know why he was so concerned for her when he had no idea who she even was.

Walking toward the corner desk, Rein addressed the stewardess. "Ma'am? Excuse me, good afternoon. Could you possibly advise me as to where Mr. Harker is staying?"

Rein was shocked at what she had just asked. It had slipped her mouth, like thoughts spilling over. She had meant to ask about her room and why each ones décor was different…but she realized that perhaps she only wanted to ask Mr. Harker about things and not the stewardess.

The stewardess's bleak face stayed stiffened. "*Traith* Harker?"

Rein paused and stuttered a moment. "I…is there another?"

"Oh, no."

Relief struck her; at least he was alone on the ship. But it was odd how mechanical the woman still seemed in her speech.

"No," the stewardess continued. "There is most definitely not another. But he isn't asked for often. He most definitely is not asked for often."

"Why not?" Rein asked; she was confused about why the lady was degrading him so.

The stewardess's eyes met and burned into her own. "You do not know him well, do you?"

Rein shook her head. "I do not. I've only met him once."

"He is the rebel of this ship. Different from the others. He is forced to stay on this ship, so he avoids us," she added.

Rein felt her eyes widen, and she hoped it didn't look as obvious as it felt.

"But," the lady sighed, "to answer your question: his chamber is two doors down from yours, further into the hall."

Rein's heart skipped a beat in excitement. If she couldn't find him lingering about the ship, she could knock on his chamber door. But it would take the courage of God for her to do something like that.

"But he wouldn't be in there now," the lady continued after a pause. "The captain ordered a meeting with him and a few others. You probably will not catch him today."

Disappointment tore her. "A meeting with the captain? He is the man with the white eyes, correct?"

"White eyes? Yes…" The stewardess words slurred.

"What is their meeting about?"

"That I do not know." The stewardess did not move a muscle, as if she were connected to strings like a marionette, and her face was without expression.

Suddenly, out of the corner of her eye, Rein saw a blur of a man headed toward the door behind her, the one leading to the deck. But the blur appeared out of nowhere.

Spinning her head, she caught a quick glimpse of the man, and realized that it was Mr. Harker. His hand was the last thing she saw, slamming the iron door closed.

She quickly thanked the stewardess and walked near to the café. She could not follow him; he was meeting with the captain, wasn't he? But he had acted like he hated…

And he was forced to be on this ship?

She felt herself curving toward the entrance door, when Romanoff walked in front of her with Saria close behind. "You saw Traith?" he said, making her stop walking. "He is headed to the private drawing room for wine with the captain. I am going, and I'm taking Saria. You are coming?"

"I…I wasn't," Rein replied politely. "How can you bring Saria and me to this meeting without invitation?"

"Oh, I'm sure you two will be welcome, dear girl."

"Come on, Rein!" Saria said with excitement. "We'll have fun. I told Edgar we'd just be down the stairs, and he said it was fine that we be alone as long as he was aware of where we were."

"Come with me," the gentleman said as he turned to the entrance door that led to the deck.

Rein was secretly itching to attend this gathering; she would see Traith Harker. But the same puzzling thought kept ringing in her mind: *why would he go?*

Had he been lying to her about the illness of the captain? It was beginning to seem so because the captain seemed friendly and because no madman could be in charge of a ship.

But Traith Harker seemed protective. Not, perhaps, friendly, but as the stewardess said, he was not accepted…or he did not accept. Had he been forced onto the ship? And for what purpose would he lie to her about the captain's illness or the danger of being around him? He had seemed rather loathing of the captain, so why would he go? In a few moments, she surely would have to learn the answer to at least one of her many questions.

chapter 08

R ein followed Romanoff and Saria out the entrance door, into the cedar hall, and out the door that led to the deck. The weather was dreary and threatening to rain again, and the bitterness in the air made her stomach ill. The saltiness she smelled and tasted were horrible.

Romanoff walked over to a protruding door and opened it. Rein and Saria followed him down a long stairwell into the bottom of the ship. Rein studied her surroundings well as Romanoff made an immediate right, avoiding a dark hallway, which led elsewhere, and entered through another.

There was a large opening in the front of the room, and Rein peered forward and saw Mr. Romanoff greet the captain and take a seat near the fire at the end of the hall. He sat at a small table large enough for only six people, but it seemed cozy enough. Standing momentarily, the captain shook hands with Romanoff and reclaimed his seat at the end of the table. Rein smiled as the two people greeted each other. She felt much unrest, in an eager way, when she noticed Harker sitting at the other end of the table, the side away from the warmth of the fire.

She was exhilarated to see that he was as handsome under good light as she had thought. His muscular chin and jaw and strong but subtle nose were illuminated under a sconce's glow, and his red eyes, nearly closed, seemed faded. His shaggy hair was a dark brown, and it matched his unshaven face. But the bristles on his face were nearly unnoticeable, about as unnoticeable as his scars. He was wearing a dark waistcoat with his collar high and covering him entirely so she couldn't see what his clothing was like.

Harker gave a small smile to Romanoff, acknowledging the fact that they were indeed acquainted, but she inferred from his informal greeting that he was not happy to be there. He didn't seem happy to see her, either; his face grew quickly solemn, and his previously sleepy eyes widened fully when he saw her; their brightness shone. He nodded to her but didn't make much eye contact afterward. What was he thinking about?

"Ah, Romanoff!" The captain exclaimed, finally, after examining Rein and Saria. "You brought guests! 'Tis fortunate that I brought extra wine glasses, just in case!"

"I thought I was told there were to be no guests," stated Harker quietly.

Rein bit her bottom lip in a sort of sudden shock at his retort, beginning to feel as though she'd jumped to conclusions about him much too fast.

"Traith, this young lady told me she has already had the privilege of meeting you," Romanoff said to him with cheer, putting his arm behind Rein's back.

"Yes, we did meet," he countered with a very low tone of voice, almost a whisper. "How are you, Miss Pierson?"

She was happy that he remembered her name. She found herself a bit stunned at his silence and short words. He had seemed much friendlier than he was acting now, although friendliness didn't seem to be one of his virtues.

She replied, and he met her gaze. "I'm fine, thank you. How are you?"

"I'm well."

"You know this beautiful dame, Harker?" The captain questioned him in a pompous demeanor, smiling with his pipe.

Rein felt herself flush, but a sniff from Saria told her she was jealous of the attention. Rein smiled.

"I do not," the laconic yet irresistible man replied, still calmly quiet. "I only met her last night walking to the foyer."

"Was he kindly to you, Miss Pierson?" The captain asked.

Romanoff encouraged her to take a seat next to Saria, who, to Rein's dismay, had taken the seat next to Traith Harker. Romanoff situated himself on the other side, across from her, next to the captain. Mr. Harker sat back and crossed his arms, blowing breath out through his mouth and staring at the questioning man.

"He was," she answered.

She watched Harker's jaw bite down with his lips together; he lowered his eyes again, as if she had made the wrong answer.

"So what is this gathering for?" Saria asked, trying to make her own conversation with the men. She was always very nearly too sociable and outgoing.

"It is just a daily gathering that I set up with these two fine gentlemen, and I see they've each a lady now to converse with in addition."

Harker did not respond, but Romanoff laughed quite audibly. "They looked a bit bored of the ship, so I invited them," he replied. "Oh, and Traith, I don't appreciate your pushing me out of my chair earlier." He grinned and laughed a little.

Harker cocked his head, and his eyebrows drew together. "I have no idea what you are accusing me of, Carden, but *I* don't appreciate it either."

"Ah! Men, beautiful ladies, let us have some wine!" the captain declared. "No quarreling!"

The captain stood and grabbed a bottle from the mantle and poured wine in each of their cups. Not Romanoff's or Harker's, though; theirs had already been filled.

Rein was stunned at how very silent Mr. Harker was being. He did not once reach for his goblet to drink. Unlike him, Romanoff gulped his drink down, as did the captain. She and Saria took sips of it. But what was wrong with Traith Harker?

"Ah, quickly! Look here," said the captain, rising from his seat and walking over to something covered by a large cloth.

He pulled off the cloth lightly so he didn't arouse dust. It was a studio camera.

"Shall I do the honors?" he said, beginning to laugh very hard.

Rein glanced at Harker. His face was intimidating with annoyance, and he was staring steadily at the captain.

"Traith, you and Miss Pierson stand together!" he said with another laugh, bending himself underneath the curtain, holding the shutter. "After all, you've met, and that is enough for a picture relationship, isn't it?"

"Uh, I do not think taking a photograph will be necessary," Romanoff said, smiling.

The captain stood and pushed the curtain off him, letting go of the shutter. He laughed. "I'm sorry. I didn't realize that neither of you liked photographs. You don't like the way you look in photographs, Harker?"

He said nothing from the end of the table, and Rein saw the anger in his previously gentle eyes. Although his voice contained all the anger she saw, he continued to speak calmly. "I don't." His upper lip nearly rose with irritation.

Romanoff stood and walked near the captain, holding him around the waist and leading him back to the table. "More wine for me, *s'il vous plait.*"

Rein was shocked at the tense manner of the men and the covered up, double meanings of the words they used with each other. The captain nodded his head to her in a closer greeting, reached across the table to fill the Frenchman's goblet again, and then began a quiet conversation with Romanoff. Traith Harker was silent and motionless.

She wasn't able to hear their conversation. Her attention on Harker muted everything else around her. Each time he glanced at her, she quickly looked away and acted like she was listening to the conversation at the end of the table. She noticed out of the corner of her eye that Harker turned down and stared at his glass. She wanted to stare at him again, at his rough but handsome face and his mysterious actions. She was wondering if she'd ever be able to read his face.

But then Saria turned and whispered to her with a joyful tone, and she had to blink fast and turn her seemingly full attention to her.

"Rein!" she whispered earnestly. "Please redo the knot in your hair. It's quite a mess, you know. You must have presentable hair, more than anything, especially to make a good impression. Nonchalantly, though."

Rein rolled her eyes and laughed at her friend, knowing that she jested in a most unusual way. She slowly lifted her arms and re-pinned her hair as well and as subtle as she could behind her. It fell out of her hands, however, and fell in wavy, black chunks down her shoulders. Her heart hit her throat in embarrassment and quickly pinned it back up, then sat quiet again, hoping she hadn't made too bad a breach of etiquette among the men. The Frenchman and the captain hadn't seemed to notice, but she caught Harker's piercing eyes dart toward her and watch for a while. She then smiled at him. His eyes became tame again in his glance, but she lost sight of them when he looked down, smiling faintly back as if he were uncomfortable.

"Have *you* ever read, Miss Pierson, about werewolves?"

Rein saw Harker's near smile turn. His head rose, and his eyes focused tightly toward the captain. He really hated that man.

She immediately turned her interest to the captain with delayed brightness, wishing to see Harker's face. "I...I'm sorry?"

He looked irritated for a moment at her lack of etiquette, but he continued. "Werewolves—you know, beasts of the night, frightful men that are doomed to change into wolves every full moon?"

"I have," Saria answered him. "I read something of it in the awful rendition of *Little Red Riding Hood* that was retold by the Grimm Brothers."

"Aha! In 1812," the captain replied. "But that was more a normal wolf than a wolf-*man*."

"Ah, classic authors of literature, they were, the Brothers Grimm," Romanoff added. "They had many a story about strange things."

"Yes, and what about you, Harker? Do you recall any good reading on horror? Of werewolves, or perhaps others?"

"None that I recall," Harker replied, his voice very calm and steady.

"Oh, come on, Traith! What about Webster's *The Duchess of Malfi*? I know you've read it, what with the library you have at your castle."

His bright eyes turned and focused on Romanoff. The stare had deeper meaning. "Oh," he said ironically. "I forgot about my library." He swirled his drink; the first time he'd grasped the cup.

Rein was intrigued by Romanoff's last words. Harker had a castle? He had a castle. He therefore must be, or must have once been, a lord or a very wealthy landowner. But a castle? Something that rare and expensive? And so young. Why then had he told her he lived on this ship?

She was still stunned by his coldness. He truly seemed as though he did not want to talk or be there; perhaps it was because she was there that he was hesitant to speak. But there had to be something more.

"Oh," said the captain with a jovial expression, "but nothing sells a good werewolf story like introducing a vampire." The man walked around smoking a pipe by the fireplace. "Leipzig, 1734. Do you know what was written?"

"The German story, I believe, about vampires," Rein spoke quietly, trying to be in some of the conversation. She knew the answer after all.

The captain stared at her with curiosity. "You've read about the vampire, then?"

"Briefly," she replied. "I didn't know it was in 1734, but I knew about Leipzig. It's all in German. I only know what I could make out, as I only know a little German, but it was awful. The thought of drinking blood is entirely sickening."

"I agree," said Saria. "I don't understand what would make someone create folklore as monstrous as that."

Rein saw Traith Harker glare, but not at her. Even Romanoff seemed on edge suddenly, looking at the captain.

"Another version was written in English, in 1732, two years prior," the captain stated again with his egotistical intelligence. "Harker! You've read it!"

He did not respond, though his animated, red eyes slowly gazed down at his cup and then back up at the captain. The captain seemed at his throat.

"Yes, Traith, I recall you telling me about it," Romanoff added.

Rein noticed that Harker always paused as if he was tiring of the situation before he spoke. "I have read it," he answered them coolly.

"Tell me, what does that make you think, then, about vampires? What do you know about them? Do you think them to be real?"

There was a longer pause before Harker answered. "I think that the vampire is described as a fearsome curse on man in books and articles." His words were quick, quiet, and not exaggerated.

"Do you think them *real*, Mr. Harker?" Saria asked him with interest.

Romanoff stared at him for a moment, and then let go of his gaze and smiled at Saria.

Harker glanced at Rein, and then down at his goblet of wine. "I do not."

"Don't you?" the captain asked, interested.

One of Harker's eyebrows rose as he stared at the white-eyed man. "No. Was I unclear in some way?"

Rein was interested in Harker's reaction to the captain's questioning when she noticed that her wine was very clear. That was, in all fact, the norm, but as she glanced down at Romanoff's goblet, she noticed that it was quite an opaque red, much thicker. She could not see into Harker's chalice, but she could see that the Frenchman's glass was already empty again, and a residue was left inside of it.

"I recall a French reading about them, too, Romanoff," the man interrupted her thoughts. "I'm sure you, a Frenchman yourself, have read it."

"Ah, yes; indeed I have! *Histoire des Vampires*, a scarce but famous history of vampires by Collin de Plancy, right? Paris, 1820. Oh, I do adore books of that nature! Such mystery and skepticism!"

The captain laughed. "Well, ladies, do you know what a vampire *looks* like?"

Rein figured he was trying to scare them, but in a good-natured way. "I have no idea," she said, finally sipping once at her wine. "I know what they do, but no author has ever really described them."

"I don't know, either," Saria replied.

Harker looked quite frozen as he spoke, his head tilted sideways. "Is this subject so interesting to you that we must speak of it?" He was addressing the captain.

"Do you not like it, Harker?" the captain asked simply.

The words Traith Harker said were enunciated carefully and slowly with clear precision, and Rein could see his immense agitation. "It is very *dull*."

"Bah!" The captain moaned, puffing on his pipe. "Dull, you say? I thought you enjoyed it. You of all—"

"Not particularly."

"More wine, then, Harker?"

"I have no desire for more, no."

"Don't you? No desire at all?"

"I should like more," Romanoff broke in, without doubt trying to stop conversation between the captain and Harker.

Harker stared at Romanoff, his eyes burning red as the captain laughed and filled the Frenchman's goblet with more.

"Traith, you know, you do not speak loud enough," the captain said with a smirk.

Carden Romanoff sat back and looked tense, staring at Harker with his large eyes full of nervousness. It was obvious by the expressions he made that there was a dark and hidden agenda between the captain and Harker.

Harker's eyes raised and opened larger in response. "Does that bother you?"

"You mumble much too much! Open your mouth a bit when you speak."

Harker stood. "If my speech so very much annoys you, I'll *leave*."

"Then off with you, Harker."

"Thank you," he said dryly.

For a moment, as he stood, she felt his eyes hook onto her gaze. He turned away, nodded his head in her general direction, and walked out the door, slamming it on his way out.

"Such an *obdurate* boy," the captain said with a laugh.

Rein noticed Romanoff's eyes grow regretful, and he stared past her at the door Harker had left from. "Poor man," he whispered.

"Forgive me," Rein said assertively, trying hard to act as if she was in shock at remembrance. They all looked at her with question. "I just recalled that I've left something…hazardous exposed in my chamber. I very much enjoyed the wine and conversation."

She had no desire to be at the conference anymore, Harker being gone, and she did have unpacking still to do. As she contemplated her unpacking, she realized she no longer wanted another chamber—not if Harker's was two doors down.

"Going after him?" the captain asked with a chuckle.

"No," she said with dipped eyebrows.

Romanoff and Saria smiled, and the captain laughed. "Very well, you may leave. Take this key," he finished. "Sometimes the entrance door locks itself."

She thanked him and stood, taking the key. Closing the door behind her very silently on her way out, she quickly ran up the flight of stairs in hopes of catching him. She opened the port door and felt disappointed when she did not see him. She walked across the deck and into the lobby of the ship, but he wasn't there either. Her heart sank when she could not find him anywhere, so she headed back to her chamber as she had proposed she would at the meeting.

She still wasn't sure why she had such strong and sudden feelings for Traith Harker, but she did know she didn't want to lose them.

chapter 09

Rein opened the door with a sigh, closed it, and locked it with a chain. She had no idea what she was doing. Why had she even left the meeting?

She walked deeper into the chamber and grabbed the water pitcher to wash her face. She shook her head and poured some water into the bowl, then cupped her hands and splashed water onto her face. She placed the water pitcher back in the indented holder and patted her face dry with a clean towel that was hung over a wall bar.

With a sigh she sat down on her bed. She was so frustrated with herself. So far she had minimally been enjoying her stay, even though only one night had gone by. Saria had fallen into another one of her many loves, and was obviously smitten with Romanoff. It was all part of the vacation, for her, as she had said. She had been expecting men.

The realization hit her; she was alone. Saria was busy and she didn't know Edgar. "Do you have a male escort?" Traith Harker's words rung in her mind. She had no brothers or sisters, no mother, and her father… she hadn't seen him for years. How could he be gone so long? So many years without word? The last letter she got was fourteen years ago. But those were the questions she silenced each day. She pushed the nightmares out of her mind at night.

But now, she was on a real steamship. She was away from the haunting she felt in Teesdale, especially at Barnard Institution. Thoughts of Carden Romanoff's teeth and the captain and Harker's bizarre eyes crowded her mind. What happened to those men? What was that accident? And the subject at the captain's meeting—why had that ugly man wanted to be so chilling?

She tried to brush it off. She was all right.

Just the thought that Saria didn't seem to pick up on Rein's fear lingered. Either Saria didn't care or didn't know. Rein had always hidden her fear from everyone, even from Saria. She kept so cool all the time. Couldn't show her deep emotions. Was she too proud to show any weakness?

She cleared her throat and wiped her eyes. She was tired of being reserved. Tired of hiding the thought of her father. Saria would listen and comfort her if she would only tell her about it. They were best friends; they would have grown up together if only Saria's parents had been allowed to take charge of her. She was like her sister.

With a smile to herself, she wiped her eyes a second time, forgetting about those things troubling her. She stood straight and walked to the table in the center of the foyer, taking out her copy of *Sense and Sensibility*. With the book in hand, she entered the bedroom hollow and lay on her side, propped on the pillow. She was just becoming settled when she felt a hard crinkling under her elbow.

She lifted herself up and looked down, lifting the pillow.

There was a letter.

Miss Rein Pierson,

I am disposed to inform you of something most important before you come to find out in your own time. You are reading this on a ship, and I understand that you left Teesdale not three days ago. This is most urgent for you, and my information is to be taken as completely reliable. It is about your father, Colonel Timothy Pierson.

chapter 10

During military stationing in France, Col. Pierson was part of a standing army ordered to watch for any French infiltration into the English Channel. You were six years of age, and as he left, you were sent to live in Barnard Institution while the servants kept your house and an agent kept your money. The year was 1828.

Being that Col. Pierson was part of a standing army, it was mandatory for him to take board in nearby houses. A native French woman invited him to stay with her. Since you were only five years old, I understand why he would not have told you about his dealings with the woman. Her name was Colette Badeau, and she was a very handsome woman, a sort of gypsy. She knew no English, but Pierson was enraptured by her. However, your father left Badeau when he found out she was pregnant by him, and he continued in his post elsewhere. He attempted to forget about Badeau and the child. He was sent back to Teesdale a few weeks later, but he left you in Barnard for the rest of your childhood.

Rein set the letter down, her hands trembling wildly. This had to be some sort of hoax…but no one knew those things but her. She was faint with shock. She thought and squinted with disgust. A child? Her father was in Teesdale the entire time she was trapped in that terrible school? Her only blood relation, and he left her?

His decision not to take you out of school will not be discussed, but you must know that he was in Teesdale for fourteen years before he was drafted again to France. He was drafted a few months before you graduated Barnard, and to his shock, he found that Colette Badeau had died of fever, leaving behind their now fifteen-year-old daughter, Taverin. Despite France being a mortal enemy of England, the girl had learned English, and the colonel claimed charge of her. France made no attempt to restrain him from removing the French-raised girl from her homeland, but she still has no citizenship in England, where both she and the colonel were headed.

However, when he had returned, you were gone—on this ship to America.

I am Mistress; someone you do not know, but will in due time. You will be something great, Rein Pierson. Do not take my words lightly. Trust whom you meet with the same nationality as your own. He is to be trusted.

Her heart was racing. She stood, trembling with the letter firmly in hand, and ran to the foyer and out the door. She struggled to keep her hand still to close the door, frustration and confusion overwhelming her.

Coincidence was not a possible explanation. Something was wrong, or the information she received was faulty. It had to be fake; no one could send a letter to a moving ship. Someone aboard had to have written it. But the mere notion that her father had left her in that awful institution…

Rein stumbled in panic into the atrium, glancing around for Saria. The hall was unusually empty, and the lounge where she had been before had two people she didn't know sitting with their drinks glued into their hands. She turned completely around in an attempt to go back to her chamber. Saria still had to be at the meeting; it had been less than an hour since she'd left.

But as she stared down the V-Wing where her chamber was, she saw Saria standing there with Romanoff. They must have been headed to her chamber to find her, but she hadn't noticed them in her haze of fright.

Saria's eyes were focused on her for a moment, and she quickly paced over to the atrium with her arms out. "Dear God!" she gasped with sorrow, holding her shoulders. "What is wrong, Rein?"

She felt weak and closed her eyes before Saria neared. She lost all sense of balance and felt herself collapse, but she never hit the floor. Her shortness of breath subsided when she blinked open her eyes.

Traith Harker's face hung over her, and his arms were situated one underneath her waist, and the other holding her head.

She'd fainted?

"Rein! Rein! Oh dear, Rein!" She could hear Saria yelling, but her voice was muted by the man above her.

"Miss Pierson?" His voice was clear and soft. She felt his fingers moving under her body, searching for an easier hold. "Can you hear me?"

She shook her head and tried to stand. A mortified feeling plagued her, but she said nothing. He wouldn't let her rise.

"Relax," he said with attempted comfort. "Give yourself a mome—"

"Rein! Oh, my darling friend! Can you hear me?" Saria's face suddenly protruded under Harker's, and he had to lean back to allow her to bend down. "What is the matter with you?"

Harker helped her stand, his hands still partially holding her, helping her over to the divan next to them. She saw Edgar appear behind Saria, looking shocked but meek as usual. Edgar quickly shook hands with Romanoff and told him who he was. She fought to overcome her light-headedness and carry herself so he didn't have to strain to hold her, but Harker made it seem as if she were light as a feather.

And then she realized that she had not been able to find him any-where before. How had he gotten into the lobby in that small time, just enough to catch her? She stopped asking questions. It was useless.

Her vision was clear again. She held her head and took a seat at the sofa that Harker had led her to, taking a deep breath. But it wasn't as deep as she wanted it to be because her bodice was so tight. She was humiliated, and in front of everyone she knew. She had never caused such a scene before!

Romanoff came up right next to Saria, momentarily looked at her, then bent down to pick up the papers she had dropped when she nearly fell. He glanced at them, but Saria snatched them out of his hands. Saria's eyes were wide, and her mouth dropped as her eyes shot back and forth against the papers.

"Oh, no, Rein," she muttered, still reading. "Rein, this can't be true. Where did you find this?"

Romanoff's eyes grayed. "W-whose name is in there?" he asked almost inaudibly, and his eyes scanned the paper from behind Saria. "*Mistress?*"

Harker stood stiffly and watched Romanoff with icy eyes. "What?"

Saria blinked a few times blankly in thought, and Romanoff took the letter from her. He spoke the last words of the letter ardently. "*Trust whom you meet with the same nationality as your own. He is to be trusted.*"

He looked up at Rein and then at Harker. "Well, you are the only Englishman here, Traith."

"You must not believe this," Saria choked, her words louder than Romanoff's. "I would have seen your father sometime in those fourteen years. You live across the street; he was never—"

"You never even *met* my father," Rein quivered to say. "How do you suppose your parents could not remove me from that horror of a boarding school? My father was deliberately keeping me there. It would make sense…" She had to stop talking to hold back her emotion, and cradled her head in her hands. She wasn't going to cry in front of them as well—she wasn't.

"Madame, I am inclined to say that what you read must be true," Romanoff said. "I know this Mistress, and she does not lie."

"You know the person who wrote this letter?" Saria asked him emphatically. "Is she on this ship now? Why, she must be! How else could—"

"She isn't on this ship," Harker replied sternly. Romanoff attempted to interrupt, but Harker continued. "It was more than likely a hoax, and I know by whom it was committed."

Romanoff was furious. "Traith, what are you talk—"

"Miss Pierson," Harker said more gently to her, ignoring his friend. "Please." His next word was hesitated upon. "*Breathe.*" He sighed. "I'll find out who has done this to you. Don't be upset. It isn't true."

When Rein looked up, the only thing that filled her line of vision was Traith Harker's trademark brooding eyes, but they were shrouding something. He was lying; the tone of Romanoff's voice made it obvious. But that gentleness she had noticed before was still glistening in his eyes. She was coming to admire it; it was the same tame gaze she had noticed him use on her before. But only on her.

"Do you want me to take you to your chamber?" Saria asked, seated next to her and fanning her uselessly.

She shook her head and sat up. The embarrassment of portraying what she thought seemed like a prim, weak girl was crushing her. "I'm fine, now," she said, forcing a smile. "I didn't mean to make such commotion, you know I hate that. Mr. Harker is right; I can't worry. I can't get back to England for at least a month anyway." She spoke with a shaky coolness, and she stood with as much dignity as she could muster.

Saria had stood and given her hand to her French confidant, ready to take leave. "I'm sure that was some sort of prank, Rein," she said softly. "Don't worry over it, you must enjoy yourself here! But I'll give you a little while to think, all right? I know how you are; you like your space when you're tense, so I'll let you go ahead." She smiled with pity. "I'll be by in a bit, all right? Promise."

"Sure," Rein said, clearing her throat and smiling. "Thank you."

Romanoff smiled with concern and handed her the letter.

"I need to talk with you, Traith," he murmured before he went to take leave. "Tonight?"

Harker never answered as Romanoff walked away with Saria.

Saria left with that concerned, motherly attitude completely abandoned, and her arm resting with sudden frivolity in his. He was smiling at her, and the two disappeared behind a few wandering people and a door.

Then it was only Edgar and Harker left near her.

"I'm their escort," Edgar said, and shook hands with Harker.

"Evening," Harker said with a nod of greeting.

"Are you sure all will be fine, miss?" Edgar asked her quietly.

Rein attempted a believable laugh at how dramatic she felt she had been. "Think nothing of me, Edgar."

He nodded with that timid smile. "I'll be in room 1102 if you need me," he said. "Don't hesitate to get me if need be, please, Miss Pierson."

She smiled to him, and he turned and went on his way.

She directed her attention to Harker, who was standing awkwardly amidst the staring passengers. He cleared his throat and took a seat next to her so he blended.

"So," he began, looking around casually and trying to strike up some conversation. "Are you steady again?"

"That letter was…disturbing," she rasped. "I pray it is not true. It is about my father, and other things that have haunted me for years, things I never knew the answers to. I don't understand who could know those things. I'm sorry for falling; I *never*—"

"No, don't apologize," he said, sympathetic, finally looking at her face. "I'm not a practiced liar, so I should clarify what I've told you."

With a knot forming deep within her, she searched his face for some kind of expression, but he was unreadable.

"You think it is true, don't you?" she pushed to say, her voice hoarse with sorrow. He had hesitated. "Mr. Romanoff had seemed so upset for me—"

"Please, Miss Pierson," he quieted her, covering his lips with his strong, pale hand. She noticed white, lifted scars on his hands, too—just like the ones on his face, but longer and larger.

"Tell me the truth," she whispered. "I trust you."

He seemed near embarrassed at being seen in the atrium and speaking in public. She could tell he was uncomfortable sitting in the open, but that was part of his characteristic reticence, and she was assured that he was truly attempting to make *her* comfortable, even if he was not.

His face changed; he wore a sudden surprised look, no doubt from her comment of trust. Did he not receive that often? It seemed to her that he was the type of man whom everyone would trust but always managed to neglect.

His surprised, essentially grateful expression slowly altered into a more somber one. "I do appreciate your trust. This may make you change your mind, but—" He chuckled emptily. "Would you invite me to your chamber?" He shook his head. "I don't mean at all to be uncouth, although that must sound terribly near to it. I would invite you to my own, but it's a bloody wreck, and I should explain to you in quiet..."

"Of course," she stuttered, wiping her eyes. She felt a very deep thrill stirring at his wish to go into her chamber. The gentleman she liked, that she wanted to speak with, wanted to speak with her. But the subject on which he was addressing her brewed terror inside of her.

Trust whom you meet with the same nationality as your own. He is to be trusted. The last words of that horrifying letter echoed in her ears.

chapter 11

I n her defense, her chamber was very tidy. But the very thought of having left something out of place haunted her. In the hall she had him trailing behind her quietly, in awkward silence to the door.

She turned nonchalantly to him with a half smile, took out the key from her pocket, and unlocked the door. He returned her smile, but his eyes focused on everything but her. She could see his coyness, and she suffered anxiety over the thought of who would begin the talking. She was usually rather timid herself, and having a man she didn't know in her chamber? She kept calm, and thought more about the idea of getting to know this man better.

Her latter feelings won out—she managed to walk into her chamber with ease. To her relief, he already seemed more outgoing than he had been before. He took a seat at her request and relaxed his long, muscular body.

"I'm sorry, I have nothing prepared to eat, but there is some wine in the icebox," she said with a sigh. "If—"

"No wine, but thank you for your generosity," he said with a small smile, his impeccable face relaxed. "Your chamber is very well kept."

She shook her head and smiled, taking a seat across from him at the table. She noticed for the first time, as he put his arms on the table, that he was scarred on more than just his hands. She could clearly see his forearms, as his white sleeves were rolled up. They were scarred worse— much worse—than his face. But the same kind of scars—long, narrow, similar to knife wounds. They must have been all over his body. But what had caused them?

To her dismay, he removed his hands from the table. "Not too formal, I suppose," he said to her dryly.

She felt so ill it was nearly excruciating. "No...*no*, I—"

"They are a long story," he said simply, rolling down his sleeves.

"Oh, please don't!" she declared with the most foolish feeling burning her up, and he stopped immediately and looked at her. "I don't care if I see them," she muttered. He watched her closely as she tried to clear up her actions. "I just hadn't noticed them before. Please forgive me if I offended you. I don't mind, really."

He said nothing. He watched her a moment, looked down, and kept his sleeves as they were. But he put them under the table. His face was down, and he seemed for a flashing moment personal and pensive. "Are they much worse than my face?"

She was shocked at his comment. He seemed more sarcastic with himself as he spoke, but not as if he was depressed. But within his eyes she could see question. She could read something, finally. But he must know what his face looked like…

She felt horrified at herself. "No. I mean, yes! No, Mr. Harker, your face isn't…the scars on your face are barely noticeable; I just…I'm sorry!" For a moment she didn't know whether to laugh or cry.

"Don't apologize," he said with a short, silent chuckle. "I was just wondering. I prefer not to look at myself in the mirror. Don't exactly *like* my reflection."

She marveled at how that was possible, but mortification still clung to her, and she put her face in her hands.

After a pause, he sighed with a trembling breath. "About the letter, Miss Pierson," he began, changing the focus of the conversation. He paused. "Rein?"

She looked at him, releasing her hands from her face. He'd said her first name. He'd actually slipped and used her *first* name!

"It isn't something you must pity," he said. "I've had them for years." When she didn't reply, he spoke with more refinement. "Miss Pierson, I don't want to have to tell you that the letter you received is truthful, but…" his regretful pause was terrifying. "I hadn't thought it was, and I said it wasn't because part of me wanted to make sure you were…well, you seem to take shock better than most women."

She sat back and laughed a little. "That's what Saria told me. But of course she is also very—"

"Dramatic?" he finished for her, and he smiled.

"Yes. She is terribly histrionic." She stopped and spoke with a quiver. "Oh, Mr. Harker, I haven't offended you, have I? I had to have; first your eyes, and now—"

"Miss Pierson, please," he said quietly. "I'm not offended." He made a slight shake of his head and toyed with his fingers. "The writer of your letter— Mistress—is a well-known woman in this ship. But she is not anywhere near it. In fact, she is in a far-off country, as of now. But both I and Carden served for her...I mean, for work." He seemed to end his speech there.

"You must be wealthy to have a castle, as I heard Mr. Romanoff say you did," she said. "Why would you work?"

His manner shifted into one of uncertainty. "I inherited it. It regrettably didn't come with money seeping out the cracks." She smiled at his unintentional humor, and he continued. "But Mistress had...*has* a tendency to *know* things. A medium, perhaps you would consider her. I wouldn't say witchcraft, but, I don't know," he mumbled. "I have not seen her in many years," he seemed to grimace. "In fact, I've needed her for so long..."

Rein felt like her heart was attempting to come up her throat. He was making this Mistress sound as though he had once loved her, and the very idea was heartbreaking.

"—so the letter you found was just as much a shock to me as it was to you. She isn't on this ship, Miss Pierson."

She took a shaky breath and blew out her fright in anger. "A witch? You think a witch wrote me this letter stating that my father left me in a boarding school when he was a few miles up the road my whole life? And brought back a French daughter five years younger than me?"

He didn't reply at first. "It is not my intention to have your personal life trouble you," he said quietly. "Nor is it my intention to even *know* your personal life, but I do believe now that what is written is true."

With a quick movement of her hand, she wiped the blurriness out of her eyes. His face was very grave but became saddened—he had noticed.

"I believe you," she whispered shakily, though she wasn't sure why she said that.

She didn't want him to think she was in love with him, especially if he loved someone else. But she found she was experiencing the wildest feelings she could dream of, and they were becoming stronger. The strangest part was that she had no way of stopping the progression of those feelings, even though she hardly knew him. The idea of falling in love so quickly was completely ridiculous to her. She hardly knew him. Why hadn't she fallen for any other man she'd hardly known? There were others; some extremely handsome, but they nearly revolted her. Somehow it honestly felt like she did know Traith Harker, and *that* made her believe him; she just couldn't let him see that.

He widened his fiery eyes. "I..." He paused, and her heart stood still. "I've never had anyone trust me so, Miss Pierson," he muttered. "I don't know what to say."

"If your 'Mistress' *is* a witch," she stuttered to reply, covering her deepness of feeling for him, "then she told me to trust you. You are the only British man I know of on this ship. Other than Edgar, of course, but I've known him since before I boarded."

He laughed softly. "Please stay calm for me, then," he said. "I realize you have been and most likely *will* be calm anyway, without my asking you to, but stay alert at the same time. We will be approaching America in a fortnight, maybe less." He glanced at the letter she had thrown on the table. "If this is true, your father will be waiting for you when you get—" he cut himself off and became quiet. "When you get back to England." He let out his breath and cleared his throat after a moment. "I haven't seen England in awhile. How is it?" He appeared to be reminiscing.

"It's well," she replied, wiping down her dress. "Hasn't changed any for years, really. Where are you from there?"

"Surrey," he replied. "New Egham. Small town, but quaint."

"Oh, south England. I'm from up north. That's odd; you don't sound as though you're from a home county."

He laughed softly. "So you simply found this letter here, right?"

"Yes," she said, getting her thoughts back on track. "This ship is so bizarre. Couldn't you explain to me why you seemed so worried when we first met in the corridor? Why was I in need of warning?"

His focus was solely on her, and his comfortable posture stiffened. "M-Miss Pierson, I..." His face was full of concern as he was about to finish his reply. He bit his tongue and sighed, his head falling into his hands. "This is so hard to understand." He wiped his hands down his face and squinted at her. "You told me you trusted me, so just do that.

There is no explanation I can give, but I can keep you safe. There is nothing more for you to worry about, all right?"

"No explanation?" she repeated in a confused whisper. "So you warned me without reason?"

"No, not without reason," he said. "Just without explanation. Trust me."

She shook her head and smiled at the way he spoke. Despite not receiving the answers she wanted, she felt inside as though she should embrace him. He cared about her situation. He said he would protect her and asked for her trust. She had been right all along, but both her propriety and the table were in the way of an embrace.

Suddenly her eyes strayed toward the bedroom hollow. He had slowly reclined himself, but as she stood, he immediately sat erect. He must've thought she wanted him to leave. He stood after her and was clearly about to bow in leave, but she walked past him toward the place where she was staring. She hadn't wanted him to leave. Something had caught her eye on the bed.

She walked almost as if she was in a trance. Her weakness returned. She was concealing the fear, anger, and sorrow she felt over the letter she had found, supposedly from a witch, but an influx of chills seized her when she realized that there were a few more pages to that letter that she hadn't seen, peeking from beneath the blankets.

chapter 12

He didn't follow her, but he glanced into the room where she was with interest. She saw him stand out of the corner of her eye, but she was paying close attention to the remaining pages of that letter which had been hiding beneath a fold in the sheet.

However, Miss Pierson, I am sorry to inform you that your timing leaving England was terrible. Your father died last night...

Her lip quivered. Her heart raced. She felt herself losing color.

"No," she cried quietly, holding her head. "No. This isn't true," she said, tears finally beginning to escape her eyes. "This can't be true! Oh, God, it can't be true!"

She fell onto her bed and cried softly with little recall of the man standing behind her, watching her every move. She couldn't hear him, but then she felt a hand touch her shoulder. He was in her bedroom, trying to be of some comfort. But she didn't care; she didn't care about him being there. She didn't even care about holding in her fear anymore—about showing the world she was strong.

"Miss Pierson, what is it?" he asked. "What's happened?"

She could not answer him. She felt as though she couldn't talk, but she had to. She held her head, breathing little breathes in sorrow. "Is this some kind of cruel joke?" she asked angrily.

But he didn't know what she was talking about. "I don't believe I understand. May I?"

His last words were hesitant, but she handed him the end pages of letter without delay. "I can't read anymore," she choked.

His eyes scanned the paper, and he slowly pulled it down from his face and stared at her. "I am so sorry. How far did you read? You may want to read the rest," he paused and looked at her with sympathy. "Did you want me to?"

She wasn't sure what kind of expression she had given, but he nodded and looked down, clearing his throat and reading from the beginning to her.

"*However, Miss Pierson, I am sorry to inform you that your timing leaving England was terrible. Your father died last night. It was determined that he had Typhoid Fever, brought on by his time spent in unsanitary places in France.*" He stopped. "This is appalling," he murmured.

"He was not yet an old man," she hummed. Her throat was dry, and her heart was crushed so terribly that she thought she had bled through to her clothes. Her only person *left*, and…

"Shall I continue, or did you want to finish it?" His voice was quiet.

"Please," she cried lightly.

"*Rein,*" he continued reading, and he stopped every few words to look at her. "*Your father's death was unstoppable, even with the aid of modern medical techniques. But I must explain to you about his affairs and your half-sister, Taverin Badeau. Since your father has died, his entire fortune goes to you and is currently in the hands of your agent; the French girl was left nothing, and your house was not left to either of you, but to the county.*" She had lifted her eyes, and she saw Harker looking sadly at her. "Rein, this is too much for you to listen to now."

Again. Again he'd said her name.

A chill ran down her spine.

"Please keep going," she entreated gently. "I must hear the rest, and I…"

"*Taverin is left penniless. Both her parents are dead. She would be working in a poor house or selling flowers on the streets, but, to her fortune, the man who has gotten claim of your home, Bruce Hall, is going to adopt her, giving her the chance to remain in your house. However, he is a heavy alcoholic; when you get back to England, I advise you to meet her promptly.*" And then he stopped with terrible abruptness.

She looked at him because his voice had fallen strangely. "It couldn't be finished," she said, almost like a question.

He didn't look at her. "It isn't."

She forced herself to recover her composure. "What does it say?"

He took a breath, and his eyebrows rose as he read the last few words. "*By now, I'm sure Traith Harker has explained my being to you.*

Believe what he—oh, this is bizarre. This is bloody—"

Rein sat up. She felt her hair; it was down and probably a mess now. Her cheeks were wet, and she dried them with her hand. Her corset made it hard to catch the breath she had lost. Her dress was wrinkled, and she could only imagine how her eyes looked. She probably appeared terribly unattractive, and with a sick feeling she froze.

The near stranger of a man she had met just the day before was sitting on her bed with her, reading her a terrifying letter, which included him. His eyes were shooting side to side; they were wide, and their bright red color gave her a mix of chills and excitement. He let the paper down and gave it to her as if he couldn't read the rest. She took it without words.

...Traith Harker has explained my being to you. Believe what he tells you, as I trust him entirely. He may have told you that I am a witch, but I assure you, my intentions are only to keep you safe, so please trust me. You have a bright future ahead of you.

You will find no more trace of me, Rein. Clear up your eyes and put this news behind you. You cannot become depressed over your father's death. He would not want you to, and I do not either. You'll be too important to me.

Mistress

Her mouth had fallen open, she realized. Who was this? Who was this woman writing to her such intimate things? Facts? She was now more angrily perplexed than she was frightened. There was nothing she could do anyway at this point. If it were all a lie, she would go back to England to her normal life, but if it were true, she would never forgive herself for leaving Traith Harker and the *Olde Mary*, and she would forever live with the desire to find out how and why all this had happened.

"I'll be too important to her? What does that mean?" she asked desperately.

He was reluctant. "I don't know."

After a short silence and loss for words, Rein forced herself to think not of her letter but of him. "Thank you, Traith," she said, wiping her eyes of anything that could be left. She noticed she had used *his* first name.

He didn't seem to mind; he didn't reply at first, and his eyes were still dazed. "I cannot believe she wrote about me in your letter."

"Please do not tell anyone," she murmured, sitting up closer to him. "For now, I must believe what is written. If my father is dead, there is nothing I can do. Nothing can exhume me from confusion over this, so I'll just have to wait."

His eyes were sorrowful for her, but still very cool. "I will not speak a word of this." He stood slowly and cleared his throat to regain his reserve. "You should stay in here tonight, and think things through. It'll be better for you. Not that you need time to solve things...you strike me as a very independent and strong girl. That isn't common." His voice grew gentler. "I do hope, despite this...you do try to enjoy yourself. Don't worry in waiting, it'll do no good." A knock on the door stopped his speech. He turned to answer it, and she was frozen, thinking with awe over what he'd just said.

Outside the large, wood-framed doorway, a servant boy stood with a large, silver tray in his hands. His shirt and trousers constituted a faded blue uniform; he was the first servant she had ever seen on the ship. "Your food, sir," he said with a foreign accent she could not place.

Traith did not answer the young boy but walked past him into the hallway. "If you need me, Miss Pierson, for any reason," he said quietly. "I understand you have my chamber number."

She felt hot with embarrassment.

How did he know that?

"I ordered dinner for you," he motioned his head toward the boy. Then he gave her a farewell smile.

"Thank you so much," she said numbly. "You have been incredibly kind."

He watched her for a moment, nodded in thanks with a crooked smile, and disappeared past the boy with the tray. She waited for him to appear again, but with a shake of her head, she backed up and allowed the servant boy to come in and set the tray on the table. He bowed to her and left.

She sat down, her numbness fading to pins and needles. When had he had time to order dinner? He was with her the entire time. And she wondered who had told him that she had found out where his chamber was. The stewardess? She couldn't imagine that, because she hadn't displayed any interest toward Harker while in her presence.

She opened the silver lid and saw under it two plates full of appetizing meat and potatoes, hot bread and dipping oil, and two glasses of white wine.

There were *two* glasses and *two* plates. One was meant for Traith. Had he been too nervous to eat with her in her chamber? He was so shy; she felt so sorry for him. The stewardess had told her as well that no one spoke to him on the ship, other than Carden Romanoff. But had he wanted to stay with her? She could see, finally, that he was no longer afraid to show some emotion to her. He was less mysterious in person; he was entirely human.

"God, what am I supposed to do?" she asked, leaning her head on her hands. She didn't have the energy to cry.

She ate what she could, but the other plate stayed full on the table, and she closed the lid over it. She picked up the tray and set it outside the door, closing the door and locking it.

She untied her corset and took a deep, shaky breath; one she had been in need of taking all day. She took off her shoes, undressed and lay down in her large, feathery bed.

Was her father dead? Had she a sister? That moment tore into a stretching, looming darkness. The knowledge revealed to her in the letter came with inevitable pain, and she felt her heart crushing like a pillar bearing overwhelming weight. Despite these feelings, she found herself falling rapidly into a deep sleep.

chapter 13

two nights went by in which she didn't leave her room. Saria had come in a few times, but Rein never told her about the last pages she'd found of the letter she received. She had just blamed her waste of those two days on contemplation over the letter. She was lying, but she didn't want Saria to know about what only she and Traith knew. She would have to explain that he had been in her chamber, and she didn't want her friend scolding.

She hadn't seen Traith since that night; he hadn't checked on her. He doubtlessly felt too awkward to invite himself into her stateroom again, but she wanted him to come. She needed to see him again, and see how he reacted to her. Was that bond she felt just an awkward accident?

Rein realized that four nights had already gone by on the ship, and she had only enjoyed a small bit of that time. This realization made her anxious. The time was quickly disappearing. She was rested and calmed enough now to leave, as another afternoon began. She had come to terms with the letter and the possibility of its validity, or else she wouldn't be coherent. And she would have no chance at being happy for the rest of her voyage.

She put on her stays tightly in the front of her bare torso. Over the stays, she put on a chemise and a waist petticoat, and then placed a more elegant, tight shirt over top. It was a little more extravagant than she was used to, but she knew Saria would like it. It *was* beautiful.

This ship was apparently only for first class citizens who could pay their ride with ease. She was one of those; money was not a problem for her, as her mother had been incredibly rich. In any case, Rein had discovered earlier that heated water was available, and she had bathed that morning in the small washroom off of the bedroom hollow, which, to her excitement, actually had a bathtub, and through another door inside it, a working privy. Those were the advantages of being on such a new ship. The advanced plumbing alone should have caught much attention, yet there were not many people on board.

Once she was clean and dressed and her hair was washed and dry, she took a seat at the vanity to do her hair. She quickly raveled it and pushed the bun forward slightly to make her hair lift a little, and then pinned it. It was simple, but trim.

With a sigh she stared into the mirror, studying her reflection. Her cheeks were rosy, and her black hair looked nice. Her lips were average. Her eyes sparkled their unique blue. Only the dark rings under her eyes revealed the stress accrued in the previous days. The letter she'd found had been weighing heavily on her.

Rein didn't think it was fair that she was excluded from the secrets surrounding the letter and the relationship between its author and the men she and Saria had befriended. That letter, and the woman's name at the bottom, was connected to both Harker and Romanoff, and yet she found she was still in the dark about it. That fact frustrated her immensely, and she wanted to get more information out of Traith Harker than he'd given. Not only because she wanted to talk to him, but because she now had a right to know. After what the two had gone through that night, she thought it should be much simpler to converse again.

With concerns and feelings spinning wildly in her mind, Rein reached for a pad of paper and began writing. Perhaps it would become a poem or story. She didn't know, but she'd always loved to write, and it occupied her for a while—got her mind off of the burden of mysteries that surrounded her. The easy creaking and swaying of the ship was calming, and outside the porthole, she saw the sun straining to make its way through the heavy, drizzly clouds.

After a few hours, she thought she'd go to the atrium and find Saria—perhaps visit her chamber or just talk and explore the ship further. Perhaps even *eat* again. She had eaten the small portions that filled her icebox the day before, but it was late enough in the day now that her hunger struck.

As she walked into the hall, quickly checking herself over, she thought about knocking on Traith's chamber door. He knew, somehow, that *she* knew which door led to his stateroom. And he had told her that if she needed him not to hesitate. She realized she needed him much more than Edgar, anyway.

The stewardess *had* told her which his room was. Two down from her own, further down the corridor. She backed up, treading a few feet deeper into the hall as softly as she could on the wooden floorboards, and she stopped when she reached the third chamber, Harker's chamber, listening for a moment for noise or movement. Unless he was sleeping or reading, Rein heard no sign of his being in, so she turned back down the hallway to the lobby: the easiest place to find entertainment. Saria was at the beverage lounge with Carden Romanoff.

She gleamed with excitement and waved when she noticed Rein. "Come here, my Rein! Are you feeling much better?" she asked enthusiastically, and as Rein nodded, she continued. "You look lovely, you know."

"Thank you," Rein replied with a smile, greeting Romanoff with her eyes.

"I'm so sorry for all the shock you've been going through," Saria said sadly, turning to acknowledge Romanoff's agreeing nod. "I don't really know what is going on concerning the letter."

"It's fine," Rein said. "I'm not sure what to think, but as of now I'm just trying to forget about it."

"It was a truthful statement," Romanoff broke in. "Mistress is a true, living person."

"But then who is she?" Rein asked, beginning to unfold her hidden fears.

He hesitated. "*That* I cannot answer. She is just someone with extraordinary abilities, in truth. She is more like a mother figure to Traith and I, but there have been…complications, that have prolonged our meeting again with her. She has been incapable of reaching Traith or I, but for some reason she reached you."

Just as relief hit Rein at hearing a confirmation that Mistress was not anything special to Traith, confusion set her back. It was like Romanoff was talking in riddles. Rein knew now that both men knew this 'Mistress' well. Either they didn't know anything more than they were telling, or they were lying to keep their secrets. That was what she needed to figure out.

Romanoff continued. "Traith was trying to break that ice easily to you, that is all, Miss Pierson. It is truly an intricate situation, but you mustn't worry. Things will work out for you."

"Perhaps you can start enjoying your trip more now," Saria said, as if the Frenchman's words had rolled off her like they'd never been said. "*And*, I must comment, now that you're here—Traith Harker!" She laughed and looked at Romanoff. "*Traith Harker*! Never have I seen a man like him!" Romanoff laughed at her as she continued. "He caught you out of nowhere, I declare, those nights ago!" She was startlingly loud. "A peculiar man indeed! He said astonishingly little at that gathering—he was rather annoyed, you know—but when he caught you he seemed so gentle!"

"I know," Rein said quietly, hoping it would quiet Saria. "His manner changes drastically, it seems."

"A prize of a man, he is, am I right Miss Pierson?" Romanoff added.

"A *prize*?" Saria laughed. "Perhaps immensely handsome, but not so valuable for women, I'm afraid to say, with such a gloomy demeanor."

"He is in a deep depression," Romanoff said sadly, "and has been since he's been stuck on this ship. To drown it out, he either submerses himself in his science or books, or trains—*exercises*—or takes to his bath. I've never known a man to enjoy bathing so. He has never been romantically involved before; at least to my knowledge. That is why he is unaccustomed to *you*, Miss Pierson. His memory of how to woo a lady has most likely withered. I most definitely have never seen him attempt to flirt before, in all his years!" He laughed, and then his shrill voice quieted. "So, he may be attempting it."

Rein prayed she wasn't glowing or turning red at his comment. At that exact moment she was thankful for having an acquaintance with the Frenchman. She was learning so much about Traith through him. He was depressed. That explained his introversion.

"Mr. Romanoff, that is quite jumping to conclusions," Rein said, smiling and trying not to flush. "I wouldn't say he has flirted at all with me."

"You say his wooing has 'withered,' but he is still a boy!" Saria replied to him. "How could such memory be withered? How old is Mr. Harker?"

Romanoff laughed with sarcasm. "He is…oh God…oh; three and twenty."

"He is merely three years older than *you*, Rein!" Saria said with applause, and Rein chuckled as Saria continued. "He is very handsome, indeed."

"Yes, he is," Rein answered with a smile.

"But I did want to ask—have you noticed the scars on his face?" Saria asked, opportunely toning her voice down. "I was nearly breathless at how handsome he was, but when I saw the scars, subtle though they may be, it takes the refined quality from him."

Rein shook her head. "He never told me how he got them."

"He has a long past with this ship," Romanoff said. "I do not even know how he obtained them for sure."

"Haven't you asked him?" Saria asked, her interest building.

Romanoff sighed with pity. "He can't remember."

Rein felt that the mystery that surrounded Traith Harker suddenly made sense. He had lost his memory. She longed to know how, but obviously that was impossible. But at least she had some sort of notion about him. Did he trust her, as she did him? Was she wrong to trust?

"He can't remember?" Saria asked in sorrow. "Oh, the pain he must feel!"

Rein was usually frustrated by Saria's drama, but this time it was called for.

"You see," Romanoff began, "something terrible happened to him that made him lose his memory of his past; he told me he remembered at least that much. That it involved a great deal of pain." He was now whispering. "The poor fellow, his tolerance to pain is unnaturally high, too. But all that he recalls—finding it even hard to articulate to me—was that there was so much pain that he still nearly *feels*—" he stopped and swallowed. "Well, anyway, he cannot recall much of anything before he turned twenty-three. I suppose that would make anyone depressed. Also, he has had a terrible family life."

"That is absolutely *dreadful*! That was his last birthday!" Saria was nearly in dramatic tears. "But didn't you know him, then, to know what happened to him?"

Romanoff hesitated. "I did, but I never learned of his past. We became better friends *after* whatever happened."

Rein was disquieted. "He mentioned a laboratory accident," she said quietly. "He said that was what affected his eyes."

"O-of course," Romanoff said with a stutter. "The accident is what contributed to his eye color, yes. But not to his scars."

"Rein told me Mr. Harker was blind," Saria said as if boasting that she knew something about him. "Although he doesn't seem it. But I see what you mean about his eyes. *Very* peculiar."

"He told you he was blind?" Romanoff asked Rein.

Rein was unsure how to reply. "No; well no. Not completely; I'm not sure—"

"He *isn't*," Romanoff said with a loss of happiness. "But his insecurity regarding his sight and his eyes are more than noticeable. He needs something to explain it with. He does see differently, though. Better."

"Better? How is that? He lied?"

"I'm sure it was only out of insecurity that Traith would lie to you, Miss Pierson. That 'accident' honed his eyesight; it didn't destroy it."

"That's interesting," Saria said, "but I want to know how old you are, Mr. Romanoff. You've failed to tell me before."

Rein stared at him when Saria spoke.

Carden Romanoff was young, but not nearly as young as Traith was. His face was slightly aged, but vibrant nonetheless. She noticed him coil a little when Saria asked him his age.

"My age?" he repeated her question to himself.

"Do you not know?" Saria asked with a good laugh.

"*J'ai cinq ans et trente ans.*"

Rein smiled in her mind. Thirty-five. It was a little odd that Saria, being only eighteen, was trying to start a relationship, as short as it might very well be, with a man his age, although she had guessed his age rather well. He had to have seen so much more of the world than Saria, and his experience in it must be vast.

"Being older than Traith, I do try to work with him about being more social. He will come around."

"Mr. Romanoff is right; he is not social at all, Rein," Saria added, just to make herself noticed in the conversation.

"But you are attracted to him, aren't you?" Romanoff asked her, and she laughed. After a pause, he continued. "Ah, but I know what you're thinking. Very elusive. He is a shy gentleman, Miss Pierson, but he is like the analogy: *a very high stone wall*, very protective and hard to climb over, but when and *if* you make it over the top, you are under the protection of the stone wall forever."

Saria laughed. "Interesting correlation, Mr. Romanoff. Would you consider yourself 'protected by the wall'?"

He sat back and held his hand on his chin with a smile. "Yes, I suppose so, though he gets quite vexed at me sometimes when I push him to do things of a sort. Ah, but it is true, he has weaknesses, though he conceals them. He is more human than he appears sometimes."

Rein suddenly flinched and turned at the creak of an opening door. She turned and saw a man sneak through the crack in the door and slam it behind him.

"That was him," Romanoff said with a snort of a laugh.

"That was Traith Harker?" Saria giggled. "In such a rush again, always out that door!" She quickly became excited. "Rein! Go try to speak with him! Follow him!"

Rein laughed. "I couldn't—"

"I would advise you to, Miss Pierson. He is hard to catch. It is rare seeing him around the lobby area." Romanoff smiled and lowered his voice. "He will not turn you away, I assure you."

chapter 14

Rein opened the larger door that led to the deck and crept through it. It was beginning to rain hard, and the crisp air greeted her with thousands of droplets stinging her face as the wind blew. It managed, as usual, to pull her well-done-up hair out of its placement and into her face. It was already completely down and blowing in front of her eyes.

Traith wasn't on the deck; therefore, she knew he was in the port door chamber underneath the ship. The ocean waves misted the top of the deck as they ran past the sides of the ship, lapping and foaming around the edges. The smoke stacks, however, that stood so tall above her, made no smoke at all. As she wondered how the ship was running, she slowly made her way to the far side of the deck.

She suddenly heard faint yelling coming from down the stairwell as she approached the door. Her hands crept up the porthole window, and she placed her ear onto the door. She could recognize Traith's voice yelling above another.

Suddenly the door opened inward, and Rein fell into him as he had come up the steps and opened it. He staggered backward but caught himself by grabbing onto the rails, a shocked expression on his face.

"Bloody hell!" he said as he caught himself and stared at her while she pulled herself up and pushed her long, wet hair out of her face. "M-Miss Pierson," he stated with shock. "What the devil are you doing out here?"

Rein immediately stood upright, fixed her dress, and cleared her throat. She noticed him slip a vial into his pocket.

"I'm sorry. I just wanted to look around a little more. Mr. Romanoff told me to go down to the meeting room, and then I heard you, and I didn't know it was raining. I didn't mean to fall into you."

He turned abruptly and shut the door behind him, just as the captain ran up the stairs yelling his name. He sighed heavily, pushed on the door for a few moments, and locked it. The captain banged on the door once or twice but then stopped. It sounded to her as if Harker swore under his breath.

"Why did you lock him in there? Why was he so upset?"

"He is unwell; I told you. Frankly I would be upset too if I were mad."

The explanation he gave was faulty; a front for his hatred.

As he rested on the port door looking back, she focused on his attire. He wore only a white, long-sleeved shirt, different than the one she had seen him in before, but similarly casual. He wore no waistcoat, and his trousers and boots were relatively the same as what he had been wearing. Because of the rain and wind, his white shirt was quickly becoming transparent, and Rein's stomach quivered with exhilaration as she observed his form. It was as if he wore nothing above his waist.

A spectacularly muscular chest and abdomen were very clear under his wet shirt. Although he was not bulky in any way, each muscle in his arm seemed to be chiseled from marble; defined, and...

"Are you all right? What are you thinking about?" he asked quietly, noticing her in a daze. He looked at the sky as it rained, blinking when the drops hit his eyes.

She laughed in embarrassment, realizing it must be obvious that she was examining him. But it was inevitable. Her heart skipped a beat, and her stomach seemed to flutter when she looked from his physique into his fantastic eyes and face. She had feelings she could not deny. He really seemed as if he didn't know how handsome he was.

Rein said nothing, but then chuckled at herself. "You are athletic, aren't you, Mr. Harker?"

He accidentally smiled, staring at the floor. "I train, yes, if that's what you meant."

"It's just, the rain made your shirt...You're very strapping." She laughed harder that time and felt herself flush.

He made a sigh of quiet, short laughter, as he always did. "It isn't meant to show off, trust me. But I suppose wearing a white shirt in the rain makes it seem so."

"Well," she cleared her throat and looked away, trying not to make him feel even more awkward, "if the captain is locked down there, who is navigating the ship?" Her embarrassment turned to uncertainty. "How could he even be captain if he is mad?"

"We have a second," he said. "Another man who does most of the navigating. The man down there technically isn't the captain, but most consider him as such. Slowly he is worsening." He stepped quickly in front of her and turned. "Let's go inside. You shouldn't be out here."

"He didn't seem unwell at the gathering," she said with charm, following him to the ship's entrance.

"Miss Pierson, were you at all part of the conversation he started?"

Rein laughed at his sarcasm.

"He is always speaking of absurd things." He lifted his tough hands up to the vaulted door-wheel, trying hard to turn it.

"Is he particularly fascinated with horror having to do with cursed beings such as vampires and werewolves?"

He grunted. "Yes, he is." Then he turned to her with a sigh of frustration. "Bloody thing seems to like locking itself from the inside. I need a key." As he felt in his pockets, she looked into his burning eyes. They slowly returned her stare.

"You two are not on good terms, are you?" she asked as he continued feeling for the key in his clothing, shifting his eyes back down.

"No, we aren't."

A moment passed. "I can't find it," he said with anger. "The madman stole my key. Bloody stole it."

Rein felt stupidly forgetful because she hadn't brought the key she had been given earlier with her. Fortunately, her forgetfulness gave them more time to be forced to talk. She didn't feel hindered by the downpour to speak to him. Despite his frustrated temperament, she managed to see gentleness underneath his hardened outer shell.

"Why were you so quiet and annoyed at the meeting he had, Mr. Harker?" she asked softly. "Or do you not want to say?"

He stood still, moving only his eyes up to look at her. "Please, there is no need to call me by my last name," he said with a sigh.

"But I feel improper calling you Traith," she said, smiling harder and with more passion.

He laughed slightly. "I suppose it could feel improper. But," he held his arms out to his sides with his head cocked, "I'm sure you understand that formality isn't something I'm known for." He let his hands fall, staring into the rain at her. "It really doesn't matter that we get inside quickly now, does it?"

He was right; they both were soaked. He left her and walked back toward the port door, so she turned and followed him.

"You did not answer my first question," Rein said agreeably to him on their way back to the port door.

He thought a moment before he replied, his ear against the metal, listening for the captain. "What was it?"

"Why were you so unresponsive during the meeting that day?"

He turned and chuckled. She saw his brilliantly white teeth to the full extent. She had never seen his teeth, not even when he spoke since he always mumbled. It was as if he had been hiding his smile, but in that momentary glimpse, she knew why.

They were as white as snow, but his top set of eyeteeth and the bottom alike were very sharp and pointed, like those of a carnivorous animal. It was only the canines on his upper and lower jaws that were sharp; all the other teeth were quite regular. The upper ones were much longer than his lower, which were only slightly pointed. She realized they greatly reminded her of Romanoff's teeth. How had she not noticed them before? He had spoken so many times to her.

He closed his mouth. "Damn," he said, turning his fiery eyes away from her and shaking his head in anger, a smile of pure frustration up his face.

She was baffled at his harsh response, and her heartbeat began ringing in her ears.

"Bizarre aren't they?" he said with an irritable look.

She felt guilty as a murderer. "Traith," she murmured. "Traith, I'm so, so sorry. But what happened to you?"

chapter 15

H e became very grave, and his eyes narrowed. "My teeth aren't cherished, Rein," was all he said. "Just like my scars, and my eyes."

Through the downpour she stared at him. She thought she was crying but it was hard to tell. She felt as though she had nearly severed her friendship with him by asking that question.

"Dear God. I'm ruining this, aren't I?" she said.

He said nothing, and there was a pause.

"I want you to trust me, Traith," she muttered. "Don't fear that I would say something about you to anyone. Please."

The fiery red of his eyes enlarged. "I do trust you," he said simply. "But there are some things that I want to keep hidden. Doesn't matter now, though." He shook his head. "I don't know what happened to me, Rein." The time nearly stood still. "I can't remember."

Through the rain, she saw his insecurity, and her heart ached for him. His quiet temperament had to be because he feared people seeing him as different.

But he didn't know *her*. Didn't know that she was unlike most typical girls who might be deterred by such differences as his. Differences that meant nothing to her.

He had told her the truth—the truth that Romanoff had told her first. He was being honest.

"It doesn't take away from you," she said as she approached him. "You're differences aren't that dramatic, and they make you *you*. To me, anyway."

He looked shocked. "Mhm," he mumbled. "Of course they do. They would have to, you never knew me as anything else."

Rein was miserable for him. He faced the port door, unlocking it slowly. A key lay on the top step of the stairwell, and the captain was gone. Traith bent down and with a swoop of his hand, grabbed the key, stood straight, and pushed the door closed, locking it again.

"Look what I found," he said in exasperation.

"I don't mind the rain," she replied. But her heart was still stinging. "Traith, please don't be upset."

He walked slowly to the entrance door. But almost as fast as he had turned to look at her, the wind picked up with ferocity and a huge wave hit the side of the ship. He felt for a rail or a door handle as the wave rose above them. Then she saw him throw the bottle that he had put into his pocket off the side of the ship.

The wave crashed down, and the last thing she saw was him falling and being thrust into a rail. She heard him hit the rail and grunt, but the wash of saltwater by that time was already over her face. Knocked down, she was sliding on the deck as the sudden rush of saltwater stung her eyes and lips. Then she hit something, a rail, and covered her face until the water washed off of the deck.

And then she felt two hands lift her up and hold her shoulders. Blinking to open her eyes, the salt still burning them, she could barely see his face through the rain.

"That was uncalled for," he said, and she saw unclearly his forearm raise and wipe across his face. "And brutal. Are you all right?"

She nodded, and when the burning sensation left her, she gazed at him. He was still holding her up with one hand, and he didn't let go. But she didn't pull away. It seemed as though his eyes were shining through the rain. His other hand took her other shoulder. She noticed that she was drawing closer to him.

Was it on purpose? It had to be. But she couldn't control herself. She was nearly in a dream, where their faces drew closer and closer…

But it ended.

He recoiled slowly, let go of her, and held his hand out for hers.

She shook her head and forgot about the dream. Had it been a dream? No; she had nearly tasted his lips. In their closeness, she had breathed in his appealing cologne through the dank, salty smell of the ocean. Nearly tasted *him*. In that sheer instant, she wasn't sure what had happened.

He led her back to the entrance door, quickly unlocked it, and brought her into the ship with him, closing the door. His head was down, and he shook his hands to remove the excess water. She felt ill. They had almost kissed. His eyes were so intent on her, but he'd stopped it.

"I can't say I've ever been hit by a wave that size before," he said quietly.

She made an empty smile. "You've been hit by a wave before?"

"A couple times out on that bloody deck, but that one was massive."

"Terrible weather," she said with a smile. "And all I can taste now is that nasty saltwater."

His eyes turned to her with sadness. Perhaps he had felt it as well—that fascination. Certainly he had. "I suppose we should change into drier clothes."

"Yes, I suppose so."

"Have you eaten yet?" he asked.

She stared at him for a moment. Out of nowhere he had become relaxed. She felt herself smiling.

"No. I haven't at all today. Barely at all yesterday, save what was in my icebox." She choked. "There were two plates, you know."

His eyes widened. "You were in your room since *then*? The entire time you stayed in your chamber?" With her acknowledgement, he shook his head in thought. "I don't recall ordering two meals." He wrung some more excess water off his shirt, and his manner took a sudden turn to graveness.

"Do you have anything else you're hiding from me, Traith?" she asked softly. "I truly want to be your friend. I want you to have someone to talk to." She was speaking without thinking, she realized after she had finished.

But to her relief, he was not acting as if she had spoken too brazenly. His eyes were focused directly at her. "No. You've learned just about everything," he whispered. "Thank you, Rein."

He took a single step away. They were interrupted with a sudden opening of a door, the one leading to the atrium. Relief swept over her at seeing that it was Carden Romanoff, and he had stopped Traith from leaving.

"Traith!" he yelled heartily and with a welcoming laugh. "God, man, did you feel that hit? The whole ship tossed! Tables are turned over everywhere!"

"Yes," Traith said, not yet facing him, "I felt it. It was cold."

"You are sopping!" Romanoff added.

Traith then turned his body to him, his voice full of no enthusiasm at all. "By the way, Carden..."

Romanoff's large eyes were filled with happiness as he paced up to the two of them through the dimly lit hallway. "Why, you both are! Miss Pierson," he said in greeting as he bowed slightly. "For what purpose were you both standing in the rain?"

"We felt like taking a bath," Traith said sarcastically.

"Was that a wave that hit this ship?" the Frenchman asked sincerely.

"Was that not obvious enough?" Traith murmured.

Romanoff huffed. "Hold that saucy tongue of yours for a mere moment, will you?" He sighed. "Once both of you *merfolk* dry off, why don't you prepare yourselves for a little tête-à-tête with Saria and I tonight? We can order dinner and sit in the unused parlor." He paused when Traith shot him a cold glance, but smiled anyway. "In the unused parlor in the *V-Wing*, yes! That room would be perfect, seeing as no one goes in there. We would have it to ourselves!"

"Do you realize what time it is?" Traith asked dryly.

"Not at all late!" Romanoff replied as casually as always.

Rein greatly anticipated the possibility. Just the four of them would be so splendid, and they could eat and spend time together. But the look on Traith's face suggested that any debate over it at all would be closed.

He began speaking hesitantly. "I don't think—"

Romanoff chimed in fast. "Just *stop* thinking and have a bit of fun, eh, monsieur?"

Traith looked at her for a moment and then sighed. "I suppose," he said nearly inaudibly, as if only his lips had been moving.

"Good!" Romanoff announced, his voice echoing in the hall. He patted Traith hard on the back, but he didn't even flinch. "I shall tell the cook to bring us food there, and we can meet you, once you both are dry and dressed, down at the West Parlor!"

Romanoff seemed to be glowing with excitement, practically lighting up the dark hallway, and he led them both back into the atrium. Rein glanced with a smile over at Traith, but he wasn't paying any attention, shaking his wet hands and looking down. It was amusing to see his frustration over being wet. When she giggled, his head snapped up, but he smiled, and she saw passion take hold of his face for the first time.

"We must look horrible in front of all these people, sopping as we are," she said laughing. Her heart was racing with chills from the cold and the thrill of the proposed dinner and what was nearly a kiss.

"They usually don't pay any attention to me." He looked around and shook his head when he noticed the people staring coldly. "Who knows? Those might be their happy faces. None of their expressions ever change."

Such sarcasm as his was intriguing to her, and she laughed at it, as did Romanoff in front of them. Then that made him smile. She realized that she felt revived and happy for nearly the first time since her arrival on the ship. The odd part was, it was because of Traith Harker, not because she had left England and seen the ocean. She also sensed that it was probably his first time feeling happy since she had boarded—or perhaps it was his first time feeling happy since long before that.

chapter 16

S he heard a knock on her door. It was nearly seven o'clock at night, and she was just slipping her boots on when a hand knocked again. She quickly buckled her boots and went to the door, opening it, and secretly lost her breath at the sight of Traith Harker.

He was dressed casually, though a little more formal than before. She remembered with chills his muscular upper half, which had been clear when his shirt was wet. It was now concealed beneath a black vest over a loose white shirt, and he had added a cravat and black string tie. His brown hair was kicked forward almost into his eyes, but it didn't disguise the fiery color of them. She was completely engrossed in every fiber of him. It felt like he was touching her everywhere at once without lifting a finger.

She was only in a long-sleeved, dark gray dress, but it was enough to look pretty, she hoped.

"Good evening, again," Traith said with a smile, and she became fully and gladly aware of his relaxed tone.

She laughed softly in reply. "You look nice and dry," she said. "I feel like I've had wet dresses hanging in my room since I got here."

"The weather is usually much calmer than this," he said.

He backed up, and she came out of her chamber, locking it and following behind him down the hall—for the first time, not toward the atrium. To her joy he stopped and waited for her to reach his side, his eyes holding a glint of pleasure in them. At the end of the hall he opened a door, one that was not marked with any number.

Inside, the room was darkly decorated, similar in design to her chamber, but she had come to the conclusion that each of the halls had a different theme to them, and her hall was romantic and dark. The wood paneling was dusky, and the walls were a deep red. There was a single large, medieval table in the side of the parlor, and next to it was a beautiful organ. There was a small shelf of books, almost fashioned as a small library. She decided that it was a quaint and likeable room. At the other side she saw Saria and Romanoff already seated within a circular pattern of furniture, including a divan, two armchairs, and three couches.

"Glad you two have arrived," Saria said with her frivolous giggle. "Carden just finished ordering dinner for us all! Isn't that nice?"

"Quite," Rein said, walking past a few of the candelabras that lit the place as brightly as she had seen yet.

She then took a seat across from Saria and Romanoff. Traith sat at the armchair in the corner, relaxing his muscled shoulders that protruded from underneath the white fabric he wore.

"The servant said he might be late with the dinner, though," Romanoff said haughtily. "*That's* why I initially protested against the captain having permitted them on board in the first place! They cause such disorder."

Traith gave a humorous grin, his lapel practically touching his tough jaw in his slouch. "You Frenchmen—always so judgmental."

Saria laughed over Romanoff's shocked snort. "The French are far more valuable than you think, Harker," he said.

"Not really," Traith retorted. "Always starting wars and such, especially with England. I *figured* you needed history refreshment."

It was then that Rein noticed the humor in Traith's speech. This was his way of joking.

"Why are we discussing the French? In any case, we don't start those wars," Romanoff said, sitting straighter and raising his voice.

"Carden," Traith returned with a single, quiet expression of amusement, "if your bloody country stopped interfering with everyone's lives, over half the war in Europe would cease, and you would save yourselves the embarrassment of getting beat all the time."

At that point, Saria was laughing so hard that Rein thought she would topple over. Her face was completely red. "You *two*!" was all she could manage to say.

Rein found herself laughing as well, but she was more interested in taking in each facial expression and remark between the two men, especially Traith's.

"If I'm not mistaken, the French won nearly every war fought with England!" Romanoff spurted.

"Well then, I believe you are mistaken," Traith answered amusingly. "One war out of many, and it was by accident anyway. But perhaps you think that way because we kept our loyalty and never cheated in order to randomly throw a ruler off of his throne for no particular reason."

Romanoff laughed proudly. "It isn't my fault you aren't French or that you are not able to have the French assertiveness," he said.

"Carden, why would I want to be? I hate Frenchmen. Their arrogance and terrible breath exceed all limits of the imagination."

She couldn't believe what she was hearing. Saria was curled over top of Romanoff in tears and even he was nearly turning red with laughter. Traith seemed to be laughing more than she had ever seen him, though he was still subdued. It was like a hardly audible chuckle when he laughed, but he was always smiling with his head cocked. She was baffled at how comical Traith was and how entertaining he could be without trying. He was content and enjoying himself, too, which made her feel content. But how the two men were friends with such differences was beyond her imagination. It was then that she noticed their friendship was as deep as her and Saria's, and just as perplexing.

"Here we go!" Romanoff burst with another snort of a laugh. "You're stooping that low, are you?"

Traith shook his head, his face balanced on his fist with a smile.

"Traith, do you know how to say your Rs? I can never quite hear them!"

Saria was having a fit of laughter, and her red face was turning blue. Rein felt herself laughing harder than before, too. Traith's British accent was actually very similar to her own. She saw Traith begin to suck in his laughter and shake with it.

"Say 'cart' or 'heart,' Traith!" Romanoff taunted on. "Go on, say them! *Ca'ht? Hea'ht?* Did you hear? Or, *heah?* Do your Rs just disappear, or can't you pronounce that letter at all?" Romanoff was laughing so heartily that the room nearly shook.

Traith was laughing, as well. "You're the idiot sticking your tongue up like a hound to pronounce anything English, so careful *what*—"

"*H'wot? H'wot?* I can barely say that!"

Traith had begun to answer, but he had to stop his speech to laugh, and Rein was fascinated to hear it.

"You aren't *supposed* to be able to say it," Traith said after he managed to subdue his laughter. "Mainly because you aren't supposed to even speak English! In fact, why don't you bite your flailing tongue, and pray quit speaking my language?"

"Ah! *Semble-t-il un peu mieux?*"

Traith made a fist and held it partly up. He let it fall limply between his knees and shook his head. "Bloody frog," he whispered with a wicked smile.

He had spoken it too quietly for Saria to hear, as she was still laughing strenuously. But Rein couldn't help but snicker when she heard him say that; he seemed to be in possession of a terrible tongue, and had only a slight guilt at speaking in any manner he pleased in front of her and her friend.

"Ha! *Touché*, Traith! What name have they for the British? Excuse me; I dare not say it, as you are the only person here *shaming* the British title. These two fine women make me begin to adore it."

Just then, a knock on the door stopped the laughing quarrel. Traith sunk lower in the armchair and pinched the bridge of his nose with his thumb and first two fingers, shaking his head and laughing downward. Rein knew he hid his face to laugh further. She knew that Saria was the only one he was hiding his peculiar smile from.

chapter 17

Romanoff answered the door. The servant who came in was a grown man this time, and when he entered Rein saw that he had a large, reflective silver tray in his long hands. Two other servants followed him, carrying other various trays and pitchers.

The way Romanoff stared at the servants proved Traith's charge of arrogance. His large, brown eyes were cut in half and his smile was just short of being a snarl, devoid of any appreciation whatsoever; his aristocratic nature was obvious. The servants quickly exited the room when they had laid out the food and drinks on the enormous oaken table.

She heard Traith chuckling as she watched the Frenchman, and she quickly turned to see his face. He was covering his face, but his shoulders were shaking in a teasing amusement.

"He's so stupid," Traith mouthed to her, pointing to Romanoff, for only her to hear in his laughter.

Rein's eyebrows rose and she bit her bottom lip to hold back an interrupting laugh. She began to feel him becoming a whole person; he had a dry, sarcastic, rough manner about him, but a gallant elegance and formality ate away half of his rawness, leaving two opposite sides of him.

She liked that. She liked figuring him out.

Rein stood. Traith, then, rose casually from his slouch and cleared his throat, his hand out signaling her to go ahead of him. He then waited for Saria, who was in a tizzy trying to fix herself without a mirror. By his silent expression, Rein noticed that he seemed slightly annoyed at Saria's dilly-dallying.

She took a seat at the table, her back to the close wall. Romanoff lifted the two ornate, metallic tray lids to reveal biscuits and butter and meats and even potatoes. Then there was the wine—two bottles of red. After he had made ready the food, he tried to take a seat at the piano, but Traith motioned for him.

"Ah, these men!" Saria burst out saying, her voice raised as it commonly was. "Are you not having a most pleasing time, Rein? I am!"

Rein nodded and smiled with a sort of giggle, but couldn't help her eyes from straying over to where the two men stood, mumbling lowly to each other. They seemed to be arguing—as usual.

Saria stopped and breathed a long, high-pitched sigh. She turned around in her chair across from Rein and yelled, "Gentlemen! The conversation should begin over dinner, should it not?"

Both men paused. Traith's arm was out as if laying down a law, and Romanoff's were both at his sides. The two men froze a moment until Romanoff cleared his throat and walked over to the table with a large smile. Traith turned his head in frustration but then scrupulously walked over and took a seat at the end of the table. He tried to seem unaffected by whatever it was they had been talking about, but he wasn't nearly as good as Romanoff was about it.

Then Saria began speaking without end. Rein tuned her out and thought she heard Romanoff say something about eating, but it seemed as though Traith didn't want to. Romanoff returned to the piano.

"You play?" Saria asked enthusiastically, stopping her personal imitation of a filibuster.

Traith seemed to cringe at the shrill in her voice, and Rein thought it amusing that her flirtatious attitude made him uncomfortable. She always did feel that if Saria wasn't a Christian woman, she could be a harlot. It had the opposite effect on Romanoff.

"Ah, my love, I do! I will eat after a few songs. Enjoy!"

My love? What had he just called Saria?

Romanoff began a simple but formal tune. It was beautiful. His fingers hit each key so quickly it sounded like a harp. Saria, during or after the song, took a little of each thing to place on her plate. Rein was hungry, but she tried to be a bit more graceful than Saria.

Traith sat still, not touching the food.

"Do you not sing at all, Mr. Harker?" Saria asked. "Or play?"

"I try not to."

"He has the potential to do very well at both, I am sure!" Carden boomed over his keen piano playing.

Rein felt herself light up a little when Traith chuckled once more. "I wouldn't say any such thing, Carden."

"Well are you not hungry, then, Mr. Harker?" Saria asked. "Why, after such a long day, I should very much like for you to eat with us!"

His face was so sober he nearly looked ill. His fiery, powerful eyes, set like a perfect work of art, shifted to Romanoff, who played unwaveringly. But his eyes met Traith's in return and he nodded his head forward as if indicating for Traith to eat.

Traith took up the right pitcher, filling a goblet. Then Romanoff became quicker and lighter with the piano beat, going up and down the scale as if to make fun of him—or to show off his playing.

Traith shook his head and smiled at the way the man seemed to play Traith's movements. "I'm not very hungry this evening," Traith said over Romanoff's music. "Swallowed enough of that saltwater to fill me for a week."

"Oh please, do have something!" Saria begged. "Rein, here, is usually uncomfortable eating in front of a gentleman who isn't doing the same."

Rein felt herself flush and her eyes widen in response to Saria. She was right, though; that was one of her little mannerisms that Saria often did point out.

Traith's face donned that gentle expression she had noticed him give her a few times before. "Perhaps I will, then."

Saria looked content and chewed on a biscuit as happily as a child. Traith reached across the table and took a piece of bread. He seemed nearly reluctant to place it in his mouth, and he did so looking down.

Rein was eating a piece of cooked meat, but she was intrigued at the way Traith ate the bread. He swallowed it slowly, and his face gave that unreadable (perhaps annoyed) gaze. It must have seemed that way to Romanoff, for he began playing more slowly and formally.

No, Traith wasn't looking at him out of annoyance with his playing. There was a hidden thought between the two she couldn't quite figure out.

"This food is just delectable," Saria said in between bites, completely ignoring the seriousness of the two men in that instant. "Don't you think so, Rein?"

"Yes," she replied, taking her eyes quickly off of Traith.

"Well, tomorrow night, there will be more than just that type of food," Romanoff announced over his music, breaking his stare with Traith. "Tomorrow night is the ship's ball. Tell them about it, Traith!"

"My *Lord*!" Saria yelled.

Rein perked up at Romanoff's words about a ball. How was that possible? Then, from the corner of her eye, she saw Traith clench his teeth.

He continued his glare at Romanoff, speaking quietly and directly. "I wasn't going." His relaxed mood seemed to have taken an about face.

The Frenchman laughed. "Don't pay attention to my friend, here," he said. "The balls are magnificent, and we're having one tomorrow evening. Perhaps you could rather say afternoon; it begins in the late afternoon. It would be far better than anything else you could spend your evening doing." Romanoff's smile always made Rein feel happy, and he motioned his head toward Traith. "He'll come."

Rein felt excited. "A ball? On a ship? That's ridiculous, but I would love to go. This ship really is a wonder."

"It is a wonder," Romanoff said. "You see—"

"You know what, Carden?" Traith cut in. "Why don't you take my seat, here, and drink with 'your love.' You've been at it all day anyway."

Rein felt as miserable as the weather when he said that, and she began to feel ignored, as if he didn't see her there at all anymore.

"Is that an invite for me?" Saria asked back on the subject about the ball, purposely allowing time for Traith to calm.

"Oh yes," Romanoff said with a finishing note of his music. "I would be honored to have you join me." Romanoff let his fingers finish out a few notes to end the song and then stood and walked over to Traith.

He looked up at him as though he were insane.

Romanoff patted him on the back. "But I would be just as honored for *you* to take fair Miss Pierson, here."

"No, it's all right if he isn't interested in the ball," Rein said. She'd tried to stop herself from saying that, but she felt too awkward to plainly accept Romanoff's words.

"Madame, you do not know any other man on this ship besides your unflattering escort, and Traith, you need to get out more. She really has no one else to go with but you."

Traith looked at Rein for a moment, and his eyes were sad. "I can't. Carden, you know I don't exactly blend well at balls." He looked at her, and she felt any excitement she had shrivel at his words. "I'm sorry."

He stood, said good evening, and left the room. Rein nearly felt her eyes watering, but she was good enough at hiding her emotions that she made it invisible to the other two left in the room. There was a deathly silence in the room for a moment, until Saria broke it.

"Oh, Rein," she said with sorrow in her high voice. "Perhaps he isn't as perfect as he looks. You must still come—"

Romanoff laughed. How he could was beyond her. She felt distant, and she felt a sudden chill of emptiness as she bit on her lip. It had felt as though he perhaps cared for her. It had felt as though he was just learning to be at ease around her, and he suddenly resorted to mystery again. And now she couldn't talk privately with him again for a while.

"Cheer up, Madame," Romanoff said, ending his laugh.

"No, no," Rein said, defending her independence. "It's fine, honestly."

"Traith will come. He probably just won't dance. But you never know."

"If he doesn't want to, I would hate for him to feel obligated," she said, trying to smile, hiding her choke.

"Perhaps you should forget about him," Saria said in a failed attempt to be soothing. "He—"

"He has a great deal of potential, Miss Kendrick, if someone would learn that he doesn't mean to drive people off with the way he acts. You need to keep at him, Miss Pierson." He paused and sat in a chair next to Saria. "I have never seen him laugh in front of anyone else but me before. Ever. He is comfortable around you. His predator-like mannerisms fade."

Rein noted the mistake he made in pronouncing *predator* more like *prezahter*, but she had not time to think of it. Was what he was saying true? To her relief, Saria made no reply.

"I know Traith well enough to vouch that he will come."

Rein paused. "What about going to a ball does he detest? Why wouldn't he dance; doesn't he know how?"

"Oh he does. Believe me, he does. He dances quite well, if I am so bold, he just chooses not to most of the time. He is so introverted that he prefers to be alone most of the time, and balls are the most social places one could be in." He ducked down toward Rein, looking at the door Traith exited. "Right now he is just choosing to be *le coquin damné.*"

Rein swallowed. Romanoff had actually, for the first time, returned fire with words by calling Traith something rather vulgar.

Then he sighed. "He is indescribable, Miss Pierson," he said, calmer.

"So unpredictable," Saria said as if she were part of a gossip chain. "He was at first so cold, then comforting to you, then hilarious with his sarcasm, and then cold again. Moody."

"I can see that," Rein replied with fading words.

"But I am working on him," Romanoff repeated. "He does seem to have a weakness for you already, despite his ambiguous responses. He does not make friends easily, and you're beginning to become one," Romanoff said, taking a long drink from his goblet. "Or, perhaps, more than one."

She laughed to lighten that mood. "I greatly appreciate your encouragement."

She knew she had done a good job lightening the mood when both her friends began eating comfortably.

"So why is Traith forced to stay on this ship?" Rein asked. "If he had a castle, as you mentioned before?" Rein continued when she noticed that she had Romanoff's complete attention. "He told me he inherited it, that he wasn't wealthy."

"Well, Madame, that would make him a flat out liar."

Rein set her fork down after taking a bite of meat and swallowing it. It went down painfully.

"He still has his castle, Miss Pierson, and he is extremely wealthy. Extremely," Romanoff replied. "He has to be on this ship, as do I, for the Mistress. She is our...how do you say? Chef. Patron. Leader, is what you say? Our work for her is done out of necessity, not money. Why, I am nearly as wealthy as he." Rein saw Saria let off a glow. "Not quite as. I would like to assume that he was being humble in saying he inherited the castle."

"No," Rein said softly. "He lied."

Traith earlier affirmed that he had told her everything. Although she understood completely that he didn't have to tell her all of his secrets, he had lied, and for no apparent reason.

She knew, now, that something wasn't right. She was being lied to about more than one thing. It struck her when she noticed Romanoff's teeth again. They had both been in some kind of accident together. They all had. She needed to find out what exactly that accident was. There had to be so much more to the story than what she had heard, and she had a strong feeling that her letter played a crucial part in that story.

After another half of an hour or so of talk, Rein thought she might excuse herself. She had only stayed that extra time to not seem as rude as Traith Harker.

Clearing her throat, she stood. "I'm getting tired," she said with a yawn. "If you would excuse me, I'm going back to my chamber for the night."

Romanoff stood at her departure. Saria stood to embrace her a moment, a gesture of Saria's that reminded Rein of why the two were friends. After she said goodbye, she headed back to her chamber.

She had to get to sleep to prepare for a ball tomorrow, a ship's ball, something that was more unusual than anything yet. Then she would wait for the possibility of Traith Harker's arrival. Perhaps she would ask him why he had lied. They were becoming friends, it seemed, and there lay a chance that they could be more than that. She didn't want there to be any secrets between them.

chapter 18

She rolled around in the soft and airy covers of the featherbed. Her room was dark, and she heard the wind whistle just outside her porthole. She was comfortable, lying on her side in the drowsy state that she found herself in each morning, but it was still dark. She fumbled her hand around the side of the bed and grasped the pocket watch that her father had given her a long time ago. It was some time past three o'clock. She tried to sleep further, but thoughts of her father haunted her. She sat up slowly, pushing her loose, black hair out of her face. Perhaps she could read for a while under a candle.

The next moment, Rein realized that the sun was up. Daytime heat had settled inside the chamber. Her eyes fluttered a moment to regain consciousness. Perhaps she had been more tired than she had felt.

Then a sudden continuous rap at the door startled her to awakening. She staggered to stand and looked outside her door through a chain opening. She sighed.

"Dear God, Rein!" Saria said with her voice raised through the chain.

Rein opened the latch on the door and let Saria in. She tottered in, entering when the ship tossed a little. Rein looked down and saw that the pocket watch was still in her hand. It read three o'clock.

"No…" Rein mumbled.

"*Yes*, Rein! It's three o'clock in the afternoon!" Saria sighed loudly when she took a seat at the table chair. "Lord, I've been knocking all day, and you didn't answer. I was starting to worry."

She had slept that late? The *ball*.

"The ball?" Rein asked clumsily. "When does the ball start?"

"In two hours!" Saria stood and circled her. "And look at you, in nothing but your chemise! Your hair is in knots," she sighed.

Rein couldn't disagree with her. Her eyes were still nearly glued shut from her haze of sleepiness.

"Shall I stay here with you to help you put on your corset? I can put it on tighter than you can."

Rein's anticipation had turned to excitement at the realization that the ball was to begin soon. After Saria tied her corset for her and left to finish getting ready herself, Rein shook with anxiety. She didn't know quite what to think about the entire ordeal. So many frightening things had happened, and it was only six nights into the trip, but the thought, as small the thought may be, of having found love outweighed her fear. However, she knew she would eventually have to leave the ship. But she could give him her address. Did she even have one anymore? Was she going to live with some man named Hall, or whoever had her house now? Was that even true? She had the money to buy it back, but the very idea was haunting. She could give Traith Saria's address if she had to, or perhaps he would come with her.

She tried to forget about that last thought, as it was entirely improbable. She wiped those kinds of thoughts out of her head; she had to enjoy herself tonight—make this trip worthwhile, Traith or not.

Rein opened her wardrobe to look at her dresses. At first she looked into it blindly, still wondering about how she could have slept for so long. She chose a yellow dress with a dark bodice and black lace out of the armoire, hoping it would fit. It was made of a satiny chiffon material, and in the light it almost sparkled with a grey haze. She only wore two petticoats to give the dress a slight widening. She refused to wear more than that.

Tying her bodice loosely, since she already had a corset on tight underneath, Rein sat down on the bed and opened her parcel. She pulled out a pair of black leather boots with a pointed toe and thin heel. After she buckled them, she spent a while with her hair, making it as lovely as she could. Dusk was beginning to set it, so she knew it was near time to get to the ball.

She headed out to the atrium, trying hard to keep her balance as the ship rocked. As she came to the end of the hallway, she noticed that the atrium was completely empty, other than the stewardess at the desk. She never seemed to move or leave that spot.

"Going to the ball?" she asked bleakly. "Down that hall, there."

She pointed to one of the halls Rein had never looked down. She noticed a small sign hanging in it, pointing to the ballroom. She nodded and thanked the lady, who looked back down at her papers.

What did the stewardess do all day? It was as if she never slept.

As she walked through the hall, through the dimness of scattered sconces and candlelit tables, she saw a large doorway to the right with withered plants and flowers in vases by it. She could hear muted music playing from inside the enormous room and the clashing of dishes and shuffling of feet. She made a quick review of herself, feeling her hair and running a hand over her dress to smooth out any wrinkles or folding in the whalebone. With her head high and posture straight, she opened one of the doors a crack and found that no one was watching her entrance. People were talking and laughing, dishes were being clanked with spoons and forks at a large buffet table, and Carden Romanoff was playing the organ beautifully next to a violinist.

With relief she found she was still unnoticed and, relaxing with a sigh, she found a corner in which to stand and observe. People passed her by and danced around her; she took a long glance around the ballroom for Traith Harker. He was nowhere to be found.

She turned, her heart, and saw Saria approaching her.

She was in a long, blue, bell-shaped gown with gigot sleeves and pink gloves. It was quite a sweet dress and was very predictably the one she would prefer.

"Do you like it?" Saria asked.

"It's charming, Saria," Rein said, smiling. "It suits you perfectly."

"You look like quite the beauty yourself, but I see you still won't widen your dress." Rein smirked as Saria spoke again. "And where's your cravat?"

Rein's eyes gazed down. "Oh. I forgot."

"I see that, because your bodice is so low," she snickered.

Rein looked down fast, hoping it wasn't too much. She hadn't paid attention to it. There always seemed to be something she forgot.

"But the low neckline does look alluring, Rein," Saria continued, nearly to herself. "Even off the shoulder, and long, tight sleeves, and an *adorable* black lace; you know, that shows off your perfect figure immensely! I do declare! Look at the bows on your lower half. Turn around. Oh, the black bows! The lace! Oh my, Rein, that dress is beautiful even without a crinoline or cravat!"

Her praise felt wonderful.

"Oh, fingerless, black gloves, Rein! You look ravishing!"

Rein laughed at her enthusiasm. "Thank you," she said. "So do you!"

"*Well*, did you see Carden playing the organ?" Saria said, glancing over at the musicians. "Oh, he's so good at it. I'm surprised he never pursued a musical career!"

Rein ignored Saria's boasting of him. "He told me that he lives on this ship like Traith Harker does," she said with a cross of her arms. "But you know that, don't you?"

"Yes, I heard him last night. Apparently he and Harker are very good friends."

"Apparently?" Rein protested. "I didn't exactly think it *apparent* the way they were at each other last night, even in jest. They are harsh with each other, without doubt."

"They were just having manly fun, is all," Saria said, giggling. Rein managed to chuckle as Saria continued. "But Carden does seem to make up for Mr. Harker's lost ground, does he not?"

Rein lost her laughter with a deep breath. "Yes. I suppose he does."

"Oh! But I just love hearing the man play! And his *adorable* accent!" She got quiet and leaned her head toward Rein. "You know, it was truly hilarious the way the two went after each other yesterday! Traith's accent is very formal, I must say. Why, I think it is extremely appealing! But you know me—all about romance. The French are known for such romantic pleasure!"

Rein laughed but followed with a serious question. "But have you ever noticed their teeth, Saria? They're—"

"They're *fine*. It doesn't mean anything. Perhaps I'll ask if it has anything to do with the accident your Mr. Harker was in. They are best—"

"He isn't mine."

"No? Please!"

"Saria, it's only been days since I've even met him!" she said casually, though somehow it felt much longer. "But you haven't seen him anywhere, have you?" She tried desperately to hide any stupid, girly infatuation that might've been apparent.

"I haven't. I couldn't imagine why he wouldn't come. It's so nice!"

Rein quieted down. "I couldn't either."

"Have you eaten? The food is wonderful. Come with me."

Rein smiled, but turned once more in search of Harker. Her eyes were searching to no avail.

Saria sat down at the table next to Romanoff, who had stopped playing the organ. Rein sat as well and quickly made a plate of finger sandwiches, carrots, and potatoes for herself. She tasted it, and it left a mouthwatering flavor in her throat. She took a cup of wine, as well, and drank it.

"I am sorry, for Mr. Harker, Rein," Saria said, turning pale. "I know you do like him." Rein smiled, attempting to maintain her temper as Saria continued. "Your beauty, I think, should be a strong lure for any man. He is a handsome man, young too. His dress is a bit plain for his type, however. He would be a good beau for you, I should like to say."

"I wish you would stop with these comments, Saria, about my being elegant in manner, or handsome, or whichever one—"

"I cannot! What I say is true! And yet," Saria spoke with a manner of more sensibility, "when gentlemen approach you to ask your hand for dancing, for tea, for different things, you decline them. It is a very foolish notion you have."

Rein smiled, placing her hands under the table. "But no one has ever admired me for anything but being appealing, and I don't like—"

"Your shrewdness is too overbearing, Rein!" Saria announced. "You should be thankful for any man who wants you!"

"Why are you drawn to Traith Harker, then, Miss Pierson?" Romanoff asked. "If men do not attract you?"

"I spoke nothing of ill attraction, Mr. Romanoff," Rein said with assertion, now fiddling with her fork. "I am very willing to admire a man, but only if he is attracted to me for a reason of worth. Traith Harker is different. He is apprehensive about me, about speaking near me, but he's slowly unbolting his own locked doors, and I feel it is when he speaks with me. He isn't the kind to like someone for the way she looks. His own attraction, if there be any at all, is not due to beauty."

"You are exactly right, Madame," Romanoff chuckled. "And do not worry. He will come." He spoke with composure and confidence. "He will show up."

Their conversation continued on a different topic for a while, as Rein chose to change it. Once they had finished dinner, Saria stood and smiled with pity at Rein but left the table with Romanoff to dance. Rein waved her on with an empty smile, but soon stood up and walked toward the back of the floor beside a pillar, feeling bare inside. Playing with her glove ineptly, she heard the quiet closing of a door and looked toward it. She smiled breathlessly to herself as she looked upon Traith.

chapter 19

Her stomach was fluttering inside to see him. He wore a dark suit with a pinstriped grey and black vest, a tall but not stiffened white collar and cravat, and his black string tie. His coattails hung behind him elegantly. He actually looked like he was dressed for a ball. He was clean shaven, but his hair was still somewhat unkempt; not slicked back or combed perfectly like most men's hair was.

He scanned the room, his eyes flickering around uneasily. Then, with sorrow, Rein saw more clearly the scars on his face. They were not disfiguring, by any means, but there were so many. They looked like they were the result of deep cuts, long and narrow. Some, or most, were where he was once shadowed with bristles.

He didn't see her, but he didn't seem to be trying to find her either. He slipped in as quietly as he could and sat at a table off by itself. She eagerly moved closer to him, and he smiled when he saw her.

"I'm so glad you came!" she said happily.

He laughed with his face down. "Yes, Carden can read me like a book sometimes." He paused and stared at her, his manner reserved. "You look striking."

She was stunned by his words, and she felt hotter than ever; an unfathomable excitement and chill jolted down her body. He thought she was striking?

"Th-thank you," she stuttered with a smile. "You do as well."

He said nothing for a moment. He was detached; he sat slouched in his seat. It was his regular slouch, one of relaxation, but she realized that it was a bit odd that he did so because he walked with a most proper step.

"Have you eaten, Traith?" she asked him, hoping it would make him livelier.

"Eaten?" he repeated, a slight quiver in his voice. "I did. In my stateroom, earlier."

She did not question him, but she had a feeling he was not speaking in truth. Again. He looked over at Romanoff, who was dancing with Saria in front of them. The Frenchman nodded at Traith with a large smile. Traith returned it and then revolved his attention back to Rein.

"Why don't you dance?" she asked gently, watching their two friends spinning and laughing as they did.

"What?" Traith paused, looking over at Romanoff momentarily, who winked in merriment as he spun Saria around. He looked back at Rein. "I *do*, I just don't enjoy the *enthusiasm* of balls." She didn't mean to, but she must've looked as deeply disappointment as she felt. "I will, however, tonight," he murmured. He was smiling his handsome, boyish smile. "May I have the pleasure?"

"Of course," she replied with a laugh, trying to suppress her ecstasy.

She knew now that he had to be fond of her, too, even if it was something light and undeveloped. He had to have some feeling. After all, they had nearly kissed!

He stood and asked for her hand with a smile, and she followed him to the center of the floor and danced to the music of the piano.

She was quiet for a while, taking in the way he moved. She spoke nothing of how deeply she admired his touch. Though Rein's manner was generally quite sensible, she felt out of control near him.

"Your dress really is beautiful," he said.

She blushed. The second compliment. He liked her dress too.

"Thank you. I don't like crinolines or anything, though," she said, laughing. "So that's why—"

"You're so different." His speech was encouraged by a smile. "I honestly hate crinolines on women, myself." His fiery eyes wandered above and around her, to all the other dancing couples. "Big, ridiculous things. Get in the way. When I was younger, women wore them so unreasonably that I came to hate them."

"What?" She replied with a laugh. "When you were younger? As a child you hated them?"

He looked at her fast and stumbled to reply. "Y-yes."

His hand raised and he twirled her around, her dress widening for a moment during the slow spin. Excitement was not part of the particular dance.

"The stewardess informed me that you have few friends on this ship," Rein said to make more conversation. "Have you met no women to admire before?"

Dear God, was that question too forward? Had she just then sounded like Saria, whom she always knew was too forward? Oh, she hoped not!

His eyes focused, but he was looking past her, not at anything of particular significance.

By now, he *had* to know she admired him. He did. For her, it was not embarrassing that he knew.

"No, I've never found love. Before." He flicked his eyes down to her. "Do they bother you, Rein?"

She moved back a little in his arms to get a good look at his expression, wondering what he was talking about. "What do you mean?"

"My eyes. Honestly, do my eyes bother you?"

She bit her tongue hard. He must have caught her staring at his eyes again, and she didn't even realize it. But she was so focused on the color.

"No, they don't. No. I'm sorry, they're just so vibrant, as if on fire." She looked away and watched Saria and Romanoff dance across from them. "Contrarily, I like them."

He looked directly at her for the longest time.

"So glad you came, Mr. Harker!" Saria yelled with a giddy laugh, hanging onto Romanoff.

Traith smiled at her laughter, and Rein saw the pallor of his face fight to prevent a glow from breaking through. He wanted to glow. She could see that he was truly trying to be untroubled and blithe, but there was a death in his face that wouldn't release him. There was clearly something wrong, but when she watched him with a sigh, she saw gentleness on his entire face.

"I just can't fathom what kind of accident could do something like that," she said, unworried. "I-I mean, they are not seared or scarred by any means, just odd in color." She laughed. "I do like them, really I do."

"Well," he said with a chuckle, "I must say, that is a first."

His gaze left her and concentrated on Romanoff, who was now dancing directly next to him. The Frenchman made a cough of a laugh at him, and he smiled with sarcasm in return. Then he looked at her, and the softness in his face filtered through to his touch.

"I know I have not told you much about myself," he said suddenly. "I can't give explanation for my mystery. I am sorry to say that, but it's true. But I want you to know something." He paused and looked past her. He looked like he didn't want her to see any emotion in him—not happiness or sadness. He focused his eyes on something other than her. Perhaps he felt that he had let his guard down. "I have never rendered friendliness to anyone because I prefer hiding myself. Only Carden—and *you*—have deeper knowledge, have seen everything about me most bizarre, so you can imagine why I avoid the public." It looked as though he was pushing himself terribly hard to speak to her. "Rein, because you've seen all my features—features nearly inhuman—"

"No! *Inhuman*? That isn't true, though!"

"Because you don't mind them, you've become something to me." He stopped. "I do trust you."

Her eyes were wide, but she felt happiness glowing within them as she smiled. Her heart was beating in quick, pounding strokes. She knew she was flushed. The burning in her heart became a fire fast. Nothing mattered in that moment but him.

"I'm glad I'm something to you," she murmured, moving closer to him. "But I don't think that your features are what make you the rebel of the ship."

"Who told you that?"

She backed up from his neck and stared at him. "The stewardess." She paused, but continued as he didn't answer. "You do consider us friends, don't you?" she asked.

He blinked a couple times and stared at her. "I would say so."

She could hardly breathe. "Then—and I swear to you I would never repeat it if you desired it to be secret—but how exactly do you see differently? How do things look to you right now?"

He stiffened, but laughed quietly. "I see a mix between haze and extreme clarity, divided unequally and constantly fluctuating and modifying itself. I can't focus on anything and truly be concentrated upon it." That gentleness in his eyes lit again. "But do not think that

I can't see you clearly." His voice dimmed to a whisper. "You give my strange, frightening eyes something incredible to view, Miss Pierson."

Rein felt herself turning red. She looked like "something incredible"? She was delighted to see how comfortable he was with her. She had never seen him speak to anyone else but Carden Romanoff, and even with him he was defensive. She realized that her own spark was beginning to start a small fire in *him*.

"Your eyes are not in the least frightening to me," she said. "I very much enjoy your gaze." They bowed apart from each other a moment, then he took her hand and began to dance again.

Traith's gaze shifted from her to the far back wall of the ballroom. She turned to see what he was looking at only to realize the captain was standing alone there, isolated against a secluded wall, and watching.

There were still deep, horrible secrets. She recalled Romanoff's voice: *"It involved a great deal of pain. The poor fellow, his tolerance to pain is unnaturally high, too. But all that he recalls—finding it even hard to articulate to me—was that there was so much pain that he still nearly feels…"* And that's where the man had to stop.

She felt ill as she wondered about what had happened to Traith. But she caught the captain waving at them from the corner of her eye, and that creepy motion cleared her mind of everything but anxiety. That man always seemed to renew her fears and anger about the letter she received and the secrecy the *Olde Mary* held. The secrets made her dwell on the letter, forcing her to try to figure out something that was impossible to know. And if she trusted Traith as he asked her to, as she wanted so badly to, all she *could* do was wait.

Traith puffed in disgust and ignored the captain's gesture. With the next turn in the dance, Rein found herself facing the captain. He repeated his gesture with a volatile grin draped on his sagging face.

Rein noticed the captain pull something out of his vest. A vial of red liquid.

A vial of red liquid?

The captain dropped the vial to the floor, and she watched it shatter and the liquid spill. The man laughed and walked away into the shadows.

"What is it?" Traith asked her when he noticed her distress.

"The—the captain," Rein said, shaking her head. "I'm sorry, I need a second." With that, she pulled from him and started to leave the dance floor.

"No, don't leave, what happened?" he asked, following her.

He was doing exactly what she wished he would: he followed her out into the ship corridor outside the ballroom. She paused in the dark deserted hall. Traith quietly closed the large door and turned to stare at her, a solemn expression on his face.

Rein knew that he hadn't seen the shattered vial that the white-eyed man had purposely dropped, but she hadn't wanted to tell him in the midst of everyone. The act scared her—why was the captain tormenting her with those little displays of his?

"What is it?" Traith asked, nearing her. "What did he do?"

"He looked at me," she murmured, dazed as if reliving and trying to figure out the meaning of it. "He does scare me—he looked at me, waved, then dropped some sort of glass vial of red—*blood* perhaps, I don't know, but that's what it looked like." She was panting and she felt her heart pounding. "Traith, I know all this connects together. You, the captain, my letter—but I'm so confused, and I'm becoming more and more restless because I know nothing!" She took a breath and became quiet. "Traith." She didn't want to say it. "What actually is a vampire? Is that what all this is?"

He looked like he'd just been smacked. "*What?*"

"I don't know," she declared desperately, her hands fisted. "Nothing would surprise me anymore, and—"

He held her shoulders, an action that calmed her. "You did the right thing, coming out here," he murmured. "I wish I could…God, I'm sorry about him, and this entire situation. Don't be frightened, please. You'll be safe, all right? Please trust me; now more than ever you should."

As hard as it was for her to suppress the rage and frustration, she did it. She cooled off and said nothing. Her eyes spoke everything, as did his in that moment. She placed her hands on top of his. Her heart felt as though it would burst in her chest.

She slowly drew her face close to him, and he did not pull away; he surrendered to her advance, and their lips met. Rein closed her eyes and instinctively embraced him. She felt his fingers grasp her waist passionately. She tasted him. The scent of him filled her with fervor. It was her first kiss—a feeling she had never experienced.

Then there was a sharp pain.

The taste of blood filled her mouth.

She pulled back, grabbing her bottom lip. She looked down at her fingers and saw blood. Traith's eyes dilated and he turned away, feeling his own mouth.

"My lip, what—?" She stopped, recognizing his chill.

His eyes were iced and his expression cold. His face was like stone after the moment of weakness that had overwhelmed them. She was bleeding. Her blood was in his mouth. He was gaping at her face. Her lip. Her bloodstained hand.

"I'm sorry." His voice was immediately hoarse. "I'm sorry, I don't…"

He looked sorrowfully into her eyes for only a moment, turned fast, and nearly ran away with his hand by his mouth.

"No, Traith!" she yelled. "Don't—"

She closed her mouth when she realized he was already gone.

She began trembling and her back hit the wall.

The next thing she knew, she heard quiet talking and laughing, and a bright light momentarily lit the hall. It was Saria and Romanoff leaving the ballroom as well, obviously looking for them. The door closed and darkness returned.

"Rein, what—where is Harker?" Saria asked.

They walked relaxed to her. It took them a minute to see what was happening. Rein could feel the blood running down her chin, all from her lip.

"Oh my God!" Saria gasped. "What *happened to you*?"

"Here," Romanoff said, rushing to her with Saria. "Use this."

He pulled out a handkerchief from his shirt pocket and held it onto her mouth. She grasped it, and his hands let go, his eyes staring at her mouth.

Romanoff was staring, his eyes opened broadly. "May I see it, mademoiselle?" he asked politely.

Rein removed the handkerchief. "Is the cut bad?" she asked with a quiver.

"Where is he?" Romanoff demanded, not answering her.

"He left," she said, holding the stained white linen to her lip. "Again."

He looked momentarily at her. Then he turned, kissed Saria's hand, and without another word left the hall and vanished into the darkness.

"What happened, Rein?" Saria asked again, pleadingly.

"His teeth," Rein whispered in a voice almost inaudible. "It had to be his teeth." She lost her breath then, and after a moment, continued. "He kissed me and then…oh God, Saria, I was so happy."

Saria took her hand and threw her arms around her. "The cut is deep," Saria said. "Oh, please don't be sad, Rein. Just think of the mortification he must feel since *he* did it! Carden went to find him, I think. He'll fix things, Rein."

When Saria let go and helped her up, she felt faint and heavy. She was tired, despite her long sleep, and she wanted to cry wildly.

She had not been at the ball any longer than an hour, and already the night was ruined. *Already.* That kiss had been so enchanting that it would always be fresh in her head. No matter what happened, or what was wrong, it would always be fresh in her head.

chapter 20

C arden rushed down the West hall. The evening was dark and the few candles still balancing themselves on the tables throughout the corridor cast only a dim glow. He quickly paced through the shadows and rapped on door 1271, the room two doors down from Rein Pierson's chamber. There was no answer, so he again lifted his fist to beat.

"Harker, open the door!" he yelled, getting agitated. "Traith, I said—"

The door wrenched inward and Traith stood with flaming eyes staring frigidly into Carden's. His face was tight and paler than usual. His stance was tense, and he had stripped himself from his coat and vest, wearing nothing more than a frilled, white, open blouse and his dark pants and boots. When he noticed his friend's look, however, his expression grew more grieved and tired.

"You left her? You couldn't be gentleman enough to stay with her?" He asked as he watched Traith already lamenting.

"Carden, not now. Go back to the ball and leave me be." His head fell when he noticed that Carden was not going to move a muscle. "*Please*, just leave me be."

"No, Traith. You look ill. Your eyes have dark rings around them as if you were in a fever."

"Don't they always?"

"And you're trembling! What do you want me to tell the poor dame? That her engagement with you tonight was nothing but a disappointment and that you won't see her?"

"Carden." Traith paused and left the doorway, indicating for him to enter. He paced slower with his head in his hands. "She said it."

"Said what?"

"*Vampire.*"

"She did?"

"She's—Carden, I kissed her—something that's supposed to be *romantic*. She was bleeding such a great deal, and I can't be around blood, Carden. I can't! I go mad! It was in my mouth, I swallowed it!" His throat seemed to jam. "I just—I can't do this. I know what will happen. I *can't* be close to anyone, Carden! He won't let me, you must know that. He brought her here just to—"

"He is fighting a higher power, you know that. Mistress is—"

"Stop saying her name!" Traith yelled with frustration. "After all these years, she hasn't found a way to get us off this damned ship!"

"It isn't her fault, just like it isn't yours."

"How can you say that to me?" Traith said with a rasp. "I've had to wait so long, and if she can get in touch with a girl she's never even *met*, why could she *never get in touch with me?*"

"She's tried to find us a way off. That's all she's been doing. I've been stuck here too, for as long as you! You are not alone in this!"

Traith sighed and trembled, laying his hands against a bureau. "I know."

"But putting her completely aside," Carden continued from nearby the door, "I am meaning to be close to Saria because I believe she is meant for something greater than we both know. She and Miss Pierson both." He paused and watched Traith tremble as if he were coming out of the disagreeable aftereffects of drunkenness. "And then you tell her you're *blind*? Come, now, man!"

"That was by accident and loss of words."

Carden sighed. "Listen, to me, my friend," he said sympathetically. "Have I not the same faults as you?"

"Yes, but you're the colder one," he replied quivering. "Every time I see her I realize all the more I cannot attach myself to her, and yet I fear that I have. I want to be able to be with someone and I can't do even that. I could so easily have her be a part of my life—I can't figure out how I so suddenly..." He was stuttering for a word. "*Fell* for her. You may mean to be close to Rein's friend, Carden, but you have yet to kiss her like I just kissed Rein. I made her bleed!"

"Stop, Traith!" Carden gazed at him with a passionate stare. "I have not and will not. But I am not letting that stop me."

"I can't ever do it again! Look at me Carden! My eyes are maniacal and I can't hide it like you are able to. I don't appear normal to her, nor do I to anyone! How could she love—" he swallowed twice.

"My eyes have nothing to do with it," Carden helped him gather himself. "I don't hide anything from her, and that's what makes us different."

"You're eyes aren't *red*, Carden!"

"I was born with dark eyes. You would just rather make yourself sick, starve yourself, and make yourself less appealing to women! Brits like you—"

"What do you mean, Brits like me? Most Brits have red eyes?" He was panting in fury. "I'm not trying to exhibit myself, Carden! My appearance—"

"Could be greatly improved, without having to be an exhibit!"

He said nothing in reply for a while.

Carden glanced around the chamber. It was disheveled. Broken glass was scattered around the room; books were spilled open onto the floor, some face up and some face down. The only table he had in his room was filled with medicine bottles and vials, paperwork and ink. Not a spot was cleared for anything other than work.

"How do you expect me to see her?" Traith finally sputtered. "How do I explain? To speak to someone like her when I made a bloody fool out of myself and everyone who saw it will know what I've done."

"You can't stay hidden in here forever, Traith."

"I may never be able to leave this ship, Carden! Think about how long we've been cursed here! Every place I dwell in I will have to be hidden." He quieted. "This is all being drawn out, and I can't stand it. I can't be sure about what is going to happen, and I let myself fall for this girl. But if I show the slightest indication to the captain that I love her he'll do what he did to nearly every other passenger on here, probably worse."

"Traith, stop thinking like that."

"And then you tell her I have a castle and that I'm rich, after you know I was trying to rid her of me."

"Why, in the name of *God*, would you try to rid her of you? You've been alive a long time and have *never* met a lady you admired. *Never*! Almost *instantly* you admired her; I could tell! Lucky for you she's not even slightly afraid of you. In fact, she continually *fights* to know you, even when you are imbecile enough to walk out on her so often. You refuse to let her know you, so I am doing it for you. Yes, she knows you are wealthy, she knows you have a castle, but does that change anything? She does not want to be with you for your wealth, Traith!"

Traith leant on the vanity that had no mirror and sighed without agreement.

"I can't sway you," Carden said with pity. "But if you love her, you must not be evasive any longer. I hide nothing. Saria sees me for what I am."

"But you haven't dared to tell her, and soon you won't even have the chance because she'll be gone!"

"I know."

Traith gave him an icy, glazed stare.

"Therefore I will never have the need. You'd better leave your room, Traith. It was not your fault."

Traith stood, then, for a long while, not facing him. His hands were grasping the sides of a tall bureau. After a few moments passed, he made a grunting wince and threw the chest over in anger, smashing it against the wall by Carden Romanoff. He panted and suddenly his eyes grew even heavier.

"Get out of here, Carden."

Carden stood. "Yes," he said. "Ignore it, because whatever is going to happen, will happen soon." He began speaking with sarcasm. "So don't worry about losing a woman who actually loves you, Traith, despite whatever you think you look like, despite what you act like to her; despite what you are. No, don't worry. Forget all about her."

Traith was silent.

"Listen to me," Carden started gravely. "You will not find someone else like her, so don't pass up the chance. Keep her protected!"

Then he left the room, slamming the door on his way out.

chapter 21

R ein continued to watch for a short time after Romanoff left, standing with Saria in the dark hall. Her thoughts haunted her. She didn't want to think that what she had said—the vampire—was real, but she knew nearly nothing about that to begin with. She was never interested in such subjects. But there was at least an accident, and some sort of "powers." The whole idea terrified her, and being lost and unknowledgeable to it all was even worse.

Rein turned to Saria, breaking her sorrowful thoughts. "I have to go," she said with a low voice, still holding Romanoff's handkerchief to her bloody mouth.

"Come with me to my chamber for a while," Saria said. "It isn't even late yet, and you shouldn't be alone. Your beautiful face shows the stress you're in, and you need comforting."

Saria took her hand and walked with her down the hall to her chamber door. She pulled out her key to unlock it and stepped inside, only to find that Rein was still in the hall.

"What are you doing? Come in."

Rein only shook her head and said nothing. She wanted to speak, but her heart was so full of emotion that words were hard to express.

Saria spoke to her again, putting her arm around her friend. "Please, come inside. Your chamber is so very far away from mine, and the boat is rocking terribly."

She tried to urge Rein inside, but she continued to resist. "I'm tired, Saria," was all she could muster. "I ache for some reason. I should like to sleep."

Saria stared at her deeply. "Sleep? You need to cry. You never cry, and you need to. You are so pale, Rein. You look sick! Why did you come with me if you will not even spend a moment in my chamber?"

There was a pause. "I don't know, Saria."

Saria lingered a moment, thinking. "I suppose, if I absolutely cannot have you stay, you should be quickly off. You've managed a hard few hours, but try to not be so grim, Rein. You'll speak to Harker many more times before we leave the ship."

"Right," Rein choked and swallowed after pulling the red-stained handkerchief from her mouth. "Do you love Romanoff, Saria?" Her voice hoarse, but present.

Saria smiled. "Oh yes. Perhaps on our way home from America we will be able to catch this ship and meet with them again."

"You aren't sick for having to leave him?" Rein asked again with a crack of ambiguity.

Saria stood still, her lips formed in a doubtful smile. "I won't know until I leave here. But I do think that there is love found in many places, Rein, not just in one."

Rein narrowed her eyes at her friend and turned, beginning to walk down the hall. "Good night, Saria."

"Sleep well, Rein. Please, cheer up. I'll come see you directly tomorrow morning. I'm going to find Carden, if I can, and perhaps find out some information for you, all right?" She gasped a little. "Oh. I wonder whatever happened to Edgar."

Rein didn't look back at Saria. She didn't care about Edgar; she felt like she didn't care about anything. She paced in angry misery. Once she had turned the corner of the hall, she slowed down, feeling sudden sympathy toward Saria. Her lip was aching as if it had its own heart, and she wanted to see how bad the injury was. She had to go to her chamber. If by some chance he was there, around there, she could talk with him. But her confusion made it so hard to hold back tears—tears she had been holding in for years that only came out as the truth did.

She approached the West Hall. She had been looking down, fixing her gloves and trying to get her mind off of Saria, and she realized that she was now standing in front of chamber 1270. She heard talking coming from inside the chamber, and she listened intently, recognizing the voices of Harker and Romanoff.

The voices were calm but serious, and Rein found she could only catch small bits of their heated conversation or argument, whatever it may have been, except when the voices raised a small bit. It did sound, however, from what she could hear, like Traith speaking of his eyes. She thought she heard Romanoff say, "I can't sway you" or "I won't have the need" or "gone." It sounded like they spoke, argued, about what had happened to her. Traith sounded so upset.

Suddenly Rein heard a voice by the door, and watched as the knob began to twist. "You'd better leave your room, Harker, it wasn't your fault."

It was Romanoff. He had spoken clearly from inside the doorway. After that, his voice faded with words she couldn't make out, and all she heard was a shuffle and the loud noise of something hard, probably wood, hitting against the wall on the inside of the room.

She ran back to the door of her chamber, her hand trembling to get the key into the lock as fast as possible. Quickly she closed herself inside her chamber before anyone had left the room.

Rein was panting against the inside of the door, her bodice heaving up and down.

She heard a door slam.

She closed her eyes and pressed the handkerchief against her lip hard. She would have dreaded being caught listening to their conversation.

Her feet, in shaky steps, took her to the vanity where she looked into the mirror. She saw the ghastly cut: a puncture mark. Seeing that the bleeding had slowed, she set the handkerchief down and started unlacing her corset and undressing.

Traith's tooth cut her lip. He cut her and was scared enough to disappear without a word. She felt so much pity for him. Only three years her senior, he was, and he had to live the rest of his life like that. Or, he didn't. Not if he was with her. But he didn't know that, and she had no way of telling him. She couldn't.

She grabbed her nightgown and the bloodstained linen and headed back out the door after a few minutes. She had changed her mind. She needed Saria; she felt guilty for leaving her. She hadn't spent that much time with her, and she needed someone. She was so hot, as if in fever, and she felt tired, but her body was not. She was bringing her nightgown to sleep in Saria's chamber tonight.

The halls were empty and silent. Everyone was still at the ball. The sun had just gone down. She reached Saria's room and was welcomed with open arms.

chapter 22

a few more days passed. The evening of the ball had been gone for some time, but the thought of what had happened lingered in Rein's mind with intense clarity. She had been so close to a complete, meaningful kiss. So close to almost beginning a relationship with a gentleman she had come to adore. So close…but since that night, she had not seen him. The thought of a relationship began to shrivel; that happy possibility was slowly being replaced with a petrifying and unnatural one.

Rein had decided to try on a dress from her wardrobe. One not as formal as the one she had worn the evening of the ball, but handsome all the same. It was cream in color, long and stiff around the stomach. There were gloves to match and shoes, all items she had discovered in the dresser.

She glanced in the mirror at herself. She looked elegant in her attire. Her hair was pinned up into a loose bun, and her white gloves were missing all ten fingertips. She sighed, however. It meant nothing to be dressed in such a beautiful gown if no one noticed. Well, Saria would. She left it on and headed out her chamber to find her friend.

She had no thought of meeting Traith Harker again. The ship was vast, and she knew he was avoiding any further contact with her. She had now been on the ship for almost a fortnight, and within that time, each meeting with Traith had been somehow ruined or had come to an abrupt halt. Her voyage was nearly over, and time was slipping so quickly that days seemed like minutes passing before her. America was coming, and this ship was going to end up a blur of memory, along with the confusion that had consumed her since she'd arrived.

She stepped out of her chamber and turned with regret, staring at room 1270. It produced for her such an intense chill, and she stood to watch the door for a moment.

No, she had not seen him for days, but she knew he had not left his stateroom in that interval of time. He had been in there since their kiss. She knew, for she listened often. She searched the ship for him with a detached air, as if merely exploring it. When she listened, she could hear him shuffling around, pacing; she heard things fall, break. She wondered with sorrow what his chamber looked like. She knew that she had heard him smash and shatter things; therefore, his room must be a broken wreck. She knew he hadn't eaten for days and often felt as if she should speak to him, but she couldn't. He was in there, just in depression. But he was in there.

She was right in front of room 1270. He was right inside, right in front of her, beyond a single door. But that door meant everything. There had been many times she had tried to knock, and every time she hesitated. Her hand sometimes even lifted to the knocker, grasping it, but she just couldn't. She would drop it slowly, without a sound, and continue the other way down the hall. She didn't know what she would say or do around him. She had not seen him since their broken kiss, and though her lip was nearly healed, she knew if he saw it, it would pain him.

Rein walked away, not having heard anything of note.

She entered the atrium and saw Saria sitting out in the drink lounge again, probably waiting for Carden. Rein could've sworn she had been there since their voyage had begun, and instead of meeting her as she had first proposed, Rein waved to her courteously and looked up at the dining hall. She walked through the entrance, and a hand on her shoulder made her heart lift. Turning with excitement, she frowned—it was the captain. She had not seen him since the ball, either.

"Good afternoon, Miss Pierson," he said. "Come to my dining hall and grab a bite to eat, won't you?"

That's what she wanted to do, but not alone. "In a few minutes," she said. "I was just thinking."

He nodded; she couldn't figure out where he was staring since his eyes were entirely white. "With your friend Miss Kendrick, perhaps. Or Mr. Harker would be fine, too."

He gave her a slight wink and removed his hand from her shoulder, entering further into the dining hall. A chill ran down her spine as she thought about the vial he had dropped.

What had it meant?

It was spilled blood. She thought about it and became quietly terrified.

But Traith was still on this ship. He was still there, and protective, and probably watching silently where no one could see. That was how he worked. But she couldn't solely rely on that theory, could she?

The captain snickered violently and stared at her a moment before turning a corner and disappearing, leaving her hanging onto a thread of valor. She was, in all aspects of life, a sensible young lady, but her coolness was beginning to give way. Too much was happening, and there was something more to it all. She turned out of the dining hall and walked up to Saria, taking a seat quietly next to her.

Saria glanced over, a bit surprised at Rein's arrival.

"Have you eaten?" Rein asked disconnectedly.

"Yes, I am sorry," Saria replied, fixing her no longer surprised look down at her glass. "Carden is coming back now, and we were going to talk. Why don't you just go grab something to eat quickly now so you can come join us?"

Rein glanced down. "All right," she said softly.

Saria meant to look sad, or at least that was what Rein figured. But as soon as she saw Carden coming from down the *V-Wing*, she brightened, and Rein left her without another word.

She was inside the dining hall again by the time she shoved her thoughts aside. When she looked around, however, she found herself intrigued with the décor of the room. Though she hadn't noticed it before, each and every one of the stone walls were carved with intricate designs: wars and battles, cupids and God, horses and carriages, show-cases and opera houses. Somehow, all were entwined within each other, making the room look dizzy and large, almost like a cathedral ceiling.

The tables, too, were old-fashioned; wooden chairs or stools occupied each one, along with candelabras in their centers, and the floor was red. As her mind wandered, she noticed a small, empty table toward the back.

A shadow of a man opened a door in the back of the dining room and took a seat as silently as possible. Her throat became dry. Traith.

Her empty heart was fueled immediately when she laid eyes on him. He looked no different, save bristles grown back around his jaw.

She glanced back at Saria, whom she could see through the dining hall glass windows. Saria was laughing. Rein saw Romanoff take a seat beside Saria, looking to the back door where Traith had just entered, pulling down his vest with a satisfied expression on his face. Then she knew that the two had done it; had set them up to meet again, for the first time since the ball.

She looked side to side and then slowly began to walk to the table in the corner without the candelabra. She figured she might as well approach him, since it was probably the hidden plan anyway between her friend and his. She'd been looking for him for days. They had to speak again. The subject had to come up, and her concern needed to be addressed.

A man placed a glass of wine in front of Traith, but he didn't even acknowledge it. He had taken up a small book. He had not yet spotted her.

She begged pardon from those she had to pass, slowly making her way to the back of the room, wondering what she was going to say to him when in speaking distance.

He looked up; his cheeks smooth and tight under bristles. But he still wasn't looking at her. His head turned slowly, as if taking in each and every person dining there. His face seemed frustrated, and for a moment she thought it might not be a good idea to approach him. But again Romanoff's words seemed to ring in her mind, lightening her uncertainty: *"He will not turn you away, I assure you."* Why was that? She didn't want to question.

He finally was facing her. His eyes immediately locked onto hers.

He did not move.

She had to.

She neared his table and smiled very lightly. She saw his head tilt down as he had done when he didn't want her to see his eyes.

"Good afternoon, Traith," she choked, swallowing hard.

"Rein," he murmured informally, gradually forcing himself to look up at her. "Please sit."

"Traith," she pushed to say, watching his frigid apprehension. She had to say it, somehow. It had to come out. "I don't care what happened—"

"You should, Rein," he countered. "I should never have kissed you." The emotion in his rough voice was enough to tell her that he was hurting, but, to her surprise, it was he who began speaking again. "I know you must be horribly disturbed as to why things happened as they did." His last words trailed off as if he didn't want her to hear them. "And about other things."

"Yes," she said, her voice as soft as a whisper. She was content that the topic had quickly come about. "I was disturbed." She found that speaking to him was becoming progressively easier. "But it wasn't because of my lip." He stayed as stone, and she went on with strained words. "It was because you disappeared like you did. For days."

He said nothing after she had spoken.

She held back a flow of tears. "I'm leaving this ship in a few days," she winced. "And I'm going to leave you. Does that make you feel nothing?"

She was throwing her respectable composure completely away. She didn't mean to; she didn't even want to, but she was pouring things out to him without control.

"I do feel something," he replied in a whispered tone.

"Then please, Traith," she said desperately. "It's not fair to let me leave without even giving me a true explanation of everything that's happened to me. I'm afraid." His head raised, and he gazed at her, and she continued at his stare's command. She was losing her voice to tears. "Don't lie to me anymore."

He was watching her with the utmost intent. He was quiet for a moment after she paused. "I'm sorry," he finally said. And it was the only thing he said. He was short of words, but his mouth moved in small gasps as if he was trying to articulate something to her.

"I trusted you, and yet you still lied to me for fear of my reaction to the truth," Rein said, despite his attempt to speak further. "And it doesn't matter what happened at the ball days ago; I don't want my trust in you to change. Don't allow me to be wrong about that feeling." Another pause ensued. "Because I yearn for it."

His beautiful red eyes always tried to gaze at her, but he pulled them away in discomfort. "I wish I could explain to you," he muttered in reply. "I just can't. I didn't mean to hurt you. I don't *want* to lie about anything."

"Then don't," she countered in aggravation. "You can explain to me. I am genuine, Traith. I can listen and help and keep secrets, I swear to you. I just need some kind of understanding, and I know there is an explanation. I know you have one, and I know something is wrong. I don't know whether I should interrogate you or let you maintain your mystery. Perhaps I don't want the real answer, but nothing can develop if you continue hiding such vital secrets." Her voice was so hoarse, and she thought for a moment that she couldn't have sounded elegant. "You don't have to hide them from me."

"I do trust you," he stammered. "I *do*." He began to wince as he spoke. "You don't understand; I *can't* tell you."

"You can't tell me?" she repeated. "But that isn't an answer."

"I want to, but I can't. I feel more than just trust for you, Rein."

She wanted to think about that sentence forever.

"I don't think anything could be strong enough," he began softly, "not trust, not even love, to handle living with…" He stopped. "You're right, Rein, about my having an explanation. Something is wrong with me, Rein. Terribly wrong. It isn't in my head or in a physical deformity, other than what you see in my features. It's difficult—no—impossible to describe." He looked down and held his hands together. He was trembling.

She saw it but found it hard to keep her eyes from him. She didn't know how to answer that. "I just wish you wouldn't have left when it happened," she whispered. "No matter what *is* wrong with you." She stared hard at him. "And I think I know what it is."

He didn't look at her. She saw his gaze was up and forward, and he wasn't focused on her, but on the captain, who she saw as she turned to see what he was looking at. He was wandering the area aimlessly. Traith directed his attention back to her, looking into her eyes, concern building up within him. He was searching inside for an answer.

"Can you begin somewhere?" She heard her voice quiver slightly. "If you will not say your problem, please tell me something. Why did you come here? You were forced to? I suppose I'm not allowed to know that either."

His face became deathly sober.

"But you came for work for the Mistress?"

He stumbled to answer. "Yes—well, I dare not explain it all. I never wanted it to be this way, Rein. Please know that."

"What did you work at, Traith? What was your work?"

"I never worked because I had the money." She didn't say anything to him, but he had contradicted himself. He had said he was not rich; he had to know he was giving her a different answer. "I've always studied medicine and science," he said, still quiet. "Mistress needed that."

"Which are you more like?" Rein asked weakly. "A scientist or a surgeon?"

He chuckled to himself without even smiling. "I am a little of both, I suppose. Not quite a doctor, but not quite a scientist, either."

"Oh," she replied quietly, swallowing. "Well, what about family, Traith? Do you have any siblings? Parents?"

"Only a sister," he said with clenched teeth. "I don't know what happened to my parents."

It wasn't enough; the information was not enough. "I think you should tell me your imperfection, Traith. Suppose you came off the ship with me in New Jersey. We can work with whatever is wrong with you."

"No, you couldn't." He clenched his jaws and cringed. "It is much too severe."

"I see nothing severely wrong about you, Traith."

"You would after a while. I am obligated to stay here, Miss Pierson; I couldn't leave, not even if I bloody tried." She became cold at his last words. "I have."

"Please," she said quietly, after a moment. "Don't call me that anymore. Not Miss Pierson. I feel as if it means you are bidding me farewell."

"That was not my intent," he said in whisper.

She felt her throat burning. "Do you realize," she murmured, "that every time I've ever talked to you, you've left me by walking away? Every time."

He didn't answer, his head hanging down.

"Would you care for a drink?" The hideous voice made Rein jump.

It was the captain, again, who had made his way to their table. He stood by and put a goblet on the table, filling it with a white wine. Traith still had the one he had been given before, but he hadn't taken a drink of it.

Wanting to quench her mounting thirst, she took a drink. She was just beginning to swallow the wine; it was different...

With a sudden whack she felt the glass forced out of her hands. The shatter was so loud that her head rung two times over. Staring ahead, she thought it had been the captain. It wasn't. Traith was standing over her with a small scratch on the back of his hand from the glass. His eyes were wide. She was staring coldly at the two men. Within a moment's time, she understood Traith's actions.

That man had poisoned her drink.

Poisoned me.

"Harker, you're so observant," he began.

Traith flared, his fist locked onto the captain's shirt. "What in God's name have you *done?*"

"You lock me away down there as if it matters. Oh, and did I tell you? There is no need to hide your true self to her anymore. She'll see in time anyway, do you not agree? Or perhaps she already has. How *is* your lip, Madame Pierson?"

Her body was so cold. Sick. She had tasted the wine. She did not reply to him, her body was in an excessive shock. A chalky residue was left in her mouth.

"No," Traith said, his face as angered as a wild animal. "*You—!*"

"Enough, Harker!" the white-eyed man shouted.

He smiled, and she saw Traith's hand fall off of his shirt; it almost appeared as if it had fallen through it.

"Can't you grasp me, Harker?"

A few ghostly couples turned and watched Traith's every move, looking very ready to intervene in the situation. She smelled it now: an almond smell arising from the floor. Arsenic? She *had* been poisoned. There was no need for words on her part. No panic. She was losing consciousness. With that little taste, she was still poisoned.

Oh *God...*

"*Jackass,*" Traith muttered through gritted teeth.

"Why such a cruel tongue, Traith?" the captain asked. "I even approached it differently this time for you." His voice hissed like a snake. "I won't do anything more. Now it's all up to *you.* Not too torturous, is it?"

He walked away, and Traith was standing more erect than ever, his eyes lit and flaming. Every time he almost spoke to her, he stopped himself as if she wasn't there. As if he did not want to. Then his white shirt slipped off his broad shoulder as if something pulled at it. Something had pulled at it. His head twisted and he knocked something from him; something she couldn't see.

Then she noticed for the first time two reddened scars on his throat.

Her thoughts were affirmed. Mental notes she had been making all along were being stitched together to form a story…

His sharp canines. His mystery. His lies. His reaction to things. His seemingly restricted hunger. His eyes. His pallor. The scars ~~hole~~ she'd just seen on his neck. The subject at their wine gathering. The scarlet residue left around the rim of Romanoff's goblet. What the captain brought up. What complemented werewolves. What was written in Leipzig. "*A fearsome curse on man in books and articles.*" "*Do you think them to be real, Mr. Harker?*" "*Do you, Traith?*"

The *vampire.*

"Please, Rein," Traith said with a trembling voice. "Go to your quarters and sleep. I will not leave your side after this, Rein, and I'll soon explain everything. Everything in complete honesty. Every detail. Forgive me, Rein." His words ran together in his sorrow, and she was too scared to return words.

Her eyes were becoming so watery that she could barely see. But Traith stood still for a moment to watch her with his gentle face.

"I truly didn't want to walk away this time," he murmured.

He hesitated, watching her eyes close, but then he turned, and she saw rage light his face like a match. He grabbed the wine glass that was set before him and threw it onto the ground next to hers. More glass shattered. Then he sprinted after the captain.

Rein flinched at the sound. She watched the liquid in his glass seep out. Red. *Blood.*

He hadn't wanted to touch the blood, to drink blood. Hadn't wanted to be near *her* blood.

Her eyes widened as the red spiraled into the puddle of her white wine. They mixed.

She stood and teetered out of the dining hall. He had been trying to hide so much. She was crying without a sound; her tears fell so quickly, but it was in horrendous fear. She knew what she had seen. She knew what his defect was. She knew she was going to die.

Rein felt her eyes slowly start to droop. She felt tired in a way that she had never felt before, and suddenly she had little control over her body or actions. With quick, nervous, and awkward movements, she staggered out of the dining hall, holding her head and wobbling back and forth, one arm out to keep her balance.

At the entrance, she found she now had to squint to see straight. Her vision was quickly blurring, but no longer due to her tears. She couldn't see properly. She made Saria out, who had been out by the lounge with Romanoff. Her body was limp on Romanoff's knees, significantly blue, and Rein could see Romanoff's shocked expression when he saw her.

She felt her knees buckle underneath her. Tears were streaming fast down her cheeks. He'd gotten Saria, too.

She heard a shout; *Edgar*. The normally submissive man sounded hysterical. He was running toward her. Then she fell to the floor, and she hit her head hard on the ground. She saw blood running down her arm from somewhere. Edgar was looming above her, but she suddenly heard him yell as he was pulled away from above her. She didn't know where he went.

Somehow, she could still faintly hear and see the crowd gathering. She heard Traith curse above the crowd and barely made out his fanged teeth. It almost sounded like his yell was a whisper.

"Get *away* from her!"

He looked at her but did not come over, his eyes grieving. She was horror-stricken and gasped for air, but could obtain none. Everything went black. She could still hear Traith through the fuzziness, fighting both verbally and physically with the captain. She barely heard the smashing of fists and yelling that was like whispers.

In her last attempt to inhale what little air she could, which was decreasing rapidly, she heard the ghostly passengers around her quietly hissing.

chapter 23

Hours struck as fast as the lightning outside the ship. The storm had finally come. Thunder sounded, and the ship rocked with violence from the wind and waves. All hallway candles were out. They were all on the floorboards, snuffed out by their fall. Corridors were darker than they had ever been.

The chamber had only a sconce lit on the far side. The dimness made it feel cold and damp, and the porthole was continually washed with saltwater, despite the chamber being above water.

His fist slammed down on the bookcase. He winced. He paced in indecision back and forth next to Carden.

"Traith," Carden said from the chamber bedside. "Listen—"

"He *murdered* them," he mumbled back through gritted teeth.

Carden stared down.

Traith stopped pacing and stood stiff. His entire body was tense as if enduring pain. "*Poisoned* them," he stuttered. "And I was able to do nothing. I was right there, and I did nothing."

"Do not lie to yourself, Traith."

"There is no lying in that!" he yelled, this time without a care of anyone seeing his four pointed teeth. "And not only did they murder the ladies but God knows what they did to the innocent man that came with them!"

"Try to control your temper," Carden declared. "We'll get nowhere if you can't focus."

"Focus?" Traith asked with a caustic laugh. "On what?" A dry swallow ensued. "He *tortured* me with things," he murmured. "He shattered a vial of blood in front of her. She was given a chamber two doors down from my own stateroom!" He shouted again. "She was staying in the West Hall, Carden! She had a *vampire's* quarters!"

Both men were silent. Traith sat on the bed in Saria's chamber, next to Rein's limp body. Her lips were still red, but her skin was pale. He held out his arm to her. She was as pale as he was. Her skin was clear and soft, where his was scarred. He bit his lip. She was dead—just as dead as he was.

"She fell," he said, choking on his words, "and I couldn't be there to catch her. I let her hit the ground this time."

Carden watched him with sorrow in his eyes. "Traith—"

"I fought with him. I fought hard, but there wasn't anything I could do. We can't *destroy* him, and I could see that Rein was still awake. God, Carden. She's dead."

"*Mon ami*," Carden began, "Saria is also dead. There is a choice you must face. If you want Rein Pierson to live—"

"She would not be *living*, Carden!"

"She is dead, Traith. *Dead*. Understand that. Her freedom is gone anyway. No matter what your human heart wants you to do, she is gone anyway. All you can do is give her a sense of life. I will not deprive Saria of that."

"Carden, neither of them would ever want to be cursed beings who have no right to—"

Traith stopped himself when Carden ran to the bedside and grabbed his wrists. His own hands were in fists, and he looked into Carden's face, biting his lip harder.

"—who have no right to even exist," he finished.

"Calm down, Traith," he said with angst. "Sometimes you are so much a human it is frightening."

Traith was silent, staring at Carden, and yanked his fists from his hold. "My mind is emptied of who did this to me or why or how," he began hoarsely. "I don't know much as it is. All that I do recall is such misery."

"Traith, it is not as much of a curse as you would think," he interrupted, obviously trying to make light of the situation. "It would be if we were immoral, wicked, but we are not. I know I fell in love with Saria and will bring her back to life under any circumstance. Did you not fall in love with Mademoiselle Pierson?"

"Yes," he said softly. "Yes, more than you could ever imagine. She loved me. She ignored everything, Carden. Everything I couldn't tell her, everything that didn't make sense. She still tried to win my heart, even after it was already hers. For the first time in so long, someone felt something…" Traith stopped in the middle of his sentence, running his fingers through his hair. "I think I've found true love in a matter of days, and now she's dead."

"Did I not tell you those exact things a few days ago? When you left her at the ball?"

"I know," he murmured. "I know. But everyone I ever became close to has died. I so, so terribly did not want that to happen to her." Then his voice grew louder. "And then things happen to me; things that ruin what few good things I can have. I bit her lip, Carden! I took in her blood with no intention to do so, and I enjoyed it! I *hurt* her and couldn't prevent it because I have *fangs* like a bloody *animal*!"

"Traith," Carden said as he backed up, staring at him as he stood, ferocious. Carden grasped his shoulders tightly. "It was not your fault. How often must I tell you?"

Traith panted and sighed with a shake as he looked down at Rein's pale, slim body. Her cream-colored dress was stained a dark crimson in spots. Blood was streaked down her face from her fall and down her sleeve on one side from how she had fallen. Her gloved hands and corset were even slightly blood-stained. But the lace on her dress and neck looked perfect, and even now she looked like she could've been an angel. The murderer must've given her a staggering amount; there must've been so much poison in her drink to kill her so quickly, from only a sip.

Traith then glanced over at Saria. Her body was unblemished too, with fewer marks than Rein's. *She* had been caught by Carden when she fell.

"If we do not bite them, Traith," Carden whispered, "you can add one more casualty to your list."

Traith turned his gaze to his friend. His eyes were actually frantic.

"Traith, please. Do what you know would be best. Rein was not yet ready to die. She will accept it."

Traith looked off coldly. He shivered at the thought of "what was best." What kind of monster bit into a human's throat and drained them of their blood? A monster like *him*. But he couldn't.

Traith felt pain and pressure raining down on him like boulders. "I can remember being human once, and the pain I felt afterward was indescribable. I remember at least that, and that's enough." His words faded off, and he looked down at his feet, putting his cold hands on his face, and then on his knees. "I don't want to bloody do this, but I can't lose her."

He reached for Rein's body, taking a seat on the bed. Her head hung back as he picked her up and lifted her onto his lap, his one hand holding her head and the other holding her hands.

Her red lips unlocked, and he witnessed her scabbed puncture wound.

Her body dropped to the bed.

"I can't," he shuttered. "Look at her."

"Traith, you have not eaten for far too long. You are what you are, no matter what you want. You'll bring her back to life, and if she is so terribly frightened of becoming what you are, let her die again. Trust me, not your blasted humanity, for once!"

Carden approached him slowly, and, for a moment, Traith thought he was going to try and comfort him.

But no, Carden merely approached him to lift Saria and drain her—

instantly, without another thought. He cut one of his wrists with his teeth and held it to Saria, allowing her to consume his running blood through her open, unmoving mouth.

Traith shifted his sight from Carden to Rein, whose head was in his hands. He lifted her once more, his body tense. Her black hair had unraveled and fell through his fingers. With his thumb, he lifted her chin, revealing her thin, unmarked throat. He turned her face, and he drew his mouth close to her jugular, feeling fresh blood that had once pumped through it with his thumb.

She was dead, yes, but he knew he had the power to bring back those in death. The body had to be fresh; if he gave the bitten his own blood, they would turn. If he didn't, they would die. Simple as that.

He could feel her blood, though it wasn't moving. He could feel it. His body became instantly desirous of it.

Why can I feel it?

His eyes closed.

What am I doing?

His mouth met her throat, and he bit down, grasping her.

It was the first time that he had drunk the fresh blood of a person, as far as he knew and hoped. He didn't want to believe it was mandatory, but as he continued to consume her blood a new and tantalizing sensation overwhelmed him, and the twinge that ate at him disappeared in a matter of moments. He yearned for more.

He pulled back. There was little to no more blood inside of her. His mouth was wet; he felt it. His fingertips were red.

He quickly wiped his mouth with the back of his hand. He wanted more, and it made him sick. Blood came slowly out of the two puncture marks left in her neck, like pin pricks, only swollen. He wiped the blood off her throat with his thumb, and with an amazing amount of willpower, wiped it on her dress.

In a state of numbness, he pulled a knife out of his boot and cut his own wrist. Blood began to flow freely, and he held it up to her. It drizzled into her mouth.

And then it was done.

Carden reminded him of where he was.

"Take Rein to her own chamber," he said.

Traith felt as though he were going to fall over with weakness in seeing his friend. His friend? His friend did that? Why was he his friend?

Though he was not an evil person, Carden was happy and complete, and the more Traith saw how happy his friend was, the sicker he felt. With regret swallowing him whole, he picked up Rein's body and left Saria's quarters, not stopping to speak another word or give another glance to Carden Romanoff.

chapter 24

traith staggered through the corridor of the West Hall. Though he was easily strong enough to hold her body, the intense swaying of the ship made it hard to keep balanced. Even through the dark blanket of air he could see her features changing as he walked. His heart plummeted when he noticed her white teeth lengthen. He swallowed his pain as he looked down at her perfect hands. Her nails had already become sharper and darker, and her skin remained as it was in her death.

He approached her chamber and glanced ahead two doors at his own chamber. He looked down at her in his arms. He withdrew one of his hands from underneath her lifeless body, holding her with only one arm. He stumbled awkwardly into the door and pulled on the knob. It was locked. With a harder twist, he easily broke the knob and entered the chamber. With his free hand, he closed the door behind him.

The sconce in her room was still lit, so there was a dim glow throughout the quarters. He laid her on the bed softly, her limp body stiffening when it met the mattress.

His thoughts haunted him. He had done something evil, something he couldn't ever fix without death. He had taken it upon himself to do it. He was still fighting in his head whether his decision was the right one or not.

That was exactly the captain's intent. To torture him by making him decide to either let Rein die, or bite her and drain her of her blood to awaken something different. The captain had murdered many people whom he'd picked off of the shores for a passage fee, but Traith couldn't have saved them, and he certainly hadn't felt love for any of them. Not for any other woman in the world but her. This ship was never going to America like Rein had hoped.

He hated that man with every ounce of himself.

It would be a few hours before she awoke. He took a seat quietly in a chair, staring around her living area. It was just as his own was, but less cluttered and destroyed.

His own chamber was dark and cluttered, with things broken and left to collect dust. He never cared if his stateroom was clean. It was never his idea to be on this ship, nor to be on it for this long.

Nor to fall in love.

He thought about going back to his chamber, but he knew he had to be there for her when she awoke.

He leaned forward and rested his elbows on the table, putting his face in his hands. He spoke to himself with muffled words. "What in God's name have I done to this girl?" he asked himself in a whimper.

Rein Pierson—a name he liked, a name he would never forget, wherever she was to go. But maybe she would stay with him. Or maybe she would try to kill him or kill herself. But perhaps not. No. She was a sensible girl. She would at least think first. She *had* to think first!

He stared down at his wrist. A knifed scar was left there from where he cut himself to give her his own blood. The wound was healed, but he'd still given himself another scar to add to his collection. Thank God all the others weren't from *this*. They were from the suffering he'd gone through. That torture when they bit him. He looked at his forearms. The scars were there too. And on his stomach and his back, and legs. And what about his face? Of course. Carden had spoken of those on more than one occasion—so had Rein.

If only he could see himself in the bloody mirror!

He glanced over at her vanity. It had a mirror, unlike his. He dared not approach it. His heart would crush under his ribs. He had been a normal man, once, and the normal man inside of him had never vanished, even if its reflection had.

He saw her small bag opened on the center table by his elbows, and underneath it, some written-on paper. He read through the papers; they were her writings. Poems, story ideas. Then he stood and picked up a book that was inside. He could smell the perfume she wore so often lingering on it. Some sort of flower, perhaps. He couldn't tell, but it taunted him. A bookmark marked her last read page. *Sense and Sensibility*. He wasn't familiar with the book, so he checked to see when it had been published: 1811. Thirty-two years ago.

He had been on this ship, then.

Just as bitterness was about to break him, he was thrashed forward and onto the floor by a fierce jerk of the ship. The table was knocked on top of him, as were her things. Rein, as if sleeping, slid to the side of the bed and fell. He scrambled to get out from under the table, but he knew he wasn't going to be able to catch her.

But she landed in his arms in an immediate flash. He kicked the table to the side and stared at her. The bed was on the other side of the chamber.

He again tried to escape his own devastation as he gazed down at her. She looked so lovely, though her life had been stripped from her.

He flinched when he felt her begin to stir, freeing him from his own mind. Somehow, she had begun to awaken in his arms. Her arm stretched and touched his neck and face, but she was still in a drugged-like state. He stumbled up with her, walked to the bedside, and laid her again on the bed. She didn't open her eyes but calmly ran her fingers over the silk sheets.

In a moment's time, he would need to explain something unexplainable. He stood, trying to prepare himself for the terror that would soon engulf the room.

chapter 25

S he felt so comfortable, so relaxed. She opened her eyes slightly and could see Traith looking out the dusty, dark porthole. She could see the canopy with black mesh above her, small bits hanging down over the sides.

She let her fingers run up and down the sheets, her mind swimming with thoughts as she was slowly recalling the events of the evening. She could remember Traith, and others, around her, and she remembered there was something wrong with him, with Traith.

She opened her eyes and saw him walk over to her, hesitation in each of his steps. "Rein?"

She stuttered for a moment before she could get words out and panicked. Her head shot up and she grabbed his loose shirt, her chest heaving desperately. It didn't work. Her breathing didn't mean anything. It didn't *do* anything.

He was pulled over her bed, his hands quickly balancing him. A distraught expression had surfaced on his face. "Rein, please, calm down. Let me explain."

Horror froze her. Her eyes were drawn to his teeth, the ones a great deal lengthened. As she pulled at his shirt, she saw those two puncture holes in his neck.

She realized her own neck was sore.

She let go of him instantly, and he glanced at the floor because she was looking at his neck. She saw his eyes fill with assorted emotions. For the first time since they had met, she saw emotion overcome him.

She placed her hand over her neck and felt two, tiny holes pierced into her skin. She felt numb with fear. She felt like a child having a nightmare. She realized there was only one creature capable of doing something like this, and it was a vampire. But they were myths. They had no true meaning. They were only pretend. Just pretend.

"You *are* a vampire," she murmured as a tear left her eye.

His eyes were large and dismal. "I would never hurt you, Rein."

She let her tongue glide across her teeth.

"And I am too." She began to tremble.

He made a sort of wincing sound and turned from her. She tasted blood inside her mouth and throat and choked a moment.

"What did you do to me?" She asked in indescribable fear. "*What happened?* You can't be..." She backed up into the bed. "God, *please* no." She stopped, feeling suffocated. "They're not real; they aren't real, Traith."

He wouldn't turn to look at her, his fingers running through his hair. Rein jumped out of the satin bed and staggered across the velvet rug to the vanity that was still standing. She caught her balance quickly and looked at herself in the mirror. She was not an image in it. Neither was Traith.

How about a picture with Miss Pierson, Traith?

"No!" She screamed. "No!" She repeated herself many times before managing to circuit around and stare at him in horror. "I'm not breathing! Please, *God*, this *can't* be!"

Traith turned and looked at her. "Rein. Rein, that damned soul *murdered* you and your friend. The captain poisoned you. I told you I was flawed. I didn't know what to do—you were *dead*, and the only way for you to live again was...You must understand..."

Rein continued to stare at him, fear gripping her. Her screaming ceased, and panic, the uttermost, truest panic, overwhelmed her. She looked down at herself. Her once cream dress was stained with blotches of red.

He wasn't lying. He finally wasn't.

She watched the striking gentleman and had no further notion of how to act or what to say. He tried to approach her, but she backed up even further and placed her hands to her mouth and felt the pointed canines that now replaced her once-regular ones. Her face and body were cold and her hands were colorless. She then felt the holes pierced into her skin and was chilled. She noticed a strange difference in her sight. An amazing difference. Better.

"Your eyes are not red because of any laboratory accident," she said, shaking, and she coughed in panic and loss of voice from her shouting.

"You can't *be this*!" she yelled hoarsely with tears swelling and streaming.

"Rein, I'm sorry; I don't *want* to be this."

"So my letter—tell me, Traith! What was it supposed to be, a *forewarning*?" She didn't know what to think about anything. Her mind was numb.

"Rein…" There was a soft, hushed sound in the way he said her name. His eyes were gentle, and she felt his humanity return.

No, he had never lost his humanity. But she had never heard of a vampire being anything more than a monster that drinks human blood. But she could feel. She didn't breathe, but she could feel and think and judge.

His hand was outstretched as if to let her hold it. His handsome face was lit through her eyes, but everything he was wearing blended into the darkness. He slowly walked toward her, hesitating every few steps. He knew she was scared of him, of herself, of the entire ordeal. He was trying to comfort her. Why didn't she let him?

Because he had bitten her. He wasn't human.

But he *seemed* human.

Her thoughts were so jumbled that she could barely hear or see.

"Oh God," she murmured. "I'm going to need to feed on *people*?"

"No!" he said, drawing back a little. "Never people, Rein, never."

Rein was lost inside herself, in a place where both her dreams and nightmares occurred, a place that she knew Traith could not follow, no matter how hard he might try.

He began to speak frantically; she had never seen him like this. "*I* don't do it," he said louder to calm her down. "I don't *feed* on anything!"

"*You fed on me!*" She felt so cold when she said that. She loved him; it frightened her to a standstill when she thought of how she could, but she did… she loved a vampire.

"No," he spoke softly to her, as if cut to the heart. "I didn't. It was only to allow you to have another chance. I'm not an animal, Rein. I'm not like that."

She thought she didn't care about what he thought, but she did. He was hurting as much as she was. How long had he been hurting? How long had he been a vampire?

A *vampire*?

How was that even real? Even possible?

Everything he had been hiding, every secret, every excuse he had given to her, it was because he didn't want her to know. But he always acted like a normal *person*.

His head was down. His eyes were closed tightly, and his eyebrows dipped down over them. She was scared for him, too. She wanted to embrace him.

Why? Why, when he had drained *her?*

Rein stared at her whitened hands and stifled an airless cry, trying desperately to recover her voice.

"Rein," he said unsteadily. "I never meant to lie about anything. H-how could I have *told* you about this?" He stopped.

He was tearing her heart in two.

"You would have been so frightened of me, and I didn't want that!" he continued. "I don't want *this*! I feel for you what I have never felt before. Rein, I didn't know what else to do."

She sat numbly at the vanity, looking into the empty mirror. Suddenly she drew up her hands in fists and hit the mirror in an uncontrollable outburst of confusion, fury, and tears, and then put her head in her hands and sobbed. She felt his eyes watching in helplessness as her shoulders shook in despair.

"It was my only choice," he said in a whisper. "I never loved before, Rein, and I...I love you, Rein. And no matter what, I can't control that."

He'd said it. She had never heard him say it. That made her even more miserable.

"I couldn't let you be completely gone from me," he said. "Your heart, your trust—I could never really believe that I had such a thing. But for that to just be gone?" He took a seat on the bed, remaining stiff and tense, as if afraid she would make a sudden movement toward him. "I only wanted you to be able to have a chance at life again, and this is all I could offer. If you don't want that, I can let you fall into death again. I'm not mad, Rein, and I know right now you might hate the very thought of me. I know your pain, but I saw no other choice. I'm still the same man you knew before." He sighed. "Now you must understand, Rein, why I couldn't tell you."

"I just…I can't feel. I'm so scared, I don't know what to think!"

"Do you trust me at all anymore, Rein?" he asked.

He had spoken quietly. It seemed as though her inappropriate, meaningless words had made him give up trying to win her love back. He didn't know he still had it and always would. She was more infatuated now than ever with him, despite whatever he, and now she, too, was.

She didn't turn to look at him, but lifted her head. So many different thoughts were spinning through her mind. What was she supposed to do now? Would she live forever, drinking blood and taking pleasure in the taste and aroma of it? Was that possible? She had to face the facts laid before her: she loved a vampire. A *vampire*. A man she so desperately valued. But he had made her into the same.

"I do trust you," she replied softly. "I am too afraid to disappear, Traith, into nonexistence. Into death. I don't hate you, I *don't*!"

She got up and ran out of the room, slamming the door behind her. Once she was in the hall she covered her face with her hands. He called her name.

She always liked the way he said her name.

She didn't know where she was going. To the captain, perhaps? To kill him? To do what? She couldn't walk far away from Traith.

She needed him.

chapter 26

☿

traith departed from Rein's quarters just as fast as she had, running after her down the ship's corridors. He knew who she wanted.

He caught up to her and grabbed her arm, but she pulled away and kept walking. "Rein, please, listen to me. Forget what I—"

"Forget what you *are*?" she cried.

"I didn't want this, Rein," he said more assertively. "I wasn't *born* a *vampire*! I was twenty-three years old, living a normal life! Twenty-three! I had so much more life to live, and now I have nothing! And I felt something for you. My intention was not for you to lose the rest of your life as I had, but he killed you, and you lost it anyway! If you don't want to live, I can arrange your death." His final words seemed to sting his lips.

She backed up, staring at him. She feared him, and he knew. "I love you, Traith," she said, crying. "But I'm *scared* of you; I don't want to be."

"Rein!" He called after her when she began to run, and she immediately stopped, never facing him. "Rein, please don't be afraid of me. Please. Hear me. Hear me out. Hear my side." His voice was quivering.

She fell to the floor in despair, holding her head. His eyes were fixed on her, and he stood back from her as she cried. Her body was tightened in a crouch on the ground. She imagined herself falling apart, having the threads of her body come undone, but as hard as she tried to want that, she couldn't.

"What can I do?" Traith asked softly after a pause, bending down in front of her, slowly falling onto his knees. "What can I do to make this easier? I never meant so much pain to come to you. Not you. Please, Rein, look at me," he said as he knelt down and lifted her face to his. "Am I that horrifying that you cannot even bear to look at me anymore? Please; I don't want to scare you."

She looked up into his pleading eyes, tightly closing her mouth.

"You couldn't imagine how much I wanted to look normal for you." His voice was miserable. "I'm sorry, please," he whispered.

She was cooling; she was calming herself down. Her panic was over. She had no more energy left to be hysterical. It was over; the shock was over.

Instead of speaking her feelings, Rein showed them to him. She threw her arms around his waist and buried herself in his chest. She wasn't afraid of him. She was afraid of the situation. Never *him*. Then she felt his arms lightly cross her back. Very lightly, as if he didn't know how to respond. She was crying in his arms. She could smell the cologne on his skin.

Then she noticed something fall from him. She pulled back and glanced into his burning eyes, and then glanced down. There was a small crucifix and chain on the floor. She had never seen it before.

"How can you wear a cross?" she stuttered and stopped herself to regain her voice. "How are you able?" She paused a second time as he spotted what had fallen from his inner shirt pocket. "A crucifix—doesn't that harm vampires, Traith?"

She sensed his sorrow and had to stop. His face was so sad. She saw his sincerity; he *was* remorseful. She knew he was. She trusted him. That letter—it was true. Her father was dead. Her house was sold. Where was she to go?

But it was finished, now.

"God holds no curse against me," he muttered. "He holds no resentment against something even as ostensibly depraved as a vampire, as long as it has a pure and just heart, and despite everything, I do have one." Rein felt relieved at his words. "My intentions were always pure," he said, picking the crucifix up off the ground and placing it in her hands, closing them. "They always were. You brought such a deep feeling out of me. I always tried to hide it, even after I met you, but the captain could see the little bit of it I must have shown near you. That's why he poisoned you, to make *me* suffer."

She knew, then, that she was sulking over something that could not be undone without death. True death. She felt such a sudden sympathy for Traith that she could not explain, nearly forgetting her own novel and terrifying situation.

"I believe you," she said. "I *love* you."

His eyes, piercing and bright, softened, and she felt like she could swim and sleep in them with inexpressible comfort. His touch probably felt so divine.

"I will kill him, Rein," he said, his gentleness turning bitter as he stood. "I will, I promise you."

"Traith?" she called.

He turned to look at her and waited.

"I'll never see America, will I? We were never going—"

"No, we never were."

"Did you always know?" she asked despondently.

He paused. "No, I didn't."

She felt as if she were dreaming. "What do I look like now?"

He watched her for a few moments without answering. "Rein, I will explain this to you, but not now. Too much has already been said. Trust me. I only want to protect you."

Just as he was about to say something else he was drowned out by a loud, deep shout. He turned his head; it was Romanoff yelling his name in the lobby a few feet down.

"Carden?" Traith murmured. His voice grew louder. "Carden, what are you doing? What's wrong?"

"She killed herself!" the Frenchman yelled from the end of the hall. "Saria is *dead*!"

Traith looked at him, bewildered, and glanced back at Rein. She was frozen. She had forgotten about Saria. Saria had been blue. Romanoff also had to be a vampire. Saria must've been bitten, too. But why was she dead? How was that possible? And Edgar?

"W-what?" Rein spoke, trembling. Her heart plummeted. "You're mistaken…you…" she burst. "You've *got to be mistaken, no!*"

"Dear God," she heard Traith mutter. "Carden, come with me!"

"Rein *stayed*?"

Traith groaned nervously as he followed Romanoff's stare over to Rein. Suddenly, bitterly, angrily, Romanoff backed up and ran out of sight, ignoring Traith's beckon. Traith left Rein and ran after him, and she heard him swear. She stood, trembling, but managed to follow him.

Traith was standing with his back to her. His legs were wide apart.

His hands were out by his sides, not touching his body. She heard him moaning lowly. Romanoff had disappeared.

By this time, the other passengers, who had been sitting and mingling on sofas and stools at chess tables, began to stare vehemently in anger at the situation. They all blurred translucent and hovered toward Traith. She nearly fell in a faint, but Traith turned swiftly to her. In a blink, she was directly in front of him by the port door.

"Oh my God, what did you *just do*?" she asked hysterically. "How did we—?"

"Trust me for now, please," Traith urged, holding her shoulders. "I will tell you everything, but not yet."

What could he do? Make himself be anywhere he wanted?

"We need to leave here, now," Traith said, trying to ignore the disgusting glares of the others. "The captain is across the deck, through the port door, and down that lone hallway. The one you never went down."

The piano began to play a tune of its own; it was a loud and carefree tune.

Traith turned and built up an authoritative voice. "Stop it!" he swore heatedly. "*Stop playing*!"

Something crashed down onto the piano keys, and a cowering shriek sounded from it. Laughing chaos roared from the mouths of the surrounding people as they watched Traith fume.

He took Rein's hand and jumped into the air, and Rein realized that she was no longer in the lobby hall but in the air above the deck.

The downpour had subsided into a slight mist. There was no more thunder, but the sky was dark with ominous clouds. Traith looked down at her, his expression hard to read. She wasn't pulling away from him.

Was he *flying*?

She closed her eyes tight. She pretended she was alone in a bed, having a dream. But she would face reality soon enough.

She gazed up at him again.

He was. And he was holding her.

But by the way Traith was looking wildly down at himself, Rein knew something was terribly wrong. *He* was confused.

"How can I…? Did I…?" he stuttered to himself as if a miracle had occurred.

To her, one had.

He landed with her on the deck. He looked ill. He had dark rings around his eyes. He looked dead. She wanted to cry, but she was out of tears.

The more she thought about her situation, the more she felt like she was going insane. There was no such thing as a vampire. In fact, one could probably be institutionalized for even speaking of such fallacies. But it wasn't a fallacy. She was a vampire, now. A *vampire*. She tried to think about that fact. She tried to think about how she would cope with herself for…for eternity?

She saw the port door. It looked more menacing now than it ever had. "That door…" she spoke with a gentle voice. "From there you got blood, didn't you?"

"Rein—"

"Traith, *Saria*! God, help me, I need to find her, *now*!"

"Please, Rein, wait for a moment. We'll get her; she'll be all right."

"Traith, he said she was dead!" She was utterly distraught.

"Why so sad, little girl? Traith can't kill me for you?"

She looked up. Traith tensed and turned to stare with a vision most piercing. It was the captain's voice.

"What are you?" Rein asked with a quiver, her eyes sodden with tears.

"A ghost, my dear," he answered, still out of sight. "Didn't you notice why Harker never succeeded in attacking me? He can't harm me. I can make his grasping fist fall right through my chest if I want."

His white eyes were the first things she saw when he came out of the blackness of the vault. He was mimicking Traith's fist by putting his own on his chest and letting it fall down, limp, to his side.

"So, you think I'm intimidated by *you*?" he asked her. He snickered and looked at Traith. "You are quite the scientist, Harker," he gurgled with laughter.

The stooped figure paused and walked out of the blackness, circling Traith. Traith was clenching his teeth hard; his eyes followed the man's every move, every step. The man tossed him a small bottle like the one she had seen Traith put in his coat pocket the last time she was on the deck. Like the one the captain had dropped at the ball.

Traith caught it and looked down, and with a sudden ferocity, he crushed it in his fist. Blood spilled everywhere, from both his hand and the bottle.

"You son of a—"

"That was a perfectly fresh bottle of blood for your beloved, Harker! I *try* to be hospitable on this ship, and you resent me! You never minded accepting one of those before! Is it because you're already full of *her* blood?"

She stared at Traith, and his eyes were as angry as they had been the night the captain had poisoned her.

"Oh, by the way, how's she coping? Not too well, hmm? You've finally decided to reveal and pass on the truth you so immensely despise? Bravo, boy, you've done it! Now don't you feel *disgusted* with yourself?"

Rein continued to sob without realization. She watched Traith in his torment but noticed his body beginning to become transparent.

"Yes," he replied.

Her heart was wrenching.

His eyes suddenly faded, as did the rest of him. He slowly became less and less visible.

The captain tilted his head to the side sarcastically. "Oh, don't try that."

Traith spun around, becoming completely invisible.

Or had he disappeared?

At that point, she was beyond shock, so she just watched, numb. She was scared. She didn't know where he was, but it appeared as though only the captain and she were standing on the deck.

He raised his hand to her, and that twisted grin formed on his ghastly face. He was going to hurt her. Could she get hurt? It didn't matter. She was frightened. It looked as though something was sparking off of his fingertips, and she nearly felt a wave of pain...

But then she saw a piece of rope lift itself off of the ground. It glowed red with energy, as did...a fist? Traith's fist—the only thing about him perceptible was his fist. The captain looked at him wildly but was too slow to retaliate.

The sparks stopped.

The bodiless figure wrapped the rope around the man's neck, and then let go. It exploded, and Traith suddenly became visible again, standing next to Rein. She ducked from the blast. Traith was standing directly in the way of the noise. After the echo of it ceased, all was silent.

When the smoke cleared, she looked up and saw Traith standing tensely, and, somehow, perfectly unharmed.

There was no sign of the captain through the lingering smoke. There was nothing but dead stillness and silence for a moment. Rein saw Traith watching her. She still refused to say even a word. She was hardly lucid.

"Rein," he stumbled to say. "It isn't what you—"

A sizzle, like something about to spark, cut him off. The hissing crackled as it grew louder. It cracked, and a boom rang in her ears. She managed to see the captain with his hand out, his fingers pointed straight. Sparks spewed from his fingertips again, and a bizarre, lightning-like flash came from them and hit Traith.

That could've been her. It all occurred within an instant. She didn't know where he had come from. She heard herself call out Traith's name. It was the first time in her life she had ever seen someone hit so hard.

Traith was jolted and forced backward. He'd been struck by lightning. He slammed into the side of the deck, grunting in a near yell. His back smashed hard into the deck flooring, and he collided into the rails. The rails bent and nearly broke in half with the force of his body.

Then he was still.

A blaze of fury swept through Rein. She still didn't know what she was feeling. She was numb and removed from what was going on around her, and humanity seemed so distant. She felt pretend.

In her anesthetized thoughts, she approached the laughing captain. He immediately threw her back into a pile of storage crates with only a nod of his head. No arms, just a nod.

Pain seized her body, but she forgot about it in a single instant. She felt the fury continually rising and heating her skin. Her hands formed fists underneath the broken crates.

She saw Traith roll limply onto his stomach. He managed to push himself off the ground, but before he could react to anything, pieces of crate panels and nails shot through the air.

She was doing it.

She was angered beyond words. She didn't know how or what she was doing, but she didn't have time to think.

Traith quickly stood up, trying with great effort to dodge and duck to escape the debris. A single nail did meet with his arm, piercing it and lodging into his flesh. Another impaled his side. However, the captain simply became intangible like a true ghost, causing the crate pieces to sail straight through him.

She glanced down. Fear spread throughout her, but she couldn't control whom she hit. She couldn't control what she was doing. But there was so much power in her hands.

A soft, bluish glow shown around her fists. The captain's eyes were wide. He was shocked. He and Traith both. She was, too. But fear of what she had done overruled any of that. She had hurt Traith. She had driven nails into him.

"This isn't p-possible," Rein heard Traith utter, trying to stand straight despite the nails lodged into him.

She lifted her hands out toward the Captain. Silvery rays came from his somewhat transparent body, and into her hands.

He looked down at himself, cowering, his sunken eyes as terrified as she had ever seen them. His body was slowly fading into nothing, and his mouth was moving wildly trying to speak. She had him restrained. A small and silver orb with a burning center radiated from within the captain's body. Rein's energy yanked it out into her hand, and she crushed it. The captain's body disintegrated and instantly disappeared, his voice echoing in the silence.

chapter 27

She had fallen to her knees on the deck. Misty wind blew through her hair and blew it around her. She was getting wet in the dark, watery breeze. She was cold. She smelled the salt, and it made her sick.

What had she done? Something as terrible as what Traith had done. Worse. She had killed someone—someone who had killed her. She had driven large, rusty, near hand-length nails into the man she loved—the vampire, who was standing speechless. The wind rang in her ears. She couldn't speak. Her throat was swollen in fear.

"Oh *my God*," she finally heard him murmur beneath the wind.

She tried to stand but couldn't. She absolutely couldn't; she was completely drained.

Then she felt that grasp on her arms. Traith pulled her up to her feet. She heard him let out a single whimper of pain, but he tried to make no more noise after that. He had pulled her up with a nail sunken into his arm.

She forced herself around to face him and saw that his arm and side were now bleeding heavily. He did not meet her watching eyes, but yanked out the large, rusted nail from his forearm.

"Traith, forgive me," she rasped. "I don't know what I did; I didn't mean to—"

"I know," he replied.

Rein still gazed at him as he wrenched the other nail from his stomach. She had been responsible, and her heart sank when she heard the noise of his muscle being tugged as the nail was pulled out. She saw him bite back the pain.

The silence was ended by a slam of an iron door. The vaulted, entrance door. She glanced up and, through watery vision, saw a swarm of passengers flood out. She thought she was going to lose consciousness, but she never did, and she stood waveringly.

Traith slowly bent and touched the base of the deck. A reddish glow pulsed out like the glow on the rope.

Was it going to explode?

"Rein," he said. "Quickly, come here, please."

His feet lifted from the ground. His hand was out.

She did not respond.

The ship lit. Blinding. She couldn't see anything. In one second…

She was grabbed by the forearm and yanked into his hold, just before the ship completely detonated. The flash was the last thing she saw, even through her eyelids. She felt herself being driven forward into the smoking air. Traith was clutching her tight and somehow shielding her from the blast.

His back was being burned. She heard his light moans in biting back the pain. He was being hit hard by the fiery explosion.

The force of the detonation drove them in a whirling of light into the air. Then the glare turned black. She opened her eyes.

Stars were out tonight; shining, peaceful, untouched. The blackness of night covered all, except for the flames from the ship as it sunk to the watery depths of the Atlantic.

She was right; his embrace was divine. He was holding her close and tight. He was so strong. After a lingering moment, she could feel him loosen his hold. They were slowly dropping from the air. Was he losing consciousness? *He was.*

So protecting. Gallant. Chivalrous. He had saved her life. What happened wasn't his fault.

It *wasn't…*

The peacefulness she longed to feel in his arms was suspended.

She never did get a chance to see his face above the water.

The next thing she knew, she was standing before a woman in a white room.

chapter 28

ⵖ

She was an old but angelic woman, dressed in a cream and lavender dress that sparkled brightly. She stood in the center of a white room that was so intensely lit that Rein could hardly see her. In the far front of the room, there was a table where three others sat.

"Welcome, Rein."

Then her head lifted off of a pillow.

She was in a dark room and seemed to be alone.

It was a bedroom, but she didn't recognize it. A small window was on the wall to her left. It was the only thing making the room at all lit. Daytime? Then she realized that she wasn't on a bed, but on a divan. Red and gold and black twirled in a pattern amidst the buttons that held the fabric on. There was a hardwood floor underneath a pale golden rug.

Had she only been dreaming about the angelic woman? She knew the rest was real; she still felt sharp eyeteeth with her tongue. She could still see profoundly well in the darkness. She wasn't in pain anymore from the collision with the heavy crates. But where was she?

As if on cue, Traith entered from a bright hallway that nearly rendered her sightless. He closed the door quickly and held it there as if someone were trying to break in.

"I think that I'm blind," he said, most likely to himself.

He approached her without another word, shaking his head as if in relief to have gotten out of the blaring light. She was grateful to see him. She didn't have to be scared because she had him.

"Where am I?" she asked, sitting up slowly, realizing that she was still dressed in the cream, bloodstained dress she had been wearing on the ship.

"It's called the Council of the Presage," he muttered. "But forget the name. You're safe, Rein."

His voice was steady, as she knew it best. He took a seat on a chair next to the divan. He had on no shirt, and she saw muscles rippled down and throughout his chest and sides. His stomach wasn't moving. He wasn't breathing. She also caught sight of the scars left on his throat.

A burnt, smoky smell was detectable on him.

The *explosion*.

"Your back, Traith?" She panicked. "Is it hurt? Where is your shirt?"

"It was burned off," he said calmly, reminding her of how he had spoken before what had happened. "And my back is rather sore."

She felt ill. "I felt us dropping," she said, breathing out. "You were losing consciousness…but you didn't let go."

He smiled a little. "Of course not."

She managed to smile back and started looking around the room, studying it. "How long ago did we get here? And where's here?"

"A few hours ago," he said. "And it's hard to explain where here is exactly. But anyway, once we arrived here you collapsed, and before I did, I laid you in here. After an hour or two I came out of it. I've been directly outside the door since, so I haven't had the chance to worry about my back."

"Traith, I can imagine your back is burnt horribly."

"It is," he replied, rough and quiet. "I can't touch fire, Rein. If I do, the wounds take a great deal of time to mend. Do you know anything about vampires?" His voice was strained when he spoke the last word. "Vampires heal quickly. They don't die. This doesn't mean less pain, but both of these advantages have the exception of the stake, and…" He paused. "Every vampire has his own weakness. The first substance a vampire encounters after being bitten becomes excruciating for him to tolerate. If he comes in contact with it again, he won't heal quickly at all. I don't know what yours is, but my own," he said, making his empty, single-breathed laugh, "is fire."

That made sense. At the meeting, he was sitting farthest from the hearth.

"Did you dream anything?" he asked.

It took a moment before she could formulate words. "Yes, about a woman, shining, like an angel."

"Her…well," he said, becoming quiet, "she isn't an angel. She's bright, I'll give her that. Nearly burned my eyes out with those bloody lights. That was Mistress. Although I've yet to speak with her, I was told that she would give you a dream."

"She only greeted me," Rein muttered.

He sighed. "I figured such. She likes to confuse people. I think she gets more kick out of life that way. I must warn you, she likes to speak in riddles, and she can be intimidating, but do not feel too flustered by her. She wants to meet you."

"Is there no way for her to turn us back?"

"I wish there were a way," he murmured, "but nothing has ever worked. Some say it's because I was bitten by an advanced vampire, one that has mutated more than normal and is much more powerful. Even though *you* might have a chance of being turned back," he paused, "to do so would result in your death. If you had been bitten alive it would be a different story. I can guarantee I would've never bitten you otherwise."

She nodded, trying to push back fear. "Traith, can I ever see day again?" she asked, the realization of the blinding light hitting her. "That blinding light—"

"It isn't blinding, Rein, to anyone else but us," he said. "But I can be out in the sunlight. It makes me weaker, but I've trained to become accustomed to it. It'll take a little time for you, however, but you'll get used to it, don't worry; it isn't *that* bad. You'll absolutely *see* sunlight again." He smiled.

But she needed to know more. The questions were flooding her mind again. "What you did, to the ship and the rope—"

"Let's just say I'm more dangerous than I'd like to be," he replied. "But you and I are alone in this." He was choking on his words. "I have never known an honorable vampire before, Rein." His voice became grave. "There were never any, anywhere, other than Carden and myself."

Her eyes blurred. "Carden! *Saria*—"

"I don't know where they are." His voice was trembling, now, hard.

He was actually afraid, and she saw it.

"The Mistress will tell me," he cleared his throat, but the quiver was still noticeable, "when we meet with her. She knows. She's got to."

"Oh God, Traith! Saria is like my sister; she can't have—"

"Rein," he whispered with his head down.

"Waiting is hard," she murmured. "That's all."

"I know," he said. "I can see your pain, Rein; I understand it."

"See my pain? Tell me what I look like," she said, wanting him to be more expressive. "Please tell me. I must know if I can't ever see my own self again. I trust you to describe me."

His flaming eyes closed partially while he hesitated. "I'm not exactly sure how you would have me do that," he said. "I can't—"

"My hair? Eyes? Face? Do I look at all *human*?"

He bent down with his arms resting on his knees, his hands becoming still and dangling flaccidly. "Rein, you don't look any less human than before. Your eyes aren't like mine. They are...subtle."

"My eyes are red, then?" she asked with a weak voice. "Blazing red?"

"No," he said quickly. It seemed as though he had taken a blow from hearing about his own eyes. "Your eyes nearly look...they're dark, Rein. Like a deep scarlet. Your hair is still black, and your skin is only slightly lighter, now. You don't look..." He seemed to bite his teeth together tight. "You've hardly changed at all. You're not nearly as obvious as I am."

She could see that he was more depressed and alone than she had ever seen him. A long silence followed. She used it to think of every possible question she could. But then when she wanted to ask him, she had to stop herself. He was lost in thought, and she knew he was too upset to answer her any further. He was bent over with his head resting on his hands, and he wasn't breathing. It was so obvious to her now, with his shirt off, that he wasn't breathing.

On the ship he had been breathing. She knew because she noticed how slowly he had done so. Had he done so for her? It was voluntary for him, and her now. They had to think about each breath.

"What about what I did?" she asked gently.

"What?" He glanced up at her, but he blinked heavily.

"Traith, I didn't mean for those nails to hurt you; I didn't. They went so deep, and you pulled them out as if they were tiny splinters. But I killed him. How was that—?"

"Rein, I don't know!"

She flinched at his raised voice and said no more. But he wasn't angry. He seemed only to know as little as she, so she bit her tongue. She didn't ask any more questions.

"I'm as confused with my own new abilities as those you exhibited," he muttered more calmly. "I was stuck on that ship, Rein. I could not get off. No matter what I did, I couldn't get off. I tried jumping, but the next moment, I was in my chamber bed. In a matter of ten seconds I would somehow be back on that ship. With that man. It was so torturous." It looked as though he couldn't finish his words. "But somehow I could, and after so many years." He stopped abruptly.

She was sitting up straight, her legs off the side of the divan. He was still leaning on his hands with his head down and eyes closed. But she reached over to him, taking no thought in the matter. It was a simple action. She lifted his head with her fingers, and when he looked at her, she placed her arms around his neck, careful not to touch his back.

He stood and she felt him go limp for a moment. Then his naked arms tightened around her, and his head touched her own. She rested her face on his bare shoulder, and she could smell that familiar cologne on his skin beneath the scent of fire. She was in love with him, no matter what she was. No matter what he was.

A vampire.

But without doubt a godly vampire.

chapter 29

He closed the latch on the door as quietly as he could. Rein had fallen asleep instantly. She was so overwhelmed, and all he could do was watch her and be there for her when he could.

As he turned from the door, he gasped slightly at the blinding effect the light of the place still had on him. He closed his eyes immediately and held his hands over them, hoping no one was watching. He needed a moment to adjust.

Then someone ran into him. He heard a "humph" of irritation from the body who hit him…or had he been inadvertently inching his way to a walk? He slowly dropped his hands from his face and tried his best to look at the man he'd run into.

"Excuse me," Traith murmured.

All he could make out of the man was a voice. "What is your problem?" he snapped back. "You blind, or something, boy?"

Traith felt himself flooding with fury. He dropped his hands entirely and squinted at the man. He was hardly a man. Young.

God, his eyes felt *ablaze*!

"Who the devil are you?" Traith shouted in question.

The boy hummed in arrogance. "We like to walk around half naked, too, do we? My name is Magellan, and I'd better not find the likes of *you* in any other place but this *infirmary*!"

The man went to walk away when Traith grabbed his shirt and yanked him back. "I suggest you know who you're talking to before you run your bloody mouth."

"Why?" the man growled, holding onto Traith's fist. "Who are *you*?"

"Don't you know?" he said in reply.

Traith finally felt his eyes doing a little less squinting, but squinting all the same. It was then that he could finally see what the man looked like; long blonde hair, blue eyes, a pale blue shirt buttoned up with a belt diagonal from shoulder to waist. The man's face went icy, and his eyes enlarged.

"*Traith Harker*?" he declared. He cleared his throat, and Traith let go of him, letting him put his hand out. "Mistress' right hand man, huh? Oh for the love of Merlin, I'm *sorry*," he replied, curtsying like a girl with a sarcastic grin. "I've only been here ten years, and I've never met you—"

"Apparent as hell you've never met me," Traith said, not giving him his hand. "Sarcasm isn't the right approach, right now. I'll tell you once and once only, that I'm not exactly a *boy*, I'm half naked because my back is nearly burned *off*, and I can't *see* out here because I'm a—"

"A vampire," the man said, wiping a golden lock from his forehead. "By gold, I've never met a true vampire before."

Traith shook his head and held it, the lights giving him a headache. "In ten years, you've never met a vampire? You must have done a *great deal* of field work, then."

"I doubt that I entirely trust you, Mr. Harker," the man dared to say.

Traith felt his eyes wanting to widen in shock. "What?"

"A vampire?" Magellan laughed. "Being that you're the only good one I've ever heard of, it just seems too implausible for you to be good when you're straight from the Devil Himself."

Traith clenched his fists together. "You've no right to speak to me like that. You're too ignorant, and you're too young—"

"Me? Young! What about you?"

"I'm *140 years old*! Does *that* change anything?"

Magellan laughed. "Your looks can be deceiving, I suppose."

"You'd better watch your tongue before I *give* you a reason to think me of 'the Devil Himself'!" Traith said, not even trying to look at him anymore.

"All I know is that I've done much more *field work* than you have; your name has never been on assignment. Does that have anything to do with the fact that you're a *vampire*?"

Traith felt a hand press his chest. A woman's hand. For a split second, he thought it was…it wasn't. It was Lorena. She pushed him back.

"Calm down, Traith," she cooed. "Magellan, you should leave, right now. Do you have any idea what power he has over you? You're a petty novice for God's sake!"

"You can *take* my next bloody assignment, then!" Traith yelled to the man as he walked away. "Do me the honor!"

The man puffed. "I *will!*"

He was still steaming when he heard Lorena laugh. "Good day to you too, Traith," she said, teasing. "Trouble never ceases to find you, does it?"

"No. It's beginning to flat out run *into* me." He tried his best to stare at her without recoiling from the bright light. "What in God's name is his problem? I never even spoke a word to him before, and he wants to fight."

"His attitude isn't his greatest asset, and I think he has a thing against vampires." She giggled, and Traith felt his brows lower in frustration. "Come in here," she said. "No shirt today?"

He sighed and mumbled. "My—"

"Your back. I don't mind that I see you half dressed of course," she laughed. "But I see your bite marks!"

He gave her a half smile of anger. "Oh, amusing."

She took his arm, and part of him felt wrong allowing her to do so. What if Rein awoke? No, she wouldn't. She'd just fallen asleep.

They walked into a room down the hall that was very dim. It was a reading lounge, like a small library. He remembered that room.

"I bet you need an update after all those years alone, don't you?" she said, sitting at a table in the center of the area.

He took a seat across from her, blinking quickly to get rid of the glare in his eyes from the harsh light. "Yes, I do. Although I was on that ship with Carden Romanoff, you know. I wasn't completely alone."

"Isn't he the one who kissed your sister, Ana?"

Traith froze with anger. "Lorena, don't start with me!"

"It was only in jest!" she said, laughing. "I thought you might need a laugh after all that's happened. Perhaps *more* than a laugh…"

"The update will suffice," he said, raising his voice.

She sighed and put her elbows on the table, leaning forward on her hands. "All right, *Grim.*" Her manner went suddenly from giddy to grave. "We lost over half the Council, Traith," she said. "Anytime we tried to avenge someone, or help someone the Mardinial Council tried to take, we lost."

He felt himself shudder.

"Does that surprise you?" She paused and took a breath, staring at him, but not at his face. "God, I never knew your chest was that scarred."

He felt himself boiling at her coolness. "I apologize for not introducing you to my *damaged exterior*." He forced himself to further hold his sarcastic tongue for a moment. "What of the Mardinial Council, Lorena?"

She shook her head. "No one, in all of the time you were gone, was able to find anything out and come back alive. Helena still lives, along with a stronger rivaling council. We really needed you. And missed you."

He felt ill at her words. He was that strong that Mistress lost half of her council when he wasn't at her side?

"All we do know, that you do not yet, is that your sister does actually know Helena's weakness."

He stood, hands grasping the table. "What?"

She nodded, not looking at him…at least not at his face. "No one has seen her since she cursed you onto that ship, but we have gotten information that she, as Helena's alchemist, was told Helena's weakness."

He felt faint.

"Having you back also brings a chance of getting more information. You're the only person I could ever imagine she would speak to."

"After she cursed me? You think she'll talk to me?" He was becoming unnerved.

"Why else would she hide away and not battle anyone?" Lorena said, slouching back in her chair. "Mistress said she feels that Ana is— was grieving and contemplating what she had done, but that Helena frightens her so terribly that she would not dare disobey her and attempt setting you free."

"*God*," he murmured.

He felt so feeble. His eyes were blurred, unfocused.

"One thing fortunate for us is that Mistress has told no one her weakness; therefore, no one from the Mardinial Council can find out about it without numerous failed attempts. You of all of us should know that either council would cease to be in existence if its leader were killed."

"I didn't lose my memory, Lorena. I just wanted an update."

She smirked. "Last I recall, you did lose your memory."

Traith turned around and attempted to leave, not saying anything more to her. His anger level was already too high. Damned woman never knew when to stop…

"*Lord*, your back looks *terrible*, Traith!" she called from behind him.

"Thank you," he replied, throwing his hand out as if to bow.

She became quieter. "But nothing else looks terrible."

He swore under his breath and slammed the door as he left the room. He could hear her laughing from inside. He needed a few hours of sleep. It didn't matter that it was daytime; he was exhausted.

But how the hell was he going to sleep with a back burned to a crisp?

chapter 30

a cool breeze whispered onto her bare throat and curled around her neck. It stirred her, and she turned onto her side under the blankets. Her eyes blinked open, and she saw through the open window that it was nighttime.

It was nighttime? She had slept through the day? Traith had held her, and that was the last she remembered.

But she'd had another dream; the same woman was speaking to her.

"You've not been introduced to anything this vast before. Unfortunately for you, you had to learn through love. My First Hand meant no harm, I assure you, and once you become used to your new lifestyle, things will start to work out for the better.

"However, you must now choose your own fate, Rein.

"You are still capable of returning to a human state, but you will also reside in death; or you can live as a vampire and continue living morally, as most humans do.

"You must clear your mind of your rancor. *You are dead.* Nothing else in the world can change your fate but this. It is not a comforting choice of destiny, I assure you, but you will be able to adapt. And if you live awhile and still detest yourself, you can always go back, though it isn't usually a pleasant experience.

"Smoke was the first harmful substance you were near after your alteration. Now you must make no contact with it. The effects it will have on you may very well be close to torture, yet it will not kill you.

"Also, you should know that it was Traith's sister who cursed him onto the ship. His sister."

Her head rose quickly off of the pillow. What had been talking to her? This *Mistress*? It was the strangest dream she'd ever had; it was words and no faces or images, just darkness, like the room she resided in now. She was still on the divan.

She sat up and scanned the room around her. Smoke was her weakness? Like Traith's was fire? What about Traith's sister? Where was she?

She nearly stood, but she heard talking directly outside the door. It was Traith. Then his voice rose.

"You expect me to wait longer?" he shouted, and his voice was loud even through the door. He moaned; perhaps he swore, she wasn't sure. Another voice was quieter, a man's voice. She couldn't hear him, but she heard Traith speak again. "About bloody time!"

She heard something hit against the door. It made her stand, warily, and walk toward it. To her surprise, she was completely revitalized from sleep. But how long had she been sleeping? She was utterly confused.

Her hand reached out and pulled the door handle down. The latch clicked, and the door opened. To her relief, there were no blinding lights. They were dimmed.

A heavy weight lifted off of the door, and she saw Traith standing, still without a shirt. His hands had been leaning on the door, and he caught himself as she was opening it. As he caught sight of her, he sighed as if to let out his anger so it wasn't noticeable.

He approached her, and she quickly backed up into the dark room again. He peeked in with an unnecessary knock.

"Can I come in?" he asked.

"Of course," she replied, taking her seat back on the divan.

He must have seen her shaking as he came in and sat next to her. "Rein, I'm sorry," he nearly whispered, looking at her hands. "What do you want me to do for you? Anything you need."

"Traith, who is behind these dreams?" she asked in frustration.

"In a few moments everything will be explained," he murmured, leaning over, wiping away a tear with his thumb. "To you *and* to me."

The gesture made her weak.

"I'm furious, Rein, that she's made you wait so long. *I* haven't even been able to see her yet. I haven't seen her in—" He stopped. He had a sort of immediate hesitance when it came to tallying years. "They told me she would see us in a few moments. Things will get easier, all right?"

She didn't reply.

"I love you, Rein," he said softly.

She was baffled at his sudden words, smiling.

"Please forgive me," he continued. "I know I can't fix this situation. I don't want you to fear me or look at me as though I had enjoyed what I had to do. I wanted to give you some sort of chance. I wasn't ready for you to die."

"I don't fear you at all, and I never did," she said, inching nearer to him. She laid her head on his arm and found the feeling perfectly cozy. His arm wrapped around her waist. "I didn't mean what I said. I don't think you made the wrong decision. I don't want to die, Traith. She told me in the dream that I could choose, and that my weakness is smoke, and your sister—"

"My sister?" he repeated, shocked.

She looked up at him.

"She told you about my sister?"

"Yes. But Traith, I want this, and I want you," she whispered. "I just have so much to ask."

His face was gentle again; that softness was there that made her feel safe. "You will get all your answers, I assure you."

She smiled slightly, but her gaze was deep. "Traith, I love—"

A knock on the door and a woman's voice interrupted them. Traith rose slowly, still looking at her.

She smiled, "you. I love you."

He didn't smile, but his eyes were immersed in her. He turned to answer the door at the second knock. She saw his back for the first time.

It was burned as though it had completely caught fire. It was damaged terribly, covered in open wounds and dried blood. It looked fresh.

"Oh Traith," she said.

He turned back, raising an eyebrow.

"Your back…didn't you let anyone try to bandage it, or something?"

He stared at her for only a moment before there was another knock. "No."

He answered and walked into the hall. It was a girl she hadn't seen before; she had smooth, darkened skin, eyes as green as emeralds, and long, curly, brown hair that flowed down her shoulders. Who was she? Not the Mistress?

The door closed partially; the brown-haired woman's hand was on it. She was whispering, but her eyes batted like she had an eyelash stuck in them. Rein felt an unfamiliar anger rising in her.

She couldn't see Traith, but she heard him softly talking to the lady. It wasn't like he did with her. Less gentle. He was frustrated.

He turned back into the room, facing her, and didn't look back at the girl behind him. "Come with me, Rein," he said. "She wants to see us now."

chapter 31

t he room was dim, and Rein was comfortable in it. Traith stood beside her. It was as if they were awaiting a grand entrance together into some sort of ball.

Some sort of ball…

Like the one where she'd had her first kiss. A *broken* kiss.

That thought made her notice that her lip was completely healed.

Traith was standing tensely. She didn't dare touch him or talk to him. It wasn't that she couldn't, but he was too infuriated. She wasn't sure about the details, but something about the Mistress made him uptight and on edge. Why hadn't the "witch" summoned them sooner?

For a moment she thought her vision blurred. A woman came into view. She was old and angelic…*Mistress.*

"Harker, I've missed you," she spoke, and the words came flowing out majestically. "You have taken quite a hit to your back, haven't you?"

He didn't make any movements. His eyes were emotionless, and he stared directly at the woman. Rein saw by the way he clenched his teeth that he was as angry as she thought.

"God," he murmured with his mouth still nearly closed and his eyebrows drawn together. "So *long*."

The old woman looked deeply into his eyes. "Traith, I tried to get you free—"

"You tried?" he said, still rigid. "You must've tried to get us both here to see you quickly and get the lights turned down, too, I suppose; you must've tried *really*—"

"Do *not* speak to me like that, Traith!" she yelled.

Rein watched him immediately look down and cringe bitterly.

"I have had many other obligations more important than this!"

His face was as bleak as could be, and his eyes looked like ice. "How did I get off of the ship?" he said through his teeth, his words enunciated.

Her eyes calmed. Her white hair draped coolly over her neck as she watched him. "I cannot say. Perhaps *this* entrance into the ship counteracted your curse." She shifted her sight to Rein. "I honestly cannot say."

His troubled face stared at the old woman, but then he turned and looked back at Rein.

"I don't understand," Rein said in a whisper, but the lady's voice outweighed her own as she spoke.

"Miss Pierson, welcome. I am the Mistress, and this is my council: the Council of the Presage. Has Traith explained anything to you about this?"

She looked down at her feet. "I…"

"He didn't, did he?"

"How was I supposed to?" he asked irritably. "I scared her out of her *mind*."

"Traith, please calm down." Her voice was loud, clear, and strict. "I will explain to you, then, Rein. The curse of the vampire is perhaps the oldest and wickedest of any. It has caused more than its share of terror and deaths; most of the vampire race gives it a sinful reputation. But it can be contained and hidden, like Harker has done. You can still act and function no differently. My council contains these right-willed creatures. But only two have ever chosen to follow this moral path. That is Traith, the only just creature of his kind that I have ever known, and Carden Romanoff. But even he submitted to his desires. Traith never did."

"*Mistress*, I'm *not* a—"

"You are a creature, Traith, whether you like it or not."

Traith glared at the floor. It was so odd the way he surrendered to her, despite his anger. But her heart went numb when the woman had called him a *creature*. He was right. He *wasn't*.

"So," Mistress continued, "it is rare for those who are moral to take the vampire form. It is indeed an evil curse, but it can be turned with the right will. It is hard to control, but it is powerful nonetheless. My council welcomes anyone who is immortal without means. However, *you* are untried. You can learn to live with this, or—"

"No or," Rein said quietly.

Traith's glare turned gentler. He gave her a casual glance, as if smiling with his eyes. That had been the answer he wanted.

Mistress motioned with her hand toward a separate room. Traith followed without thought, as though he knew where he was going. She followed him. The woman sat down in front of them at a smooth table inside the new room. Traith took a seat, and Rein sat beside him without a word.

"Just tell me what happened to Saria," she said, and the words triggered her sorrow to return in tears. "I won't ask anything more, but I must know what happened to her."

Mistress nodded, closing her big, grey eyes. "I understand you had a strong bond with Saria Kendrick, Rein, but she did not wish to remain what she woke as."

Rein held her forehead with her pale hands, closing her eyes tight. Traith's face fell at her teary-eyed response. His red eyes began to glisten with dejection as if he were being read his felonies by a black-masked executioner with a rope in his fist. He was full of guilt, depression.

"I am sorry, Miss Pierson, but everyone on that ship has died. Saria did, the man brought with her, Edgar Johan, is also dead. He died as the ship went down."

"I *killed* him?" Traith asked frantically. "W-with the *explosion*?"

"No, Traith. I will not say how he died, but it was not by you."

Rein's head was in her hands, and she cried softly.

"Rein," the woman said after a moment, "there is much to tell you, so please try to bear with me. You did receive my dreams?"

"Yes," she replied hoarsely.

"Traith has mentioned the stake to you."

That the woman knew as much only verified the letter she had written her; she knew things that no one else could know.

"But other than that, *blood* can easily kill you, if you do not consume enough. Not enough, without doubt, will make you increasingly weak." She gazed at Traith, who was slowly gaining depth. "Refrain from being like Traith, here, who attempts to go for over two days without his sustenance."

Traith still said nothing, his eyes freezing again. His poise stiffened with her remark. "I should go to Hell for such a misdeed," he whispered.

"Drinking blood will not make your human heart any worse for wear. You must do it, regardless," Mistress countered back.

Rein would not give the woman her stare.

"Being a vampire does come with advantages, however."

Traith spoke with a face of stone and assertion, his eyes slowly turning and staring at the leader. "Mistress, you cannot possibly believe she will be able to swallow all of this now. I will tell her when she needs to know."

The dazzling lady paused. "Indeed, I understand you, Harker. I trust you will explain to her rightly, but I must know she understands what I still must tell her. I need to explain to her the history of the councils."

chapter 32

Since the beginning of the world—since the first two people ever created sinned—we have been. As soon as the fruit of Satan was bitten, evil formed in the hearts of man; it is the evil nature. Although blessed in the image of God, man's nature is sinful. So as this evil was created, a council formed: the Mardinial Council. Helena, the council's leader, is the offspring of both a demon and a vampire monster from Hell—like the spawn of Satan himself—and she possessed the first murderer in history, *Cain*, who murdered his brother *Abel*. She, like a black hole, devoured her human host and merged with him, and thus began her havoc, infecting men forever more.

"However, at the same time Helena was growing and infecting, I began my reign. Although man has an evil nature, he has a good one as well. The two, developing throughout time, have always fought. Finally, originating from the souls of man, immortals came to be. I have revealed to no one my exact circumstances of origin, but I created the Council of the Presage—this council. I have only *created* minor immortals to aide me—more or less harmless, purely moral spirits. Immortals are people who will live until the end of the earth. Reversely, there are *curses*—thirteen to be exact—that exist today because they came about through Helena's bloodline, though most of the time, not directly from Helena. Any immortals who become cursed choose good or evil, therefore choosing councils as well. Those who follow Helena, I find and try to sway.

"Cursed immortals have a monstrous nature. Evil *physically* marks the immortal, while at the same time affecting him psychologically. It is the internal fight that is hardest to overcome—for the vampire, in particular. This is why we have only Traith in our council…and now you. But I know without doubt that you are strong enough to win over your vampire impulses, Rein.

"So have you a better idea of how this came about, and how I am? Think of it like this: there is Satan below; his earthly force can be carried within Helena; then there is man. Above man is God; I carry out His will by balancing the evil nature with the good. Good rarely wins on earth, Miss Pierson, but the time has come that we begin to."

Rein heard Traith huff. She looked at him, wondering why he was giving the impression that he didn't exactly agree with Mistress.

She had tried to listen to the Mistress while she could. She was beginning to get her answers, but they were too awful to bear.

"Do you understand what I've explained, Miss Pierson?"

Rein nodded, fingers holding her head.

"I will clear up only a few more things for you, and you shall be free to go. You did something inhuman on the ship, did you not? Something that frightened you?"

Rein looked at her with an agreeing stare.

"A vampire has many aptitudes that are also beyond human capability. All are different. For example, Traith controls kinetic energy, which is how he caused the ship and the rope to explode, and how he can become invisible at will. You displayed one of your capabilities when you destroyed the captain of the *Old Mary*. You took his life in a single instant. Rein, I believe you can exchange, or, in some instances, *take* life or death or pain—to or from whomever you wish. I may not be entirely accurate, but I think you can remove any pain except that caused by a weakness. You could not remove something like Traith's back wounds, for instance. They were caused by his weakness; what he is *not* immune to: fire. Does that make sense?"

"Pf," she heard him murmur. "That's a bloody shame."

Her mind began racing. Mistress was silent, then, for a long time. Rein felt as though she shouldn't speak.

The woman sighed heavily. "You have acquired one of the most powerful—and mysterious—abilities I have ever been acquainted with." She paused and sighed. "I do know, Rein, that you will become great in your mental capabilities."

Traith, having let his head fall, sprung up with his eyes keen with question. She didn't know what to think. What did that mean?

"I'm prophesying it to you; listen carefully," the Mistress said. "Only you can learn how to use your abilities. No one else can help you or teach you because this power will be your own, and it will work in a way only you will understand. You will only learn from error." The woman watched her intensely. "You used part of this ability on the ship, Rein. You will soon be capable of hearing thoughts, being in someone's mind and existing in them, changing people, mixing memories, moving or changing things with your mind…but understand you must stay coherent through your pain. You will continue to learn more, so do not feel so overwhelmed."

What was she talking about? What pain? Her body was numb with fear. *Great in mental capabilities*…did Traith know what that meant? She glanced at him. His eyes were wide with disbelief. He had to know what it was.

"Is this a joke?" he asked finally. "Rein? Powers can take *years* to kick in, and I just turned her. How could she possibly—?"

"Allow your mind time," the woman said gently to Rein, ignoring Traith. "It *will* become easier. Do not fear it." She paused. "You are also in want of answers regarding your home's state, and your father, no doubt."

"Father," Rein repeated her. "It is all true, isn't it? You really did write me that letter, didn't you?"

"I wrote you, yes. I had to prepare you for something, as the emotional pain for you would have been much too great. Taverin Badeau is living in your home, as it were, with a Mr. Hall. So you must decide where you want to go now. To live."

"I can't go home," she said. "My father is dead. God, I missed him by *days*." She let her face fall into her hands again.

She felt that hand—that touch she was learning well, the touch she felt when she had been lying weeping on a bed in her chamber days ago, the touch she felt when she was in the hall on the ground. She waited and then looked up at him. His eyes were tight, looking from beside her, and he removed his hand slowly.

She wanted to smile for him, but she couldn't. "I can't," she swallowed. "I won't go back home. I don't want to go back there. See Saria's family, and say what? And my home…" Her voice was scratchy, and she couldn't keep back her emotions. "It isn't even mine anymore."

"Rein," the aged lady said again. "In all truth, I can make it seem as though you have died to any of those who have known you. You and Saria, both."

A chilling feeling overwhelmed her. She would never see her father again. Saria, who was like a sister, and her father...*dead*.

Rein could tell that Traith was attempting to conceal his panic for her. "Mistress, what of Carden?"

"He is gone," Mistress said wearily.

"To where? Where did he go?"

"I do not see him anywhere. His presence is blocked from my mind, somehow. Perhaps it is he who is causing that. I am truly sorry for you, but there is nothing I can do. I understand your pain."

"You understand nothing," he said quietly, gritting his teeth. He held his head.

The old woman stared deeply at him for a moment. "I will not reprimand you now," she said. "Your heart is full to burst, I know. Both of you. But Traith, don't you dare think you can address me in that tone afterward."

"But I still can't understand," he said from under his hands. Then he removed them and let them hang down limp on his knees. "How was it possible that I came off the ship? I was trapped with Carden. You do know, Mistress, I know you do!"

"Perhaps," the woman began. "Perhaps your female friend was more destined to be here than you think."

Mistress smiled, and Traith gazed at her with an angered glare.

"If only I could speak with Saria for a moment," Rein whispered. She glanced up at them.

Traith looked immeasurably tense. His composure, as hard as he may have been trying to keep it, was deteriorating.

Mistress looked back up. "But it is all over, now. Rein, the last statement I must make is important." The lines in her face became softer. "Keep a sharp eye for Helena; she and I, as I have explained, are the council leaders. There are only two councils, which means Helena's is always making ready to weaken us in any way they can."

"All right," Rein said, staring vacantly.

The old woman paused and watched them. "I just wanted you to know that we are not alone. Please keep it in mind. I am finished. Are you taking her with you, Traith?"

Rein glanced directly at her. The woman's eyes wrinkled in a near smile. Her eyes were actually kind, but Rein saw a hint of mischief within them. Traith continued to look down.

Rein then began trying to feel more tranquil. She was trembling hard but slowly regaining a poise that had disappeared. She was thankful she was at all alive, despite everything sinister that had happened. She just had so much to learn and accept.

Traith's tenseness was gone, she could tell; his slight motions and mannerisms told her so. Was he hoping that she would stay with him? The more she thought, the happier she became; she was brought to life by a man who loved her, no matter what was wrong with him. But she still needed time to mourn. The only two people she had in the entire world were just dead.

Rein turned to him, her eyes glazed over. "Traith? Look at me."

He continued his downward stare for a moment and then turned to look at her. His stare was wet, as if he were holding back more emotion than she could explain.

"Traith, I *love* you," she whispered. "Despite your eyes, despite your teeth and scars, I've always loved you. I felt something when I saw you, something protecting and loving, whether you knew it or not. I wanted that because I have no one. I always knew you had noble intent, but I'm just scared. The man I fell in love with…" she had to stop. "Please," she said, forgetting the woman sitting in front of them. "Don't be so cheerless. I just feel like my life has been breathed out of me. Like it was never worth anything." She bit her bottom lip. "Like it never *mattered*."

He was looking at her still. "You matter so much more than you think," he said. He opened his mouth once more, but closed it again. It wasn't the time to speak about their relationship. "I have a home you are welcome to, as you have heard," he said.

"A *castle*," Mistress declared with a smile; he turned his head in her direction, but never made eye contact. "It had once been his home before he and Carden were cursed on the ship by someone in the Mardinial Council. Harker's own *sister*, no less. For many, many years."

Traith took an unnecessary breath at the mention of his sister, and he seemed to tire of Mistress's speech. Rein wondered why. She had to find out about his sister.

"There is no more I must tell you. Traith's home is located in the eastern side of Romania, close by the isolated region of Bacauan. Here, your home awaits you. I wish you no grieving." Suddenly a light shone out of her hand, and a vial of blood appeared. "You may want this, Rein."

Mistress handed it to her, and she took it with a tightened fist. The woman waved her arm. Rein felt weak. Where was she?

She was going to see Traith's castle. Harker Manor, she imagined it called—a castle in the countryside, just the two of them, like a fantasy. Except Romania was desolate and secluded, a place where she would be free only to mourn.

No, not unless she made it that way.

chapter 33

t he night weighed heavily on Rein. He could see it. Traith watched her from behind; she was seated on a chaise lounge in the library of his castle.

It was a beautiful castle, full of richly medieval, complexly designed furnishings and wall décor. It was entirely made of stone and hundreds of years old, as was some of the furniture. It was overwhelmingly old when he had first come across it in the eighteenth century…in the *early* eighteenth century.

She had been sitting there idly for almost an hour. He felt like he couldn't do anything to ease it for her. He had brought this upon them. It was also the first time he had ever been in love…he wasn't sure what to do.

He would try to help her. Be with her, so she wasn't alone.

He noticed her left hand hanging open over the armrest, the small vial of blood on the floor, untouched. Then she turned her head to him.

Her face was pale, but she captivated him even further. She didn't even look that different, save her eyes and teeth. Her eyes were dark.

"Traith?" she called, staring at him.

He stepped silently into the library.

"Please sit with me," she entreated.

He walked and sat in a chair behind her, farther from the fire. He thought briefly about smiling, but chose not to. He sighed and stood again, forgetting about his discomfort around fire, and sat next to her on the lounge.

"Rein," he said, "I just wanted you to have a little time alone. I thought you needed it."

"Thank you." She casually wiped her eyes and laughed softly.

He put his head down. He had to say something. He had to reassure her somehow. "You're safe now," he said. "You're safe. You'll never need to worry about being alone." He looked up at her. "I have never known a woman, ever, that could see deeper into my soul than what I show. Love never meant anything because I rejected it. I didn't feel I deserved it, perhaps. But you broke through my—"

"Your stone wall," she said, as if recalling something.

He looked deeply into her eyes. "Yes," he said. "You made me remember how to feel. I imagined you with me, and I thought for a moment it could happen. I know your pain; I feel it often still. I just never came to terms with it."

Should he not have said that?

She was watching him with sad, dark red eyes, but with a smile. "I will be fine," she whispered. "I'm alive. I love you. I'm just lost in thought. Saria was all that I had. We were so close. I have no family, save my father. But he left me at five years old and left me in a boarding school. And apparently he was in Teesdale the whole time." She had to pause to maintain composure. "Only yards from me for thirteen years."

"I'm sorry," he whispered, looking at the fire.

"Then he had to leave again, just before I was let out of school. And just after I left to travel with Saria, he returned, finally waiting to see me." She sighed with an empty smile. "Terrible luck. I suppose maybe I should be angry at him, but I'm just more heartbroken."

Traith glanced down. "I lost family too, Rein," he said. "So I do understand what you're feeling." Beneath the words, he felt ill. What he had done to her was still scratching endlessly at him. "Rein, I know—"

"Do you love me?"

He shut his mouth and felt feeble at her words. "Yes."

"Then I'm yours, now. You don't have to worry about where I stand. I am with you now, and I will stay with you because I love you, Traith."

His heart left his throat. "Rein, I didn't want you to feel pain. You understand that's why I didn't tell you the truth, don't you?" He stood, the fire making him uneasy, and he walked over to the wall, placing his fist softly upon the cold stone with his other hand in his pocket. "I was always scared that if I showed you love, something would happen. I was right. The captain was waiting for me to slip."

"Don't worry yourself anymore, Traith," she said, and her words puzzled him. "It's just that everything is so far from normal that I'll need a while to get used to this. Come back next to me. Sit *with* me, Traith."

He reluctantly took his seat next to her again. "I'm sorry, Rein. Just the fire. God, this sounds so idiotic, I know."

"Traith, can you tell me the truth?" she asked sincerely, holding the cross he'd earlier given her in her fingers. "The whole truth. Tell me everything. Please. No more lying. There couldn't be anything that I cannot hear, now."

"About?"

"About *you*. It is easier to be scared of someone whom you know almost nothing about. I love you, your demeanor, personality, your intentions, and every one of your characteristics. But I don't know anything past that."

Those words hit him hard. "I didn't lie to you when I told you I lost my memory," he said. "They took it from me—the Mardinial Council. I was told by Mistress that their founder, Helena, was the one who bit me. I was twenty-three, so I know what it feels like to have life at such an early age taken away." He was straining to talk about his past. "But I can't remember her, or the incident. I lost nearly everything." He paused. "I was close to my sister; as close as blood could get. I was close to my parents, too, but I have no idea what happened to them. I can't even remember the majority of my childhood, my adolescence, or what I did after she bit me. I could've done anything. But I do remember I was scared, and I suffered. I suffered, Rein, badly." He stopped.

Her eyes were full of sympathy for him. "Where is your sister?" she asked.

He bit down. "They took her from me, too. She's in the Mardinial Council."

Her fingers were by her mouth. "Why?"

"I…" He winced, looking down at his hands. "I don't know. That is one of the vital things I try to remember every day, but I just can't."

"Does she know you lost your memory?"

"I've never had the chance to find out, but I know she cursed me onto the *Olde Mary*. Some sort of black magic spell she found, or learned, or…She despises me entirely, now; I know that. She wants to destroy me."

He was glad when she broke in. He couldn't say anymore that moment. It tore him apart.

"Traith, I am so, so sorry. You don't know why she is in that other council?"

"I know they lied to her," he murmured, forcing himself to stay clear of conveying heavy emotion. "She was told that those in our council did this to me, and I stayed with them." He sighed with difficulty. "They even made her immortal through God-knows-what sort of measure, so she could kill me. 'Free me' of this curse, as if I am no longer me, but some sort of monster." He took a trembling breath and held his hands still. "It's been hard, Rein."

"You have not had the chance to speak with her or tell her your side of the story?"

"Yes, and that is what got me cursed onto the bloody ship."

Rein looked down. "What is her name?"

"Ana."

There was a long silence. He really hadn't wanted to think about Ana. He wanted to think about Rein. Talk about her, what she enjoyed and how she felt about everything. It was already apparent to him that she was accepting facts with much less hysteria than he ever had, which made him think…

When Rein moved closer to him, he stopped his thoughts. He had wanted to hold her before, help her, and make her feel safe. But he hadn't been sure what she would feel.

She reached out and touched his throat, where puncture scars were left. He still didn't have a shirt on, or else he would've kept them covered.

He almost began to pull back, but he didn't. He leaned in.

"You have nothing to be ashamed about, as I think of it," she said, her eyes sparkling up at him. "Were you ever really in an accident, then?"

"No," he said ruefully.

"And your vision is perfect, isn't it? Like mine?"

"Yes."

She sighed. "Why did you say your transformation was so painful yet mine was not?"

"I was alive when I was bitten," he said quietly. "My body was rejecting the poison, which, in turn, caused havoc inside of me. You were dead, so your body did not try to fight off my…my toxin." He paused another moment.

"And that was all the pain you remember?"

He hesitated before speaking again. "There was torture also."

She shook her head contemplatively. "I can't imagine, but I feel better to know that you can relate so much to me; at least to my internal pain. I never suffered physically." There was a break in speech to swallow the spoken thoughts. "What does it mean to 'become great in mental capabilities', Traith?" she asked, her heart beginning to break down again. "All those things she said I would do, and that they included pain. That does terrify me."

"I know," he said. "I know." He looked down and shook his head, then met her eyes. "I can imagine that means you will someday be capable of doing nearly anything regarding the mind; another's, or your own. Rein, that means you'll be powerful beyond your imagination."

She hugged him in a closing sorrow. But she hugged him. He smiled, but she didn't see. He refrained from talking anymore because he felt her hands begin to tighten around his lower back, below his main wound. She drew closer to him, as he did to her, and their lips brushed.

He tasted her kiss with a fiery passion he had never felt before. He was kissing a woman. A woman he loved.

He *loved*.

chapter 34

t raith was walking in front of Rein down the hall. His shirt was still off, and she saw that his back had not even begun to heal. It must have only been a day or so since they were on the ship. She was going to ask him again about his back; she was going to ask him about how much time had gone by.

There was so much to ask about, and only a few hours had passed since they were in the library together. The castle was so large and extravagant. Did he inherit the castle as he said, or was that one of the lies? She had to ask him about that, too. As soon as they had another chance to sit, she would.

He opened a large door at the end of the long, stone hall. As soon as he opened it, he froze. She couldn't see much from behind him.

"I haven't been here for so long," he said in a daze. "Nothing has been touched in here for years; but it's *clean*."

Then she wondered how old he really was. When was he born? How long had he been on the ship?

He finally walked forward, and as he did, she saw that it was a bedroom. More like a bedroom chamber. It was the largest bedroom she had ever seen.

Although everything was made with stone, there was a bed the size of three average ones to the left, with a canopy and sheets and blankets full of feathers. With a glance around the room, she noted a vanity, a sitting area, and balcony doors.

"Look," he said, and he walked forward.

He unlocked the iron and glass doors and walked out onto the balcony. Wind blew his hair to the side, and the muscles tensed in his shoulders. He turned and motioned for her to come next to him.

She approached the end of the balcony and looked over the edge. They were on the highest floor—at least 100 yards from the ground.

"Dear God," she whispered.

He watched her with a smile, but she could see that he was still tense. "Rein, I didn't inherit this castle. My family was rich, but our home was in England. I came about this castle…"

"How?" she asked.

He turned to her slowly, and then looked down at the ground from the edge, his arms propped on the rail. "I wish I knew."

It was sad to see him trying to remember things in vain. He truly yearned for his lost memory.

"When *were* you born?" she dared to ask. "You aren't really twenty three, are you?" She walked forward and rested her arms on the rail beside him.

He glanced at her for a moment, and then looked ahead. The pine-scented air blew harder, and it felt good on her face. She looked at him until he was forced to return her stare.

He sighed loud. "Rein…"

"Please tell me when you were born," she winced.

"In…" He shook his head and looked at her, as if in disbelief himself. "I was born in 1703, Rein."

Her heart sank. He was watching her with gentle eyes. Rein calculated his age; 140 years old.

One hundred and forty?

And she was only *twenty.*

She let out a breath and closed her eyes. "Something about you didn't seem only three years older than me," she trembled.

"I grew up in the 1700's, Rein. Not the 1800's. And in a hundred or so years, the world changes more drastically than you could ever imagine; especially if you've lived it. Not that I can remember much of it, and even if I did I was stuck on that ship for most of it."

She was silent.

"Listen, Rein," he said, leaning close to her, but she cut him off.

"That's why Carden said your way of wooing a girl would be withered, and why you said you hated crinolines, because when you were young they were too big."

"What did Carden say about me? Couldn't woo a girl?"

"Traith, you were three and twenty over a hundred *years* ago."

"I know." His thumb touched her cheek. "But it doesn't matter, it doesn't. I've never changed."

"I know it doesn't matter," she said, staring despondently ahead. "But everything is just so…unbelievable."

"Rein, tell me about *you*," he said, changing the subject. "We can tackle what you're facing as it comes. I've never accepted myself, but suddenly, because of you, I'm beginning to. Pretend nothing happened for a moment."

She smiled vacantly. "Well," she murmured. "I grew up in a boarding school my entire life, alone, without parents. My mother died in childbirth and my father…" Tears instantly came to her eyes at that term.

"Don't say it," Traith said, and she felt his hand touch her back. "Tell me the rest. No siblings, I assume."

"No. Saria was as close as it came…"

"Hobbies," he said fast, turning her face to look at him before she broke down into tears. "What do you like to do? Do you greatly enjoy reading and writing? I saw some things in your chamber."

She nodded with her lips tight as she was regaining composure. She smiled to think happier thoughts. "My two favorite."

"Any piano? Singing? Drawing?"

"Drawing. I love to draw—not paint though. Not very good at that."

"The worlds dumbest could surpass me in art," he said, smiling.

He managed to make her laugh a little. "Really? I'm sure you aren't that bad."

"Oh, yes I am," he objected adamantly, laughing softly.

"Are you an animal person?" he asked.

She stared deeply into his eyes. She was numb in that place on the balcony—it was like days were passing by in those minutes. She was looking again at him as he had been before anything happened, and an old happiness returned to her.

"I love animals," she replied, curling her escaping hair around her ears.

Suddenly a strange feeling took hold of her—something of a headache, but worse. Something—maybe dizziness. Weakness.

Traith's expression changed. "What?"

"My head hurts," she mouthed inaudibly.

His hand fell, and he stepped back to watch her closer. "I'll help you with this, Rein," he said, and with his words, their social conversation again became surreal. "But you must stay strong about it. Don't ever, ever let go of your grasp."

He was talking about her mind. It was expanding, and she felt it. It seemed so insane to say, but something was going wrong inside her head…going wrong or just becoming something different. She was hearing things, now…

"Do you hear me?" he asked. "For me, don't ever let go."

"I won't," she whispered.

He turned to leave the balcony. Then she got another clear view of his back; she could not take her eyes off of the blisters and open, burnt lesions.

"Traith, your back." She didn't know how to finish the sentence.

He turned and looked at her, half-smiling. "That *is* why I'm not wearing a shirt."

"How long ago did it happen? I can't exactly tell. I slept in such strange successions."

"Two days ago," he said. He was about to leave the balcony, but waited for her to go with him. "Come with me; I'll show you the rest of the castle."

"Do you want me to clean and bandage it for you?" she asked, ignoring his beckon. "It'll heal faster."

"No. It'll be all right for now," he replied.

"You can't see it, can you?"

He hesitated. "No, but—"

"Then let me fix it for you. Please. It's awful."

He smiled. "Thank you, Rein." He watched her for a moment. His eyes crinkled as if he were going to laugh. "I'll let you wrap it up later, or do what you want to do with it," he said with slight hesitance.

He still trusted her. He had as much of an issue with that as she did. In an instant, she was no longer upset. It was over. The only things left to mourn were the possibility of what was to become of her mind, and the lost lives of her loved ones. She needed to open her mind and take everything in—learn it, and accept it for what it was. She had no other choice.

He walked off of the balcony into the bedroom. He held the glass door's handle. "So this is the highest floor, the hall with the two master bedrooms," he said. Then he stopped his speech and sighed with a smile, his head down. "Mistress had someone here," he said with his voice lowered, almost as if speaking to himself. "She had someone here keeping it ready for if...when I returned."

He looked momentarily interested about something, and when she followed his gaze to a side door in the bedroom, she saw his face light with shock. She neared him hesitantly.

"What is it?" she asked.

He almost laughed. "Plumbing," he said in a daze.

She looked through the door and saw a beautiful bathing area with a bath larger than any she'd ever seen, and through an arch on the right, a toilet with piping, extravagantly decorated.

He shook his head. "I can't believe this."

"And in a castle," Rein added. "Mistress did this for you?"

"I suppose," he murmured, still surprised at the notion of it. Then he nearly began talking to himself. "So they must've added a boiler room a floor below..." He turned, holding his chin, and left the washroom. Then he held his hand out for hers. "Want to explore my house with me?"

She gave her hand to him wholeheartedly.

He spent the rest of the night and early morning showing her the grounds and rooms. The castle was vast, yet it appeared lived in. Exactly how long ago had he been cursed onto the ship and forced to leave this beautiful place?

It was nearing dawn. She could see light forming in the sky from the open doorway they were approaching. They were going to an outside bailey.

It was a courtyard, with grass and iron fencing. Dawn was breaking in the sky above, and it was shedding minimal light around them. Clouds were coming into view. Then Traith stopped, and shocked registered on his face.

"*Horses?*" he gasped.

He jogged to the fencing and leaned in, his jaw slack, with his palms grasping the fence that kept the beautiful creatures in.

Three horses stood eating. A silver one galloped briskly over to Traith, and he held the horse's muzzle with both hands. The horse shook his face free gently, and Traith let him go join the other two.

He rested on the rail, head shaking. "I wonder who—"

"Yoo-hoo!"

Neither of them had spoken.

chapter 35

⚥

traith snapped his attention completely forward and his arms lowered tensely to his sides. Rein was puzzled. It was a girl's voice that had called.

From a stone entry on the other side of the courtyard, a woman slowly walked out, her hips pushed out meretriciously as though one of her legs were shorter than the other. Rein was sure that one of the lady's legs was not shorter than the other. Was she trying to look like some sort of harlot?

Traith turned and looked at her before approaching the woman.

Was that the same person she had heard speak to him before when she was in that bedroom? Long, curly brown locks and bright green eyes.

"Do you like what I've done with the place?" the woman asked him.

"You did all this?" Traith asked, walking around the fencing.

She walked into the courtyard toward him. "Well, Mistress wanted someone to keep your home clean while you were gone." She paused and stared at him narrowly. "One hundred and ten years, Traith…"

Rein watched his response to that. His face was grave. "Lorena, believe me, I tried to get off that ship nearly every day of every one of those years." He looked down and held the fencing inside his fists. "You kept this place the entire time? *You* did?"

"Why do you act as if you are in such *shock*? Am I that incapable?" Then, as if she hadn't noticed her before, she looked at Rein with surprise. "Who is this?"

"Rein Pierson," he replied, giving his attention to her and taking it from Lorena. "I already explained her to you."

"Ah," Lorena said. "You're the lucky human being who stumbled upon my vampire." She giggled.

Rein's heart was in her mouth. She couldn't answer, but she was beginning to feel like she had thought wrong about Traith never being interested in another woman. He was, after all, born so long ago, yet never lost his handsome, young form. That thought made her tremble: 140? And just because he hadn't *loved* doesn't mean he never *played*.

"Don't start with me," was all Traith said in return.

She laughed. "I am sorry; I'll wait until we're alone again to discuss—"

"Lorena, I'm here now," he said with his usual calm, but his eyes shone with fury. "You can leave."

He glanced at Rein. She was praying she didn't look too awkward, but inside she was steaming. Who was this woman?

Lorena's face was mischievous, and she bit her lip. "I'll speak with you later, Traith. I'm glad you so greatly *appreciate* what I've done for you all these years."

"Thank you, from the bottom of my heart," he said, bending as if bowing to her. He wore a small, sarcastic smile.

Lorena's lips curled in satisfaction. She hadn't caught the smile.

"Oh, and Miss Pierson," Lorena said with a sneer. "Seems you've managed to get blood all over you. Might want to—"

"Get out, Lorena," Traith countered.

She laughed, then, and slowly her legs began to fade. Then the rest of her body did the same. She was gone.

Traith looked at Rein almost immediately. "She is a lady from my... our council. She's a priestess." He watched her closer, and neared. "She thinks, or, she likes to make it seem as though we have a past, but we don't. At least not the kind *she* was talking about."

Rein still didn't know what to say. She did have blood all over her from her fall and...

"Are you all right?" he asked, now merely a few feet from her. "Don't worry about her," he said.

She shook her head and lay onto his chest, holding his neck. He returned the embrace, but pulled back to see her face. She was so excited that he loved her, and she loved him, but that encounter with Lorena had made her a little uneasy.

"Are you tired yet?" he asked.

"A little."

He sighed, and his broad, muscled shoulders relaxed. "I know you have more questions for me, don't you?"

She nodded.

"Let me take you to where you can sleep, and I'll answer them for you when you bandage my back," he said, laughing gently.

"How long will it take for that to heal?"

"It'll take longer than *I'm* used to, but not as long as a regular wound would. But it never stops hurting. It'll take about a week or so, I suppose. Sometimes a little less. It's been three days. Doesn't look better, does it?"

"No, it doesn't at all."

He bent into her and kissed her, holding her tight. One of his hands gently held her face. His fingers caressed her.

She felt as though her dreams had come entirely true.

Except she was a *vampire*. The realization occurred to her when she felt the sunlight beginning to make her weak. And she was so hungry…

"Rein, we'll come out as much as possible to get you used to this again," he said, pulling back from their kiss.

She felt ill at his statement.

"It didn't take me too long," he said, motioning for her to follow him out of the bailey and back into the castle. "It never gets as easy as it once was, but don't worry. It will get easier, soon." He paused mid-step, one foot not yet entirely down. "It was a long walk down here from the bedroom, wasn't it?"

She was right behind him. "Yes," she replied, forgetting her momentary sadness.

"I can make the trip a lot quicker."

She knew what he meant. He could go from place to place in a blink of an eye. He smiled. He held his hand out for hers, and she took it without hesitation. The image of the surrounding horses and courtyard almost looked as if they merged with another picture, one of the master bedroom. He let go of her and took a seat slouched forward in an armchair by the side of the room, by the bed.

"Faster, wasn't it?" he said, arching his back as if to crack it.

She felt her eyebrows raise is agreement, and he laughed, relaxing. She looked down at herself, at the bloodstained bodice that had once been an ivory color. She undid the frogs, and took it off. Under it was a corset, but it made her much more comfortable to have taken off the bodice. She eventually undressed into just the corset and a petticoat.

She looked at him and smiled. He smiled back and didn't even appear astonished. He appeared more…dreamy.

"I hate looking down at that," she said. "Made me truly *feel* like I'm dead. Anyway, it's more comfortable off."

"Fine," he said. "Did you want me to get rid of it?"

She nodded, smiling at him. With his hand out, Rein watched as her dress suddenly dematerialized and disappeared. She felt like the sad and frightened part of her vanished with it.

"So do you have gauze? Salve?" she asked, her hand on his shoulder, looking at his back. Her nose crinkled in disgust at the severity of the wound.

Rash-like blisters had begun to form on his marred back.

"It looks terrible," she whispered.

He stood and headed toward the bathroom. "I used to always make sure I had *materials* to help burns in the past, considering fire wounds call for that and I can't heal them myself." He paused with a look of thought. "Let's see what my new bathroom has within it."

He stood and walked to it after carefully striking a match and lighting a candle. He set it in the bathroom wall sconce. Rein sat on the edge of the huge bed, and after a moment of being alone, Traith returned with a large roll of dressing and a jar of what she figured was salve.

"I have everything here," he declared with astonishment, smiling. "Are you sure you want to do this? As of now I should think that it would revolt you to be doing this. It would revolt me without doubt."

"Just a little," she said, laughing softly. "But I don't mind." She patted just next to her on the luxurious bed in signal for him to sit.

He did and handed her the supplies. She crossed her legs beneath her and opened the jar of salve. With a piece of the gauze, she wiped the salve down his back. He arched it and held his breath, then let it out and simply bore the pain quietly. After she'd covered his back with it, she began unraveling the gauze. She slowly put her hand under his muscle-defined arm, which he lifted, and began to wrap it around him. He winced a few times, but he didn't make any further indications of pain.

"Does it hurt awfully?" she asked.

"Yes," he said, trying not to laugh. "But the worst is the feeling of my *skin sticking* to the bloody linen." He stiffened his back each time dressing met with it. "So, shoot."

She continued wrapping. "What?"

"Interrogate me," he said, letting out a breath. "I'm ready."

"All right," she replied, smiling a little. "Who was the captain?"

"From the Mardinial Council," he answered. "They put him on the ship just for me. Like a departing farewell gift."

"What are my weaknesses, now? All of them?"

His head was hung down. "Other than the ones you are familiar with, garlic is terrible—painful, rather. I touched it once." He cringed and shook his head, hair hanging in his face. "And blood is the worst of all. It's hard to go without for any longer than a day or two." His last words were choked on as they came out.

"Yet you go without for longer than that, don't you?"

He sighed. "I do; I *try*, but the desire for it eats away at me until I consume it. I would die without it, or become savage, I don't know. But when I tasted yours, Rein, I felt like I wanted more and more. It was horrible. Shows how easily it can consume you. If I were ever to do that again, I would starve myself until death afterward. The feeling was haunting. Demonic. It's something I wish terribly would cease to linger in my mind."

"I tasted blood that night," she spoke lightly. "It was yours, wasn't it?"

She watched him; he didn't move a muscle. "I regret to say it was."

She broke the silence that followed as soon as she was able to force out words. It was hard to after what he had just affirmed.

"There," she murmured after tying the end of the dressing so it wouldn't come undone. He winced as her fingers skimmed the wrapping. "The whole thing is covered now."

"Thank you." He turned and put his knee up on the bed so he could face her. "Any more questions?"

"What can *you do*?" she asked quietly, slowly lying back onto the bed.

He didn't reply for a moment. "You've already seen each one," he finally said.

"Remind me," she murmured, her eyes closed.

She heard him make a low sigh. "I can materialize myself to any-where I want, something called *teleportation*. I can *fly*, for lack of a better word. Become invisible, control potential energy; you know, the whole rope display. I apparently have incredible strength," he said.

She forced her tired body to sit straight as she looked at him, ignor-ing the heaviness that was taking over her eyes. "Really?"

He chuckled with his chin resting on his fist. "All vampires have greater strength than normal people, but I have an ever greater amount than all vampires." He sighed. "And...well Rein, you'll get an ability that is nearly impossible to use, because it's painful, but it is incredibly powerful." He became silent. "What you did on the ship...that was... I've never seen anything like it, ever. And that isn't even the aptitude I was talking about."

"What is yours?" she asked. "The one that is painful but powerful."

He didn't reply.

"What is it?"

"I can instantly...*destroy* certain..."

Her tired eyes opened wide. "What?"

"Humans," he whispered. "Or lowly immortal beings. Not like us," he said. "We're too advanced, I suppose."

She finally let herself fall back onto the bed comfortably. "Have you ever used it?"

"Not that I remember."

She turned toward him onto her side. "Are my upcoming mind 'powers' the ability you said is powerful but painful?"

"No." He waited a moment before speaking again. "And that is what strikes me as so odd. Immortals never receive abilities until a good amount of time goes by. Your case is highly unusual." He paused in thought. "Do you think you could replicate what you did on the ship?"

"I don't know," she spoke softly. "But I don't want to try tonight."

"Oh, I didn't mean for you to," he defended.

A gap of silence occurred. Her head was now resting comfortably on a pillow. She was nearly falling asleep, and it was daylight. Traith had closed the velvet curtains over the balcony windows, making the bedroom as dark as if it were some time in the night.

She yawned. "Aren't *you* tired?"

She couldn't see his response because she had closed her eyes.

"Not really. I try to…"

She didn't hear the end of that. She was falling in and out of consciousness. When she caught herself and opened her eyes a crack, she saw him sluggishly stand and sit carefully into an armchair beside the bed. He whispered a goodnight to her, though night had not yet come.

Then her eyes closed a final time as she drifted into sleep.

chapter 36

She heard a rustle that caused her to open her eyes. It took her a few moments to work up the courage to look around in the darkness. The warm breeze blowing through the open balcony doors felt good against her skin.

Traith was gone.

She felt terrified. She had fallen asleep as he was talking last night. Rather, last day. It was night now. The thought that she had slept for more than two days in a row, waking only in the night, scared her.

But Traith was gone. He had been in the room with her. Then she recalled seeing him asleep in the armchair on the other side of the room once when she was turning over in her haziness of sleep. He had finally fallen asleep. But he was gone.

Panic began to set in. She stood and walked slowly to the dark, open balcony. She was walking on bare feet, and the cool stone was a reprieve from the hot weather and wind. She was still only in a corset and chemise. Nothing on her arms, nothing below her knees, making her cooler still.

There was nothing she could see out there, only the enormous pines and other trees swaying heavily in the wind below.

Why would he have left? She knew he had; she just heard him. That rustle. He had gotten up and gone, but where?

She wanted to call him, but a fear of breaking the silence stopped her. Clouds covered the sky, and the moon peeked through a hole in them. It was almost as if she could reach for it and pluck it from the sky.

She turned to check the bedroom further. Her steps were hesitant, and she tried to step as quietly as she could. Her hair stopped blowing in her face as she reentered the bedroom, leaving nothing but ominous stillness. The door to the hallway was closed. She approached it slowly, her hand out to turn the knob. Her nerves were making her throat feel as though she was being throttled.

The door creaked open as she pushed it. The hall was darker than the bedroom was. She left the only room truly familiar to her for the dark void beyond. Despite her novel, heightened sense of sight in the dark, she didn't know what to expect. Anyone could be out there. She was beginning to feel ill with fear.

"Rein."

She spun around to face the bedroom entrance from the hall.

It was Traith.

She sighed. "You left me alone."

His face was as black as their surroundings were, but she could still see it. "I was forced to leave for, well, I didn't know how long, but thank God it was only for a few minutes."

"Who forced you?" she asked.

"Mistress." His voice was rougher. "There is a man in England that needs my help. I was *furious*. She bloody told me I have to leave Romania the day after I get back to my home. But I fought her request, and some-one else is going in my place."

"I don't understand," she said, nearing him. "What are you talking about? A man in England? Who?"

He sighed as though he thought the very idea of it was idiotic. "His name is Jacques Campbell. Some doctor that got bit by a—" he stopped abruptly. Then he sighed again. "I'm the Mistress's First Hand, Rein. I'm the next in command, as foolish as it sounds, so when the council needs to find someone, I'm its detective, per se. That's basically all the council is for: keeping evil at bay by going on missions to coax victims of immortality into our council, before the Mardinial Council does. But I have you now, and I don't want you to be exposed to such things yet. I don't think you're ready to leave here. You aren't ready for this, so I finally persuaded her to get someone else to go in my place. See, they make me go on assignment, usually only two or three times a year. But now, over half our council has been destroyed, all when I was on the ship. So it might be even more often than that. This was one of those assignments."

"What happened to him?"

"It wasn't a vampire, Rein," Traith sighed. "I don't know any other vampires. It was a *werewolf*."

A chill took over the warmth she felt. "Who is going for you?"

He scratched his neck with a slight shake of his head. "A man named Magellan. I'm hardly familiar with him, save a near fight yesterday while you were asleep," he smiled. "But I don't care—"

"A fight? A physical fight?"

He laughed quietly. "Yes, but never mind that. I told him then to take my next assignment, and he did. Mistress can be as angry as she wants, but I'm not going. I have too good of a reason to stay."

She smiled.

He turned and went into the bedroom, and she followed. He fell limp onto the armchair he seemed to favor, and she took her seat on the bed again.

"So you're able to stay here for awhile now?" she asked.

He tightened. "Yes." His red eyes softened as if he saw her fear. He stood. "A werewolf, Rein," he said, taking a few steps to the bedside next to her. "I was going to have to converse with a werewolf." He looked down, shaking his head and sitting.

She smiled and wrapped her arms around him. "You're here now," she said. "And for that I am thrilled."

She was suddenly entwined within his heavenly embrace, and his face was in her hair. She moved it and sucked in the taste of his lips. She had no one in this world to call her friend but him; she had no one to stop her from making love to him, either.

"Can I ask you something?" he said, pulling away from her.

She watched him closely. "Of course."

His face was so handsome. He had a beauty in his expression that she couldn't explain.

He left the bed suddenly and walked over to a bureau, opening a small drawer. "I bought this a long time ago," he said, fiddling with something he drew from it. "It was the best one I could find…in hopes of one day finding a woman I loved. You won't see another one like it—especially with its early-last-century authenticity."

He walked back to her and held out a ring in his two fingers. It was a most brilliant ring: gold with sapphire and pearl within it—and diamonds…

"Traith!" she said, her voice uncontained.

"It's entirely gold of the highest purity. I never thought I would use it. In fact, for a long time, the thought of having bought it haunted me. I gave up on love, Rein," he said softly. "But then I met *you*. You *are* the only woman I have ever loved, and the only one I ever will. And I want to solemnize our relationship." His voice dropped to a whisper. "I don't want to lose you, ever."

Her eyes were swelling, this time, with tears of nothing close to sorrow.

"So, Rein?" he asked, his voice as masculine yet as gentle as could be. "Do you think you could marry me?"

Her heart seemed to burst with excitement, and she felt her mouth open in shock. She gasped with laughter a few times. She felt herself smiling hugely. "Oh, absolutely!" she said with exhilaration. "I will marry you! I love you! God—you'll *never* lose me, Traith!"

He handed her the ring, and she put it on.

She threw her arms around him on the bed, lying nearly on top of him. "I love you," she said into him. She pulled back to look at the ring again. "Traith, it is magnificent!"

He was laughing. They kissed again. She curled into him under the blankets, and laid her body on his, being careful about his back. She rested on his bare chest as he embraced her, taking in his sweet cologne.

She was *engaged*? *Engaged!* There was now an excitement within her worth everything in her world, and for a moment, she wasn't scared.

chapter 37

She couldn't recall the exact number of nights she had been with Traith at his castle, but she was deeply in love, something she knew was definitely a true feeling. It was a feeling that could not be taken from her, no matter what conflicts came their way. Even though she had been a fortnight on the ship, the entire terror of it seemed so distant in her mind. Having love recovered her sanity regarding vampires ten times as fast.

Making terror more distant still was the fact that Traith had taken her back to England, to enjoy time together among other things. To talk more about each other's pasts; their likes and dislikes, only for Rein to find out that, beyond doubt, she really was *infatuated* with everything about him, a term she had never used in thought of herself in her entire life. Traith had taken her to some beautiful places in Yorkshire, mainly to buy whatever sort of clothing she wanted. She had only had a single bloodstained dress when she had arrived which they'd thrown out, so Traith went in the first shop and purchased a good one with her measurements. Once she had put that on, they continued to shop and bought more.

And that particular day, he was going to take her home—to Teesdale. To meet a sister she never knew.

She put on a beautiful ivory and blue bodice and skirt that she had purchased in order to go quickly to her home. Perhaps, if her things were still there, she'd take some of her old clothing back to the castle with her. She hoped, also, to regain her money she had left behind and keep it with Traith. She also thought she might speak to Mr. and Mrs. Kendrick. But the thought of doing that made her ill. It would be so painful—Saria's death was still a fresh wound. But she knew pain was inevitable until she was familiar with each aspect of immortality, or *vampirism* for that matter.

Traith knocked on the door of her dressing room. She finished tying up her bodice and spoke for him to come in. The door opened, and he entered with only a few steps before he leant on the wall. It was a room within a castle turret, at the end of the bedroom hall, so all the walls were circular.

A handsome smile rose up on his face. "I take it you're excited to see your sister?" he said, his arms crossed.

"I'm anxious," she said, walking to him. "I don't want to cry." She forced a smile. "You know, crying honestly is something I never do. Hasn't seemed that way lately, has it?"

"Don't think about it so grimly," he said.

His hands crawled up her shoulder blades, and she looked up, turning her head. She savored the taste of his lips and felt as if time stood still. But then he pulled back and pushed her away.

"What is it?" she asked.

Her hands fell through his, as if he were an apparition. He was disappearing. She would've fallen through him if he hadn't pushed her back.

"What is it?" Rein asked more keenly. "What?"

"No," he murmured.

She searched his face for an answer. "*Traith*—"

"A meeting," he muttered angrily, and his hand reached out to her face.

She couldn't feel it.

The next thing she knew, she was in the council, with Mistress in front of her.

"What is going on?" Rein demanded.

Staring with hostility at the old woman, Traith began to yell. "A meeting? Mistress, you're assigning me to a—" his mouth was still open, but his speech was stopped. His eyes turned to Rein in apology, and his image slowly disappeared.

He was gone.

"A meeting?" Rein asked, still staring at the spot where Traith had been only moments ago. "I don't understand."

"Yes, a meeting," the woman said. "And perhaps he is angry with me, but I can deal with him later. Perhaps you are also, but he *is* my second in all of this, and there was something important for him to head. He was able to get out of going to England and chancing a werewolf for you, but I was gracious in letting him do so. I know his feelings about you—"

"He proposed to me," Rein said quietly with a smile, twisting the magnificent band she now wore on her left hand. "We're going to—"

"As important as that might be to *you*, I have no interest in the matter."

Rein stared, rather squinted, at her with disgust. "How could you have just said that?"

"Listen, Rein," she said. "I must speak with you about a matter more important than that. Follow me. He is right next to this room, leading the meeting. We mustn't disturb them."

The woman took her hand, and she realized that the room had literally molded into another. It was completely white, as was every other room she had ever seen the Mistress in.

But she couldn't think much about the room. She was still so stunned and disgusted by what that old lady had said…He had *proposed* to her. He was her *fiancé*, and she could say nothing to that news? After dedicating himself to her service for over a hundred years?

Rein sat down on a sofa. "What is it that you want of me?" she asked, trying to hide her anger.

The woman paused, thinking. "I am a Presage, Rein," she began. "I must meditate for days upon months—perhaps, as in your case, I must meditate longer than that."

"About me?"

"Has your mind been different to you lately?"

Rein felt strange at her words. The woman seemed to know what she was thinking.

"Yes," she replied. "Why?"

"You have a connection to Traith, don't you?" Mistress said. "You can tell where he is, talk to him…even when he is not present?"

Weakness began to set in. Her eyes were wide. A connection? She did. She was beginning to hear things. With a strange suddenness her ears began to ring. Left. Right. Straight. No. This Way. Turn Around. Wrong Direction. There. Over Here. Look That Way. Back Here. Forward. Random words mixed with her thoughts.

"What did you do to my head?" Rein asked nervously. "What did you do?"

"I only prepared you for it," she replied. "I wanted you to be here when you experienced—"

"What?" Rein asked frantically. "What in God's name are you talking about? Those words—what *was* that?"

"I am a Presage, Rein," the woman said, "as I have told you."

"What *is* a Presage?"

"I can see future occurrences and learn the whereabouts of those I choose. But I cannot do what you can."

"What can I do? Mistress, I don't know if you're aware, but I—"

"Say nothing, Rein," she said sternly. "I will explain. I sensed that your abilities had developed; your *mind*. You are metaphysically peaked in mental activity *now*. And it is just beginning."

"You said you meditate to find out about those in your council?" Rein said, almost ignoring her. "Then what about Traith? He's been in your council for over a *century*, and you could not even tell him his own forgotten past?"

"He has not simply *forgotten* his past," she said. "He's lost it. It has been nearly erased, and it is impossible for me to find it because it was the doing of the Mardinial Council." She got quieter, and her words became quick. "When I first came upon Traith, he was hysterical. So much more than you ever were, or ever will be. He tried everything to fix himself. He would've killed himself had I not persuaded him against it. He attempted quite a few times, Rein."

Rein held her tongue, though her mouth was gaping. She was learning more about him…He'd tried to kill himself? He hadn't told her that yet.

"When he first got his power that lets him control a fiery energy, he was more scared than I've ever seen anybody before. He would touch things and they would explode. He couldn't control it for a long time. Then, at times, he would turn invisible without his knowledge. Then teleport places unintentionally. He was literally in pieces, and I never could understand why my own beyond-immortal heart felt such a wrenching for him. I helped him more than any other I've ever dealt with, and in the end he pledged me his loyalty. That's why I made him my First Hand. Then seven years later, Ana…" She cleared her throat, and her eyes widened. "I apologize," she said assertively. "Please, don't ever speak to anyone about this. Can I trust you with that?"

She hadn't meant to tell her those things…

Rein was taken aback by her manner. "Yes."

"Then back to you, Rein," she said, clearing her throat once more. "You must learn how to use your abilities, with more control than he had."

"How long did it take him to learn to cope?"

The old woman sighed. "Rein, I said I was through—"

"Please," she returned. "I'm sure he won't tell me like you could. I'm so in love with him, Mistress. I want to know as much about him as I can, without having to constantly ask him questions he doesn't want to answer."

She hesitated, her eyes scanning. "Traith…well, he improved every year within the seven years he was with me, before he was cursed onto the ship. But I don't believe he entirely gained control of his abilities until he was actually on the ship, where all he could do for so many years was practice." Rein saw the lady snicker a little, unbelievably. "I had to laugh when he'd run into things suddenly because he'd teleported into them or even when he'd disappear in front of me, talking, or listening, and I'd have to explain to him that I couldn't see him anymore."

Rein found herself feeling partially better as she watched the woman chuckle, and she giggled too.

"But the only time I had to be staid with him was when he'd touch something and it set fire or ignited and exploded. He'd get so frustrated. Most of the time he'd hurt himself, and I actually felt bad for him." Then with a shake of her head, "Oh, I cannot believe I'm telling you this. I'm finished!"

Rein casually cleared her throat. "Thank you," she said, smiling. "That's all I wanted to know." She took a breath. "So what am I, a *clairvoyant*? Can't you please elaborate?"

"A *clairvoyant*, yes. I have never seen, in all my years, someone progress as quickly as you have," Mistress said with concern. Her temperament almost changed to one of fear. "You have progressed so greatly, and so rapidly, and there is something about you that makes it impossible for me to see anything about your future. Or your fate."

"You have tried to see my fate?" Rein asked, frustration setting in.

"Calm down, Rein, and listen," she said, but the strictness in her manner was gone. "I *never* seek to find the fate of *any* of my council members without reason. But for you, there is a difference. You carry an aura around you. One that seems changeable at will, as if so was your fate. That worries me. You will become so powerful, Rein, that you will be..." She stopped. "Just don't lose hold of what your mind wants," she finished. "It will get worse until you learn to control it. If you do not take the time to control it, you could easily go insane. But once controlled, your abilities will be unlimited. I cannot affirm exactly what you will be able to do."

Rein hid the disappointment she felt. Something about Mistress infuriated her. The woman knew more about her than she was saying, and more than she was comfortable with. She had a right to know. But it was so quickly dismissed, and she knew she would never find out the ending to Mistress's previous sentence.

"Rein," she said calmly. "I brought you here to test your power. The very basis of your mental abilities is working. Right now."

chapter 38

t raith found himself standing by his meeting desk in the front of hundreds of immortals who had come due to a certain issue brought up by an applicant. His job was too bureaucratic. He didn't always want to be so serious and focused on his council, but it was the first time he had to for *years*.

The timing could not have been worse, however. What did that blamed crone want with Rein? What exactly was she learning without him? About her abilities? About his initial reaction to his turning? Damn—had she told Rein he'd tried to *kill* himself? His absence of control? Her fate? His fate? *What* had she said about his proposal?

He grabbed his head and held it.

"What the devil is going on?" he whispered to himself.

He was hearing her. Hearing *Rein*.

What was bloody *going on*?

The woman's wink from beside him stopped his thoughts. He held his fury at bay as the meeting opened. It was Lorena; the romantic that was everything any man could lust for. He rolled his eyes and turned away, still holding his head, his elbows now resting on the desk.

How am I hearing what Rein is doing? Saying? Thinking?

"Traith Harker, this meeting has been adjourned," a loud voice rang out, "due to the victim's demand of trial suspension. He claims he is yet insufficient for an assessment."

Suddenly the crowds of people arose and began to talk amongst themselves, and the announcer left the room.

Traith stood up and attempted to leave the room, but, as soon as he began to transfer himself back into the room the two women were in, Lorena grabbed his arm.

"Well met, Traith! Were you ignoring me? I see great tension in you."

"Is it that obvious?" He jerked his wrist out of her hand and cleared his throat, smiling uneasily. "I have to go."

"There is, isn't there?"

"What?"

"Tension."

"Isn't there always?"

Her beautiful green eyes narrowed. "What is it?"

"I need to see Rein."

"Traith, my *dearest* Traith. Do you actually *love* that woman?" she asked, laughing.

He hesitated to reply to her. He didn't want to have news of him in love spread like a disease. If Lorena knew, it would. Or it would get distorted.

"It isn't any of your business," he said quietly.

"Uh," she replied, walking directly in front of him. "So after all those years of being amorous for you and taking care of your home, I see I still cannot appeal to you. What must I *do*?"

"Lorena, I don't have a taste for women who throw themselves onto men like they're part of their clothing."

She puffed out a laugh. "Don't fool yourself. Little Miss Pierson is probably expecting you to return in a few hours, when the meeting is through, and in the meantime, you and I could—"

He held his head again. "The meeting *is* through."

"I hardly believe that you actually hold such a magnificent position in this council, for surely you don't act as if you do! Please, Traith! Come with me for a little while. I promise I'll bring you back, soon. I don't bite much. You, being a *vampire*, of *all* immortal creatures should like that in a woman anyway," Lorena said, fingering his waistcoat.

He backed away. "No, I don't."

"Oh please!" She neared him and spoke quieter. "I'll let you take a bite out of me, Traith. I missed you so!"

"Lorena!"

"I want you to! You don't like biting women, Traith? You bit—"

"Get *away*!"

"Ugh. I take that as an insult!"

"Being told that I like biting women is an insult!"

"You're a *vampire*! You'd best soon learn to live with it!"

"Pray for me, then," he answered her dryly.

"Really, Traith, you need to give a girl her due. After all that time being on a lonely, old ship, I would like to think you would want attention from other people—from me."

Traith smiled with exasperation. "No, not really. But there are a few men over there that might. Or were you already planning on frivolously greeting each of them after I left?"

In an instant, she nearly fell through him. She stood up awkwardly, angered. He smiled in return, winked, and in a moment, found himself in the same room he had been in before.

chapter 39

H e heard a terrible noise, crashing, coming from a distant room. Then pained crying. He ran to the doorway and froze, gripping the jamb.

Things were moving in mid air, hitting the walls, ceiling, and ground. Mistress stood to the side, staring calmly. It was the woman on the floor in front of her—*Rein*—that made him sick. She was holding her head as if in pain, curled on her side on the white floor.

"What is happening to her?" he asked Mistress. "What is she doing?"

He tried to run to her, but Mistress stopped him. She stopped him mentally from a few feet away. "Listen to me before you lose your temper," she said calmly.

He was nearly panting in bewilderment. Rein was in pain.

"This is one of her abilities, Traith," Mistress said, directing her attention back to the girl on the floor.

His *fiancée*.

Suddenly everything—the chairs, the sconces, books—left the air and fell to the floor. The room was a mess, but Rein was herself again. Her black hair was down and cascading over her shoulders, and her blue dress was crumpled and twisted on her slim figure. She wiped her eyes while still covering her face. Her body shuddered, recovering from whatever trauma she had just been through.

Mistress bent down in front of her. "Rein? Are you finished?"

Rein glanced at the woman with angry fear in her dark red eyes. "Finished? I didn't want to do any of that! What is wrong with me, what did you *do*?"

Her voice was becoming hoarse in her fury of what she couldn't understand. Then she saw that Traith was there for the first time. She murmured his name. He walked over and knelt beside her, lifting up her head and touching her face.

She grasped his hands. "Did you see what I just did? God, I don't know what is happening!" Her eyes searched his for a moment, and then she became nearly inaudible. "You didn't see what I did earlier, Traith," she whispered.

He returned her stare for a moment, and then looked up at Mistress, letting Rein hold onto his hand and put her face in it. "Mistress, can you stop this prolonging of an explanation? Stop speaking in blasted riddles and just explain what is going on to her!"

Mistress gave him a sharp glare. "All of Rein's abilities are functional."

He felt a near faintness come over himself. "What are you talking about? That isn't possible; it doesn't even make sense."

"But she has gained them nonetheless," Mistress countered. "Rein Pierson is a mental giant. You felt her, Traith, didn't you?"

He gave a sharp stare to the old lady. "Yes."

"My point should be taken, then. Rein can do nearly anything she wants with her mind, but she must learn to harness those capabilities. She is *telepathic*—able to communicate in a mind, *empathic*—able to both render and sense feelings in a mind, *telekinetic*—able to move physical things with her mind, and various other techniques such as a form of healing, levitation (although that is already exclusive to the vampire), shape-shifting, *and* she can cut into the time barrier, with a good deal of discomfort."

He narrowed his eyes. "Cut into the time barrier?"

"Stop time. As we all just witnessed, Rein has just learned to *use* her telekinetic ability. At least, for the first time since she had accidentally used it on the ship. The nails?"

Traith gazed at Rein, who was staring in disbelief herself. She suddenly took a breath and closed her eyes. He took her in his arms and held her tight.

Her fingers were grasping him. "I love you," she whispered.

He turned his head to Mistress for only a moment before holding her tighter to him.

"And…the werewolf…it didn't work," Rein murmured.

"What?" He receded and looked back and forth into each of her eyes, and as Mistress sighed, he instantly glared at her. "What is she talking about?"

The woman held an ornate cane between her hands and looked back at him wearily. "I sent Magellan to persuade him to come—it resulted appallingly. Campbell didn't consent; not at all."

"So what does that mean?" he asked.

"You must go. He must concede."

"You—"

"Traith, you cannot say I didn't *attempt* to make you happy. I found this out momentarily ago, and you must go. I can keep Rein here."

"I'm not staying," Rein protested from beside him, now standing.

He didn't know what to say. Fury was nearly spilling over the surface. "I am supposed to take Rein to see her sister."

"It must wait," she said austerely. "This man may, at any time, be taken by the Mardinial Council, and there are many, many unfathomable things that they can do to him, and we need to replenish the numbers of our council. The Mardinial Council uses force. We shall not. You are the best persuader I can use."

He laughed. "Me, the best persuader? Mistress, you've got to be—"

"Traith, I give you no less than a day. Take Rein. Use a few hours to go over her abilities with her. Then you had better go."

"Go over her power with her? I hardly know what she can do; that's what you're supposed to be for! I have no mental powers, I can't explain them!"

"I cannot teach her, Traith. She must learn herself. You can assist. That is all."

"But—"

"Traith, I *said* that is all."

He groaned and took Rein's hand. In an instant he was back at the castle.

chapter 40

H e cursed the old woman as he took a seat in the library, holding his head. "This is ridiculous," he said quietly. Then his voice rose. "Rein, come here."

She swallowed her emotion, taking a seat on a sofa close to the unlit fireplace. The stone and dimness of the castle made it cool inside, which was a nice reprieve from the outside heat.

"I cannot believe I have to converse with a werewolf," he said. "I hate them more than anything I have ever come in contact with."

Rein's anger was beginning to cool in the shadows of the castle. "When are we going?" she asked, taking a breath of release.

He lifted his head up and looked at her in return. "Tomorrow. Evening. Tomorrow evening." He smiled halfheartedly. "Consider this your beginning taste of Mistress's thoughtfulness."

When she saw him so solemn, she thought about how hard Mistress had said it had been for him. At least she had someone to help her through it. He hadn't. For some reason, each time she gazed at Traith, her own sorrows shrunk completely.

She heard him thinking deep thoughts. Thoughts about her. About how much she was capable of doing.

"I know," she said.

His eyes widened. "What, Rein?" He was staring at her.

Her heart dropped. "I'm sorry," she said, numbness engulfing her. "I read your mind. I'm sorry…I don't know how I…I won't do it again, I swear it!"

His eyes were still large. "All right," he replied.

She was shuddering with her head in her hands. "Traith, I didn't even mean to."

His voice was quiet in response. "I know you're just learning how to use this…mental *power* you have, but make me a promise, or as best of one as you can."

She looked at him apologetically and felt horrible.

"Don't go into my mind without my consent," he said, fiddling with his waistcoat chain. After a moment he smiled. "That would not only be unfair, but it would take the fun out of everything."

"Of course," she said quickly. "I'm s—"

"Don't say it. You don't ever have to say it again, Rein."

She felt his original peculiarity return with that and sighed with a slight shake of her head. A sort of chill came over her when she thought about what she had done. She had read his mind. She wouldn't do it again. She wouldn't.

"I can turn things into whatever I want?" she asked, or rather affirmed. "I can pause time, I can read minds, be in minds, switch minds. Take pain, take life, control people, move things without touching them. God, I must be going mad. Or I *will* be going mad."

"You aren't going *mad*," he murmured from the other chair, laughing a little.

"But think about all I have to memorize," she said, rubbing her forehead. "When I have to use what, what all I can do…Traith, how *can't* I go mad with all this? I got the impression from Mistress that I could—"

"No, Rein, you won't," he replied. "I promise you. Just don't let go. Don't ever, ever lose your grasp on these mental capabilities, whatever they entail. I will help you as much as I can, but I can't think for you. I don't have any sort of mental power over anything. What I can do is strictly physical. But you…" he sighed, stopped, and chuckled lightly. "Everything will be fine."

She finally gave up and accepted his answer to her ranting—the one she had wanted. She softly leant on her palm with her elbow resting on the side of her seat. She glanced down at the large and stunning ring on her left hand. She managed to smile. "So what does this ring actually have attached to it, Traith?"

"Hmm?"

"You know, what comes with it?" She grinned when she noticed him perk up to the seductive tone in her voice. "Does it have anything to do with 'the fun in everything' you mentioned?"

He cocked his head. "Why, what kind did you have in mind?"

He suddenly disappeared in his seat, the image of his hands folded with his chin resting upon them, gone. Then he was beside her. "Something like…"

He leaned over and nudged her chin up with his, kissing her neck. She laughed, and in a single moment she felt a bed beneath her; he'd taken them to the bedroom. She fell back onto it, lifting her arms up around him and running her fingers through his hair. His head turned, and her lips tasted his. His tough, strapping body became instantly soft and gentle as if he was a god holding a mere person in his palm. She pushed him up a moment and began to unbutton her vest, then her bodice. He peeled the blouse off of her shoulders and down her body, until her dress was off. Next thing she knew, she only had her tiny corset and chemise on against his bare, muscular chest, and she could feel the bristles on his face tickling her, making tingles run from her neck, down. She was burning for him, and his skin was hot to the touch…

chapter 41

t he shore breeze tossed Rein's dark hair around her face. She grasped the reins tightly as she rode her horse through the marshy, muddy fields of Gravesend. The wind whistled as it curled around the sporadic growth of trees and cattails that surrounded her. The sky was clouded, and it was nearing evening. Her surroundings looked rather like a desert with steep hills, but not quite as vast.

"Are you with me?" Traith asked as he rode next to her.

"Hmm?" She turned and looked at him.

He pulled and twisted the reins to get his horse to slow down.

He brought the horses only because he didn't know exactly where Dr. Campbell was. He had had time to get over the initial anger he felt toward the entire situation. A werewolf. Something about the way Traith spoke about werewolves gave Rein the impression that he was almost scared of them. That made her *twice* as scared.

Traith slowly halted his horse, and Rein did likewise.

"I think his home is right up there," he said, but his manner was detached. It was wholly focused on her. "Something's wrong isn't it?"

Her mind clouded with voices she didn't understand. They flooded together as if trying to tell her something…then stopped. Her mind became clear. "Oh God," she murmured.

"What?"

She winced, shaking her head. "I can't…"

He stared at her. "What? You can't what?"

Throbbing began to overtake her. She stared down at her horse. "My head is aching, Traith, it's starting," she murmured. "I'm sorry. I won't say anything—"

"Won't say anything? Rein, this…" His eyes flicked around uncomfortably. "This isn't even possible," she heard him whisper to himself. "I don't know what to do, Rein, I'm sorry."

She shook her head and squinted momentarily. "I love you," she said.

He stared at her for a moment, his face to her, so intent.

She felt something wrong. A chill ran down her spine. Something was skewed. A sharpness pierced inside her head in a rush, and things grew quiet. She glared at Traith. He was watching her in shock.

"You told me Ana looks like you, right?" she said.

"What?"

He had told her one night about his younger sister. Her average stature, dark blonde, short hair, brown eyes; he said that they had looked alike.

Rein could see it.

"Go," she murmured.

His eyes were narrowed as if annoyed. "*What*, Rein?"

She waved him on. "Go!"

He didn't listen. He watched her in bewilderment.

She jumped off the horse and ran to a tree.

"Rein! What are you—?"

"*Stakes*, Traith!" she yelled. "Your *sister* put *stakes* on a—"

Sparking—popping triggered from the huge bundle of sharp wood set on the tree branch. She tried to get back to the horse, but instead she jumped forward, into a pile of high grass and behind a tree. She didn't have time to say anything more to Traith but to call his name.

She had heard him get off his horse to reach her, but suddenly a boom sounded. She could hear the pointed pieces of wood driving through the air only a meter or so above her. She heard the horses screeching, and it sent terrified chills down her body. She held her ears.

Then it was over as fast as it had begun.

She dropped her hands to the ground as silence ensued. She grasped grass between her fingers and, with a breath, slowly inched her way up to look out to the trail they had been on. Both horses were dead.

She immediately searched for Traith, calling his name in panic.

She heard movement.

She glanced at a briery thicket ahead of her and smiled with relief when she saw him attempting to get out of it. Her smile turned at the widening of his eyes.

"What just bloody happened?" he asked, grabbing his hat from amidst the thorns.

He was scratched up a great deal, and she felt such pity for him. He always seemed to be the one getting hurt.

Rein felt wonder come over her. "I saw Ana," she said. "Behind there. No, she had *been* there, but I didn't exactly see her…"

He stared at her, neither blinking nor moving.

"Traith, look at the horses!" She ran to them. They lay unmoving in grotesque positions. "Traith, can you pull out the stakes? I can't…"

His half-dazed eyes slowly left her face and met with the gored horses. "My God," he breathed. He looked grave as he limped over to her. "Can't you heal them? Or try to, or something?"

"I can't heal something dead, Traith," she muttered. "I know I can't…" she paused and felt cold. "I *know* I can't." She wanted to smile at the fact that she knew what she could do, somehow, but the horses' screeching rang in her mind. "Look how many stakes," she murmured, her eyes filled.

He held her shoulders and turned her to face him. "Stop looking at them," he muttered. "But you—you saw my sister?"

"Not really, no. In my mind, as though just in front of me." She had to pause in talking. "Though obviously she *had* been right in front of me."

He waited for her to finish, then he sighed. "After over a hundred years away from her on a ship, she's still too afraid to confront me. Instead she wants to kill me in greeting," he said quietly, brushing himself off. "Campbell's warehouse of a home is right up here," he murmured. "I think I see it, so I can take us there."

She took his hand and watched as the trail they left turned into a foggy, dreary shore.

"Here it is," he said with an empty smile. "Just as I figured."

She glanced at him as he walked ahead of her, still shaking his head in disbelief at what had just occurred. Her stomach sank.

chapter 42

t raith placed his hat on his head, covering his messy, brown hair. He looked so handsomely sloppy; his body was hidden inside his overcoat, and his hat covering most of his face. It was now pulled down to cover his flaming eyes. All she could see was his upper jaw, sideburns, and chin.

She took in, then, the repository ahead of her: it was old and run down, with broken windows and boarded doors. There was a large gate that ran all the way around the warehouse, and she wrinkled her nose as the pungent, marshy smell became noticeable.

Traith approached the gate and pulled at it a few times, but it was locked. He slowly felt toward the ends, his arms out wide, holding it by the hinges. He tugged once at it and broke the gate.

He turned and looked at her with a grin. "Easier to get in that way," he said. "Magellan couldn't get through that, I assure you. Or didn't have the nerve to." He sighed and set the gate to the side gently, tapping the top of it in sarcasm.

She followed directly behind him as he walked up to the old door. He knocked hard a few times. In each pause of his fist, she glanced around at the bizarreness of the area. She happened to glance up; a dark figure appeared and leaned on one of the broken windows.

"Up there, Traith," she said, tapping him.

"Dr. Campbell?" he called. "I need a word with you!"

The man didn't answer and left the window.

Traith shrugged inelegantly and looked back down. "Things can never just be easy, can they?"

Rein watched his anger rise, and he protested under his breath when they heard the man lock the door from the inside after a few minutes. She knew Traith genuinely didn't want to be there.

She then heard a faint grunt, or cough, as if Campbell were ill. Following Traith's alert spin of head, she saw the man reappear by another window on their floor, but about twenty yards away.

"Look at him, Rein," he whispered. "He looks shaken and intoxicated."

"How do you mean?" she questioned him.

"Without doubt from the medicine he takes to try and contain himself. The curse of the werewolf is the only other which is as uncontrollable and as frightening as our own."

She watched Traith jump over the side of the entrance fencing, his black military boots digging into the dirt when he landed. He casually approached the man by the window.

"Can you let us in?" he asked with a cheerless disposition. "I just want to talk with you."

Campbell left the window Traith was approaching. She thought she heard Traith curse at him as he headed back to her. Then the door unlocked.

The door creaked inward. By then Traith had jumped the fence again and stood next to her, staring, as she was, at the doctor. Sweat was dripping down the doctor's face, and his bifocals were misted over. Half his shirt was untucked, and he was wheezing hard as he leaned on the doorframe.

"What?" the doctor asked loudly waiting for an answer. "Why have you come?"

"Dr. Campbell," he said, "I'm Traith Harker. This is Rein Pierson—"

"Your woman? I see." Traith shut his mouth with a slight smile, his head cocked and eyes closed as the doctor continued. "Well, I *do* apologize, but I don't want anything to do with *you* or *anybody*! I'm— I'm a—"

Traith seemed tired of the waste of breath. "You're a werewolf, Dr. Campbell. I'm very aware. I'm a vampire."

"You think you're a joker, don't you, Mr. Harker?"

"I'm entirely serious," Traith replied, still calm.

The skinny man was struck with more anger. "That man…that man earlier!" His eyes widened. "He was with you, wasn't he? The one who knew what I was—*Magellan*!"

Traith sighed, then cleared his throat. "Yes, he is with me, though I rather loathe—"

"Then like I told him, I'm a monster, you cannot change that, and you cannot protest against it! Nor can you fix it, so why have you even come?"

"Dr. Campbell," Traith replied calmly, though Rein noticed his hands were clenched tight. He talked with his teeth slightly gritted. "Do you understand even the slightest bit that we're saving you from a future of pain, brainwashing, and sick experimentations? There are councils, Dr. Campbell—"

"I don't want to hear about those councils anymore!"

Rein looked at Traith questioningly.

"Here you're vulnerable, Jacques," Traith said. "You—"

The doctor fell back through the doorway and staggered inside, leaning on the old sofa, interrupting Traith's address. Rein turned and noticed that the moon, now, was shining in a hole in the clouds. A ravenous look appeared in the doctor's eyes as they began to turn yellow with rage. She felt utterly revolted as Campbell shook his head with intensity, falling to his knees. A nervous feeling swelled deep within her, and she saw that Traith, too, had a sudden apprehension. He had stepped in front of her by then.

Campbell stopped, took a deep breath, and stood back up shakily. "Please, come in. The moon's covered again. As long as it covers fast enough, I won't turn. Sorry for the…moroseness. I'll hear you out, but if I do not consent, you must leave at once."

Traith cleared his throat in an awkward manner. "Thank you," he said with half a smile, ducking under the doorframe.

Rein followed.

"Let me take your things," the doctor said to him, once in the sitting room.

"I wonder if bipolarity runs in your veins, Doctor," Traith replied. "Don't trouble yourself."

Rein took a seat on the sofa and watched Traith take off his overcoat and slouch hat and hang them up. She noticed how he tilted his head downward after turning toward Campbell, hiding his face like he used to when he first met her. She supposed that he simply had that habit with new acquaintances. He looked apprehensive, like he usually was with people before he knew them.

"Do you see?" the doctor said. He took a deep breath as he sat across from Rein on a settee. "This medicine…" the doctor continued, "do you see how frightening I am? I'm frightened of myself. I'm a monster, and I can't control it or do anything about it. I've tried for hours, days, *months* to find something that will cure me. I can't *do* anything. I change into the horrible beast whether it is day or night, as long as there is even a smidgen of a moon! Doesn't help that now there is a full one. It's taken over my life."

Rein pushed her fear of another of his sudden transformations away as she heard his story. He wasn't secretive of it at all.

"You're vampires. You're cursed too, then. You tell me if it makes sense to listen to two other *creatures*. Besides, the idea of your particular *infection* makes me bothered."

Traith laughed as though shocked. "Bothered?" He looked out the entry again at the sky and took note of the clouds' position over the moon. Then he turned back to the doctor and walked toward him. "Quite frankly, your_*own* curse tends to make *me* terribly uptight, so we're speaking on the same level. In any case, you do not deserve to die. I do understand how you feel because I went through this as well. The Mardinial—"

"Don't talk about any councils to me; I told you!"

Rein glanced at Traith's puzzled expression. He had walked behind her, leaning with his hands on the sofa back.

He stared at the scrawny man in front of them. "We may never be able to be normal again, but we can use these curses to our advantage. I know...or would *hope* that you're a good man. Would you not rather be used for good than for evil? You still have one reasonable option left."

Traith was speaking as though he had said that a hundred times. How often had he had to do this with other people? He didn't seem to remotely enjoy being the Mistress's First Hand.

The doctor looked curious for a second but then let out a blood-curdling scream. Rein stood in alertness, and Traith's hands grabbed her around her corseted waist.

Campbell fell to the ground and grabbed his head, screaming bitterly. "No, no,_*no!*_I won't...hurt...*her!*"

"Interesting," Traith laughed, though he thought nothing was amusing. "He's never even spoken to you, yet he'll have no problem hurting me."

Rein looked at him for an instant, but she had no time to speak. The doctor looked up; his eyes again became bright yellow, and fangs slowly pierced through his gums. Rein turned away, her stomach feeling empty and low. She felt Traith's iron grip around her waist tightening as well.

She suddenly heard Traith speculating about his own transformation; had it been so traumatic? Wait, *speculating*? He was thinking and she heard. He knew her own change had been smooth and graceful and, most of all, painless, but his was far from such.

He turned her around, his expression shocked. "Rein, I felt you in my…Were you…?"

He abruptly twisted back and realized that the cloud covering had dissipated, and the full moon shown again. Even though it was the very late afternoon, the sun was still perceptible. The dimness of night would come within the hour.

"I'm sorry," she started, but he interrupted her, speaking rapidly.

"The door! We need to close the door!"

"That doesn't…*Get out of here*!" the doctor yelled frantically. He was rolling back and forth in front of her.

A sudden excruciating pain shot all the way up her leg. She let out a shout and glanced down, only to see an animal-like hand swipe around and clutch her ankle. It was Campbell; he was driving his large nails into her skin. Blood was flowing freely. She dropped to the floor with a groan of pain and began trying to pull his furred, deformed hand off of her foot. She was calling Traith's name.

He had inadvertently let go of her, but he was by her side in seconds, ripping Campbell's hand off of Rein. It was no longer a human hand.

The entire man was no longer human.

Rein managed to stare at the wolf clearly in that second. His snout was long, and his teeth had saliva hanging from the sides. Pointed ears were facing completely forward, and his body was a twisted amalgamation of man and animal. Clothes were ripped entirely off. The dark hair that covered his entire body was matted with what looked like some sort of liquid.

Traith looked shocked by the sharpness and size of the hostile claws he was holding. Pain flared in Rein's leg when the creature's claws were removed, and she cringed, gritting her teeth, trying to ignore it.

The furry, blood-covered hand yanked from Traith's grasp and shot back into his face, knocking him backward into a china cabinet. Rein froze at seeing the man she loved hit like that. He grunted as he fell, shaking his head and wiping his forearm over his face. Blood covered it.

A sudden howl came from Campbell's lips. He immediately stood and ran almost blindly at Traith, who hardly had time to react. He put his hands out as if to catch the beast. She saw how wounded his face was from the claws' backlash. But then he teleported just as the blow of a bestial fist smashed into the already-destroyed cabinet. Traith was standing, swaying, behind the werewolf. Two hind legs shoved back and slammed into Traith's abdomen, throwing him back again, this time into a dining room table on the far side of the room. Traith groaned and slid to the side of the floor.

Rein glanced down at her ankle; the wound had stopped burning. It was healed. A fear she had never felt before began to settle inside of her.

The werewolf had just turned his yellow, bloodshot glare at her. She dove at him and grabbed his calf, twisting it. The beast crashed to the ground. When she landed, she couldn't see where he or his elongated jaws full of massive teeth were. She was scared out of her mind that she would feel those teeth in only a moment's time.

But then there was nothing. She glanced up. Campbell seemed himself again, though still inhuman. He tried to speak, his voice terribly altered.

Rein couldn't try to listen to him. The smell of the blood that stained the sofa and her leg began to haunt her so terribly. She couldn't touch it. She craved it, but she couldn't. The restraint she used to distance herself from it was antagonizing.

The wolf turned at the sound of Traith scrambling out from under the wreckage. He jumped toward him, landing and rolling on the floor, but Traith was holding the wolf's jaw between his strong, rough hands. They had blood everywhere; she saw how bloodied Traith's face was, and it turned her stomach. He let go of one side of Campbell's snout and raised a fist to it. It cracked against the brute's face, thrusting him into the flooring. Traith rolled to the side and pushed himself up with his hand, shaking the other, which had been severely cut during the blow.

A new yet hauntingly familiar feeling overwhelmed Rein; strange, ethereal. She wanted the werewolf to become tame. It was the same feeling that had risen in her on the ship, just before she killed the captain...

"Stop," she said, her voice suddenly fused with the doctor's. "Be still." *Clairvoyant.*

She was a *clairvoyant.*

Minds were hers to control.

She stopped. Her eyes, which had felt wider and different, felt regular again. She watched the beast lay motionless on the ground. Traith was standing, now. He was staring, not moving, not even blinking. Just staring at her. His handsome eyes shifted from her to Campbell when a shriek sounded from the beast. Slowly, horrifyingly, the monster altered back into his regular self.

What had she done?

chapter 43

raith walked to her and held her, his face concerned and smeared with blood. But there were no more wounds on him. He drew her back from the faint man lying on the floorboards. Traith's hands moved upward softly, and he held her cheeks, staring gravely into her eyes in question.

"My God," she said, gazing at him and taking in his movements.

"Rein," he said gently. "Rein, don't think about it. It'll make sense; give yourself time."

She felt her hands begin to tremble wildly. "Are *you* all right?" she asked. "How could you even stand after what he just did to you?" She felt the side of his face and spoke gently.

"I heal," he said. "And unfortunately, though I heal, I feel all the pain no differently." He clenched his teeth and smiled. "Rein, your ankle… I'm sorry I let go of you; I didn't mean to."

She shook her head. "It doesn't hurt anymore."

A low moaning sounded. He let go of her and turned, taking a few steps around the sofa to get a better look at the doctor. He was lying quietly on the floor, with ripped and tattered clothes hanging off his body. His hands were fists, his back was wet with perspiration, and he was panting rapidly. Rein figured he probably couldn't, or didn't want to, get up to face the both of them. The mortification…

She scanned his home. Although it was only a warehouse, he had made it his own. It had a large sitting area that was scantily decorated. Its only décor was china cabinets and chests, a sofa and some other minor things, but most of it had been ruined by the impact of Traith's body. Broken glass and furniture was scattered everywhere.

"Kill me. Please. Kill me." A soft voice sounded from the floorboards in the silence that lingered.

The doors were still wide open, and the warm shore breeze blew quietly throughout. It blew her hair into her face. She looked outside; the moon was covered with heavy rain clouds, so it wouldn't be shining again that night.

Traith shuffled to the door and looked up at the sky. He let himself fall onto the doorframe, his hair blowing to the side powerfully. His muscles were tense and noticeable through the rips in his shirt.

Rain was starting to fall rapidly, pitter-pattering on the metal roof. The tall cattails were blowing hard, and a loud, whistling noise came with the wind.

Then she heard Campbell's moaning from the floor again. "Kill me. Quickly."

She looked at him, her eyes narrowed. "Are you *mad*?" she said. "Kill you?"

Traith turned his head to her, and for a moment, she thought she saw amusement in his eyes.

"Please, quickly—"

"Dr. Campbell, you have no right to blame yourself for what you've just done," she said. "I cannot kill you, *nor* will I do so quickly."

"Y-You must!"

"No, honestly…"

He began to wriggle himself up to look at her. More at her leg. "Your ankle," he murmured. "Is it all right?"

"We can heal ourselves, doctor," Traith said faintly from the doorway. "You went after me more than her anyway."

"He did say he would," Rein said. She could only barely see him smiling.

Campbell glared up from the floor at Traith. "You sound, dear Mr. Harker, as if you do not *care* about how badly I could have…how badly I did hurt her. She's your confidante, is she not? And you treat her *like*—?"

Traith turned on him furiously. "You have *no* right, old man, *no right* to question *my* intentions *regarding her*! I think I know she's my—"

"Traith," Rein cut in front of him.

He was becoming threateningly angry with the doctor.

"Leave it alone," Rein said to him quietly. "Please, don't lose your temper now."

Traith wouldn't look at her, but he backed down and turned back to the rain outside the doorway. He swore under his breath. "Lucky I want you alive, you—"

"Dr. Campbell, please use reason," she said. "I'm fine, and he knew I would be. This isn't what we're here for. We need you on our side. Please. If you don't come with us, there's a chance that someone could force you to go with them. Isn't that right, Traith?"

He didn't turn, but he more or less grunted. "Yes."

He was acting cold and emotionless, now. She knew that between the beating he'd just received and the way the doctor was talking to him, Traith wasn't too happy with the man.

"I can't go with you," Campbell said. "I can't. I almost…"

She noted how tightly focused his eyes were on her leg. She glanced down and saw that there were five small, light scars left there. But they were too light for him to see. So why was he…?

He pulled himself up with the assistance of the torn, bloodstained sofa next to him. "You saw what I did," he began, clearing his throat and finally looking up. "If I can't control it, how could I possibly be used for good? It's evil, so how could any of what you're saying be possible?"

"It's not evil, Campbell," Traith said angrily as he left the doorway to get his coat and hat from the fallen rack. "But it's hungry—ravenous. It knows no good *or* evil. It's more like a wild animal than a monster. Rein and I came to help you, but if you're not going to at least try to bloody work with yourself, you might as well give up. The only thing left coming for you is something much worse than what we have to offer, I assure you."

Traith looked down and buttoned the sides of his coat sleeves, wiping off dust and blood. He took his hat from the stand and put it on his head.

"My life is about over anyway," the doctor said, standing straight.

"Someone I know can help you greatly," Rein said, turning to see where Traith had disappeared to. "Please come with us, Doctor." She crossed her arms tightly. She was cold. "This is all new to me, too," she finished quietly.

The doctor looked deeply at her, and then walked over to a lamp. His hand trembled as he picked it up and put on the lampshade. He brushed himself off. Rein was surprised that as neglectful as he seemed to be, he was clean-shaven and had been well kempt. He was so thin, however, that it seemed as though he would break if touched.

He dropped his head in agreement. "Then I will go."

Rein nodded her head, smiled, and walked out the door. "Come with us, then."

"You are a...blessed couple," he said apologetically.

"I'm sorry?" Rein replied.

Traith turned and looked at the half-dressed man.

"It seems to me that God Himself must watch over you both quite closely," he said.

"Yes," she replied quietly, with a strange expression.

Traith laughed in his throat, but she could tell his mind was elsewhere. He was probably thinking about his sister...where she had gone, and why she had even tried to kill them that day in the first place.

His own sister had tried to kill him.

And he loved her so dearly.

chapter 44

"thank you," Mistress said.

Traith did not reply. Rein knew he was still angry with the woman for sending them after Campbell in the first place.

"He is in the recovery with some others."

Traith shook his head and laughed as if her comment was stupid. "May I go back home now and be undisturbed for a little *longer* than a day?" he asked.

The woman glared at him, but it took her only a moment to lose her fury. "As much as I am grateful for your loyalty, sometimes I wish you were—"

"*Stop* wishing for me," he said with an unkind smile. "It's never worked before, and I doubt it will *ever*."

Mistress sighed. Then Rein's vision blurred, and the woman was gone.

The next thing she saw was the inside of the castle foyer. Traith immediately hit the wall and yelled a curse to his superior, and then he walked into the library, scuffing his feet. He was furious.

For a moment Rein felt very alone. She had never seen him so upset, and he'd left her in the entry. But a month had already gone by since they had gotten off of the ship. Somehow still, she wasn't independent enough yet to be without him. She knew that she had to begin to be.

She didn't follow him, for the first time, as he walked into the library. Instead she began to walk up the stone steps to begin her way to one of the gallery rooms. But as soon as her heels hit the stone step, she heard her name.

"Rein?"

She smiled to herself. She was quick to leave it behind, however, when she walked into the library. There was a fire in there, now. His shadow was elongated on the stone. Shadow flickered on his face as he turned to her.

"I'm sorry," he said. "I shouldn't talk like that. I can't help it."

She smiled. "That's all right. I love you anyway."

His eyes lit a little, and she knew he had regained his equanimity. He rubbed his chin and shook his head. "She just shouldn't do that. I have no true freedom, Rein. Being hers to command like that."

"Why are you her First Hand? If you don't want to be?"

He sighed. "I was in debt to her, and I did anything and everything she needed, or wanted, me to do. After a few years, she asked me if I would serve her. I acquiesced, and I've been here ever since. But lately she's been so harsh, and I've only just gotten off of the ship I was on for..."

He always stopped as if he couldn't say aloud how long he had been stuck there. She didn't press him.

"Are you interested, now, to see your sister?" he asked without motive. "I'll take you to see her whenever you want. She's your sister and you've yet to even meet her. I of all people should know the desire to see..." He sighed and stopped. "I suppose it would be nice to see your sister and not have to worry about her trying to *kill* you."

His agitation over Ana distressed her. "I wrote them a letter about my relation," she said, trying to avoid the subject of his sister. "I thought that perhaps it would be better to do that instead of just showing up. I still have to wait for her guardian's reply." She sat next to him and touched his face. "I'm so sorry for what Ana's doing," she spoke softly, hugging him.

"I can take you to see her, still," he said, not replying to her statement about his sister. "She doesn't have to see *us*. Just to get a look at her beforehand."

She stared at him a moment, and then she showed gratitude as much as she could with her kiss. He let go and stood, motioning for her to get up. She did so, and he held her hand.

Her vision blurred again.

The next thing she saw was a familiar room. Her old room.

It was the one that she had owned for twenty years. Everything was the same: the wallpaper, the desk in the back, her bed...but most of the furniture was gone. The window was behind her, and she turned to look out of it, expecting to see the house that had previously almost been her home: Saria's house. She felt stiff.

It was completely different.

The Kendricks must have left.

She knew they had to have, because there were no flowers or gardens.

She turned away, her heart heavy. She pushed back the memory and swallowed. Then she felt Traith's hand on her arm.

"Don't speak loudly," he whispered. "She can hear us but not see us."

She couldn't see him either, but she could feel his touch. There was a worn-in bed with a girl sitting on it. She was crying to herself while brushing her hair. Rein knew that was her sister. *Taverin.*

She was a little girl—petite. Her hair resembled Rein's in color and length, and her eyes were blue like Rein's used to be.

When she was a little girl, Rein recalled many people saying she looked much more like her father than her mother. She figured that the townsfolk had known her parents when they were young and newly together. But Taverin's face didn't look like her own; it looked very different. Probably like her French mother.

Rein didn't say anything for fear of being heard. She wished she could see Traith and what he was doing or wanting to say, but she stayed silent. The girl was crying for some reason, and it was so late that she had expected her to be asleep.

Taverin missed her father. Rein's father.

"Oh Traith," Rein winced in a whisper. "I know why she's crying. If only she knew I was here and that I felt the same way."

She felt a hand cover her mouth. A nearly silent, "Hush."

The girl abruptly looked up, staring into the dimness of her room. Rein knew that no matter how low she had spoken, anything was audible in the silence they were in. The young girl's eyes were red and swollen, and that in itself made Rein's heart break.

She collapsed with her eyes closed into Traith's chest. She opened them, finding herself in the castle's master bedroom, Traith holding her up.

"Rein…"

She knew he didn't know what to say.

She let go of him and lay on the bed. "I'm tired," she murmured, fighting back tears. She wouldn't show him her face.

"At least you're tired at night," he said. "But that isn't a very good excuse for avoiding telling me the truth."

"I'm not avoiding…" she had to stop. Then she broke down and cried her heart out into the pillow. She couldn't hold it in. "Saria's dead," she sobbed. "Her parents aren't there. I missed my father alive by only a few days. A sister I don't know is alone and crying for him as well. My father lied to me. Traith, I just can't…I'm sorry, I don't want to seem selfish, but I…" She re-buried her face into the pillow. "I just—one more release."

His arms surrounded her and his lips brushed her ear. "Cry hard, Rein," he whispered. "I'm here."

chapter 45

the next morning was bright, and the sliver of light that shone through the balcony drape must've hit his eye just perfectly. She heard him grunt and put his hand up fast to cover his eyes, and then he rustled until she heard him leave the bed. She blinked a few times and turned, but when morning vision blurriness finally subsided—

Morning vision? It was morning. It was morning, and she was waking up. It was the first time in so long.

With much effort she pushed herself up, but Traith wasn't there. She stretched and stood up, wiping her eyes to make them clearer. He wasn't in the bedroom at all anymore.

After a few minutes she made it down to the library and saw that he was sitting in his grand armchair reading a book. There was an empty vial by his side.

His head shot up, and he closed the book. He coolly took the skinny glass and it disappeared in his hand. "Good morning, Rein," he said awkwardly.

She smiled and walked in, the stone cool beneath her feet. "I'm going to marry you," she said. "I think that you should not attempt to hide those anymore."

He shook his head and acted as though he was continuing his reading. "You do the same thing, Rein," he said. "And that girl, by the way, looks nothing like you."

"She has only my father's blood," Rein said as she took a seat on a sofa.

"How old is she?"

"I think she'll be turning sixteen," she replied. "Four years younger than me. But no, there is no such resemblance between us as there is between you and *your* sister."

She'd seized his interest. "Me and Ana? Rein, you've never even seen her!"

"But I did. I saw her clearly, at least mentally, and you look—forgive me—she looks just like you." She smiled. "One might say you were twins. Those eyes, and—"

"Twins? I think that's pushing it some."

"I don't."

He disappeared in his seat, and she flinched when he appeared right next to her on the sofa. "I have something for you." He held out his hand, palm up, and in an instant a letter appeared on it. "I managed to get to the town that's miles away from here. Believe it or not, this old castle of mine *is* on the Romanian map, and the mail carriers acknowledge it."

"Aren't the villagers curious about this place?"

"Not really," he said, and he chuckled.

"What?" she asked, propping herself up on her knees on the sofa beside him. "What's funny?"

He shook his head, still snickering. "Well, they're…scared, in a sort. Before I was cursed onto the ship when Carden lived here with me, we played tricks on the villagers so they never came around here."

She shook her head. "That's horrible."

"Well, now they all think this place is haunted. They don't dare come near—it's in their folklore, I'm sure, by now. They're a rather primitive society." He laughed. "Yet this castle still receives mail."

She laughed and leaned on him, opening the letter. Her eyes darted back and forth reading it. It was from Bruce Hall of Teesdale, Taverin's guardian.

This was the reply to the letter she had written to Mr. Hall inquiring about Taverin originally. The letter she'd sent was regarding her half-sister's future, explaining very little about herself, only her relation to the girl and their father's death. She told Mr. Hall she had been separated as a child from her family, but not her inheritance, which, of course, was not entirely accurate. She said she needed to speak with Taverin about the parting, which had never been fully explained to her. The letter from Hall said that he would speak with Taverin about everything before they met, and he gave the date in which Rein and Traith could arrive. Two weeks.

She jumped up with excitement and threw her arms around Traith. He fell backward onto the armrest, surprised.

"Was it that good?" he asked.

"Yes! One fortnight, Traith, and we can go. I think he figures we need that time to get to England from Romania."

"Ha," Traith said. "Doesn't he know who I am?"

She kissed him, and he melted underneath her.

chapter 46

Lightning continued to strike the foundation of the bastion outside of the canvassed bedroom. Candles were lit, placed at random around the rugged floor and on top of dressers and steps, melting into their positions, and the shadow of two people moving in a bed was clear through the veiled curtains. The room was red, with red, laced lining pinned over the walls, and the velvet rug sparkled vibrantly under the candled bed.

A shadow sat up and leaned out of the curtain shelter. It was a woman with large wings protruding from her shoulder blades. She was dressed in translucent chiffon, and her hair flowed down her back, covering some of what was easily seen. Her arm reached up and smeared across her grinning, red lips, wiping away blood. Her tongue rubbed across long fangs, blood still staining them.

"What are you brooding about, my dear?" A gasp of a voice asked from behind the curtain.

Her grin turned into a scowl as she licked the side of her lip. She blinked slowly and stared out the window, tucking her wings over her shoulders. "I want them gone," she hissed vehemently. "Traith Harker, Rein Pierson, and Rein's last of family—Taverin Badeau."

"Why are we thinking on this now?" the man asked. "Give it time; let us not think about them, and come back to—"

"Time? We have had time enough. Neither of them is going to give in. Neither of them is going to be able to be kept restricted." She slammed a fist onto a bureau. "We've had chances to kill Harker before, and we didn't! Chances to torment him until he *shriveled*, to beat secrets out of him until he was *smashed*, and instead, we let Ana do with him what she pleased."

"She ridded us of him," he responded. "We had time to become stronger, while Mistress and the rest weakened without him. Think of those we were able to kill with him gone; a whole half of the Council of the Presage! The Mistress is not as strong as she would have us believe, and their council is small now. There was nothing Harker could do about us when he was on the ship, and we destroyed over half their council."

"And in all that time, Traith Harker *still* didn't give in to us, even cursed on that ship! Ana just ruined things. Then our man did the worst possible thing he could do. He toyed with the woman and made the grave mistake that ended his life, thank the Devil. But now there is more than one, and the new Ms. Pierson will become more powerful than their leader. She nearly has. She'll be unstoppable. Their council is very powerful, Ben, despite their small numbers."

The man stood up and stretched. "You really think she is stronger than Traith?"

"Not in sheer strength, but in power and proficiency." The woman unlocked her bedroom door. "We need to surprise them. Traith has always been cautious when it came to us. He is hard to surprise. But both their minds will be distracted when they go to meet the girl, Taverin. Ben, they need to be weakened now. I do not care how many of our own die in the process; those two must be stopped before it's too late. First, we must get rid of the girl they are going to see. Make them weaker. Then we can try to restrain them once more. If it doesn't work, I don't care how powerful either of them is; we *kill* them. Tanya!"

After a long silence, another woman came down the hall with a small candle in her hand, covered in blood. Her long, auburn hair was tied in a braid hanging over her shoulder. "Interrupting a vampire during a perfect massacre of humans is unwise, Helena."

"Tanya, I need you to do something for me. I want you to kill the girl that is the last of Rein Pierson's family. Make her writhe."

The woman cocked her head in amusement. "You want me to kill her?"

"She's a damnation, Tanya! A human! It would be so simple! And now is the precise time to act. Traith will take Rein to see the girl in a fortnight. We will show up uninvited."

"How do you know this?" the man asked, pulling on a light robe. "The exact date, time?"

"How do you think I know? A small raven told me. Fool! My insight works in many ways. But be careful, all! We must kill the girl, not Rein or Traith yet. She'll suffer. Then he will suffer. Remember we want them alive, but if that is entirely impossible, we have no choice but to murder them."

Tanya looked at the small flame of her candle, put her fingers around it, and closed them tight, snuffing out the fire. "Murder is a virtue in my book, Helena."

chapter 47

t he street was filled with life, as was regular in those parts of town.
Ladies held umbrellas high to shade their delicate skin from a blistering sun, and gentlemen walked against them with a stride most
casual. It was a rather common-man town, but it was a wealthy one
nonetheless. The houses were quaint and lovely; gates swung open and
wagons parked in the dusty stretches of road; fields stretched across the
plains. But the plains were barren now, as if life outside of people was
dead. No horses made their homes in the grasslands any longer.

The area was *still* beautiful, but the hospital had enlarged itself, as had
the bank, the grocer, and the wine house. Old Mr. Henry's baker's shop
was gone, and the auction barn had been changed into a teahouse…
all in a few months. It was obvious that the fright of two people in their
village having disappeared had stirred something.

On the main corner, across the railroad tracks, on Sherwood Street,
there was a large, beautiful, dark green house with a black-shingled
roof. The shutters were old and rustic, and there was much acreage behind it. Grass covered the whole lawn, with small white flowers growing
in different, little patches around the sidewalk.

It was her old home.

Back about a mile was a boarding school. Barnard Institution—the
boarding school in which her father had left her.

She was walking slowly to the porch of the old, regal house.

"You have beautifully even teeth, Rein," he said with a stifled voice,
staring straight ahead of him at the door.

Rein wiped hair out of her eyes and attempted to put the stray
strands back into her chignon, staring at Traith with a low feeling. She
had vehemently been working with her powers the past two weeks. It
wasn't as hard as she'd thought it would be; but in particular use
that day was her ability to transform things with her mind, transform

herself. Whatever she willed, she could become. She could even will what others looked like.

It was odd…Rein thought Traith, at realizing her shape-shifting ability, would've been excited to be able to see what *he looked* like. She could become him, if she wanted, but he was entirely against it. He had said that it was something he didn't want to see again…the way he knew he looked. That, and he hated the idea of seeing her as a man.

Anyway, with that mastery, Rein was able to appear as she did when she was human: no red eyes, no pale skin, no *fangs*. She knew for a fact that Traith didn't like her resembling her old self. He was trying to forget her old image. She knew it haunted him.

"Traith," she finally said. "I can make you—"

"Please, Rein. You've never seen me when I was human, and I'd prefer you didn't get used to a more normal form of me."

"Do you not trust me?" She cocked her head and smiled.

"It's got nothing to do with trust, Rein, believe me."

She gave a rough sigh and said nothing more, knowing she could not win over his opinion. She approached the door, tapping the knocker.

"Do you even know anything of this man?" asked Traith.

She shrugged. "I don't."

She heard him sigh just as the door was opening, and a portly man with a head of combed over hair and thick eyebrows stood there with a blank smile on his face. She figured it was Hall.

"Good day," he paused a moment, scanning Rein. "You must be Rein Pierson. Stunning."

She chuckled with embarrassment, but a sudden caution took her over when she smelled whiskey on his breath. Traith stood still, his expression unwavering but intimidating nonetheless.

She recalled the brief mentioning of his alcoholism in Mistress's letter written to her. To go to Taverin promptly. There was danger brewing in her old home, and suddenly, Rein could feel it.

"Taverin's kin, right? I'm Bruce Hall," he said as he shook Traith's hand, and made a slight face.

Traith eased up a bit as he noted Hall's expression and realized the firmness of his own handshake. He smiled with apology.

"And you're her fiancé, are you not?" Hall gazed at Traith for a long spell. "Your eyes are quite strange in color. Mr. Harker's the name? Are you blind, sir?"

She was shocked at the curt frankness of the man.

Traith laughed quietly. "No, I can see." He glanced for a moment at Rein and then back at Hall. "It was a laboratory accident."

"A laboratory accident? My God, what a disfigurement! It must be awful for you to have to live with eyes like that." Hall stopped when Traith did not answer. "Forgive my bluntness and insolence; come on in! You made remarkable timing getting here."

Traith was acting peculiarly formal, but Rein knew he was fuming inside over the man's words. She sighed at him after Hall had gone in.

"Quite a disfigurement, Rein?" he muttered, lowering his head. "That isn't how you explained it to me."

She looked away from him and said nothing, shaking her head slightly. Although he was trying to annoy *her*, part of him joked in annoyance at *himself*, as always.

"And did you smell—?"

"Yes," she murmured. "Alcohol."

With an eerie feeling, she walked ahead of him, following Hall.

Mistress' words: *She would be working in a poor house or selling flowers on the streets, but, to her fortune, the man who has gotten claims of your home, Bruce Hall, is going to adopt her, giving her the chance to remain in your house. However, he is a heavy alcoholic; when you get back to England, I advise you to meet her promptly.*

Rein suddenly feared something terrible, but couldn't place what. When Hall even looked at her, she became instantly alarmed. It was as if someone was screaming directions at her within her head, yet it was her own voice, her own feelings. She just knew things, without reason. She knew that Hall was dangerous—had been dangerous—had done things—was not as innocent as he appeared—had Taverin scared. And after the incident with Traith's sister and their encounter with death, Rein knew better than to ignore any such feeling.

"Thank you, Mr. Hall," she said when she neared him. "Thank you for all of this. I know I didn't explain much in my letter."

"You're very welcome. She's upstairs, if you want to talk to her now. She's ready for you. I told her you were going to get here probably today or tomorrow, just so she would be prepared." He got quiet and leaned in. "Between you and me, I wasn't actually expecting you for another few days." He stood back and laughed. "Ah, do you want something to drink?"

Rein glanced at Traith, hoping he'd get the hint in her gaze that told him to acquiesce. He returned her stare once and immediately seemed to understand.

"I'll take some," he murmured hesitantly.

"All right then, one moment," Hall said, smiling and leaving for the kitchen.

She waited for Hall to leave before explaining her thoughts. "Traith," she whispered. "Something is wrong. We need to take Taverin from here."

"What?" he asked, checking to make sure Hall wasn't coming back yet. Why, now? We just got here."

She fingered her forehead. "I feel it. He's done bad things, and I want the girl out of here. My entire house reeks of whiskey. This man's turned it into a—"

"Here you are!" Hall announced, walking back into the foyer then handing Traith a small glass of a yellow-brown drink.

Traith's awkward smile told her easily that he was discomfited by the man's character, but he had to take the glass. "Thank you."

In his letter Hall had seemed like a man of intellect, but by his tone and cracking of voice, and by the smell on his breath, Rein's anxiety continued to develop.

"We can see her now?" Rein asked the stout and upsetting man.

"Oh yes. She just might be doing lessons in her room. Alone, of course."

Rein looked at Hall with a smile, but it left her face almost instantly when she began to feel ill again. Her anxiety worsened and became extremely foreboding. She realized that it wasn't only Hall that was making her head become so jumbled and disturbed. There was something more. Something more was going to happen. Something in connection with the evil she had yet to confront.

Without a second thought, Rein walked up to Hall and put her hands over his head. He grunted, but then he gradually looked baffled, then dazed, then expressionless. She dropped her hands to her sides and caught his suddenly limp body in her arms, slowly letting him fall to the ground.

She had played with his head. Erased part of his memory.

"Oh my God!" Traith exclaimed. "What the hell did you just do, Rein?"

She took a breath to turn the horror of what she'd just done into calm. "They're coming," she uttered, blinking hard in continuous attempt to remove fear from her mind. "Someone from that other council. I erased his immediate memory. I erased it up to his buying this house. I erased Taverin from his life."

Traith was staring at her in astonishment. "Are you serious?"

"Yes," she said, beginning to smile with contentment at the idea of avoiding such danger as she felt was coming. "Yes. He'll recover consciousness soon. Let's go talk to Taverin. We must bring her back with us, Traith." Her smile turned. "They'll kill her."

"Kill her?" he asked wildly. "You can feel them? The Mardinial Council?" When she didn't reply, he nodded slowly in agreement. "After you, then."

chapter 48

Her head was swimming with warm memories of her old home—
memories that made her ill with emotion when she stopped to
look around in silence. She turned into the hallway and walked up the
old, creaky stairs, Traith just behind.

As she climbed the stairwell, she saw an old, dusty, faded portrait
hanging on the wall. A portrait she was intimately familiar with. She
felt suddenly burdened with sadness, and stopped walking, staring at
the frame.

"What is that?" Traith asked.

Her eyes blurred. "It is a painting of my father when he was young,"
she murmured, "Standing in front of a portrait of my mother. She died
just after I was born. I'm the baby he's holding. All of us together, if
only for once."

Traith was silent, looking down after her words. He didn't know
what to say. Just as she began walking again, trying immensely hard to
stifle any sign of emotion, Traith spoke. "Look." She did, and saw that
he was holding the picture frame, only to make it vanish before them.
"It's at *home*, now."

She smiled with full gratitude, but felt as though she didn't have the
time to reminisce anymore than she'd already done *or* express her deep
feeling of thanks to her love—at least, not just *yet*.

"Thank you," was all she said before turning to finish the stairs.

It was so odd that that picture was even still there. She wondered
if that was how Hall believed her so willingly. That picture was of the
French girl's father, too, and he would still be recognizable to her.
But they would know that the baby in that picture wasn't Taverin;
it was Rein.

She saw an open door at the top of the stairwell. Her stomach began
fluttering, and she slowly approached the door, making sure Traith was
not more than a few feet behind her.

She peeked into the room that was once her own, knocking lightly.

The young lady was sitting on her bed, and she looked up and stared when she saw her, her eyes large and blue.

"May I come in?" Rein asked. "Taverin…right?"

The girl lit up and smiled. She jumped off of the bed and walked quickly over to Rein. "Oh my! You must be…Are you my sister?" she asked with excitement. "Rein, yes?"

Rein could immediately detect her French accent, and she smiled. "Yes."

The girl threw her arms around Rein tightly. Rein noticed a certain familiarity in the girl's manner and enthusiasm. Something about her dark hair and dramatic expressions. She reminded her of Saria.

"I can tell that you are! And *you*?" The girl asked, looking at Traith.

"I'm Traith Harker," he replied, smiling timidly.

She ran up to him and stared at him, her blue eyes wide. Rein could see him flinch a little at her approach. He clenched his teeth uneasily within his smile.

"My Lord, you must be ten feet taller than me!" She whirled around and hugged him, laughing. "But you're terribly handsome… *and* strapping."

She seemed a bit younger than fifteen because of her childish eagerness. Traith's arms hung limply in discomfort from her embrace.

He smiled oddly in gratitude. "T-Thank you."

"My! You two are not married are you?"

"Not yet," Rein replied, smiling and staring down at her ring.

"I knew not that my father had another daughter until Mr. Hall received your letter," the girl said, standing back. "But then again, I hardly knew about my father's life here in England."

Rein nodded, feeling the ice already breaking when the girl laughed with greeting. "I can tell you're from France," Rein said to make steady conversation. "How were you able to learn English so quickly?"

"I studied hard," Taverin returned with a merry giggle as she turned and plopped on her bed. "Father used to correct me on every little thing I said wrong, so I learned the language quickly."

Rein hated the idea of someone else calling her father their own. She was an only child. An only daughter.

"But there is no one here to speak French with," Taverin continued, "so I do not use it often. I want to be as English as I can."

"That's good," Rein said, forgetting her uneasy feeling. "You'll speak less and less broken English. I know French myself, but I was taught in school. Traith as well."

Rein took a seat on a sofa in the corner of the room, and Traith did the same. He relatively mimicked her every move because of his lack of knowledge and his shyness of the situation. But Traith had to be put at the back of her mind for the time being, though she found that extremely hard to do.

Looking at Taverin, Rein felt a little charmed in noticing how the girl's black hair resembled her own.

"It might seem odd, I know…" Taverin began with nervous laughter, "and I do not know how, or-or when, but I can…I can almost remember you both from somewhere, as if you were here, in a room like this once before."

Rein looked oddly into her half-sister's eyes, head tilted.

The girl looked a little dazed. "As if I've heard your voice before."

"I don't know how you could possibly think that," Rein said slowly, casually shooting Traith a wary glance. "I've never been to visit you before, but I'm glad I got the chance to today. I was never…" she swallowed the pain of her lie. "I was never told about you, Taverin. That's why I just came now. I would've been to see you so much earlier if I'd only known."

The girl was looking down. "I was not either. That is so terrible, isn't it?"

Taverin smiled, but as her eyes turned completely up, Rein noticed her expression weaken. No, it didn't just weaken; it turned to one of fright. She saw; something was wrong. Rein felt she had blown it already, yet she had no idea how.

Her heart sank at the girl's face; it was as if she was scared of her for some reason. Taverin's stare shifted behind her. Rein realized that there was a mirror behind the bed; a mirror neither she nor Traith were in.

Taverin stood up, her eyes large. They were darting back and forth between her and the mirror. Her voice cracked. "Why aren't you in my mirror?"

"Oh boy," Traith sighed sympathetically, keeping his head down to avoid any part of the conversation if he could.

Rein continued to study the mirror before meeting the girl's glare. She blinked hard, wishing her form would appear. They had just ruined their chance at secrecy. Had she even been planning on keeping it secret from her? They had to take her that day, that *hour*. Danger was coming; it was like the calm before the storm, and it ate at Rein's composure.

Taverin began speaking again before Rein could. "I know what you are," she said in a high, nervous tone. "You may be part my blood, but you are something different as well!" Her voice rose, horror stricken.

Rein looked for a moment as if she was unaware of what Taverin spoke of, but she realized that it would be hard to hide much else from the girl. The girl already knew. *She knew.* Rein could feel it in her head.

"Let me see your face," Taverin said, beginning to cry.

"Please, Taverin, what are you talking about?" she returned.

"You aren't in the mirror, Rein! You aren't an apparition; I *know* what you are, so show me!"

Rein felt desperately ill. "I can explain this to you if you only let me—"

"Your true face, you're hiding it. Can't you tell me the truth? I want to hear it from you." Her voice was hoarse. "I want to know the real truth about my sister and what happened to her when she disappeared. Show me what you really look like."

"What are you...How do you think you know this?"

Rein stopped and saw in the girl's mind that she indeed was scared to think the truth: that Rein was a vampire. But she knew. Somehow, for some reason, *she knew*. What was she to do? She couldn't possibly *show* her.

"Please," the girl murmured. "I know you *died.*"

She was unsure what to do.

The girl stared at her, as if waiting for her response. "Please. I won't be afraid."

Without more thought, Rein felt herself changing. She felt her teeth lengthen. Her nails instantly darkened. Her skin became pale. Her changes were in full view for the girl to see. Rein met her eyes directly, as if piercing through her haze. Taverin's expression stiffened when she stared wholly at her. She sat a moment and studied her, and Rein fought to say something. But what? The moment was too awkward to address. She had to wait.

Traith was sitting stiff, trying to avoid eye contact so his eye color would not be pointed out to add to the confusion of the situation.

"I know what you are. I knew I did. That's why you changed yourself!" Taverin stared, the hint of terror in her eyes suddenly gone. "What *are* you? Please, tell me." She looked deep into her eyes.

Rein stood and slowly walked toward and sat on the bed beside the girl. She put her soft hand over Taverin's worried cheek. "No wrong will come to you from me, I assure you. I *am* your real half-sister; I've not once lied to you. I've done nothing for you not to trust me, have I?"

"What *are* you?"

"Do you trust me?" Rein asked sincerely, staring hard at her.

It was imminent. They only had minutes left.

"I...yes, I do," Taverin whispered in fear.

"Then you must come with me. Your life is in grave danger, and I can take you somewhere safe. But I must do so *now*."

The girl did not reply, but stared at Rein with her large, watery eyes. Then she nodded.

Traith quickly gave his attention to Rein. "Are there any...things you want from here?" he asked. "I can...I mean, furniture, anything. Are there clothes left?"

"I don't know."

"Yes, Rein!" Taverin declared. "I found an entire room full of clothing up here. Hall won't come up here. But are all those beautiful clothes yours? They're all so lovely!"

Rein was stunned to the point that she couldn't reply for a few seconds. The girl had gone from being quite scared to comfortable. "My clothes are still here? I wouldn't know how to thank you, Traith, to bring all this..."

"Always my pleasure, Rein. Take her down the steps to the entrance and I'll take care of everything as quickly as I can. How long?"

"Minutes."

He nodded and left the room.

"Where is he going?"

"To gather any and all of my things to bring home with me. That is where I'm taking you, Taverin. Home, with me."

While Traith transferred furniture, clothes, the painting of her family that hung on the stairwell wall, and numerous other things back to the castle, Rein had made her way to the bottom of the stairs, careful not to let Taverin see Hall lying unconscious on the floor.

Barely a minute had gone by when Rein heard a set of quick and light footsteps coming down the stairwell. Traith appeared from behind the corner, nothing in his hands and standing straight. He walked to her and smiled at her as if letting her know everything was taken care of.

"Anything and everything," he said, winking. "Are we ready?"

chapter 49

raith gently let both of them out of his grasp. He'd brought them to the castle, into the tower spare bedroom—the only other tower bedroom besides the master bedroom, which was just down the hall.

Before she even had a chance to react to the sudden change of setting, Taverin gasped in awe of the room he'd brought them to. Although Rein's previous house was definitely grandeur, it was common architecture for the time. His castle was built in a Romanesque fashion; Medieval, with grand ceilings and stone from top to bottom; something he had always found antiquely enjoyable.

"Do you like it?" Rein asked softly.

Traith found a shadowed corner and stood in it. After all, this technically wasn't his conversation to be had. Rein had to talk to the girl relatively alone, but he had that funny feeling that she wanted him there. So he stayed, merely to watch and speak if needed.

Rein looked like a beautiful, elegant girl with an unbearable stress laid upon her. Her dark chunks of hair were slowly falling from her casual attempt at a knot, and her face looked tired. Even her once vibrant dress seemed to fade out with the strain Rein was feeling. She was in a difficult situation—just after his own transformation he hadn't had anything to recover from but depression over his unearthly state. Rein had that along with having to deal with *him*, an "experienced" vampire, mental powers beyond his own imagination, and the surreal world; all that, not even to mention a sister she never knew who would present a problem in either natural *or* supernatural realms.

But, as with every situation he'd ever seen her presented with, she handled it with grace and poise. Somehow, when she spoke, her voice came out soothingly enough to make even the word "vampire" seem ordinary and attractive. For someone so young—in reality, still only twenty—she was highly mature and wise.

He left his thoughts on Rein behind. He, who had always been a concise man, could go on and on about each appealing detail Rein bore. But it was the girl—Taverin—who needed attention.

She seemed ecstatic over the view of the chamber, but she calmed herself down to think clearly; to ask the questions that needed to be asked.

"What *is* going on?" she pleaded, slowly sitting in a chair in the side of the huge chamber. "How am I *here*?"

"Taverin," Rein began, but she was stopped.

"Just tell me what you are, Rein," she spoke, becoming impatient for the truth. "I want to know what you *really* are. Tell me."

Rein looked gravely into her eyes. "I'm a *vampire*, Taverin."

Taverin backed up a little in the chair. She blinked quickly a few times. "Oh…" she stuttered. "I…I'm not scared of you. It's a strange—t-terribly frightening. Things like that…they aren't *real*. But I…how can this be? You *lied* to everyone about your death?"

"No," Rein replied swiftly. "No, I did not lie. I *did* die. Do you suppose that I should've let my own father see me like this?"

"You don't look that different at all," she said.

Rein swallowed her words. The girl shocked her; she shocked *him*. She wasn't even scared. Traith saw an expression surface on Rein's face that warmed him, especially within the problematic state of affairs they were in. An expression of *relief*. Taverin had said she didn't look different at all, and that small sentence, no matter how many times he were to say it, meant so much more to Rein in hearing from fresh lips.

"I just saw you change," the girl said. "Just…change. That would've been frightening for him to see. But not for me."

Rein's eyes narrowed. "Not for you?"

"I *knew*," the girl said.

Rein couldn't reply for a moment, and she finally took a break and sat on the bed to be comfortable. "How did you *know* about this, Taverin?"

"I am not sure. But I did. Somehow I did. I *do* trust you, even though I do not know you. That is why I can easily learn to live with it; because somewhere in my heart I knew."

Rein was as bewildered as Traith was.

A tear unexpectedly fell from Taverin's eye, but she embraced Rein. "Oh please," she said as she held onto her, "I can stay here, can I not? I don't know what danger you took me from, and I hardly know you, but I have no other family, and Mr. Hall is…" Her voice died down to a whisper. "Rein, he is a drunk. He is hardly ever lucid, and I…he makes me—"

"He makes you nervous," Rein finished with despair.

She hesitated in her words. "Yes. I want to be on your side so I never have to worry or be frightened. You met me today, so if *you* meant to hurt me, you would have by now." Taverin spoke fast and between sharp breaths of sorrow as she cried.

Rein watched her, confused. A sort of dumbness overwhelmed her. The girl's manner changed from second to second.

She stood and took a seat next to Taverin. She lifted the petite girl's chin. "I knew I would need to tell you about this," Rein said. "You are old enough; that is, in fact, why I came to see you." She looked at the small smile beginning to creep up the girl's face. "And I wanted to get to know you, Taverin," she said. "Really. I do."

chapter 50

the faint sound of the breeze hitting the balcony doors woke Rein, and her eyes opened slowly. She blinked to get the drowsiness out and sat straight, her neck stiff from how she'd slept. Looking around, she saw that Taverin was curled in the huge bed, sleeping soundly and peacefully. After an hour or two of talking, the girl had fallen asleep—in the middle of some explanation Rein couldn't exactly remember as she, herself, had been just as exhausted.

She couldn't understand how Taverin was actually peaceful—like she wasn't scared at all, even though she'd been told all about Rein's transformation, love for Traith; really everything. It was, in reality, rather inspirational in the way it was handled by the girl.

Rein weakly lifted her arms and let her hair down, still seated in the giant armchair she'd fallen asleep in while talking to Taverin. Her head was sore from where the pins were holding her hair up. She scratched her head softly, enjoying the alleviating feeling of her hair down and long around her face. She stretched out her legs, untucking her feet from underneath her, and then stood. She tried smoothing out the wrinkles in her grey dress that resulted from how she'd slept, but found it useless.

Although she didn't want to leave the girl alone, Rein wanted to find Traith. After looking once more at Taverin, Rein left the chamber for the hall, trying very hard not to let her boot heels click too loudly. It had to be extremely late; the spare chamber had been so dark that it obviously was still some time in the night.

She opened the door to the master bedroom as quiet as she could, in case

Traith was asleep too. He fidgeted at the noise of her entrance but eventually grew still. Since she wasn't tired, she simply walked past the bed and out onto the balcony. She leaned on the rail, the wind blowing her hair around her face. She began thinking.

Her mind was developing at a tremendous rate. It was almost as if she *could* see with both her eyes *and* her mind. It was like an unfathomable advancement in vision and in thought. She could know things if she wanted. She could change people's minds. She just *could* now; no training was needed. It was just a matter now of channeling that near limitless power. And there were so many questions she had about it; so many things she wished could be answered to make her life a bit easier. But that was impossible.

The only answer she *had* received so far was that she needed to *enhance* whatever power she had. It was a close call at her old home; the Mardinial Council, or someone from it, had almost been there. If they'd come, there would've been an altercation, and she would've had to fight—she would've had to use her powers against them.

Mistress had said she would become extremely powerful; she realized she needed to begin that transformation by becoming stronger in her heart. She was a vampire. She had to work with it.

She shook her head and held it, resting her weight on the stone railing. More than that was on her mind, though. Taverin—how was she going to adjust to having a sister? How was Traith going to adjust to having a young girl with him? He wasn't used to people, especially not adolescent girls.

A rustling, then a masculine moan sounded. She turned from the night sky and her thoughts and realized she had left the balcony doors wide open. Traith must have felt the breeze, and she saw him sit up slowly, staring at her.

He murmured her name and got up, fumbling out the doors in a haze. The wind blew through his hair, and his shirt was off so his scar-scattered muscles rippled sleekly down his smooth abdomen.

She touched his face, and he gently held her wrist. "I want to know something."

"Do you?" he asked as he rubbed his eyes, his words slurred a little by the lingering fatigue. "What's that?"

"Tell me about the people in the other—the Mardinial Council. Explain them, and how you know them."

He smiled in his perplexity. "Why?"

She paused in thought. "They were almost there, Traith," she murmured. "I almost had to fight them, and I wasn't prepared. The only conflict I've ever had was with Dr. Campbell, and that was alarming enough. I would've been utterly useless facing more than one immortal; *experienced* ones nonetheless. I've still only got the knowledge that an average twenty year old girl would."

"Not really," he said. He sighed and stepped back a little. "There are four you should know about, I suppose. The rest are just aggravating creatures that seem to multiply. Tanya is the Mardinial First Hand, a vampire. She's nasty. Cruel—nearly worse than Helena, whom you've yet to meet. Helena is just hideously seductive. Terrifying yet beautiful. At least to men, for some reason."

"Beautiful?"

"In the most grotesque way, yes," he said, laughing. "There's her 'husband,' a werewolf, Ben Smoke." Traith shrugged. "Ben is mostly controlled by Helena. He's her toy. And the oaf is completely void of any personality. And lastly, there's my sister."

Noting the way he said that, Rein didn't press him further. "So what would they want Taverin for?" she asked, recalling the eerie feeling that beleaguered her just before they'd left the house.

"She is your blood, Rein," he said, his voice hoarse. "Anything connected to you, now, could be in danger. It hurts to say, but…maybe you should be thankful you don't have family."

She didn't reply, then, but looked at him. He was right, in a sense, but it *did* hurt to say. He was staring out into the wood, and despite the severity of the situation, she couldn't help but experience those wildly in-love feelings that were excited each time she looked at his perfectly toughened face, worn from years of fighting, yet so handsome.

"They wanted to attack differently by attacking your heart," he said, completely oblivious to her desiring thoughts. "They don't want us *dead*—or, at least not worse off than we already are—but they want us. Just, for some reason, not yet."

She was slightly confused, but she didn't question him for a moment. He looked so lost in thought, like he was trying to figure things out.

He turned his gaze to her, and it was grave. "Rein, that council has thousands more people than our own does. Especially now, after my absence. They destroyed half of our council because I wasn't here."

"How, exactly?" she asked, lifting herself to sit on the rail.

"Battles," he whispered pensively. "Assaults on us. We don't create people like they do, that's what differentiates us. Apparently our council did *nothing* while I was gone. They lost everything each time they fought; each time they tried to help some victim that the other council had taken. I didn't realize that I was that powerful in this council, but apparently I am—or was." He paused. "I noticed when I returned, with you, that many of those I once knew were gone. Lorena is the only one left that I knew before I was cursed. She has always fought alongside me whether I asked her to or not." He smiled. "She never acted this desperate until she recognized I'd found you."

"How reassuring," Rein said, smirking.

"She gets her head in the game in the right times, but every other waking moment it's in the clouds."

Rein nodded, but couldn't say anything. She didn't entirely like what he'd said, but she would get over it. He was honest, and she knew that.

"And *you*," he abruptly enunciated. "You are something so different for this council, Rein. You're becoming so powerful." He nearly laughed in amusement. "I mean, you can do almost anything you want with your mind. I've yet to see you do the same thing twice! In thousands of years, even, Mistress said she has never seen anything like you before."

"I hate it when you do that," she said quietly, hopping off the rail.

He looked surprised. "What?"

She rubbed her finger down his neck. "You confuse me. So now, I believe, I should just stop asking questions and state what I do know."

"And what's that?" he asked, pulling her close, seemingly forgetting any and all of his thoughts about the councils.

"Well," she said, smiling and cocking her head to the side, "you *tempt* me so. I cannot be entirely serious with you right now."

His arms enveloped her. "And how am I tempting you?"

"Well you stand there and give me full view of your handsome face, and you have no shirt on…"

"I assure you I had no intention of distracting you by my half-dressed state and what you call 'handsome' features, darling."

"You assure me? Oh, thank you, Traith. I love your archaic speech."

He laughed in the dawn at her teasing response. "*Archaic?*"

"In the best way," she murmured, drawing him close. "A man that looks so young that speaks so old-fashioned. I do adore it."

"I doubt I can marry someone who mocks me," he said wryly.

"And then you always ruin romantic moments with your sarcasm," she said, crossing her arms in a huff, smiling at him and leaning back on the railing.

He chuckled, winning back her retreated form and holding her. "My sarcasm changes the fact that I'm romantic, does it? My towering opinion of you doesn't ever change that quickly."

"My opinion of you never *changes*," she protested.

"Not even when nearly everything I try to do goes wrong? You know, I'm more like a lure for disaster."

Rein turned and faced the blackness, and she felt his head rest on her shoulder, and his hands make their way around her waist.

"You know, I never thought of it before," he murmured.

"Of what?"

"Purchasing your home."

She spun around and gazed at him fast, thrill hitting her. "*What?*"

"I mean, why not? Hall doesn't need it; not in his state. You have money of your own even without mine to the point that we could technically buy anything in this world. I know it means a lot to you, and even if we live here, we always have a place in England, where our hearts belong. It's perfect. And because we aren't always there, we can hire live-ins to take care of it."

"Really?" She felt chills run down her body in excitement. "Traith, I—that would be so—*oh!*"

He went to say something, but it was muffled under the restraint of her passionate kiss. He laughed and returned it by dipping into her, holding her body within his.

"You really are wonderful, do you know that?" she gasped, holding back and almost shaking with ecstasy.

He shook his head and laughed. "Why are you out here anyway?" he asked. "Didn't you want to sleep?"

"I'm not very tired." She rested on him, and he took her up in his arms. She laughed. "But I'm not in opposition to you *luring* me into bed, being the *lure* that you claim you are."

"I don't think I need to lure you," he said. "You seem willing enough."

They faded into the darkness, the cool wind caressing them as they turned to leave the balcony.

chapter 51

𝄆

a bird song filled the quarters despite there being no window. Taverin heard him singing through the stone walls and iron and glass balcony doors. She awoke from her particularly peaceful sleep the next morning with ease. She opened her eyes and blinked a few times. But when she sat up, she felt her stomach knot. She glanced around her.

She was in that lavish chamber.

She slowly began remembering what had happened last night. Nervousness swelled inside her, and she felt ill. So much had gone on that she felt lost for a moment. She breathed in deep, settling her heartbeat. She had been so exhausted.

Taverin Badeau thought back on her relatively recent departure from France, when that man came in and said she was his. She was, she supposed, but he had still taken her from the only world she knew: Cherbourg, France.

*Cherbourg…*where handsome girls met dashing men, where theater and balls were common, where she was able to sit at parties and listen to beautiful piano music with friends and the suave William Treau. *William.*

No, she would not see William again. She hadn't seen William since she left France months ago. And on top of it all, she had been thrown into a world she had never thought to be real. A terrifying world. A world in which neither she nor anyone like her could ever feel safe.

But she now had a sister. Rein Pierson. Almost a brother-in-law, too.

She put all doubt aside; it was going to be her first real day in the Harker Castle, and she was anxious to explore it. It was so vast. It had to be. The chamber she was in was as large as a ballroom!

She shoved off the sheets and, in her bare feet and nightclothes, ran into the bathroom. The air was warm, yet the stone cooled her feet. She smiled into the mirror of the washroom and saw that there was a hair rat already placed on a stand next to her. She curled and tightened her hair into a bun with it and then brushed her teeth with a toothbrush. When she had finished, she walked back to the bedroom and noticed her slippers placed under the large, medieval bed. She yawned, tiptoed to the bed, and grabbed the slippers, tying the laces around her ankles. She spent a few moments admiring the silk and lace surrounding the exterior of the shoes; they were slippers her father had bought her. She walked over to the door leading to the hallway and opened it, but she didn't walk out. She turned and quickly ran to the balcony windows and opened them. She wanted to see what it looked like out there, and how high she was.

She stepped out; it was terribly windy outside, and she quickly peered over the rails. She had looked out there the previous night, but wasn't able to perceive the ground in the dark. Now she could see that there was a large plain a couple hundred yards or so down. She was on the highest floor, and she saw that the castle grounds were cut off and engulfed by cool, dark woods.

Suddenly the wind picked up and whistled, blowing intensely. She turned and ran back inside, closing the doors and leaning on them, panting heavily. The wind was coming on strong, and the drop was too terrifying to stare down at. She smiled, still panting, when she noticed Traith standing in front of her in the hallway.

"Good afternoon," he said with a small smile. "How was your night?"

"Afternoon?" she asked, her voice slowing.

He made a short, quiet, half-laugh. "You've been asleep the entire morning. It's past twelve."

"Dear," she replied, surprised, finally ceasing her panting. "That gave me quite a scare. We're rather high up here, aren't we?"

"Yes," he said with a smile.

She liked his smile; it was boyish and innocent.

"Um, before I fail to remember, I put your belongings in the closed over there," he said, pointing to a closed door within the room. "I got them from Rein's—er, your house."

"My *things*?" she asked in a high, sharp squeak. "*Really*? Oh *thank* you! Thank you, Monsieur Harker!"

"Don't call me that, dear," he spoke, rubbing the towel through his hair to dry it. "Traith is fine."

His hair was hanging in front of his face, somewhat damp. He had a white blouse on, but it was obvious his body was shining with sweat. She shuddered when she saw how scarred up he was, and a chill stung her when she saw the scar at his throat. The bite mark.

She snapped out of her stare. "O-Oh, sorry," she said. "I was just in awe of your scars. I didn't mean to stare."

He glanced down at himself and looked back up at her. "I'm used to that sort of first impression on people—'I'm sorry; I didn't mean to stare at you.'" He smiled, almost laughed. "I know; there are a lot of them. Like souvenirs."

"From fights?"

He hesitated, but returned words amiably. "Yes."

"You must have been through a lot, by the looks of all those," she said in a quieter voice. He didn't reply. She smiled at his silence. "You are quite a shy one, aren't you?"

He smiled a bit fuller, a little shocked by her question. "I am, I suppose. I guess I'm just used to frightening people without the intent to do so."

She shook her head fast. "Oh no, not at all!"

"Well I just heard you slam the doors from the hallway on my way to shower off," he said, still with a dashing smile up his face. "Rein and I were in the training foyer." He threw his towel over his shoulder. "Rein's…practicing some things. She…well, if you need to eat or anything else you should go talk to her and she can make you anything you want. She can *make things*, in a manner."

Taverin sat on her bed cheerfully. "Rein can make my food? She has many powers, doesn't she? Like what she can do with her mind…and you can put or bring people places, right?"

He sighed and leaned on the door. "Yes. Teleportation."

"What are some of your other ones?"

"I'll show you them another time. The others aren't so…sociable. But go see Rein. She's two floors below us. God, you know what? I'll just…"

She must have had a confused look on her face, because she saw him smile and tilt his head back. He waved two fingers around as he walked away, and suddenly Taverin realized that Rein was standing right in front of her.

She was in the training foyer. A few sconces hung from the otherwise bare stone walls, and strange equipment filled the large room from corner to corner. There were obstacles made from barrels, bags filled with sand, and targets made out of odd things. Guns of all sizes were around. There were swords and daggers on the ground, and every one that had been thrown into the targets had hit the bull's-eye.

"Those are Traith's hits," Rein said.

Taverin quickly shifted her focus toward Rein.

"Mine are not quite as good, but I'm getting there."

Taverin stared back at the targets. "My."

"It was convenient he brought you down here," Rein said as she walked toward her. "I was headed up to see you just now. I checked on you earlier, but you were still sleeping. You slept a good while."

"Oh," Taverin murmured, still in awe of the hall she stood in.

Rein smiled and sighed. "You must be hungry. If you tell me what you like, I can fill the dinner hall up with food for you. Unfortunately Traith and I have no need to use it." Rein cleared her throat and forced a smile.

"How can you make food if you don't—?"

"I can generate things, in a sense." She wiped her forehead with her arm. "How was your night?"

"It was extraordinarily comfortable, and I actually slept well."

"That's good." She paused. "I was thinking about something. You miss France, don't you?" she asked.

"Yes—you said you wouldn't read my mind, Rein!" Taverin replied.

Rein turned her head to the side, her dark hair bunching on her shoulder. "I let that thought slip. Something as important as having a lover somewhere can drastically change what you miss, can't it?"

Taverin's eyes widened. "Rein!" she said, finally smiling. "You have so many different aptitudes!"

"Who is your lover, Taverin?" she asked, placing her hands on her hips.

Taverin felt her face flush as she struggled to respond. "Well...his name is William..."

"Handsome name," Rein said. "Well, Traith can send you to...?"

"Oh, it's called Cherbourg."

"Well, Traith can send you to *Cherbourg* in a heartbeat whenever you want. And you can see dear William."

Taverin felt as though her heart had exploded with joy. She let out a squeak of excitement and then threw her arms around Rein.

"Does that make you a little more at ease, Taverin?" Rein asked.

"Oh, so much so!" she replied with unfathomable exhilaration. "Oh thank you!"

Rein smiled and lifted her arms to her hair to fix it. "So are you going to make that list or am I supposed to guess what foods you like to eat?"

chapter 52

"W here are you going, Rein?"

Rein laughed and ran around the shop square. "Come on, Saria! I want to show you something!"

Rein watched Saria laugh and follow behind. She looked ahead and witnessed with building excitement the store she was bringing her friend to; the large, exquisite dress shop a little outside Teesdale.

It was the largest, most expensive shop in that part of England. Rein knew the owner, due to the fact that she went there often with Saria. But today was different; she had a different sort of dress in mind today.

The two entered the shop slowly, and Rein always seemed to just lose her breath when she gazed upon the thousands of dresses in the store. She went to the counter and whispered something in the clerk's ear. He smiled and turned back through a door behind the counter.

"What is this about, Rein?" Saria asked, huffing out of breath.

Rein bit her lip. "Just wait!"

The clerk reappeared with a brilliant, long, full, white dress in his hands. His arms were high trying not to let it touch the ground; he even had a part of it draped around his shoulder.

Saria gasped from beside her. "Rein! My Lord, Rein!"

Rein laughed. "Isn't it beautiful?"

"The absolute most gorgeous, darling dress I've ever seen!" Saria's eyes got larger, as did her smile. "Your wedding dress, Rein?"

Rein opened her eyes to see a stone ceiling above her. She sat up and shook her head. She was on a sofa in the dressing room in bare feet and a chemise with the dress she was to wear beside her.

It wasn't a wedding dress, and Saria was nowhere.

Rein fell back down upon the sofa and held her head. She could hear Saria's voice in her head, the only person in the world that would be so happy about her engagement. The only person who would love to help pick a dress, or choose a hairstyle, or…

But she was gone. Rein had not yet accepted that. It had only been a few months, yet the time had dragged on for an eternity.

Rein sat up again and tried to forget about her dream—the same one she'd been having since Traith proposed. She stretched her arms and then stood, picking the dress up that had been partly lying on her. It was half wrinkled. She sighed and went to hang it up.

At least her old home was hers again. To Rein, owning it kept many memories of her normal life alive and warm, especially ones of Saria. Traith had gone to England and bought it off of the county, who had taken hold of it because of Hall's inability to pay. He had even hired people—maids, butlers—to live in and keep it up while they weren't there. It was the most perfect thing Traith could have done.

Then the door brought Rein back to reality. It swung open, and Taverin came frolicking in with merriment.

She had been in Cherbourg the past fortnight staying at a friend's estate. During the time, despite the entertainment the girl was enjoying there, Rein had kept a close eye on her without showing her face to the people. Taverin had not known she had been watching, either.

"Rein!" the girl called, running in and throwing her arms around her. "Traith made sure to bring me here at exactly six o'clock as he said, even though he is in a meeting with the council!" She was laughing with pleasure.

"Was your stay agreeable, Taverin?" she asked.

"Oh, entirely! William Treau came to visit most every day! He is indeed tremendously dashing! His manner is so amiable and…Are you well? You look sad."

"I just woke up," Rein said, hinting a smile. "I dozed off when I was organizing my clothes. Had a bad dream, that's all."

Taverin quietly took a seat on the couch. "What was it about?"

"Nothing," Rein said, shaking her hands. "Don't worry about me."

"Honestly, what?"

Rein turned and tied the bodice on the hanging dress. "Just…about Saria, the girl who—"

"Died. Your best friend, right?"

Rein paused, nerves causing her to wipe down the dress to try and get wrinkles out, trying hard not to show deep emotion regarding the subject. "Yes. It's hard…she was my dearest friend, and now she isn't here."

"I can be your new best friend, Rein," Taverin said, looking down.

Rein felt her chest tighten and a glimmer of a smile touch her face. She slowly turned to face the girl. "Yes, you absolutely can," she rasped.

"I am younger some, and we do not know each other thoroughly yet, but I want to be there for you when you're sad like this, Rein, since Saria cannot. Traith is there for you, but he is a man; it is different, I understand. I have nobody either, so I yearn for that."

She left her wardrobe and sat beside Taverin, looked at her for a moment, and then hugged her tight. "Thank you, sweetheart," she said in the girl's ear. She loosened her arms from Taverin and sat back. "So tell me more about William, then. What does he look like?"

"Well," she began with a blush, "he has long, reddish-brown hair he usually ties back in a ribbon, and he is a very well respected man, as his older brother and sister have quite a fortune. Not at all as muscular as Traith, but his humor is remarkable! He must always be the center of attention. Very sociable."

There was a knock on the door, and Rein looked up to see Traith standing there. He appeared stressed.

"What happened?" Rein asked, sitting back from the girl. "Why do you look so upset?"

"I found out that the Mardinial Council is cloning more and more—"

"What is cloning?" she asked, standing then nearing him.

He looked down, and he took a breath. "Duplication of a person into another, or two other, or three other; mainly duplication with additional synthetics like disfiguring the clone into having claws, or hands of knives, or I don't know—anything they could possibly desire to transform a body with."

"Humans? Like civilians?"

"Yes, but also vampires, werewolves, witches, ghosts…Do you know what a Minotaur is, Rein? Or the undead?"

"Isn't a minotaur a man merged with a bull?" Traith nodded as she asked the other question. "And aren't…we, undead?"

"Yes, but these are different—these are hideous corpses come alive and that can only be destroyed by beheading..." Traith stopped and looked at Taverin. "Forgive me, girl, I didn't..."

Rein turned and looked at Taverin, but she only seemed shocked rather than frightened. She seemed more like a sponge soaking in the information willingly.

"No, no, pretend I am not here, Traith," Taverin said. "It does not frighten me; I want to know what you must do to fix these things."

Traith hesitated, his mouth open. He closed it. "You are as odd as your sister, then," he said, smiling. "Perhaps not quite."

Rein cocked her head. "So why are you telling me all this, anyway? What else happened?"

Traith leaned back on the wall, sighing, and ran his fingers through his hair. "They outnumber us, from what average we can assume, at *least* a hundred to one. And they have an attack planned, but they're holding it for something. Once they unleash their attack, it is inevitable that one council will cease to be, and it looks as though the odds are in their favor." There was a long silence. "They want us, Rein. You and I. Alive. I was the most powerful person in our council before you, and now you will be more powerful than me. That's what they wanted when I was on the ship—me to surrender to them. And that's what they want now. It just worries me to think what they will try in order to persuade us to give in now." He turned as if to walk out the door. "I'm sorry I scared you, but I needed you to know. I need to *think*..."

And he disappeared.

"Dear God," Rein said softly. She shook her head, trying to get foreboding thoughts out of her mind.

Or was her mind telling her something? It was so hard to differentiate between what were thoughts of *possibility* and what were thoughts of *prophecy*.

chapter 53

the next day was as dreary as the last had been. After Traith's panic about the Mardinial Council, Rein knew she had to get her mind to stop playing with the matter, and Taverin's mind *off* it. So with the transportation aid from Traith, Rein took Taverin to the expensive dress shop just outside Teesdale—the largest one in that part of England, and the one in her dream.

Taverin was a material girl; she liked shiny things. So they laughed and bought a few dresses each, and Rein felt herself growing much closer to the girl. She was indeed a good replacement for Saria, if there could be one.

But, despite the few words and mental signals exchanged to get to and fro, Rein hadn't spoken with Traith since the previous day. When she returned to the castle with the girl, Traith had been barely awake. He was deep in thought for the remainder of the night, and she had left him sleeping in his study, with notes and papers and quills about him.

And he was still in there upon daybreak.

Opening the near-vaulted door as quietly as she could, Rein could see Traith, now awake, concentrating deeply on his writing.

"I missed you last night, Traith," she purred.

His head shot up fast. She saw him smile. "You're startling, Rein, you know that?"

She had her hands on her hips, but dropped them as she walked in. "And what is that supposed to mean, Traith?"

She bent down, wrapped her arms around him from the back, and leaned her face against his, staring down at his paperwork. The enticing scent of his skin triggered the hair on her arms to stand on end.

"Stunning is a synonym," he replied, turning his face to her. "If you prefer that one."

She kissed his cheek, and walked around to kiss his lips. He pulled her to him on his lap and smiled as he gazed at her.

"So what do you dare interrupt me for?" he said, trying to act serious.

"I want to know what's going on inside that handsome head of yours. I passionately hate reading minds unless I must, so you have to explain."

He tilted his head back against the cushioned chair they sat in. "Taverin is in grave danger. I knew that. So I've been searching for a tactic—something I could surprise them with, but, thus far, I've come up with nothing. It is only a matter of time until they try to kill or, more likely, take Taverin hostage in an attempt to get one of us to surrender on her behalf. But you *do* know that if they get her and all works as they desire, they'll murder her *anyway*. If we beat them in that rumble, they'll send all they've got after us, and we have to fight to the death."

"That's terribly morbid, Traith Harker, for you to sit for a whole day and contemplate over."

"I've contemplated over worse." He gently eased her off his lap, and stood up beside her. "Just keep a close eye on Taverin, because they will strike when we least expect it—hours, days, months, or even longer than that."

"Of course," she replied. "I have been."

"Where is she now?"

"Just across the hall, in the lounge, doing English grammar work. I told her for those dresses she got she had to work her mind a little."

He smiled and sighed, closing the book on the table. "I just wish it would happen sooner rather than later. Get it over with. I'm ready now, and the suspense of not knowing when is the worst—"

"Now sounds about good," a voice hissed. "I'm ready, too."

Rein's head shot around.

It was a tall, thin woman, and her auburn hair was tangled in a mess around her face—covering pitch black eyes. She was covered entirely in blood—the most disgusting and monstrous woman Rein had ever seen.

"Nice to see you, Traith," the woman said, grinning. "It's been so many years, and I've missed rivaling you! It was...how long? One hundred and ten years ago? Right before you were cursed onto the *Olde Mary!*"

Traith jumped over the chair, and shook his head with a crooked smile, tossing a glass paperweight in his hands. He held it as it fell from the air for a moment. "Thanks, Tanya," he said. "No more suspense. What, were you waiting for your cue?"

"You think you have this all figured out, don't you, Harker?" she laughed, licking her teeth.

"Aw, come on," he replied, holding up the paperweight, studying it. "Give me a little credit, Tanya. I've been doing pretty well at predicting you all so far, considering I was oblivious to this world for a hundred years stuck on a *ship*."

Suddenly he lit the paperweight and pitched it at Tanya, and it shot with perfect precision through the air. The glass ball exploded just before it reached the woman, and she was impaled by the shards of it. The glass shaved into her so deeply that Rein couldn't see them anymore.

Tanya looked down and dug her fingernails into her side through the flesh. The whole hand nearly disappeared, then reappeared completely red with a shard of glass in its grasp. Then she did it again to the one in her cheek and the one in her arm. She threw the glass pieces onto the ground and licked her hand. Her head was cocked, and as the blood stained the area around her lips, a grin stretched.

"We left you a little cloning surprise, too," she said as calmly as if she hadn't felt pain at all, beginning to snigger wildly.

Rein had no idea what that meant, but she realized she needed to get Taverin as fast as she could. She ran to the door, but she heard a crack, and, turning to look back at Traith, she saw Tanya's form nearly on top of her. In the next moment, all was black.

Traith shook his head from under the stones Tanya had thrown at him, and he vanished from under them as fast as he could. Rein and Tanya had disappeared instantly, and he had no idea where to.

They hadn't taken Taverin? They wanted Rein first?

He ran to the doorway where Rein had been and came to a halting stop at the sight before him.

Bodies.

There were *bodies everywhere.* They lined the floor, and extended all the way down the hall. He squinted in disgust and had to take a step back at the stench.

Blood, flies, and corpses freshly beheaded or mangled were strewn everywhere he could see. Innocent people.

How long had Tanya been in the damned castle?

He phased into the room across the hall that Taverin was in and saw her running for the door he was suddenly in front of. She ran into him, and after a moment of shock, looked up at him with fright in her eyes.

"Lord, Traith, what just happened? What's out there?"

He held her shoulders and thanked God that he'd made it to her before she saw what was outside the door.

"They came...took Rein—"

"*Took Rein*? Why won't you let me out the door?"

"Just...I don't want you out there, all right? Stay in here a moment. I need to look at something."

He vanished back into the hall and materialized standing on a body. He jumped off fast, onto the bloodstained stone. He shivered; *so many*. He looked around, trying to find someone, just someone, alive. Maybe one, barely alive. But as he stared around him, the hall like an unearthed graveyard, he realized that everyone was dead, and a part of each body was cut off somewhere or another. It was a demonstration. The Mardinial Council was giving a demonstration of what they were capable of, in both mass murdering and cloning. And now he would have to dispose of everything—but not before he won the battle that needed to be won.

He heard a gasp, and his heart dropped. He turned and saw Taverin standing in the doorway, the door opened inward. Her hand was over her mouth in a mist of panic, her face pale, tears falling.

"Oh *God...*" she choked.

"I told you to stay *in* there! *Damn you*, why didn't you *listen* to me? Did you think I was trying to hide something *good* from you?"

She ran back in fast, crying. He sighed and ran after her. "Taverin come here, please. I'm sorry—listen to me, all right? I only want you safe."

She buried her head in his chest, and he felt her nod.

The next second, Traith and Taverin were enveloped in white.

In the council.

chapter 54

She thought for a moment she was dying. But the next thing that came clearly to her was not something of death.

Bars surrounded her. She looked past them and saw unbelievable controls; controls like she had never seen before. She was in some sort of instrument panel room. There were machines and technology, the likes of which she had never seen before. So advanced, but then again there was so much she had seen in the past month that was entirely unbelievable.

She ran forward and gripped the bars. She yanked at them, but they wouldn't budge. She was cold, and darkness enveloped her. She screamed Traith's name. She grabbed the bars again, trying desperately to pull them open.

She couldn't think. The spiraling walls and twinges of aches hurt her head. She was an empath. A *clairvoyant.* It was so terribly hard to sift the arbitrary thoughts and pressures pounding into her head because of where she was and the confusion of everything.

A mocking laugh rose above her crying mind. It was Tanya, and following close behind her was a grisly werewolf: one so much more ugly and terrifying than Dr. Campbell was. It was almost black in color, and larger, with yellow, sinister eyes staring at them. A woman stepped out from behind them, and Rein grew sick when she saw her.

The emerging woman had all the features of a devilish beauty, but as her mouth opened and she hissed, Rein saw that her fangs were twice as long as her own or Traith's were. Her eyes lit yellow in the darkness, and her pupils were slit like a cat's. Wings that hooked with talons on the ends, that looked as though they would feel like the skin of a snake, flapped once as if in triumph of the capture. Her jaw extended; fin-like bones were visible in her cheeks.

"Good evening, Rein," the woman teased. "Do you know who I am? Of course not; I am Helena, dearest—the most advanced form of a vampire that has *any* human attributes whatsoever, and I consider those *physical* attributes. Fancy your cell? Even further unlike anything you've ever seen, isn't it?"

Rein felt as though insanity was ending her. "What…?"

"Pierson, you thought we were after the puny girl, your proclaimed 'sister,' didn't you? We're trying something different, and so far it's worked. We have *you*." The winged woman walked toward her. "You foolishly let Tanya touch you, and she brought you here. Behind these bars, your powerful mind cannot be used." She laughed. "Such a powerful girl, and yet you seem not to know. Either that, or you're completely stupid."

She was speechless for a moment. "My head…" she whispered to herself. But she became more defiant. "You took me to get Traith to come? Doesn't seem very clever; too cliché, really."

Helena stopped, and one of her red eyebrows arched. "Traith?" she paused. Then she let out a shriek of laughter. "Dear girl, Traith? If Traith were to come, which he will, that would be a nice bonus. Of course, he has no notion as to where we are. But our decision in taking you hardly deals with that man at all. Having you gives us…*numerous* potential benefits, and I am more than willing to do whatever it takes to attain them. Your mind will develop with our tactics, which will make for better brainwashing, my dear!"

A jolt of pain hit her. She grunted and fell to her knees, still holding the bars. Tanya had struck her with a sort of bolt. A sort of electrical bolt…

Rein forced her head up and stared past Helena at a militia of maimed and disfigured creatures. They just *appeared*.

"We wanted you and Traith to be ours," Helena said, straightening her back and twitching her web-like wings. "We always have. Not dead. You are too valuable to kill. *Especially* you. So powerful…Traith does deserve some credit for realizing something as obvious as that."

chapter 55

t anya dropped her head as she closed the great, iron door, leaving Rein Pierson behind. For some reason, she actually had become nervous; a feeling she hadn't experienced in over a *century*.

Helena unfolded her wings and flapped them angrily, staring at her. "Damn you, Tanya, what is wrong?"

"Helena," she started uneasily. "It's just…"

"What?"

Tanya looked tensely at the werewolf, Ben, who shook his head and walked by them. It was funny how little power he had over his wife.

Tanya fingered her dress's sash. "Helena, Rein could have killed me—*easily*, if only she had known what it was that could—"

"What is your point?"

"That vampire has been blessed with abilities that no other creature could ever possibly acquire. She's more than just a vampire. She's more potent than even you, Helena, and with everyday she becomes stronger, whether she realizes it or not…"

"Are you saying she'll *prevail*?" Helena circled her with a grin, her wings wide and ferocious. "Destroy us? Win for her council? What are you *speaking of*, hmm?"

She hesitated. "Now that I've thought about it…see, I've been through Ana's notes. She's watched Rein, and now…I just don't know. I'm feeling doubtful. I believe we would be better off leaving her *dead* than *alive*. While we have her powerless."

"What?"

"If not, we could all die, Helena. She, by herself, may even be able to destroy our council, and nearly alone too if she channels herself right…"

Helena gasped in fury and then smiled harder. "So your doubtful, Tanya. Have you not seen my militia? Have you not witnessed us turn and transform thousands of people into bloodthirsty ravagers? Doubtfulness has no hold on *me*, and the foolish murder of a most powerful vampire doesn't seem to tickle my fancy, when she could be ours. *Hear me?*" she enunciated with gritted teeth, her fangs jetting down below her lip.

A door opened and interrupted Helena's direct attention. Ana Harker slid timidly from behind it.

"Ah, Ana," Helena cooed. "Tanya says you take wonderful notes on your brother's doings. Is that so?"

Ana straightened. "Yes. S-strictly research, however. Because, you said you wanted any information—"

"Of course, of course," Helena replied, patting Ana on the back. Then she bent down and whispered into her ear. "Then study your notes and find me the best way to lure him and his pet, Rein, *into* my council. Last chance, dear Ana. Or I'll murder him gruesomely. I will not wait any longer for him to join us."

Tanya felt herself boiling when she saw Ana flinch at Helena's words.

"His loyalty is strong, but I think we can break him," Helena said, jaunting toward a locked door. "We will win him, this time. We must." She laughed, and her fangs sparkled under saliva. "Now come along, Ben. Let us make love until someone must die." She laughed again spitefully and took Ben's arm, who very ungracefully transformed from his wolf form into his human form, and both of them disappeared behind the door in a single instant, leaving Tanya and Ana alone.

"And you," she spat, turning and facing Ana coldheartedly. "If you show even the slightest bit that you care at all, I'll—"

"Care...care at all about what?"

"Your *brother*, you idiot! When he comes, and I do say *when*, you'd better fight him with everything your puny self has got, or I'll murder you myself!" With that, she turned and walked down the remainder of the hallway and through a door.

Ana's eyes slowly filled with tears. She wiped her face so Tanya wouldn't see. Ana had so far proved her loyalty, but Tanya knew that for over a hundred years Ana hadn't had to worry about her brother. Now that she had to, Tanya feared she would not be strong enough, and Helena seemed to rely on Ana. Of course, that could only be a front. But Tanya knew that Ana would not be dedicated enough to kill her only brother and one remaining relative.

Truth be told, she would love to be the one to murder Ana.

chapter 56

Rein listened quietly to the periodic dripping in the cell. The bars that locked her in were grimy and wet. It had only been moments ago that she found herself here, and she sat on her knees in silence, the dampness of the stone below her chilling her legs. She was hardly dressed as it was—she'd been in the chemise she'd slept in when Tanya showed up at the castle.

The quiet, repetitive dripping was drowned out by the opening of a door.

It was *Ana*.

Rein caught eye contact with her for only a moment, but she walked quickly by and looked ahead. She began to press buttons on some type of machine Rein had never seen before.

Rein let out a breath and forced herself to stand. She leaned against the bars, and with that noise, she got Ana to look in her direction.

Rein said nothing.

Ana hesitated and then awkwardly looked down again. After she hit a few more buttons, Ana turned to check something beside the cell.

Rein reached out and grabbed her arm.

Ana gasped and gritted her teeth. She tried to rip out of Rein's grasp, but that was useless.

"Shh, I need to talk to you, please," Rein whispered. "I can't *do* anything to you from in here. I wouldn't anyway."

Ana relaxed her arm, but her stare was tenser than ever.

"Ana," Rein said, "Don't let them hurt your brother."

"What?"

"Traith *loves* you. You don't have the whole picture of him—you couldn't. Why are you so desperate to *kill* him?"

She shook her head continuously. "I do love him, but I will not…" She began to whimper and back up. "I cannot be with him anymore. Let *go*."

"*Why? Why* not?"

Ana paused, and they stared at each other with a deep gaze. "Because he'll kill me," she said trembling.

Rein was puzzled. If Ana *did* love Traith, what did she mean?

Ana looked down, and a tear fell to the ground. "I want him back," Ana murmured. "But he can't ever come back." Her voice was shaking as tears fell down her cheeks. She looked up at Rein sorrowfully. "He isn't the same. He can't be. Not after what he did to me. To us. And I have to *kill* him for it. I must, to avenge them."

"Avenge who?" Rein watched Ana's face closely.

"I was alone," Ana whispered, grasping the bars. "Alone, standing in a deserted road, calling out for Traith. A dark figure appeared in front of me. It dropped two bodies onto the dirt road in front of me. It was both my *parents, dead.* The figure looked up at me, eyes glowing in the night. They were red. Wet fangs glistened in the moonlight. I backed up and screamed, crying and covering my mouth." She was crying as silent as she could, checking with frightened speed to make sure no one was around. "The dark figure in front of me was Traith. He had disappeared only a few weeks before."

Her brother…killed…their…

Rein put her hands on her head and shook it, falling to her knees. "No," she murmured. "No, that isn't…"

Ana backed up and flinched. A slamming of a door—Tanya.

"What are you doing in here?" Tanya asked, waltzing in with a face full of malevolence.

Ana shook her head, trying desperately to hide her tears. "I was *doing* what I was *assigned* to do, Tanya, with the generators."

All the pain was so real. The anguish and the anger and the feeling, all so real and in her head, almost—*without having even read Ana's mind*—almost as if she'd *lived* it. Jolts and flashes corrupted her. She thought she was going insane. Thoughts, whether they were her true memories or simple thoughts, were spiraling. She didn't want them in her head. They weren't hers.

How were they not *hers*?

She couldn't use her powers in that cell, but somehow she fed into Ana's mind. She'd gotten into Ana's mind and not even *purposely*.

She could easily go mad with them. If she broke down…

She couldn't. She had to maintain something to keep from caving in. But she was a *clairvoyant*. She couldn't always block out thoughts, especially because she'd stolen a memory and lived it in a matter of moments—especially by *accident* and *impossibility*. She could hardly think straight.

She looked up at Ana, mouth open. "No, he…d-don't *believe* that, Ana! Traith didn't—he couldn't have!"

Ana stood, the anger in her eyes turning soft. She was having a hard time lying in front of Tanya. "What are you talking about, Rein?"

Rein couldn't focus; she couldn't focus on anything but her head. All she could do was hold it and speak thoughts quietly, sorting thoughts out. She was receiving more than Ana's thoughts—she was receiving parts of her memory, living it—and most vital of all, pieces of Traith's past.

How was this happening? It *hurt*. Suddenly she couldn't even *think* about Traith without seeing…

"He doesn't know," Rein whispered through the piercing feeling in her head. "He doesn't remember—he doesn't *remember anything, Ana!* This council *took it from him!*"

Ana's stare became grave, but she was forced away by Tanya—the person Rein didn't want to see, because with her came pain.

chapter 57

S uddenly in an abrupt flash of light, Traith saw Mistress standing in front of them. He was in the council. Taverin was, too. His leader's face was concerned. Actually concerned. He heard the girl beside him gasp.

"Harker! Where is your partner?" the Mistress asked angrily.

Traith wanted to say something sarcastic, but refrained with difficulty. "Don't you know?" he asked. "She just disappeared with Tanya, I was hoping you—"

She cocked her head and curled her lips in anger. "She only lets *you* feel her, Traith. Can you not?"

"What?" he questioned, shocked. "You cannot see her?"

The leader paused. "So you cannot feel her."

He wanted to say yes, but... "No," he murmured.

"I knew this was coming," Mistress said to herself. "It was foolish of me not to search deeper. Fortunately I know how to get you into the Mardinial Council, where I am more than sure she is. But getting you back will be a problem. It is located in a place neither in this world nor on another—in a place between consciousness and unconsciousness. Between darkness and light. A place from which your teleportation might not be able to reach. Ah, I sensed a great hardship coming." She paused a moment. "Taverin." Mistress walked up and put her hand on the girl's head, not completing her sentence.

Traith stepped aside and watched the girl stare anxiously. "You can keep her here, can't you?" he asked.

"No!" Taverin protested. "No, please! I can help—give me a weapon, something, I'll do whatever I can to get Rein back, please!"

"Miss Badeau," Mistress spoke softly. "You do understand the gravity of what you have just asked?"

Taverin swallowed and wiped her eyes. "Yes, but if they need me, I want to help. I am not a little girl, I can at least try."

Mistress looked at her for a moment. "I believe fighting for her sister may very well be better for her," she said.

"*Mistress*," Traith cut in, exasperated. "She's only a mortal girl, and a frail one at that! Why the devil are you possibly thinking this would be *good* for her?"

"I have a book I can let you use, Taverin. A spell book. Speak an incantation, and its effect will be activated. You need no training to use it." It suddenly appeared in the old woman's hand. "I have arranged that only *you* may use it."

"Oh my Lord!" Taverin proclaimed, shaking a little with a mixture of both excitement and fear, taking the book. "I will use them, and wisely!"

Traith was in shock, his mouth open and his eyes steady. Mistress returned all her attention to him and nodded. Her eyes turned bright blue, and a wind blew hard around them. He felt Taverin latch onto him like a lock.

And suddenly, he was in a place between darkness and light.

chapter 58

S he reached up and felt her lips; she wiped blood from her mouth. She withstood another crack, and then threw her fist out to hit something: one of the creatures that was teasing and tormenting her in the cold, wet cell. They teleported and whirled around her, scratching her, and making her bleed. Because they couldn't kill her, the pain merely grew worse with every blow. She didn't know what was going on, and the pain felt too overwhelming to allow thought.

Traith? She could feel him. But she couldn't call him. Couldn't show him where she was. The cell she was in prevented this, but not the inexplicable phenomenon that had just occurred—receiving Ana's thoughts.

But she could feel Traith's longing touch, and tried desperately to disconnect the murderer that she witnessed and the man she loved.

Then she could feel him more.

There was a sudden break in her attacks, as though the creatures were tiring. Her pain numbed for a moment when she had time to look around her. Tanya was standing directly in front of her outside the cell, watching her intently with a distorted grin on her face. The vampire was enjoying her torture.

"I'm keeping watch for Traith for you," Tanya growled.

She attempted to get into the woman's mind, but she couldn't. She couldn't shape shift. She was so weak.

"Go ahead," Tanya said. "Try to hurt me from in there. The angrier you get, the better the chances of your mind progression, and the faster we'll be able to use you."

It was supposed to be silent in the room, but the thoughts she'd recovered from Ana's mind were fiercely reenacting in her own. She could see clearly, and there was no noise coming from anywhere.

The woman laughed, but suddenly a flash of color whizzed by her face. Rein was sinking yet ecstatic.

He was so close now.

It was Traith...and *Taverin?*

He knocked Tanya to the stone and then spun around as Rein cried his name. Taverin was frozen, eyes looking from one person to the other, not uttering a word.

"Thank God, I found you," he murmured shakily.

Her heart lifted with relief, but anxiety pushed it back down to the pit of her stomach. *He'd murdered his parents. He didn't know?*

And *Taverin...*

"Why is she here, Traith?" Rein asked, her voice choked up. "She'll die." She was frantic, looking at him and trying to picture how on earth he could've done such a thing.

She grabbed her head tight. Her mind began stabbing at her. Pain, torture—he *murdered* his parents. He was feral. Wild. Uncontrollable. Frightening.

"Ana's thoughts..." Rein stopped in agony. "I saw everything."

His eyes deepened. "What? Rein, what happ—" He was yanked back.

His painful grunt as Ben banged him into the floor tore her up inside. And seeing Taverin cry at the sight of her and Traith made that tear burn horribly.

And *still* Ana's terrifying thoughts hit into her like a hammer—thoughts she was hysterical over having received *involuntarily*. Her head was so loud. She had to stop her mind; she was hearing Traith, and Ana, and...She attempted to drown out the thoughts by speaking to herself. She tried to rearrange her mind, immobilized by fear. If only she could fabricate some sort of barrier around Ana's stolen memories, nightmares; she could think...

But then she felt another hand grab her. The disfigured creatures had reenergized in those few moments it seemed.

Rein watched her sister spin around and stare at the iron door that burst open. Ana ran in, along with a calmly walking Helena and a few mutilated creatures. She quickly found that Ana's eyes locked to her own in a moment of pain and confusion.

Rein glanced at her fiancé, blocking out all else. He threw out his fist hard, and Ben was flung backward by its force. Then Taverin screamed out some sort of spell, and there was a screech. Flames burst and enveloped Tanya, whom had begun to charge at Taverin. The girl had a small book in her hands.

Traith turned and yanked a panel off of some sort of machine, making it glow an amber color in his hand. It was a huge piece of metal and wires, and he was holding it with one hand, enraged. That was the first time Rein had ever seen him lift something so heavy.

He pitched it at the werewolf, and it knocked him into the ground. He was lying stiffly under it for a moment, the huge mass of machinery pressing on him. Traith teleported over to Taverin and threw her behind his back.

"Taverin, you worry about my sister, Ana," Traith said quickly in a single breath. "I'll take care of the others."

Ben lifted the debris off of himself and threw it back at Traith. It hit him directly, burning him into the floor.

Ana looked down at him in what appeared to be hesitation, but then Taverin bowled over her. Rein reached a bloody hand out toward Ben, who had tackled Traith.

If she could only reach past the bars…just past them enough… She was straining with all that she had to extend her arm. And she made it.

Mustering up the energy, she suddenly shifted Ben into a regular man, without the capabilities of a werewolf.

Traith threw the pieces of different heavy, steel structures off of himself, particularly at Ben, who now had a much lighter body. Traith lunged forward from the ground and grabbed one of Helena's wings. Her clawed hand lashed out and grabbed Traith's neck, wrenching him closer to her. She lashed out and, with one finger, dug her nail deep into his face, fast. As if it were a knife, her nail ran through his skin and lanced him, gashing his one eye as it dug down his face.

Rein's heart hit her throat when she heard him shout in pain, but he still managed to light up her webbed wing, and part of it exploded. She shrieked, and he toppled to the floor. He was holding his eye on his left side. He quickly shuffled back up again, and she flinched when the next second he was directly in front of her.

His entire left side of his face was gored and bloody, starting from his forehead and reaching down his eye to nearly his lip. It was so deep.

Rein knew he couldn't see out of that eye; her stomach was wrenching at the sight of him. She had to *get out...*

He lifted his hands and clutched at the bars, trying to melt them. But they didn't budge, and only his fists lit with the fury of eruption.

"Rein, what's holding you in?" he asked, wincing. "What's—" He stopped and his expression changed into one of revolted shock.

He couldn't speak. His voice was altering with his last words.

She turned slightly and struck a few creatures off of her. They were weakening. Or dying from her own blows.

"How c-can you do this?" he forced out, until a strange, deep howling sound was all that remained of his voice. He immediately shut his mouth.

"I don't know," she cried. "If I reached far enough...I don't know! I'm turning you into a..." She paused when she saw him staring at himself.

Dark hair was beginning to grow from his arms and out his gloves.

"What are you bloody doing? Rein—No, no, *don't...*"

She was turning him into a werewolf. He would be stronger that way.

But then she was forced backward by another creature, and her eyes were torn off of him. A sharp pain hit her head. A nauseating feeling was rising within her, and it made her shiver. She gave Traith a second's glance.

He was an animal, his hands, everything.

Not daring to finish speech, he awkwardly tried to get her attention. But he let out a yelp as he was crushed against the bars by a heavy object. Rein barely caught sight of electricity surging through him. *Tanya.*

He almost lost consciousness, but he managed to pull himself up and flip around. Tanya lunged at him, grabbing his face and tearing at it more. A surge of agony ripped through him. He staggered backward and fell.

"Only more scars, Traith," she hissed. "Only more to add to the collection. No one will notice a few more."

He shook his head and leapt onto Tanya as she went to electrocute him again. She hit the ground breathless and stunned. Within an instant Traith threw himself on her, locking his animal jaws around her neck, tearing it with his new teeth. She was bleeding. But he was pulled back by Helena, whose lips curled back as she attempted to bite him. He shoved her backward and watched as Tanya's body reacted to his werewolf's bite. Her body convulsed and slowly split open, her cry deafening.

She was dead. The remains of her body shriveled into ash.

"That was it?" Helena said in horror. "A petty *bite* from a *wolf* killed her? God, that's sickening!"

Traith stood over the remains of Tanya. Helena cursed at him and charged with hatred, her nails suddenly grown longer and her face twisted into almost an animalistic appearance. Saliva hung from her mouth, and her eyes brightened to yellow as she snarled. He jumped over and rammed her into a dirty, bloody examination table. She flung backward with the table, her left wing, damaged from Traith's last exploit, caught on the side. It tore in half with the sound of ripping flesh. Blood shot out as the wing split. A screech of pain.

Traith turned around and looked at Taverin who was fighting hand-to-hand with Ana—a skill in which Taverin had none of and which Ana had much of. Taverin was punched over and over by Ana, and in the midst of Traith's distraction, Ben had latched onto his ankle and was twisting. Though he was transformed into a human, his strength remained. Traith yelled and dropped to the ground, watching as Taverin fell too, holding her face.

Rein felt so helpless. She had finally managed to kill the few creatures behind her. She was so disgusted when she looked at what was left of them.

Traith stomped Ben's face down, and as he got free he ran to the controls. He was trying to find some way to get Rein out. Before he could reach them, however, Ana knocked him down. Still a werewolf, he spun around and grabbed her, looking at her.

Rein knew how desperately awkward he felt with her in his large, clawed hands. He was an animal that couldn't speak. What was he to do? How could he not feel awkward?

He tossed her to the ground. She looked at the remains of Tanya's body and looked back at Traith. Then she got up, backed away, and ran through a door to her right.

"*Coward!*" Helena spat. "Your sister may not harm you, Harker, but I *will!* I am finished trying to win you—you're *dead!*"

A pitch-black darkness enveloped them all as Helena absorbed all the light in the room. Traith looked as if he wanted to make a nasty remark, but Helena laughed. "Can't you speak to me, Harker?"

Rein followed the spin of his head to Taverin, who was fighting blindly in the dark. Rein was trying desperately to bend or break the bars, but they still wouldn't budge. *Please...*

Creatures swarmed in and began to hang on Traith, scratching through the fur on his sides and into his flesh. He looked at one of them, and it suddenly dropped. His eyes were ablaze with ferocity. All the creatures hanging on him suddenly dropped dead. Traith staggered a moment, the pressure on his head crushing. He fell to his knees.

He had instantly destroyed lower immortals. People. *Clones.*

He turned his eyes to Taverin. Ben was pounding on her. Her lips were bloody, and her arms were cut open by his claws. Ben had somehow regained the ability to alter into his werewolf form, allowing him to see through the darkness.

Rein was weakening. She felt it.

Traith leapt on top of Ben, claws out and ready, teeth clenched. They both slammed into the ground, screeching and howling at each other. Helena smiled and pulled a wooden stake out of her sword's hilt. Rein watched helplessly, screaming Traith's name, as Helena raced forward. Time felt slow when Tanya's clawed arm rose with the stake. She impaled it into Traith's back on his left side, where his heart lay.

He howled viciously, and it slowly altered back into a deep scream as he transformed back into himself and fell limp on the floor. Ben scrabbled up and stood beside Helena, smirking.

"Traith! Traith, where are you?" Taverin cried as she tried to see where he was through the blackness.

Rein felt her heart nearly working, pounding. "What did you do?" She was trembling wildly. "Traith? *Traith!* Oh God—No!"

She felt anger so wild; her eyes filled with tears of fury. It felt like her heart had hit the bottom of her stomach and began to bleed. She curled back her lips and bore her teeth like a dog. She cried out desperately. Everyone grew still as light filtered into the room, as if a black fog drained out. Her scream intensified, and suddenly the bars snapped back as if they were straw, without the aid of her hands. She walked out, her eyes lit with fury and sorrow. All her scratches and bruises disappeared. Her powers had returned, and her psyche was in full control.

"Ben!" Helena screeched. "Get Harker's body and the girl out of here now! I want him to die suffering, and the girl to watch—and I want this woman all to myself!"

Ben nodded as he grabbed Traith and Taverin by their collars.

"No! Rein! Don't let him take me! Rein, *please*!" the girl screamed, struggling to break free of Ben's arms. She disappeared behind the door, along with Traith's body.

chapter 59

R ein's arm shot up in Helena's direction. The sinister woman stuttered and grabbed her throat. A great amount of pressure was hammering into her neck, and she was lifted off of the ground. Trying frantically to break free, Helena pulled intensely at her throat trying to get the incredible weight off of it, flailing her wings in a futile attempt to escape. Rein pulled her hand down, and Helena went down with it, denting the ground where she'd been smashed. Ben ran from behind the door. He had yanked the stake out of Traith's body and held it in his furry fist; an expression of fervent rage lingering on his face. He jumped onto Rein, sending the two of them crashing backward into the cell.

She screamed and fell to the ground. She twisted, and Ben drove the stake into her side—not where he had wanted it to go. Rein touched him, and he was crunched backward into the stone cell wall. He lay still.

Rein's head shot up, her teeth showing with anger and her muscles tense. She stood up and yanked the stake out of her side. She tried to spit out the blood in her mouth, but it kept coming up from her throat. She gritted her teeth. She ignored the excruciating pain. The tears that were speeding down her face, the blood that was everywhere…she ignored it all. Helena was all that filled her vision.

She felt something more flare up inside her: more anger and frustration, more unceasing hate, more power. *Somehow…more power.* It was a strange sensation beginning to take over her. She wasn't going to let the person who may have killed her lover survive.

Helena flew to her and slashed her across the face. Rein grabbed her hand and snapped it. Helena shrieked, and in that moment Rein grabbed the stake and plunged it into her heart with all her might. Helena was forced backward with the might of Rein's dig. She crashed through a steel door and into a metallic hallway. Ben twitched from where he lay and slowly began to rise from his position.

She didn't care about him; she needed Traith…

God, if he was dead…

She flinched when she realized that three people stood outside the cell she was running from. Lorena, beside her, Jacques, and Magellan, ready to fight.

She looked at them gratefully, but ran as fast as she could into the doorway where Traith was lying. The door slammed closed behind her, and the hall was dark. Taverin screamed her name with happiness, but became instantly terrified.

"Rein—he mentioned something with your name—'I told you I was a lure.' Does that make sense? God, Rein!"

A lure…

Traith was lying limp, bloody and bruised. His face was still gashed, down his eye, everywhere. He hadn't healed. *Why?*

She crumpled down beside him, her hand on his face. "Traith?" her voice broke. "Traith, can you hear me? Please be with me…"

She ripped and pulled off his shirt to expose the gaping chest wound in the midst of his already wide geography of scars. Blood trickled from his mouth, and he didn't speak. She cried to herself as she shakily ran her hands over his body, trying to take something from his bloodstained chest into her own body. If he was dead, maybe she could take his wound and die with it. But if he wasn't, she wouldn't be able to remove any of his pain; it was from a stake.

And then she felt it. *Dear God, she felt it.* Somehow it was working. Somehow she was breaking all limits ever known. She was taking his wound. She watched as the hole in his chest began to grow smaller and smaller. It was as if someone were quickly, but carefully, stitching his chest back together. She couldn't let him die. She could—c-couldn't let him…

Let him…

chapter 60

H is sight was foggy as he blinked; he slowly managed to flinch and then move. His muffled hearing rapidly regained its sharpness; Taverin was screaming Rein's name. He saw Rein gazing at him on her knees, leaning over him. She looked as though she was going to fall over; her eyes began to turn back in her head. He stared in shock; his heart sank. She buckled onto his chest. Trembling seized him in panic as he quickly lifted her from his chest. Her eyes were open but glassy. Vacant.

His body was healed.

A long gash suddenly riveted down her left eye. He suddenly realized that the vision had returned to his. His face had healed. Hers was doing the opposite.

And there was blood everywhere.

"No, Rein! *Rein!*" he screamed, fighting back tears. He held her head in his hands. "No please, Rein—please don't do this to me!"

"Traith, don't let her die!" Taverin screamed, wild and frightened. "*She took your wounds!*"

He looked up for a mere second. "A stake," he stuttered, staring back down at Rein. "A bloody stake." He was hysterically petting his lover as if that would revive her.

God, she'd taken it. She'd actually…

Taverin fell next to him on the floor and began to cry, grabbing Traith's once frosty-white, silk shirt that was lying beside them on the ground. It was torn apart and almost completely red with his blood.

Red. It filled his sight.

He suddenly couldn't get his mind off it.

His body wanted to rear up and inhale it.

He closed his eyes tight and held Rein close. It couldn't get to him. Not now…but he had held off too bloody long…those vials…he hadn't taken one in days, and…

"I was in here watching you *die*, Traith," Taverin spoke through tears and sobs. "I think you were really dead!" And she could say no more.

"God, I hope not," he murmured. "If I was, then she…I must have been; she couldn't have healed me if I wasn't." He swallowed blood that had been in his throat, and he felt as though he was almost losing control. "Taverin, get away from me," he said, sniffing.

His heart broke when he saw tears still running down Rein's face. She was still slightly awake. She was scared to die but would for him.

"No, Rein…"

He was getting intoxicated just from the aroma of her blood. Hers, he knew, too. Not his own, which seemed splashed everywhere. His body had a taste for *hers*…

"*Please*, Taverin, leave," he whimpered.

She stared at him curiously through tears. "Why?"

"Just trust me and go, please!"

"But *they're* out there!"

With a wave of his hand she was gone from his sight. He broke down. He was losing. His human instinct was losing. His mind clouded.

He tasted her blood in his mouth. He was swallowing.

He'd licked it. Tasted it.

Damn—what the devil have I done?

It lingered pungent in his mouth.

He was losing his mind over it.

His lover might be dead, and he couldn't refrain?

"Oh God, please, Rein, no!" he cried. "I'm *sorry!*"

A damned *animal!*

He turned and struggled to his knees, holding her. His vision was blurred and watery; her eyes were still open.

She had seen him drink her blood. Only a moment ago. She was still holding on.

And that was the last thing she was to see? Him drinking from her like she was a bloody *fountain?*

He felt his lips again with a single hand and began to tremble when blood covered it. He dropped his hand. He felt her body tense.

"Rein," he whimpered. "God, I don't know what's wrong with me; Please! Please put it back…please. Let me die, Rein; I deserve to die. Why did you—How could you do this to yourself? No, put it back. *Rein…*"

Then, for the first time, she became heavy and hung down limp.

He stared in fright at her, putting his hand on her chest, trying to stop the bleeding. It was spewing like a geyser, soaking into her clothing and into his hands. He felt his eyes continually drawn to the hole ripped into her as it bled without end. And the gash down her eye... He had had that, too.

And it was taking *everything he had* to not become wild over the scarlet that covered nearly *every inch* of his vision.

Just don't become a monster, please...

Why had I? That had never, ever, happened before... Why?

He heard screams coming from the other room. He was covered in blood, both his own and hers. He'd lost blood, so his body was going raving mad trying to replenish it.

He gently laid her head down on the floor. He stood up and ran out the door, trying to get even a fraction of the demonic thought of blood out of his head. To his shock, he saw Lorena and a few others fighting a newly strengthened Helena and Ben.

Taverin ran to him from a corner, her eyes swollen and pink. "Why did you do that?" she screamed. "What's wrong with you? Is Rein dead?" She quieted. "Lord, look at you..."

He blinked slowly but firmly. He bit back emotion with an uncanny amount of power. He was covered in blood from head to toe.

"*Lorena!*" he yelled. "Get Taverin and everyone else out of here, *now!*"

Lorena's stare was full of emotion; she nodded without questioning. She looked up, and slowly she and the others, along with Taverin, who was yelling for Traith to let her stay, disappeared.

Helena looked over at Traith and started running toward him. "How do you live again?! I *killed* you!" she screamed as she flapped her wings in fury, one side straggling.

"You killed me?" His voice cracked with uncovered panic.

He closed the door forcefully, hearing her beat into it, and melted it to the wall with his hands. "My fiancée sacrificed herself for me *because of you!*" He bent down, grabbed Rein's body, and touched the base of the floor.

It glowed red for a moment, and then everything began to collapse. He held Rein's face close to his. "Oh—" He swore under his breath. "I have to get Ana."

He shoved in the door that he had melted, crushing Helena behind it. Nearly in the same instant, Rein in one arm, he grabbed a chunk of metal, charged it, and flung it hard into Ben. The werewolf flew backward onto the ground and didn't move. Traith ran out of the room as it blew up and into another room to the right of him into which he had seen Ana retreat. Ana was curled on the floor crying.

"Ana?" he murmured.

She looked up at him, and her eyes were momentarily terrified, but then they became angered. "Get away, Traith, just get away—"

"Ana, just listen to me, please; this whole place is going up in flames and—"

"No!"

"Damn it, I won't *hurt* you! Listen to me!" he yelled frantically. "You'll *die* in here! I can take you with me; Please!"

He glanced down at Rein. Her head hanging back in his arms.

Smoke.

Her weakness.

He might've just killed her by exposing her to it.

His heart was so torn. His sister or his fiancée?

"No!" Ana answered him after a delay. "Because of you I want to *die* anyway!"

"It doesn't..." He paused, grunting as he ducked falling debris. "It doesn't need to be like this! Please, Ana!" He ran to her and bent down. "Are you scared of me, Ana?" he questioned.

"Get away!" she screamed, standing and running off.

"You think I'm going to hurt you?" he shouted. "The only other person in the world with my own blood, and you think I would *hurt* you?"

She didn't reply.

"Ana?"

She had disappeared past the flames and boiling metal that now engulfed the floor. His heart wrenched inside his body. He'd taken too much time. He held Rein close, covering her wounded chest with his bloodstained hand and, straining, successfully entered into familiar surroundings.

chapter 61

I t was dark. No candles, curtains drawn. The door was closed, and the room was quiet as a graveyard. He was too worn out to panic anymore. His head leant on his folded fists. He was exhausted.

But what if she woke? There was always that slight chance she could.

Traith studied her. Her long, black hair was slicked back and damp from exertion. Her lips were red as roses, and her thin arms were draped over her with perfect elegance. Her one eye still had a wound down it, but it had stopped bleeding and closed.

Her body was limp.

She had brought him back to life. He had been dead…truly dead. She took that death. His only hope was that she could fight it off better than he could. She was stronger; she was a clairvoyant. But then that smoke had infused her body…

The stake. He'd felt that stake. It hit him so hard, and he couldn't reach it to pull it out. It took a while for him to lose consciousness. But he felt it, pain that inflamed the very skin of his fingertips down to his legs. That stake had hit the very edge of his heart. Not directly, but it was obviously enough.

But there was a chance.

All he could do was watch her, lost in some dark, unwelcoming world, and she was the only one that could free herself of it. Her life was in her own hands at that point. Her body *must* heal the small part of her heart fast enough. And if it couldn't, she would collapse and die, like he had.

But there had to be that chance.

He looked down sorrowfully as he remembered his younger sister, too. It seemed as though everything he treasured was dying. Slipping like sand through his fingers. The worst part was, he knew that his sister still loved him. Somewhere, deep down inside of her. She had refused to hurt him.

Then there was Taverin. She was fine, mending. He hadn't seen her, yet. He hadn't left his current spot for three days. He had drunk two vials of blood in that time.

He would never make that mistake again.

He had heard what was going on outside that metal door he was thrown behind with Taverin. He had tried to get up. Tried to push it off. Taverin was screaming for him to wake up. He had been awake, but he was not listening to her. In those last few moments, he was listening to the ghastly sounds outside that door, and he could not go to help her. His fiancée. His lover. He couldn't move. So much had been going on out there, and then he heard her running. She held him. He felt it. Then things left his sight. Had he died? Helena had told him he had. Rein was so frightened when he awoke.

And then he drank her blood.

He dropped his head and held it tight.

He drank her blood. In one smooth action, he brought her blood to his mouth. And she had seen him do so. He regretted so vehemently not having had a vial the day before. It would have been enough to keep him from going crazy. He'd *never* lost control before. Now he knew that Mistress had been speaking the truth all those years—that if he didn't drink at least every other day, something like this could happen.

He held Rein's hand as he sat in a chair next to her bed, waiting for the flinch or movement that would free him of fear. Then a knock on the door reminded him of where he actually was, and he looked up.

"Hello, Traith," the Mistress spoke softly. "How is she?"

"I don't know."

She came into the dark room, out of the brightness of the hallway, and sat next to him after closing the door behind her. "I'm so sorry about all of this, Traith. Taverin will heal quickly, as you know."

"More than can be said for Rein."

He put his head in his hands. He had to stay strong. Life would go on, with or without Rein.

No—what the bloody hell am I thinking?

He couldn't think about life like that. He used everything he had to hold back a tear. Mistress looked into his heart.

"Why do you choose to blame yourself like this?" she asked. "I know what you are feeling right now, Traith. I know what happened with Ana."

"It's my fault Rein's in this condition, balancing between life and death. I killed her once. Now it seems I've done it again. She…" he choked a moment, and anger overwhelmed him.

"You never killed her, Traith."

"But I—" He stopped. He couldn't tell her what he'd done to Rein. How for a moment, he'd completely lost control. She probably knew, anyway. "She might *die* because of me," he continued hoarsely. "And I lost my *sister*, Mistress! You couldn't possibly understand how much I still love her._You can't imagine the feeling, knowing that even your own family thinks you're a monster! The only family I've got…She's scared of me, Mistress! My own sister is scared of me, and she might be dead now, as well!" He winced. "I never asked for this."

Mistress touched his face gently. "You are not evil, Harker, and it is not your fault. You couldn't have prevented what happened to you. You are not a monster. And your sister chose not to harm you. As for Rein's actions…Traith, you were…" she paused a moment. "Dead."

He looked up at her, wearing a look of discontentment.

"You had been lying on cold, hard ground for too long with that stake in you. The only way Rein could've saved you was by doing what she did."

"But now she might die," he said quietly. "And Ana might be dead also. She preferred to die rather than come with me. It's as if I have done something to her, but I don't even know if I have because I can't remember!"

"Come, Traith. Come see Taverin."

He looked up at her after putting his head in his hands again. "I can't. Not right now. Taverin will heal. Rein might not. I just…I *did* this to her."

"Traith, it is all over and done with," Mistress said. "There is nothing more you can do about this. I'll leave you, now," the Mistress said quietly as she stood up. "But you fought bravely, Harker. No other leader could have a First Hand as noble or as loyal as you." She stopped when she reached the doorway. "Remember something, though. There is a possibility that Rein has the ability to heal much faster than you." At that, she left the room.

He put his head on Rein's hand. A single tear trickled down his cheek and onto her hand. He panted silently into her palm in anger and pain, cringing in fury, nearly crying with it.

Then it happened. He felt that flinch. The movement he had wanted. His head shot up.

The gash down her eye slowly vanished.

She was healing.

"Dear God," he murmured with a large smile, watching as the horrible slice wound disappeared and left no scar behind on her beautiful face.

She smiled weakly back, eyes still closed, and held out her hand. He stood then and gently embraced her weak body.

"Rein..." He held her with such tenderness, relief filling him more than ever.

"It worked," she rasped. She seemed quietly excited. "You're all right?"

"I'm fine, Rein," he choked. "You almost...You shouldn't have..." He held her tighter. "Why did you do that, Rein?"

He laid her down and stood over her with unbearable contentment.

"I couldn't let you die, Traith," she said, her voice becoming less of a whisper.

"And you wanted me to live and watch it happen to you? All over again?"

She said his name gently and held his face in her hand. "I had a better chance of surviving, I knew." She tried to sit up. She grabbed her chest a moment and then slowly let go.

"Ana...she told me..."

"Ana talked to you?" he asked intensely.

"You lost control, didn't you?" she murmured, her eyes sad for him.

His heart sank, and he felt ill as if he had no breath with which to speak. "I'm sorry," was all he could manage to say.

She tilted her head and smiled warmly. "I heard you the first time," she said. "I knew it wasn't you...just like it couldn't have been you *then*..."

He felt so mortified that he wanted to thrust a stake into himself, but he was also confused. What was she talking about? He'd find out later when she was stronger; the revolting thing he'd done to his fiancée clouded his mind. How could she brush it off so easily? There was no reason for his actions. No bloody reason to drink her blood again.

"But you made up for it and took care of me like I knew you would," she said with a crooked smile.

He didn't reply. His head was down, and his fists were locked. "God Rein—I made up for nothing."

"Please, Traith, I know what you felt," she murmured. "Don't be angry, please…I forgive you."

He met her eyes and could only be thankful.

"I love you," she said slowly, closing her eyes.

He could hardly bear to hear those words from her because of the repeating thought of what he had done to her. It was so hard to get past, but at the same time, he almost wanted to cry for happiness.

"I love you, too," he said hoarsely.

She would live.

chapter 62

after quietly leaving the room, Traith squinted in the intense bright-ness of the hallway. A few yards down to his left was the room where Taverin was recovering. She had been up and lucid the past few nights, but he had not moved from the seat next to Rein.

He peered through the door and quietly leant on the frame, watch-ing her as she read her book, cozy and warm under her blanket.

Her left eye was swollen, and she had bandages on her arm and waist.

She looked over at him and smiled brightly. "Traith! Traith, you're all right!"

"How are *you*? Are you in any pain?"

"I am a little. But it's nothing I can't walk on." She paused. "How's Rein? Is she all right? D-Did she wake up yet? You're smiling..."

"Yes. She'll be fine," he murmured in pleasure.

"Oh, thank goodness! That's wonderful!" Taverin paused and looked apprehensively at Traith. "Did we beat them? I blacked out, and I don't remember much. Just that you were dead." Her temperament changed with a sudden chill. "Traith, they put me there with you alone when you were really dying. You tried to speak to me once—"

"I did?"

She started to get flustered, and her eyes glazed as she recalled that night. "Yes...you were *choking* on your own blood. You couldn't really talk, but you tried so hard to!"

"I don't remember."

"Traith, it was the most frightening thing I ever saw in my entire life! You were dead after a few minutes, but before you were...Traith, you grasped my hand, but you couldn't talk over the blood that flooded your mouth! Then you didn't move at all. And Rein...then her chest started pouring out blood as if it were a tilted bucket of water, and then your chest was—"

"Taverin." He walked over to her bedside, stopping her panicky talk, and she began bawling with fright, holding onto his hand and holding it up to her cheek.

"Don't think about it now. It's over, and we won," he said. "And we're all here."

She took a few deep breaths and looked at Traith's face, staring at his eyes.

"What is it?" he asked quietly.

She let go of him. "I'm just studying you," she answered him back.

He laughed a little in surprise. "Oh?"

"By the way, when are we allowed to go home?"

"When we want to, I assume. I'm fine; I've been fine. You and Rein were the ones who needed the healing. I'm not sure you can leave yet, although you seem healed, but I must go home to tend to a man with a rapidly deteriorating mind."

A nurse walked in and smiled at him as she switched some pillows on the bed. "Hello, Harker," she said.

He nodded, only partially acknowledging her.

"You two can leave whenever you like—Mistress' authorization. Rein must stay awhile, though, because she can't yet walk. As soon as she's capable, we'll send her down. Oh, and by the way," she changed her tone. "Mistress would like to see you both. She's in the main lobby." The nurse hesitated, and Traith felt her stare hard at him. "Traith, I see you have a new accessory!" she exclaimed.

He flinched. "What?" He looked at Taverin.

"The scar on your eye, yes. On your left side? Oh, never mind."

The nurse smiled kindly and winked at him.

Scar...It'd gone back to him? The gash had gone back to him as a scar as Rein healed. Since she didn't have the scar, he did. *How the hell did that happen?*

Traith nodded once more, dazed, partially ignoring the nurse. "Is that why you were examining me?" he asked Taverin. "Is it bad?"

Taverin shook her head, hesitantly choosing her words. "Well, yes, in a way. It's not disfiguring, just long and a little jagged down your left eye. I'm sure you'd be able to feel it."

He didn't know whether to react angrily or ironically at ease as his fingers brushed over the long, lifted scar now down the side of his face.

He sighed in frustration. "You're right."

"It is quite fine though. It makes you look stronger!"

His eyebrows rose. He had to give a weak laugh. "I don't exactly know about that, but I know that this one did hurt terribly." He felt around the left side of his face once more. He met her eyes. "Are you sure you're well enough to go home?" he asked.

"*Sans doute.*" She immediately quieted down when the woman left the room. "Traith," she whispered, "who was that nurse?"

He turned but the nurse had left already. "I don't know, why?"

"Because she was looking at you quite well, and rather examining—"

"Taverin," he cut her off immediately. He accidentally smiled at her as she laughed, and he noticed that her humor lifted his spirits a little more. Especially after hearing about a new, big scar down his face. "Don't speak," he said, half-smiling. "You're all too bold." He sighed. "So you said you can walk?"

She laughed. "Yes, I can walk myself, do not worry."

She followed him down the long infirmary corridors that led to the main lobby. She watched as he nodded to people down the hallway and shook hands with some of the men. He had to know them; he didn't have a choice, being the Mistress's First Hand.

About two wings away from the infirmary itself, they entered into a large domed room, which led into the grand foyer. There the Mistress stood, seeming as if she had been waiting for them all night.

"You wanted to see us?" he asked her casually.

"So she lives, does she?" Mistress said with a smile.

He didn't reply and put his head down.

She nearly frowned. "I see you like your privacy. Well, I thought that you might want to know that your sister is alive. She has fled to a nearby island along the coast of Ireland and is alone at this time."

Traith's stance straightened, and he smiled in relief. All that sand slipping through his fingers had managed to stop its landslide. Ana was alive, too.

"Excuse me, M-Mistress?" Taverin asked shyly from beside Traith. "Do you know anything about Helena and the others?"

Mistress smiled at the lack of enthusiasm in the young girl's voice. "Taverin, do not worry yourself about something that cannot be prevented. Helena is immortal, so she has not died. We still do not know her weakness, as you do not know mine." Mistress turned her gaze back on Traith, and he thought he could almost see her smiling. "Traith, you are lucky the fire didn't harm you. It is odd that the thing you control can harm you so horribly."

Traith let his stare fall back down, but he felt a smile rise on his face.

"Although Ben still lives, with thanks to you, Tanya does not. This has bought us much time, as Helena is mourning over her own First Hand's death. They will need time to replenish themselves, but they are not to be underestimated. Helena has many more followers, and she will convalesce quickly."

Taverin looked deeply pensive, and her eyes seemed sad. It was easy to tell that the trauma of the battle was still fresh in her mind.

"Rein will be out soon, right?" Traith asked.

"Do not worry about her; you need to go rest at the castle."

"But—"

"Go to the manor, Traith."

He hesitated and felt a little stunned at her words. "You want me to just leave? Rein's still here, and I plan on—"

"No! You cannot wait for Rein. Let her alone; she'll sleep for awhile. She's weak. Give her some time."

He shut his mouth, glaring at his leader, but then he faded away into nothing, as did Taverin beside him.

He was terribly eager to talk more to Rein. He didn't want to go home.

What few words she'd mentioned about Ana showed him that something had happened between them…and he had a feeling it was important.

chapter 63

t he cold wind was intense, blowing outside the window, and Rein could hear the faint sound of a raven call in the distance.

Rein jumped up out of her sleep, the sweat from her body soaking into her blanket. She was breathing heavily, and her hands were shaky. Traith jerked at her quick movement and looked at her, startled.

"Rein?" he whispered, smiling, his white teeth actually fully showing. "Finally."

She looked around. She wasn't in the council anymore. She was finally at home in their bedroom. Looking down at herself, she realized her clothes were torn and bloodstained, but despite it, she was comfortable and warm in the bed under silk blankets. She began thinking about everything that had happened to her.

"Are you all right?" he asked.

She sat up, rubbing her eyes. "Yes, I...*wait.*" She looked toward the door, pulling out of Traith's embrace. She suddenly threw off the silk covers.

"Wait for what?"

"N-No, something's wrong. Terribly wrong. Taverin!"

As Rein tried to jump out of bed, he grabbed her dress, forcing her to stay in place. "No! No, it's all right. She's safe and sound. She's in bed. No more injuries."

Rein looked into Traith's eyes.

He gently pulled her close and caressed her. "Look at your chest," he said gently. "There's a—*my* bloody hole there." He sighed. "But it did stop bleeding."

Her blood turned hot within her. She recalled Ana's memories as she felt him embrace her.

"God—Traith, I have to tell you something," she said, her eyes suddenly tearing up.

"Tell me what?"

"I spoke to Ana." A haunting feeling rose within her. "Before the fight."

"What? What happened to her?"

"I saw her mind, Traith. I know how she feels about you, and why she feels that way."

"How? What did she say?"

"She walked by when I was in the cell; I grabbed her, and she told me. Then somehow I received her thoughts, her memories—they were awful—more hostile than any I've ever seen!"

Traith sat up, stiff, as he watched the tears fall down her face. He shook his head slowly; his red eyes were squinting and full of pain and fright like a small boy who wanted to fall apart. "What did she tell you?" He took a breath. "Oh Rein—it was about me, wasn't it?"

"Traith…" Rein almost burst but felt only tears falling. "Did you kill your parents?"

chapter 64

Ψ

He got out of the bed and backed into the wall. Rein had just asked him the most unexplainable question: Had he killed—*murdered*—his own parents?

He slid down the wall and shakily touched his forehead. The details of his past flooded back to him so abruptly; every hole filled. His head jerked a few times. He tried to answer her but couldn't force anything out. There were no excuses. Rein looked into his eyes, reading his dreadful thoughts as he stammered.

He knew that nothing would be able to help him answer that question now. No one had known, ever, except his sister. The nightmarish memory had been lost in his mind for so many years. It was those sessions. Brainwashing sessions. Whips. Electrodes. Things mortals didn't even know existed. Neither had he, until then. *He remembered.* The Mardinial Council. Hell itself.

Hell.

He remembered everything.

He did; he brutally murdered them. A tormenting and bizarre flashback replayed in his head, over and over. He saw what he himself had done to his own parents, whom he had loved. He recalled exactly how he'd murdered them and Ana's face during the process.

How had he forgotten?

He could now abruptly recollect his own metamorphosis and everything that happened before that. His childhood, his adolescence...

He remembered feeling Helena's breath on his neck just before she bit him. He remembered his fright and naivety, the pain, and seeing himself in that old dungeon mirror. He remembered his heartbeat stopping, the guards, and the lantern...

It was all rushing back to him, as if he were reliving every moment.

Rein sat up tall and held her face. She was waiting for an answer. One he couldn't grasp.

"Oh, God. Oh God." His voice was entirely hoarse. He clenched his teeth hard, fighting back tears.

"Traith, I just want an answer. I…" Her soft voice faded in sorrow.

His head fell into his arms. "Rein, the Mardinial Council, they're the ones who killed me, who turned me into this *creature*. Oh, I can remember everything! My entire memory is so clear now: the cell, the pain, and what I looked like as my reflection mutated. They programmed my mind, Rein; they bloody controlled it, and taught me to be the true *damned* soul that I am. They ordered me to kill them, and I didn't want to! What was left of my human soul fought so hard to make me stop." Traith looked up at her. "And right in front of my sister… God, how could I have forgotten something like that? I *did* kill them! I made them *suffer*—and then they made me forget!"

Rein's hands covered her eyes.

"They *tortured* me, Rein," he uttered shakily. "They tortured me. They gave me these scars. They did it with whips, wires…"

Rein held her mouth frantically. "Traith—"

"Rein, they put me in *Hell*." He held his head and cried out loud, remembering the torment, the agony. After a moment his thoughts, again, focused on his parents. "I can hear them! Oh dear God—How could they have taken all that away? *How could they have done that to me?*"

"Traith…oh, my love, I can see it." Her tears were streaming, unchecked, down her cheeks.

She forced herself out of bed, ignoring the jabbing pain in her chest, to try and reach out to him, but he leapt up and turned a little, his hand out.

"Get away; don't touch me, Rein," he cried.

"*Why?*"

He was distraught. "I don't want you to be scared of me, Rein, I—"

"I'm not scared of you, Traith, I love you! You won't—"

"I'm a murderer! Rein, I'm dangerous! I just got done inhaling your blood and now—"

"No," she said. "Don't be afraid to be near me, Traith."

As soon as she tried to near him again, he vanished before her eyes.

Did he think he was doing this for her own good? He actually thought he was going to hurt her?

She stood still, leaning against the wall, her mind whirling. It felt like a lightning bolt piercing her every time she thought about what Ana had seen—how animalistic Traith had looked. It made sense that Ana was frightened of him; she would be scared of someone who did that to her parents as well; she would have the same animosity.

Rein was sobbing uncontrollably as she listened to his smothered cries and curses from beyond the wall. He'd only gone to the hallway. She held in her tears and breath and slowly walked over to the smashed door. She peered into the hallway.

He was on his knees, his fist leaning on the wall, clenching his teeth together. He turned and glanced at her, his eyes heavy with sorrow and anxiety. She approached and fell down beside him, wrapping her arms around him. He didn't pull away as she thought he would, but he didn't return her embrace, either.

"Rein, please forgive me," he stammered, looking into her eyes. "That wasn't me." She felt him slowly tighten around her as if he were going to fall. "The pain I remember…I feel so powerless. Ana has full bloody right to hate me! God, *God*, Rein, the image is imbedded in my head. I taunted them, and I hurt them before I killed them. They must have thought the same thing my sister does. She must think me a bloody terror to not have remembered…to *speak* to her as if I was untainted and flawless. They've been dead for so long, and I can't fix it! I never knew what happened to them! She undoubtedly wanted to put me out of my misery, so I could die and be freed of this curse!"

"You never said you were flawless, Traith," she said, looking at him tenderly. "Even she knows that. She knows you've always struggled with yourself. You have absolutely nothing to be…" She stopped as he continued to crumble in her arms. "Traith, please, it's all right…It's all right…It's over."

"It's not *bloody over*, Rein!" He yanked away from her and that movement sent a jolt down her body from her wound. She gasped, grabbing her chest. His eyes widened.

But he was beyond any further apology. What would that do?

He raked his fingers through his hair, doubling over, reliving the pain of everything he had once numbly endured.

It was hard to speak. She knew the best thing was for him to calm down, but that would be hard. But he needed to. She needed to. They both needed to lie down and sort out their thoughts, put them in the past where they belonged, but it was complicated. Everything was so fresh. She had seen everything as he did. She couldn't think that he would be capable of it all.

She was actually scared.

"They erased my memory," he whispered softly. "And until now... It isn't fair for you—"

Rein placed her soft, pale finger on his lips and pulled herself into him. "Please calm down." She stopped, and he returned her embrace tight again, struggling with his thoughts. "I love you," she whispered. "Don't ever doubt for a second that I would *ever* want to leave here."

He lowered his head to his knees. "I—*damn, I didn't mean to...*"

"You couldn't have prevented it," she continued, trying to soothe his broken heart. Then, reaching out and pulling his face toward her, she looked deep into his wet, red eyes. "We both know the down sides of being a vampire."

"And that's my fault, too, isn't it?" he said. "Oh God..."

She watched him hide his eyes from her, feeling helpless, unable to think of anything more to say that might uplift him. It couldn't be done.

They held each other, and this time he was quiet. She felt his fingers grasp her. Underneath the strong and encouraging spirit she tried to show him, she was terrified. Not of him; she was terrified when he wasn't himself. She felt protected and impenetrable with him over her, now, embracing and holding her. He always protected her. Would fight for her. Die for her. She loved that part of him. But now she had to find a way to help him through a worsened depression—one he had just begun to break free of.

chapter 65

Taverin felt so much calmer and cleaner after she washed and changed into a comfortable dress. She quickly brushed through her long, silky, black hair and twisted it into a braid.

Staring at herself in the mirror, she had to smile. She had no pain; no wounds from the fight. They'd healed her. And although at the time she had been hit and wounded more than she had ever been in her life, and experienced more pain than she ever had, she was glad to know that she was part of something so important. She actually felt stronger rather than weaker, mentally, having witnessed so much blood and gore—more than anyone should ever have to see.

But she thought on about how Rein felt. *What* Rein felt. Having gone from being entirely normal to being a *vampire*. Plus not being able to heal the stake wound in her chest, and being left with a *hole*. She was asleep in there now, with Traith.

Rein had just been brought back a few hours ago, after Traith had gotten frustrated that she wasn't with him. Before he fought and actually won to retrieve her from the council, however, he talked with Taverin for a little bit. It was nice; he wasn't as intimidating as he seemed.

He'd told her something interesting, as well.

"You know the old saying, 'we all have demons in our closets?'"

"Yes," she had replied to him.

"Well, I work the same way, but instead of the demons being *in* my closet, they're loose and in the house, and I'm constantly fighting them instead of being able to hide them away all the time."

She laughed when thinking about it; she'd laughed when he told it to her. He did too. Rein was lucky to have him.

Then she thought on about her own love, William. She hadn't talked to him in ages, it seemed. So much had been going on that it hadn't been safe for her to leave recently, and he had no idea where she had gone, other than home. She felt horrible thinking about the last time she'd seen him: she had spent a long night talking and dancing with him at her best friend Catherine's estate. They'd exchanged a first kiss. Smiles. Touching. And she had said she would see him soon, but had not been specific. As she left, she'd figured she would see him in a week or so, but that night had been at *least* a month ago. What would he think, having not heard from her after their first kiss? She would hate for him to think the wrong things. William was now twenty, and he could so easily meet another girl, one closer in age to him.

But Rein said he would wait...

Suddenly she heard loud voices.

Traith's voice sounded from he and Rein's bedroom across the hall.

She sat stiff and quiet, listening for a moment; she heard crying. Something had happened between them, but it was hard for her to tell what.

After a few long minutes, it became silent. Taverin hesitantly stood and walked toward her bedroom door. As quiet as she could, she turned the knob and poked her head out, and she accidentally gasped when she saw Traith and Rein holding each other on the stone floor in the hallway.

Rein looked up when she heard Taverin's gasp.

Traith suddenly vanished, and Rein sat back, still crying, staring at the spot in which he had been sitting.

"God," she said, her words muffled as she held her head in her hands.

"I'm sorry," Taverin said like a mouse from her doorway. "Rein, what happened?"

"He murdered his parents, Taverin."

Taverin held her mouth as Rein cried.

"Many, many years ago. Helena brainwashed him and then wiped his memory. I rekindled it. He's devastated."

"Oh my Lord," Taverin said. "Rein? Are you going to—Is Traith going to be all right? Where did he go?"

"I don't know," Rein answered in a frightened whisper, pushing her straight, black hair out of her face. "I cannot do anything for him. He needs to escape into himself for a while; and by God, he'll have to fight hard; no wound has ever cut him so deeply."

chapter 66

t he room was very dim; the only light came from the sconces that hung from the ceiling in each of the four corners of the area. Metallic generators and machines were all beeping and ticking loudly, eerily, and there were tall, cylinder-shaped tubes leading up to the ceiling with test subjects in them.

A special agent had been sent to locate and recover the body they were searching for. It had been considered "missing" for some time. But during that time, secret searches had been going on. After tedious searching, the body, or at least, the remains of it, was found. Not much but bone and dissolved meat was left of the wet corpse, but even that was more than enough needed to carry out the experiment. Now that same body, or rather the soul of the person who once owned that body, was drifting up and down in a large test tube with metal wires and patches attached to her head, torso, and lower body. She was stark naked and sickening to look at due to long saturation. In the tube next to her, there was another body: a woman; she was young and beautiful, but lifeless. She had been created from a number of different people. The soul of the mutilated body next to her was transferred into her, allowing her to have life. The newly created female convulsed in the tube and, suddenly, opened her eyes.

"The process is complete, Helena." A shaky voice came from a dark figure, not visible in the dimness. It was Ana.

"Good. Good. Bring her out. Dispose of the old body."

Ana nodded and punched a few buttons into the operational panel, draining the chemicals in the tube, forcing the woman to stand on her own two feet for the first time. Two pipes hissed as the testing tube rose. The woman staggered out, ripping off wires that had been transferring data into her mind. Two creatures placed a robe around her nude body, and the woman searched the darkness.

"Where…where am I?" The girl's voice was hoarse.

"Good evening, dear."

"Who am I? Who are you?"

The winged mistress turned and smiled wickedly. "Your name was lost quite a while ago, but to refresh your memory, your name is Saria Kendrick."

"*Saria.* What did you do?" The girl looked away for a moment, apparently recalling old memories.

Helena turned and laughed. Ana, from the back of the room, walked up to the girl and delivered her a message without her leader seeing.

"Carden..." Saria began rambling. "Rein...strange memories... Carden? I loved him. What happened? How long have I been—?"

"Ah, yes, about Carden," the leader said as she faced them again.

"What did he do to me? How long have I been asleep?"

"He did nothing; an evil man murdered you. I merely brought you back to life, allowing you the chance of revenge on a murderer."

"Where is Carden? Still on the ship? How long—"

"Carden is gone. And your dearest, most precious friend, Rein Pierson, was his murderer. She killed your beloved with the fangs that she now bares in her mouth."

Saria stepped backward. Her eyes were full of tears. Her new hair was cut short and strangely colored due to the chemical process of the re-embodiment. She was taller, now, and well-developed, with odd eyes: one sapphire and one violet.

"Rein Pierson brought me with her so we could get away from England. She k-killed him? But she would never...I can't believe that. How long has it been? How long have I been asleep?" Saria began walking frantically toward the dark silhouette.

"For *months*, my dear girl; months at the bottom of the ocean. But don't you worry...I'll allow you your vengeance."

Ana slowly backed away from Helena and the girl, and ran off down a hallway. She was not seen by the Leader, but ran quickly; she was terrified.

chapter 67

t averin was sitting at her vanity table toying with her hair and thinking. She was becoming restless in the silence. Taking leave of her chamber, she made her way to the bower two flights below her.

It was used so little by Rein, and since it was the room laid aside for women's use, Taverin liked it. She liked many of the rooms in the castle, really. Each was entirely different; there were baileys, courtyards, the library, the kitchen, the ballroom, training hall, gallery, armory, study, and so much more. The only place she really hated was the grotto, the part of Traith's castle that was underground and looked like a cave. It was in between empty cellars once used for wines or food. It was, to her, a damp, dark, scary room, but it opened up into a beautiful conservatory with glass walls and a glass ceiling. Once you made it to that part, it was rather amazing.

Rein normally liked to be with her betrothed, who always preferred to sit in the master library, the master drawing room, the study, the grotto, the conservatory, or their master chambers. That was usually it for Traith, but after what had happened—his regaining his memory— he had hardly even spoken once to Rein.

Taverin took a deep breath as she opened the door to the bower. She had to get away from the tension between Rein and Traith. She loved that room; it had a piano, a shelf of books, an atlas, and materials to draw and paint with. She had never been a skilled artist, but she enjoyed dabbling occasionally. She opened the large door, closed it behind her, and sat down on the piano stool. She played a simple but cheerful song.

As she sat there, however, she thought about her situation.

She was now sixteen years old, and she loved a man; she loved William. But he was twenty. He enjoyed her company, but she felt that he thought her still a bit too young to love.

She was starting to wonder if she had really made the right decision in coming to live here in isolation. And because Traith was technically inaccessible to even Rein at the current moment, there was no way she was getting to Cherbourg anytime soon. Her eyes were welling up with tears when a knock on the door interrupted her thoughts.

"May I come in, dear?"

She turned and wiped her eyes quickly as she answered the call. It was Rein, tall and refined as she entered from the shadowy hallway. She walked in and sat on a sofa near Taverin. She looked stressed, but her elegant, soothing manner still made Taverin feel better.

"You're crying," Rein said quietly. "What's wrong?"

"Nothing is wrong. I just haven't seen anyone from my old home in a while."

Rein leaned back against the sofa. "You know, when I brought you here, I knew it wasn't going to be easy for you to leave your entire social life behind. I know there's really no one here for you to talk to."

"No, no. It's not like that. I wanted to stay. Really."

Rein raised an eyebrow.

"Oh, I know I am not fooling you. I'm just so scared about everything. It's hard when you or Traith are upset. Especially now, after…" Taverin burst into tears and hunched over the piano.

After a moment of sobbing, she looked up at Rein. Her perfect face looked so miserable, so distant.

"Oh, Rein!" she gasped. "I really do love living here, and I love you! I honestly—"

"Soon, Tav. As soon as this is through, you can go back over to France. I just want you safe." Rein took a seat next to her on the piano stool and pulled her close. "If William loves you," Rein murmured, "he will wait for you. He *will* wait for you."

"Rein, honestly? You…you are confident?"

"Confidence has nothing to do with it."

Taverin smiled and then laughed. Rein knew what would happen, and with that reassurance, Taverin sat still in her half-sister's arms. But was Rein entirely correct? Would she be hurt before any of that could happen?

chapter 68

t he fireplace burned brightly, throwing shadows across Traith in the
darkened study. Everything was quiet except for his frequent curses
and the crackling sounds coming from the beakers and canisters of
laboratory equipments. Rein opened the door, quietly but not subtly.
He spun around and stared at her from the darkness; she swallowed
and took a seat at the far end of the room by the fire. She looked
straight ahead into the dancing, crackling flames, but she could feel his
eyes watching.

His voice began in a shaky whisper. "Please, Rein…"

He was suggesting that she leave.

"No," she replied, just as softly, but more aggressively.

She heard him sigh quietly, and his stare left her. He again immersed
himself in science and study.

She was actually excited that he hadn't left the room. His memories
and thoughts seemed to constantly haunt him. She knew how ashamed he
felt in front of anyone, including her. He had hardly spoken to her since
he'd regained his memory. He had wanted his memory back so terribly,
but it had brought him only more horrors to consume his thoughts. She
was happy that she'd only received Ana's perspective, as well. She hadn't
relived his entire life, just the murder. And it was *gruesome…*

He remembered everything. He had full right to be desperate to
get his mind off of it, however he could. It seemed that whenever he
was finally getting over something, something else knocked him back
down. But instead of letting her help him, he vanished whenever she
neared him.

Rein's face darkened as she looked away from the fire toward him. He
put down his papers and turned to face her, feeling her inside his head.
She smiled and, taking a chance, stood and walked across the room. He
didn't recoil. Her hands met him; her fingers ran down his chest, and she
breathed him in. She raised herself on tiptoe and kissed first his neck,

then his chin, then his lips. He finally relaxed and returned her kiss. He wrapped his arms around her and easily lifted her off her feet, setting her gently on the couch by the fire. She laughed quietly; it was due to both his caress and the fact that she knew she'd eased his mind. She knew he was thinking only of her—finally.

The door to the study swung open. He looked up, startled, standing. Rein squirmed out from underneath him and stood up just as Taverin walked through the door, a serious expression on her face. As soon as she saw them, Taverin's face flushed red.

"What is it, Taverin?" Rein asked, recomposed.

Traith cleared his throat and turned away, walking back toward his study.

Taverin looked awkward. "I—I'm sorry, did I interrupt? Oh, my, I did, didn't I?"

"No, no, no. Did you need something?" Rein's eyes followed her lover for another moment.

He grunted as a loud pop came from a small vial he had picked up off his desk. He threw it at the wall in aggravation, shaking his hand as if he'd hurt it. The glass shattered, and chemicals spilled and dripped down the wall. He gripped both ends of the table, breathing deeply, trying to calm himself.

Rein tried her best to ignore his frustration. She held her hand out to Taverin and led her out the door, leaving Traith alone in his study.

Taverin, once in the hallway, looked up into Rein's eyes. "Rein, was it me? Was he angry with me?"

"No, not at all. He's just...He's still broken inside, Taverin. Every moment he's thinking, replaying things. I imagine it would be hard to regain a lost memory to begin with, let alone a terrible one. He has a lot of mental working out to do."

The young girl looked down in sorrow. "I see."

"So what is it that you want, Tav?"

"I've just been thinking about what you said to me when I first came to live here with you." She hesitated.

"And what was that?"

"What you told me in the bower...I've been thinking about it—"

"Taverin," Rein looked thoughtfully into her young sister's eyes. "I know what you want; your own life, your own love. I understand. You want to go home now. To William."

Taverin's face lit up. Rein looked toward the study door in an attempt to hide the twinge she felt in her stomach.

"You read my mind, didn't you? William said his sister would like a companion…" She paused. "Rein, I love him. I love you, but I love him."

"Then you may leave whenever you like, Taverin," she murmured with a smile. "I trust you. You know about…*this*, now. But you must realize that you could always be a target. Take the spell book Mistress gave you. Use it if you ever must, promise me."

Taverin nodded and threw her arms around Rein. "I promise, Rein!" Then she turned and ran off down the hall, squealing with happiness.

Rein sighed painfully. She knew she had probably made the wrong decision by letting her have the answer she wanted so quickly. She wouldn't be safe living in France.

She brushed it aside. Traith was consuming too much of her thoughts. It was late, and by the time she made it back to the study, Traith wasn't there. Her heart was sick for him. He had kept himself secluded since that disquieting night. He had not slept in the bedroom for the past few nights, but in his study or somewhere alone. It was killing her.

She walked to the master bedroom, praying she'd find him there.

She opened the door, being careful not to make much noise.

He was lying silent in bed.

Her heart rose in her chest with silent thrill at him being there. She heard his thoughts. He didn't want her to know he was awake.

But he was awake.

She walked to the bedside and dropped her robe, revealing a thin nightdress, and sat on the bed beside him.

"You're not asleep," she said quietly.

He made no reply.

"I got a message today," she said, running her fingers through his hair. "It was from the council, informing us about the date of the All Hallows Eve Ball in Bangor, Ireland."

When he still didn't reply, she sat up on her knees and threw one leg over him, straddling him. His head turned fast at her movement, and his piercing red eyes gazed up at her.

"Traith, I've never been to the ball before," she continued. "I haven't been to a ball since…since you bit my lip." She knew she had his attention when she felt his muscles tense underneath her. "And I never even got the chance to finish one dance with you because you left me."

"Why do you *do* that?" he asked almost inaudibly, sitting up.

She slid off him and lay down on her side. He turned his back to her, letting his legs dangle off the side of the bed and resting his elbows on his knees.

"To make a point, Traith. You're so bad-tempered about—"

"And you think that makes your point? Having punctured your lip gives me all the more reason to detest dances as well as everything else! Do you honestly think this is what I want to think about now? Rein, it's been a mere two days since my life was shattered, so I'd appreciate it if you didn't remind me this moment of how I *ruined* yours!"

"Don't raise your voice to me," she retorted. "I wasn't trying to make you feel worse. I just think you need to get out and stop thinking—"

"Stop *thinking?*" he asked. "Do you realize what I've just recalled? You may have learned about what I did, but even still you cannot possibly think for a *second* that you can understand my pain, whether you saw what I did or not!" He broke down, head in hands. "God Rein," he whispered. "I can't think at *all* without…"

She was silent for a moment, but she reached out and grabbed his elbow, pulling him to face her. "Don't you leave," she enjoined. "Don't be afraid to be near me. I'm not afraid that you'll hurt me."

"You bloody should be!" he shouted, ripping off of her, but he sounded choked up. His hands were balled tight. "I can't be near you right now, Rein," he murmured. "That doesn't mean I don't want to be…"

"I *am* afraid of something, Traith," she uttered softly. "I'm *terrified,* and it's because you feel that way."

His head slowly turned to look at her.

"You and Taverin are the only two people in the world that I have. And when you act like you're a burden to me, or that you're frightening, I realize that you've changed. When you act like this, I feel utterly alone."

"No, Rein," he replied. "It isn't—"

"I don't want you to fall backward down the hill you've been trying to see the top of for so long. I felt like you were so close to accepting things, Traith, and now that this has happened...granted you're distraught, but...I need you to see that we can get through this. We can get through everything that comes our way, but only if you accept what we are, and that I will always love you."

He stared deeply at her, and his hand lifted and touched her face.

She pulled him back down onto the bed and held him. "Traith, you know that was not you. Not even remotely. You were being controlled. Why can't you be happy about the lives you've *saved* instead of dwelling on ones you—"

"*Took*? That can never be atoned for, Rein!"

She laid still, stiff. "I'll always be here, and I don't think you understand that. You aren't alone in this world. Never again. And all sins can be atoned for, Traith, but that begins within your heart. What happened is even less of your fault than it would've been if it had been an accident. You were forced into a position where you weren't yourself at all."

"That isn't the point," he whispered. "I was their *son*. They were proud of me. I was in a university. Ana and I were so close. She dreamt of attending the same university I did. She wanted to get a real job, a kind that women were never supposed to have. So much would've happened right. They had to watch me as I prepared to *torture* them. As I *was* torturing them. And they loved me, but died in fear and confusion as to why I was hurting them!" He held his head. "I remember fighting so hard to drive out that part of me," he rasped. "With that scene imbedded, I can't imagine you not fearing me, or not fearing that I would do the same to *you*. I'm so thankful you don't, Rein. Please don't think I take that for granted."

"You would never *hurt* me," she cooed in his ear. "So stop saying that." She buried her head under his jaw. "All I want is for you to be yourself again, Traith. I just don't know what it will take to get you there. I understand—"

"You *don't*!" he yelled, his voice echoing. "You didn't drain your parents of life, Rein! You never pumped out your lover's blood and drank it of your own will!"

"Then at least I don't dwell on how *horrible* my life is with a *murderous man* I *love*," she said sarcastically, hoarse in anger. "I try with all my *might* to understand what you went through. What you did. Would you prefer me to be scared of you? I've forced myself to accept so much in the past months, and I've accepted you. The more you do this, the harder you become for me to accept, and I *hate* that!"

He had been silent a while. "I'm sorry." He shook his head. "I just don't *want* you to understand, Rein. You shouldn't have to."

"Traith, look at me," she said sighing, becoming passive again. "I have fangs like you. I have red eyes like you. I know your fears. And guess what? I'm successfully living with the *severe problem* you told me I couldn't live with on that ship. I'm stronger than you think."

"You *are* strong. So strong, Rein. I don't know how you even stayed."

She cocked an eyebrow in disbelief. "What?"

"Have you no notion of why I avoided you on the ship?" he continued. "I was fond of you, Rein, but I knew what would happen. I tried not to speak much; I tried to appear—"

"I know you avoided me, and you probably would've been successful if Carden hadn't given explanations to all of your actions. You would've been happier if I had left you alone? So you could live life without me? Do I mean that little to you?"

There was a long pause as Traith grasped for words. "You mean more to me than life, Rein," he whispered in agony. "And I don't know what to think. If we had never met, none of this would've happened to you. He never would have killed you if you hadn't been close to me."

"So you're sorry?"

"Never," he replied throatily. "I will never be sorry. Maybe that's why I feel so guilty."

"You've no right to feel guilty," she said, her voice gentle. "And that is your greatest fault: you refuse to forgive yourself like you've been forgiven. For once," she murmured. "For once, let's not think about this. Don't ever be afraid to hold me."

After running her fingers down his face, she let go of him and left the bed, headed back toward the hall. He sighed, slowly sitting up.

"I hope that when you do accept your life," she said from behind him, "you will actually tell me what you now remember about it." She took the crucifix he'd given her off her neck and tossed it at him. "Perhaps all you need is to have a little more faith in *this* than you do."

Just as he turned to look at her, she was leaving the balcony.

"Rein," he said after her. "Rein, we'll go to the ball, all right? Your happiness would be the best medicine."

She paused in her step. Her eyes closed tight before closing the doors.

chapter 69

ana could hear the gruesome noises coming from behind that door. Helena was having a meal: another poor victim, found somewhere alone in the world, without any more chance of having a regular life, or rather, having no chance of life at all.

She was happy to be living. It was a chance unlike any she had ever come across, and it was only given to her because of her brother. But she lived in fear and sorrow. It was such a cold life. Minutes felt like hours to her. And the hours, days. It was almost unbearable. The lengthening of her life was a blessing when it had first happened to her. But over one hundred years had gone by since she was given immortality, and she had spent that time thinking without end about her brother. Perhaps she was in hell, burning in it…

The aroma of death shattered her thoughts. She stood at her bedside and held her head as she heard Helena call her name from the doorway.

But then, there he was again. Rising up in her mind, as he always did.

Traith.

A knot formed fast in her stomach as Helena called her name again. She had hardly seen Helena since the day she'd run from the fighting— from having to fight her brother. She'd seen her when awakening Saria, a few days ago, but she had not actually spoken to her. She knew she would be punished, somehow, but the suspense of the *how* was torturing her enough. It was as if Helena had been making her wait just to build up her fear.

"*Ana!*" she heard once more. Helena was yelling fiercely this time, and she opened the door slowly to approach her leader.

In the darkness, she saw Helena wipe blood from her mouth. She did so much more than simply kill her victims. She only ever took men, despite her marriage to Ben. Ana knew he was not with her by his own will. She was partly controlling him. What if Helena was doing the same to her?

"Why do you not answer me?" Helena asked with a glare of intent. "Are you thinking about where you last left your brother?"

Ana looked down and said nothing. She knew the leader had read her mind. She tried to prepare herself for what was coming next, but she couldn't. Helena could do anything to her.

"I was just lost in thought, Helena," Ana whimpered.

"You're always lost in thought, Ana. But today, as most every day, you were thinking of Traith, weren't you? Oh, but did you not fight him? Your brilliant mind must be clear. I cannot have you wavering, dear Ana."

Helena's tone was different as she continued to speak. It was strange, almost sarcastic in tone, as if she were joking. Ana felt her becoming more and more threatening.

"Forgive me, Helena," she said barely louder than she had before. "I don't know why I fled. I understand you're going to punish me, somehow, but there is something I cannot understand…" She paused, fearing Helena could sense she had lied when asking for forgiveness. "Why, if he is so demonic, do *you* kill more than he does? Why do you drink the blood of innocents, and he is so adamant that he will not? He's continuously begged for my forgiveness, as if he didn't know what he did. I don't know, it just seems…"

Helena gazed at her with mockery in her eyes. "You saw what he did to your mother and father, didn't you?"

"But he seemed so regretful," she carefully protested. "He doesn't kill people without reason, Helena. Not anymore. Not *since*. But you do, why is that? Why do we brainwash people? I've just been thinking so much about it, and it just isn't right. I think, now, that he is. And his council…they're moral. They don't do what we do." Her voice trailed off in confusion at Helena's expression.

She was beginning to grin, calmly. "Bravo."

Ana stared at her with full attention. "I don't quite—"

"I bit him."

Her throat tightened. "W-what?"

The woman smiled. "You are without doubt the stupidest woman I've ever met," she laughed with a sigh.

"No," Ana cried, shaking her head. "You said…"

Her heart seemed to detonate inside of her; she was shaking with uncontrollable fear.

Helena sneered at her as she fell against the wall. "Is that a *fit punishment*, dearest? I found him and toyed. I sank my teeth into him. Oh, and the taste of that bite. The spiciness of his blood. The bitterness. It was more than a minor refreshment. He filled me for months."

"*You?*"

"I brainwashed him with the same technology I used on Kendrick, and on you."

Ana crumpled to the floor, succumbing to panic. "He never lied to me like you said, and I—?"

"I forced him, against everything in his being, to do what you watched him do. And the most *amusing* thing is," Helena paused and gazed with laughing eyes at Ana's grief. "I obliterated the part of his mind that recalls his past. So he had no idea what he had done. He didn't remember."

Ana's body was entirely numb, but her mind was pounding as if there were a heart in her skull.

Traith was out there somewhere, and he didn't know what she now knew. What she now understood. He was somewhere living, listening or speaking, sleeping or riding, training, reading...he was doing something, and she wished to God he could be there next to her for just a single moment.

"Then of course," Helena continued, "*you* came along, and I stretched the story." She called for Ben, laughing. "You were beginning to fold, my dearest Ana," she said afterward. "Instead of murdering you for your betrayal, your refusal to kill him, I am telling you the truth. It may be worse than death itself. I am now forever finished with you, Miss *Harker*."

Ben was running down the dark hallway, and he grabbed Ana.

"Why are you doing this?" Ana screamed in desperation. "You killed him! You lied to me and tormented his mind!"

"Yes I know, thank you," she cackled. "It strikes me as ironic how your brother is so clever and so saucy, yet you are so naïve! It is a shame you had to let your mind fail like this. You now have as long as needed to think and cry about your poor, unfortunate, darling brother. I will not kill you. Yet."

Ben tossed Ana down into a dirt-floored room.

"So lose yourself, Ana," she hissed. "You will have more to think about than you ever had before, thanks to these last, minor details." She paused and stood straight-backed, flapping her webbed wings and holding the iron door open in her hand. "After Traith managed to escape from me, Mistress found him and took him in. Do you know how many attempts he made at *suicide* after that, Ana? How many times he tried to kill himself because he didn't have the mental strength to drink blood or live without a reflection, but live with the knowledge that he not only *looked* like but *was* a completely monstrous vampire? Even though he never knew what he'd done, because he'd been brainwashed and tortured. Then you cursed him, Ana, so that he would be forced to live on a ship with a Mardinial captain for one hundred and some odd years without the capability to commit suicide? Lucky he didn't go mad. So now, being that you hated him, and being that his lover, Rein Pierson, witnessed your memories, Traith recollected what he did. He recollected about two months ago and has been distraught ever since. So now that he still thinks you hate him, and that he is a vampire, and now that he knows he brutally murdered his own parents…how far from suicide do you think he is now, Ana? And how will you get to him *now*?"

Helena laughed hysterically and slammed the iron door, rousing dirt around Ana, who was curled on her side in the middle of the room. She heard the door lock. After a few moments, all was quiet. Her head was spinning.

He hadn't known?

Just months ago, she'd indirectly returned to him his memory?

He had killed their parents against his own will?

And she had tried to kill him, all these years.

Did he hate her?

What was he thinking now?

Taverin was solemn and distraught. She felt more than all of those things. She cried louder and longer than she ever had. Hours may have gone by without her knowing. She was filled with fear and sorrow. She wasn't going to be killed. She wasn't going to be physically tormented. But she was being tortured with so much more vindictiveness than she could have imagined.

She had to find him. Be near him. Tell him. Do something. She had tried to kill him so many times. Cursed him onto a ship for longer than a lifetime. He still ran back to her after it all, every time he saw her. She had to speak with him, one last time. She knew, despite what Helena had said, she *knew* she would be killed. They would give her enough time to approach Traith, and then they would kill her.

She started up, looking around her for the first time. Through watery vision, she realized they had thrown her in the potion storeroom. On purpose, perhaps, but she didn't care. She mixed a glass and threw it in front of her, and she vanished.

Helena laughed from the outside of the doorway, her ear against it. "She's gone," she said to Ben. "And I know where she's going."

"Why did you tell her? She was useful, smart—"

"And insignificant."

He huffed. "But is it not better to have an insignificant woman in *our* council rather than throwing her over to Mistress and letting her know the truth so easily?"

"I didn't tell her easily, Ben! She's been slowly figuring it out since Traith got off that ship. I'm surprised she decided to listen to us rather than her own brother in the first place!" She held her chin with her first finger and thumb, cocking her head. "But you understand that we are not at all at a loss here. We may no longer have our familiar chemist at hand, but we have an army—one more powerful than any that the Council of the Presage may have. We'll follow her after giving her a bit of a head start."

"As you say, Helena."

chapter 70

It was the 31st of October; it was pouring outside the ancient Irish castle. Thunder boomed around Rein, but the cheery voices and music were loud enough to overpower the rumbling. It was the night of the All Hallows Eve Masquerade Ball. The organ music filled the Cathedral fortress, along with low operatic singing and laughter.

Traith was spinning her. He was not enthused, but she was happy that he was dancing at all. It all seemed routine for him, ironically. His movements were better than hers, more elegant. She had never been an expert dancer, but he was so graceful; it seemed like he wasn't even trying.

The people around her were dressed in beautiful gaud, with high pompadours and top hats. Women's breasts peeked out from the tight corsets they wore, and men's necks were held stiff by their collars. Colorful and sparkling masks were placed against their dancing faces, changing appearances from all angles. Some wore masks with long noses, or large eyes, or animal-like characteristics. Each couple was dancing in sync, twirling and walking about, the fancy dresses lighting up the room. Some occasionally watched the act above where men were walking a tight rope. Jugglers and fire breathers were stationed above each pillar, entertaining those dancing below.

The castle ballroom was the largest and grandest she'd ever seen. It was decorated with dark, romantic paintings, ribbon, and curtaining. Gold tassels hung down from every corner of the room, tied around beautiful rose bouquets on the walls.

The music stopped, and loud clapping filled the air before another song was played. Traith pulled down his mask and turned to leave the dance floor. Rein followed behind him, still clapping.

"This is beautiful, Traith," she said. "I *can* understand why you don't like it here, but I wanted to experience it at least once."

He leaned back on a pillar with his mask in his hand, looking at everybody. "I do hope once is enough," he said sarcastically, but he looked to her and smiled.

She circled behind him. "You are an incredible dancer," she murmured. "One might say you used to dance often."

"I had to at one point." He held his head high. "When I was young, before I was turned, I went with Ana often."

"Did you never enjoy it?"

He shrugged, "Of course. I could dance and see myself in the ball mirrors at the same time."

He glanced over and looked at the mirror that was hung on the wall next to him, and neither he nor she was in it. There were mirrors hung all around the fortress.

He was beyond perturbed. She felt the intensity of his discomfort when she looked into his burning eyes, but he was keeping himself calm and attempting to be pleasant for her. Attempting was at least the first step to recovering from his trauma, so she didn't pester him about it.

Traith looked up above him at the man walking the tightrope. The man lost his balance and fell, plummeting toward Traith. Everyone gasped, and Rein took a few steps back, but the man fell right through Traith. Traith didn't move a muscle, but closed his eyes when the ghost fell through him. The ghost giggled and stood only to disappear and reappear back on the tightrope. More clapping echoed, and others laughed happily at the stunt. Traith gave a smile devoid of amusement and took a seat in the back after another song began.

Rein had meant to ask him about what had happened and how he had known the man wouldn't hit him. She had known, too, that he was a ghost, but Traith was beyond apathetic toward the man, as if he had been part of a stunt like that before. Rein was suddenly pulled aside before she could follow Traith back to the lone table.

"Hello, Rein," the man said, laughing. "Very nice stunt your fiancé was part of."

She turned and smiled vacantly. "Good evening, Dr. Campbell."

"You look more handsome tonight than I have ever seen you," he added with a smile, letting his eyes travel the length of her body. She smiled and nodded and attempted to leave his presence, but he began to speak further. "Your hair is done just beautifully, and your dress is the most attractive here. It's your simplicity!"

She sighed and turned to Traith. He was some distance away, but he was watching her intently, cautiously gazing. She felt his vigilance.

"Thank you," she replied. "You look…nice, as well."

She knew as well as any that Jacques was not a handsome man. His features were bland, and he was so thin that he always looked ill.

"Traith does not seem to be enjoying this," Dr. Campbell added with a swoop of his hand over his light brown hair. "And neither do you."

"I am trying to enjoy it," she said, smiling. "Traith isn't making it too easy, though."

"Well, I must tell you that I am forever in debt to you for saving me," Jacques said on a more serious note. "My life now, in this council, is far better than I thought it could ever be. Why, I even finally tamed the beast, Rein!"

"Fancy that," she said vacantly. "I'm glad Traith and I *did* help."

He laughed and turned his head to face the mirrors next to him. "We make a lovely couple," he said with a giggle. "You and Harker are the only two vampires here, you know. The only two vampires in the entire council, which makes you the only vampi*ress*!"

She felt Traith tense as he watched.

"Excuse me," she mumbled as she turned and walked toward Traith.

"It was only in jest," Dr. Campbell called out with a smile, but he turned away, back into the crowd of dancers from whence he had come.

"I *left*," she said as she approached the table, a crooked smile glimmering up her face.

"I didn't say anything." His head was cocked when he responded to her, but then as the organ began to play louder, she saw him perk up.

It was a familiar tune to her: it was a song called "Portrait of Romanticism." It had been one of her favorite songs, but now it pained her to hear it. It was the one Carden had played during the last ball she'd been at—one of the last happy times she had had with Saria, and also when Traith had bitten her lip, and the captain dropped the glass vial of blood…

"Carden always did play well," she heard Traith say faintly. "It's a shame he disappeared."

Rein looked at him and saw the sadness that he couldn't hold in anymore. It had been months, and still he hadn't been the same. His birthday had even come and gone—only a week ago—and he refused to celebrate it at all. He hadn't even spoken of when they were to have their wedding.

She looked back at the pianist, her voice gentle. "Don't think about the song. Carden might still be alive somewhere, Traith. He's a vampire; it would take a lot to kill him."

He did not reply.

"Saria liked his playing, too, you know," she whispered.

Traith turned to her with heavy eyes, but swallowed his sorrow when Mistress began to approach him. He stood and met her at the pillar where he had been before.

"One moment," she said and walked aside to speak with someone else. Rein watched in wonder as a beautiful woman approached Traith from behind. It was Lorena, and she neared with an extremely erotic demeanor. The priestess's fingers gently crept onto his shoulders, and he turned around in astonishment when he felt her.

To Rein's relief, he knocked her hands off immediately. "What the devil are you doing, Lorena?"

Rein felt her heart hit her throat.

The seductress held her hand. "Traith, that was *naughty*. I was only playing."

Traith turned and looked at Rein, who smiled when she heard his silent requests for her to stand near him. She left the table.

"Ooh," Lorena murmured, touching her fingertips to her mouth. "That new scar is quite an accent, I must say, Traith."

Rein saw his eyes narrow. "Thank you," he replied with a sarcastic bow. "Do you fancy it as much as the others?"

"Oh, more!" she continued, either oblivious to or ignoring his sarcasm. She laughed and pulled off her mask. "And there she is," she said, grinning. "Are you still Rein Pierson, as you were? Or have you married yet?"

"Not yet," she answered, approaching Traith. "But my last name will be different soon." She smiled to herself when she felt the woman's jealousy. "See my ring?"

The beautiful stones and diamonds shone brilliantly in the light of the chandelier as she held up her left hand.

Traith cracked a slight smile, and she felt his hand feel around her waist. That charming deed made Lorena even more envious.

Lorena cleared her throat. "It is dashing, isn't it? But haven't I seen that ring before, Traith?"

Rein stiffened.

Traith chuckled at her response. "You wish you had, don't you?"

In the way his voice was calm and controlled, Rein knew Lorena had never seen the ring. Lying, just to get her to feel like an imposter.

Rein wanted to say something, but she forced herself to keep quiet. Traith had kept quiet while watching Jacques.

"Lorena, please get away from me," he finally said, keeping his reserve.

"You want me to leave?" she snorted. "Bah! Your left hand could be *my*—"

"Stop being a—"

"Ah, Traith!"

To Rein's delight, the Mistress greeted the two of them before Traith could finish his words, and before there was a conflict. Lorena walked away angrily with her mask back on as the Mistress approached.

"And why haven't *you* pointed out the newest addition to my collection, yet, by the way?" Traith asked Rein with sarcastic frustration. "The apparently jagged scar I have down my eye that everyone so kindly told me about? You know, soon I'll have racked up so much scarring on my face that I can only imagine I'll be quite hard to look at."

She had to giggle slightly. "Jagged? Traith, I don't need to point that out. It doesn't make you look any different. Besides, I like it."

"How did it even come back to me, when you took it?"

She shrugged. "I have no idea. Must've been something in my power."

Just as his eyebrows rose and he gave a quirky half-smile, Mistress chimed in. "I'm sorry for making you wait," she said. "A more important matter was brought to my attention."

"There's always a matter more important than me," Traith commented quietly, crossing his arms tight.

Just when Rein thought the woman was going to make a remark about what he'd said, she sighed softly. "I'm sorry, Harker. Did I interrupt something between you and my mage?"

"Nothing you would want to hear," he said indifferently.

"I know that you're not happy, Traith. What with the reminiscence of your murders…"

Traith's reserve collapsed and his face tensed; he swallowed a few times. "I guess you haven't noticed my attempt to get over that."

"You aren't exactly that *apparent*, you know," Mistress countered.

"Oh, thank you! So is this important enough to ruin my night over?" he scoffed hoarsely. "Or for the rest of my life are you going to remind me daily of what I've done?"

"Oh, I'm sorry," she quickly said. "I just thought that you would like to know that it will get better."

"Get better? Are you—?"

"*Slightly* better. I know it will never fully heal."

He stared at her, waiting for her to continue. "Well?"

"You will see," she replied with a smile.

"What?" he asked. "That's it? You're not going to give me even a *hint* about what can make my sorrow better in the midst of your bloody riddle? *God*, I *hate*—"

"You will see," she said again.

"Of course," he mocked. "It's always a riddle. Always a damn riddle!"

"Always," she repeated him and smiled.

Rein noticed Traith staring past Mistress. His red eyes held a mix of confusion and shock, and he held Mistress's shoulders and moved her aside in a daze. Both she and Rein watched him with curiosity.

Mistress had been blocking someone different in the crowd, someone who stood out. She didn't see who it was, but she knew. Something snapped in her head, and she knew…

It was Ana.

chapter 71

a na?" Rein whispered.

Mistress walked away, smiling, unnoticed.

"Yes. It's Ana." He answered her distractedly. "She's crying." He watched his sister flow through the crowd of dancers.

Rein stared at him. Her head was pulsing.

"*No, not now…*"

Rein could hear Traith's unspoken fears.

"*I can't explain to her…*"

She was reading his thoughts involuntarily—again! She tried to suppress her panic, but then she could hear more than just Traith's thoughts. She could hear many more.

"Rein?" he turned, only half focusing on her.

Rein backed up and leaned against a pillar, and, in pain, she collapsed to the floor. Traith called her again, but she didn't answer. She could only see his mouth moving. Her mind was screaming at her, but she couldn't understand why.

My mind is expanding still?

Turning out of Ana's sight, Traith took Rein's arm, and in a moment, she felt cool rain tingle her face. Then it all stopped; her mind was silenced.

"Aw, it's bloody raining." He cursed, blinking as the rain hit his eyes. When he spoke again, his voice was gentler. "Are you all right?"

He pulled her up, and she gained her balance as quickly as she had lost it.

He immediately let go of her. "You read my mind," he said. "Without permission. Why?" He stared deeply at her. "Can you hear me?"

She glanced around. She was on the balcony outside the castle ballroom with no one near her but him. "Yes, now I can," she said with a shake of her head. "But Ana—"

"Why did you collapse?"

She didn't answer quickly enough for him.

"Is it your head? What's wrong, Rein?"

She was nearly speechless in shock. "I don't know. But it stopped. Traith, I think something bad is going to happen. I think that's why it happened."

He looked tense as ever. "I wouldn't doubt it, but please try to stay on your feet and keep clear-headed. Please. I...Ana...she looked right at me, as if she were here to *talk*. I don't know why she's here, but I don't want to talk to her, not now," he finished in a bewildered manner.

"Traith, you must explain—"

"You want me to explain to her?" he asked in frustration. "That I honestly didn't remember killing my parents in front of her, and that I wish I'd known, because if I had—" The raising of his voice stopped abruptly, and he swallowed before speaking again. "I would never have asked for her forgiveness," he finished, his words as quiet as the breeze.

They both heard a sharp intake of breath, and then sobbing behind them.

"Ana," he murmured, shaking his head slightly.

Rein watched Traith's face. He refused to turn around and look at his sister; his eyes were focused on Rein; he was tense. Rein tried to push his torment out of her mind. When he finally forced himself to turn around, Rein backed away. Ana's face was bleak as death itself. Rein stood straighter, ready for a meeting that would change everything between the two.

Ana stood silently, staring deeply into her brother's red eyes. She had heard what he'd said. Rein felt Traith's heart wrenching; she knew his sister was alone. But her hope of their reunion was shattered when Traith suddenly disappeared, leaving the women alone.

"He cannot face you, Ana," Rein said softly. "What are you doing here?"

Rein realized with terror that she had to fight harder than she ever had before to keep a clear head and not read thoughts. She *was* becoming more powerful as time passed, but for Traith's sake, and everyone else's, she had to maintain control. She could still hear his thoughts, but they grew quieter and quieter until they stopped.

He was so unsure of what to do.

And Ana's mind was screaming to her, too. Ana was beside herself.

"I need to talk to him," Ana cried. "They're going to find me and kill me, and I need him. Oh, please, trust me! I don't know what else to do."

Rein stood still, her head cocked in wonder. She knew Ana was sincere.

"They'll kill you?"

"I'm sorry—I trust you, I...I just need to speak with Traith. Please get him," she cried hysterically. "He would want to know..."

Rein could not hear Ana's last words. It began again, the same way it had moments before. So much was streaming through her mind that it shut the world out. Rein closed her eyes, fighting pain. She opened them again, praying she had blocked Ana's mind from her own.

"*I did not know,*" she heard Ana's voice in her head. "*I had not known that Traith lost his memory. Saria...*"

Ana knew something else.

"Saria?" Rein asked, her vision blurring, tears running down her face.

Ana stared at her with a frightened gaze. "How did you—?"

Alive?

A cold, familiar wind tingled Rein's neck. The smell of icy smoke burned her lungs.

Her mind quieted.

Then there was relief, but anxiety.

"God, they're here," Ana cried in panic.

They *did* want to kill Ana. She was in as much danger as Rein or Traith. No, she was in more danger.

A flash of light hit the stone in front of Rein, startling her out of the snare of her developing psyche. The terrace cracked to pieces under her feet. Rein regained her balance. Helena was the next person she saw, then an army of warriors behind her.

But it was the person standing next to the army. The person who was obviously many people merged into one. Obviously someone she knew; she felt. Even though the person didn't look a thing like her, Rein realized with terror in her heart that it was her deceased, dearest friend, Saria, standing aggressively. Waiting to fight her.

chapter 72

"D amn," Traith whispered to himself quietly when he realized where he had brought himself. "The middle of the dance floor? Of all places…"

Turning to get off the dance floor, he found himself face to face with Mistress.

"I feel it," she said to him.

"What?"

She frowned at the look on his face. "You may want to go back to your lover. Something is wrong."

"My sister is here. Wait," he said. "Rein?"

"It was not Ana who brought the Mardinial Council, Traith."

"What are you talking about?" he asked. "You think she's alone?"

"Do you not trust her?" Mistress said with a smile.

"Trust her? Are you mad? I used to, but she tried to kill me, more than once!"

"Can you see no sincerity in her now?" answered the old woman. "She yearns for you without words."

"Yearns for me? What?"

They were interrupted by the cracking and smashing of stone above them. Rain began to fall, and it chilled him.

The organ stopped playing, and the dancing ceased. Revelers gasped as the castle walls and roof collapsed inward and a militia of creatures poured through them.

Traith staggered backward. "Rein was right," he muttered.

"*Council!*" Mistress cried in authority. "Attack! Hold nothing back!"

The castle ballroom was suddenly transformed into a battlefield, council against council. Traith ran behind Mistress and found himself on the rainy balcony by Rein. He heard his sister's scream.

This was the perfect place of attack—a time when the entire council was together. They were massively outnumbered by Helena's army.

Helena gripped Ana and lifted her into the air by her neck. "Ah, Traith," she growled. "Do you see this? Do you see this traitor? She is not mine any longer! I knew where you would go tonight and that she would follow, and now I have the pleasure of killing the two of you together!"

He was so confused. Could it really be that Ana was asking his forgiveness, begging for his protection?

"Was it not she who led you here?" he questioned.

"No you fool!"

Helena threw a small bottle toward him, and it ignited in his face. A gas quickly formed, causing him to cough and grab his face.

He was too late.

Everything went grey. Then black.

He couldn't see.

Poisonous gas? His eyes were burning.

He smelled garlic. The chemicals in the gas must have somehow been combined with garlic, and it made his head throb. It scalded his hands when he held his face.

"Dear God!" he shouted, falling to his knees. "My eyes! What the hell did you do to my eyes? I can't see..."

He heard Rein scream for him, and someone—no, it was Rein—touched him. He wouldn't move his hands from his eyes. Her hands were trembling on his jaw. She was trying to heal him.

Then he felt nothing. A grunt.

"Rein?" he asked.

There was no answer.

He clutched his head tight. He could barely think until a slight numbing took the place of the fiery pain. But he didn't like the anesthetizing feeling.

Helena cackled viciously. "Oh, I am terribly sorry. By the way, I think you should know that Ana did come here to seek your forgiveness. She thought you knew about what you did to your family. She thought you were a *vampire*."

Then he was hit; it was Ana's body, smashing him. He slammed against the wall, but held her in front of him. His senses were so dulled. Numb.

The next thing he felt were shackles behind his back; he was in some place as cold and damp as him…

Rein's mouth was released. She forced her way out of Saria's immensely strong grasp. Helena had done something to her, something cruel. But at that moment, Traith, as well as Ana and Helena, disappeared.

Rein's mind was silent. It seemed as though anytime something bad happened, her psyche would leave her alone, to think her own thoughts. Or was she finally controlling her mind?

Creatures had, in the meantime, poured in through the cracks of the castle and through the walls. She killed a few of them. Transformed them into dust. Others, she fought brutally for a few moments until they dropped. They were not strong, but each one had a different tactic or power, which made things complicated. There were so many more of them than there were in her council.

But then she was grabbed again, with a might greater than that of any of the creatures she had been fighting. She turned.

"Saria," Rein said, sobbing. Her best friend, stuck within a body that was not her own. "Is it really you?" Rein asked pleadingly. "Why are you acting like that? What has happened to you? What did they do?"

Rein looked at her arm. Saria's grip was loosening. Then she let go. Rein backed up and saw how intently Saria stared at her. Her stare was irregular. It was programmed.

They had programmed her like they had done to Traith.

Rein saw her fighting it, and it crushed her.

Rein tried to speak but was stifled. Invisible fingers suddenly gripped her neck, and she began to feel light-headed. Saria wasn't touching her, but her arm was out and her hand looked as though it was gripping something. The squeezing, painful grip that lifted Rein off the ground…that was Saria.

"Rein," she said with her familiar voice. "I know what you did to my beloved Carden, and I will kill you myself for that. I know what happened to you. I can *see* it! Your eyes, skin…everything has changed! You're a sinful beast!"

Rein could barely reply. It wasn't that she couldn't breathe; it was the force on her throat; it was crushing. "What are you talking about?" she rasped.

She could not break free. She was stunned at the force acting on her, squeezing her through to her bone. The aching became stinging.

"Carden—disappeared!" she made herself scream. But then she stopped trying to speak. "You of all people should believe me, Saria," Rein spoke to her without words. "Know that I would never do something like that. No one knows what happened to Carden."

Saria loosened again. She had heard Rein. In a moment of relief, Rein broke free and attempted to regain her friend's trust. "Saria, believe me. I promise you I have not changed—"

"Rein, I..." she paused, and Rein felt that force constrict her throat again. "Liar!"

Saria threw her off the balcony into a tree, not losing her mental grip. Rein whimpered in agony as she crashed down through bare branches.

Rein suddenly changed into her old self as best as she could without a moment to think. Saria followed quickly. Shaking her head, she knelt down toward Rein, trying to speak to her.

Rein was astounded. Saria seemed to be pleading for forgiveness.

"Rein!" she gasped, grabbing Rein's hand. "Lord, do you know what they did? Do you know what they did to me? Can you see me? With your eyes...My lover, you...he's dead! Did you kill him? Rein, did you do it with your terrible—?"

"No! No, stop talking like that; I'm not what you think." Rein had to keep swallowing to relax the muscles in her throat. "Carden vanished; because you were dead, Saria, he vanished. He couldn't live without you. I...I was killed, like you; I just..."

Rein paused, and Saria's eyes widened in pain. "You stayed a vampire, didn't you? With Traith Harker...no!"

Saria grabbed a rock and bashed it into Rein. Her head was ringing; she yelped and kicked Saria off, holding her throbbing face.

"You're not yourself," Rein cried toward her. "Try, Saria! Please! Maybe I don't have to lose you again! But—"

Something thwacked into her cheek, and she fell.

"I'll have to kill you," Rein whispered, crying.

Rein was hit again; this time, close to her eye. It took a second to regain her senses, and in a quick movement, she felt under her for the large stick she had landed on. She got to her knees, and when Saria was about to hit her again, Rein yanked her close and drove the branch through her stomach.

Saria screamed.

After a moment, Saria swallowed hard. Rein still held her, the branch still in her hand. Saria pulled out the branch slowly. She dropped the branch and began to fall, scraping her nails down Rein's neck. Rein cried, falling to the ground with her friend.

"Why did you make me *do* this?" Rein screamed hoarsely to her.

Saria looked human. "I…a girl told me…" Her body convulsed violently, making it hard for her to speak. "I know…you didn't kill him…I was put into a canister of liquid…with little wires on my…"

Rein's tear hit Saria's cheek. She didn't speak. She knew she didn't have time. They must've brainwashed Saria—just as they had Traith and perhaps Ana—but it must have not been long or hard enough. Not enough, because her true self was trying to break through, although it hadn't prevailed. Perhaps it was because she was dying.

"I know…" Saria kept pushing, "the winged woman's…w-weakness."

t raith was cold. Everything around him was wet. He could feel the rusted shackles that restrained his wrists begin to make them raw. His powers were disabled. He couldn't pull free, disappear, or hear his lover in his head.

Where was she?

He still couldn't see, but the burning sensation of the poison had finally subsided.

He ignored the fear and pain. He had to ignore it. He was locked up across from his sister. He had to think about her. He was desperate to know what she was doing. She had to be watching him; she had to be. He heard her crying, still. *Was* she sincere? *Had* she finally abandoned the Mardinial Council? Did she actually want to reunite with him? It seemed too improbable. But Helena had threatened to kill her. Ana was his sister, for God's sake.

What she had done to him couldn't rival what he had done to her. He wasn't…that wasn't him…but it was. No matter how he approached it, it was the vampire in him who had killed his parents, and he did so in front of her.

He shook his head and thought about the Mistress. She had said Ana was sincere. Or, that he should believe she was. But, then, what was he to say?

He said nothing at all.

Conversation seemed useless. She continued to cry quietly, probably at the sight of him. He didn't know what else he could do when he heard her. The situation discomfited him.

"T-Traith?"

His heart rose, but he made no answer. She was too excited with fear.

"Traith," she choked. "Forgive me. I thought…" she stopped, but he made no movement. "I thought you knew."

"I do," he whispered.

She broke down, almost hysterical. "No, no, please! Do not say it like that!"

"Like what, Ana?"

"They made you do it! Like they made Saria."

Traith sat up abruptly. "They sent Rein's best friend after her?"

"When they tried programming Saria's mind, I realized something was not right. Ever since Tanya died, I began to realize I had too many unanswerable questions; things were not as they seemed."

"Glad you understand that now," he said.

"Traith, I was lied to! I was told you were deceitful and—"

"And you believed a stranger, over me?"

"They had me twisted," she said. "I didn't know who to believe, and they seemed to know…but I realized, also, that I could never hate you. I knew suddenly that they had lied to me about everything. I found out what they had done to you, and it was…horrific."

"You're right."

"But Traith, I *watched* you kill our parents! I couldn't understand it! Though I heard you plead, how could you *not* have known? I just… I can see you there, Traith. I can see what you did!" She took a shaky breath and continued. "But you didn't want to do it. I know it wasn't your fault; I don't blame you anymore. Helena told me things…She told me the truth about what she'd done to you. I had nowhere else to go, no one else to turn to. They locked me up when they told me… when I figured it all out. I needed to find you because…I wanted my only brother's protection. And his forgiveness."

"My forgiveness?" He felt her eyes burning into his flesh as the silence stretched between them. "Ana, I can't trust you," he said hoarsely. "I'm afraid to."

"I can rebuild what I've broken, Traith. I love you. I do! I can't believe I…perhaps they did things to me as well! I don't know how I could have done all those terrible things to you—awful things!" She pulled angrily the chains confining her. "Forgive me, Traith! *Acknowledge* me!"

He still didn't move, despite her cries, his body tight, his eyes facing the ground.

"*Acknowledge* me."

"I hear you, Ana."

She stopped struggling with her shackles and bawled hysterically, her words filled with true misery. "Traith, I don't care about what you are anymore," she said. "It means *nothing* to me now. Helena told me they tortured you! Victimized you! And I know the pain I've added. But what can I do? What can I do to even *begin* to mend things? Where can I start? To make you forgive me? I found out that you had forgotten—that you were deprived of your memories. I didn't know."

"I despise myself, Ana. I never *meant* to kill them! I loved them! I loved them so much. And the thought—the fresh picture keeps playing over and over and over in my head like live theater. It won't go away, and it never will!"

"I didn't—"

"I died once already, and somehow I am still here. That doesn't even include my being bitten by your damned *leader* and being cursed for eternity! I don't want you to be terrified of me, Ana, but I can't fix it! I wanted to be normal. I tried for years to train myself to become accustomed to the light again; I tried to live without blood; I even tried to sleep at night, but none of it ever works. It just isn't possible."

"You tried to kill yourself?" she whispered sadly.

He didn't answer.

"How many times?" Her voice was desperate to know.

He sighed. "I attempted many times. But Mistress always stopped me. She made me live. And I don't know whether I love her or hate her for that."

"Don't ever *think* about trying that again—"

"Look, Ana." He pulled the collar of his shirt down and revealed the two scars on his neck. "*She* did that to me. Helena. She's why I'm like this! I was used, tortured unconditionally." He pulled his collar back up. "I'm not right, yet—not since I regained my memory. I don't know what to do."

He was calmer after a few minutes, but his body was still tense at the thought of what was going on outside the cell at the old Irish castle. His lover was fighting there. Alone. He tried not to think about his sister, but it was useless. She was right there staring at him with eyes he could not see. He didn't know whether he would even be capable of seeing ever again.

She still watched him from across the cell, probably trying to come up with the right words to say to him. Even now, after repenting, telling him everything, he felt her lurking fear of him. All she had to do was look at him: his long, sharp teeth and pale skin. He looked so different than he had before. He thought of the mirror in the last cell he was in.

"What did they do to you, Traith?" she asked quietly. "When they turned you? How bad was it?"

He did not reply for a moment. "They did everything imaginable, Ana." His words hung in the air. "Everything."

"For how long?"

"Until I escaped, hardly what I would call alive. I was found by Mistress, and seven years later you cursed me onto a ship for one hundred and ten years. And I can't be angry at you for that because of what I've done."

"Oh Traith," she answered, weeping. "I *want* to be able to fix what I've done. I mean…you look so dejected, Traith, and I—"

"Are my eyes included in that one-word description?" He stopped and swallowed. "Damn it, I can't *see* you, Ana!"

"I know that I can fight my fear of you, Traith, but you must help me. If you were in my position, what would you have me do? *Please* help me see you again. The way you were. I want to *see* that you are still the same."

He didn't answer her. He squinted as a sharp sting hit his eyes.

"Do your eyes hurt?" she asked quietly, and he knew she had been watching him. "They look terribly—"

"Just cut off the 'y,' and I'm sure you'd have it."

"You can talk to me, Traith! You can trust me, now. I trust you!"

He grunted. "They're beginning to ache. I can't see at all, Ana."

"You can't see anything? No vision has come back at all?"

"No. No vision has come back at all." She said nothing, and Traith sensed her anxiety. He softened his voice. "I'm sorry; I just…I'm still constantly lost in thought about my childhood, Ana. Do you know that I forgot all that, too? Not only my crimes, but everything."

"Look at me, Traith."

"For what bloody purpose? Doesn't matter where I look, it all looks the—"

"I want to see your face clearly. To see you, my brother."

He considered her request. He wanted to see her so badly. To see how she looked now: if she was sad or angry or plain distraught. He wondered whether his eyes were seared, or if they were just clouded.

Slowly, he lifted his head and tried to steady his eyes, setting them forward as if he were looking at her.

"Do I look like your brother, Ana?" he murmured sharply.

"Yes," she replied with a trembling sigh. "What have they done to you?"

He made no reply, and again there was silence.

"Your eyes are merely clouded, Traith," she began. "I...created that poison..."

"Wonderful," he said with a hollow chuckle. "So then get to the damn *point* and tell me if this is permanent!"

"I can't believe they used it on you."

"*Ana—*"

"Your sight will come back, Traith."

He didn't like the way she said that.

"When?" he asked anxiously.

When she didn't immediately answer, his heart dropped.

"I don't know."

He squeezed his eyes shut.

"The shortest time I've seen it take to come back was...was a year."

"A year?" he asked desperately. "I'll be blind for over a bloody *year*? What was the longest?"

He heard her sniff. "Ten, give or take a little."

He tugged at the shackles, curling in his tender, skinned wrists despondently. "Damn," he rasped.

He thought of Rein. Would this change things? Would she still want there to be a wedding?

Would they even *make it* to a wedding?

Rein would have to pull through. She would have to find him— wherever the hell he was.

chapter 74

She tasted it. The bitterness in the air. The bitterness of the rain mixing with her tears: a salty taste. But she tasted death, too. The dying cries and clashing of men above her in the castle was horrifying, not only to hear but to see. Death and murders were everywhere she turned. Even in her grasp.

She cried hard, but it made no difference. No one could hear her. She was alone. The rain drowned her out. Saria was dead on the ground in front of her, but before her death, Rein had learned the key to peace. The key to the end of this war.

Helena's weakness.

But Ana knew it, too. And if she was on their side, now, Helena had to know that the information would get out. Unless she had lied to Ana.

Mere moments had gone by since words had left Saria's lips. And just like that, she was gone. By her own hand with a tree bough, she had slain the very person who was like a sister to her.

But she had to finish it. If they found Saria's body, they could do it to her again. And she couldn't be bitten a second time in order to be saved.

She held Saria, and in a moment, her body disintegrated to ash in her hands. The ash ran through her fingers and stained her palms, and it burned her even worse inside. But it was finished. Everything would be fixed if she just did what Saria had spoken to her. Wherever Traith was, he would be free if she found Helena and killed her.

But what if he was leverage? Helena knew things, just as the Mistress did.

Before he had vanished, Traith looked as if he were in excruciating pain. His eyes. He was screaming about his eyes. He could heal, but he didn't. Perhaps he couldn't. She had seen him holding his face.

Rein continued to try to reach him. Hear him. Feel him. Anything. But all she heard were the terrifying cries from above. All she felt was darkness and dampness.

The violent screams and noises going on in the castle above her were worsening.

Rein stood and squared her shoulders. She had to be ready to win a war.

But then she heard her name. She spun around, brushing pieces of stringy, wet hair out of her face. Her body tightened. Her eyes widened with disbelief. Her hands that had been clenched opened limply.

"Oh my God," she said to herself as she backed up a few feet.

In the shadow of the moonlight, a small yet familiar face walked toward her, drenched by the rain.

"How did you get here?" Rein asked hoarsely in a daze.

The girl ran and threw her arms around her. "Oh, Rein," she said. "I'd just settled with Will's sister in France—"

"Get down." Rein said, pushing her behind a bush. "How did you get *here*? We're in Ireland! Traith brought you to France only days ago, and I haven't heard from you since!"

Taverin's eyes were growing more serious as she spoke through the downpour. "I used the spell book, Rein—a spell that can bring me to wherever you are." She paused to wipe away the rain water from her face. "Unfortunately, in a war."

"Do you see what is happening?" Rein asked. "I mean—" Rein stopped and sighed. "Just stay here. Do not move."

"No!" Taverin said defiantly. "I can help. I have this." Rein saw the little spell book in Taverin's hand. Taverin looked harder at Rein. "Are you...? You are; you're crying! What happened? Why are you down here alone?"

Rein shook her head and closed her eyes, but opened them with determination. "I have no more time to talk. I know Helena's vulnerability. Both councils are in that castle. One of them will be destroyed by the morning." She turned away from the girl. "It will not be mine."

"Is Traith up there?" she asked.

"No."

"Where is he?"

"I can't find him. Helena disappeared with him and his sister," she cringed. "Fine; you can come. Take my hand, and please be careful."

When Taverin gave it to her, she landed with her up on the nearly demolished balcony. Rein shoved Taverin down to the broken stone floor, covering her face. Arrows flew through the walls and open doorway. They were still in the midst of a treacherous fight.

"All right, you must stay here. Fight whoever comes out, or hide if you can. Please, be careful."

Taverin did not object this time; she stared into Rein's eyes deeply for a moment, and then she nodded. Rein then left her there, trying to focus on the battle at hand. She walked through the broken doorway, taking down a few Mardinial immortals that approached her.

First she had to find Traith, and then she would find Helena. She had taken him, so with any fortune at all, they would be together.

Rein formed a plan.

Wings emerged from her shoulder blades, and her thick, black hair became lengthened and lightened to red. Her soaked and muddy gown became a brilliant gold and black cloak and dress, identical to the one Helena had been wearing. Flapping her new, dragon-like wings, Rein walked into the room.

Glancing around, sending a mental note to those she knew as to who she really was, she spotted a teleporting creature flying in and out of her own councilors. She asked it to bring her to the council. It made no noise, and then, as she wrapped herself in the cloak, she heard no noise at all.

But then there was a drip. And another. She heard sizzling wires. She was alone in a quiet lab. The creature had believed her. She walked around quietly for a moment, scanning the control panels for a clue as to where her fiancé was. She knew he wasn't fighting, nor was his sister.

Then she heard a noise so quiet it would have been practically inaudible to a mortal ear. Voices. She opened a door and walked down a hallway. Then another. She silently approached a dark, metallic door, and as quiet as possible, twisted the knob. It was locked. Without hesitation she jerked her fist back and took the knob with it, opening the door. There inside, she found whom she was looking for.

t raith?" Rein ran into the damp cell.

His head shot up, but it quickly dropped again, as if he didn't want to meet her eyes. Or couldn't. He was chained to a stone wall, and her eyes narrowed when she saw how tightly screwed the wrist shackles were.

"What happened?" she asked in a gentler tone, kneeling beside him.

He turned to her, squinting. "Rein. Could you hear my thoughts so far away?" His tone had a ring of sarcasm to it.

"Your eyes…" she whispered.

The once fiery color of his eyes was now gray and milky.

"I suppose this is what I get for lying and telling you I was blind when we first met, huh?" he said. He chuckled vacantly, twisting his hands around, searching for a more comfortable position for his wrists. "Ana said my eyes looked *fine*. Did you lie to me, Ana?"

"No, Traith, I…" Ana stopped and sat back without another word.

Rein turned around and glared breathlessly at Ana.

"I-It's all right, Rein," she swallowed. "His sight will come back."

Rein held his face and tried to fix his vision with her own healing ability.

"It won't work," Ana insisted. "I knew what you could do."

Traith pulled away from Rein with his eyes closed, and then began blinking relentlessly in pain.

"We need to find Helena," Rein said, bending into him. "I know how to kill her." She had whispered those last words in his ear.

"You know her weakness?" he asked quietly.

She felt her throat close up. "Saria told me."

"I suppose I'm out of the loop, then," he replied with his head cocked. "Ana knows…" His sauciness ceased, and his eyes looked ahead. "Did you have to kill her?" he asked with a scratchy sorrow in his voice.

She made no reply.

"Oh, Rein," he muttered, sighing quietly. "I'm sorry. Is she…?"

"Yes. She's dead." Trembling, Rein unchained Traith, then Ana.

"You're crying," he said gently. "Rein—"

"No," she replied. "And I don't want to think about it. It's over."

Traith sighed. "Thank Heaven," he said, rubbing his bloody wrists as they healed. His powers had returned. He still kept his head down, as if looking at his hands, still holding his wrists.

"Can you still bring us to the castle?" Rein asked, holding his hands. "Taverin is there, alone."

"Taverin? What in hell *happened* while I was gone?"

"It doesn't matter. We need to get to the castle. Please, hurry, Traith."

His expression grew tired. "I'll try my best, but my lack of sight will probably interfere with where we appear."

Ana approached him uncertainly and held his arm.

Then the rain hit her face again. He had done it. They were on the terrace. He lost his balance momentarily on the cracked and broken stone, but managed to right himself.

Rein found Taverin curled on the outskirts of the balcony, foggy through the downpour. She was soaked through, but her heart seemed to fill when she saw Rein, and she jumped up to greet them.

"Rein!" she exclaimed. "Traith! Oh, I killed one! There was a man, running toward me, and I cast a spell that made him disintegrate—it was unbelievable!"

"You're brave," Rein said with a smile. "But you mustn't leave the balcony yet. Take care of whoever comes out here, all right? If you need me, I'll stay in touch." Rein touched her head.

Ana let go of Traith's arm and he yielded to her move. She was staring with grieving eyes at him, but he didn't know it. Rein knew, though, that he did not want Ana to see him weak. He didn't want anyone to see him as that. He was staring down, brushing rain from his face.

"Rein?" he asked.

She ran over and kissed him. He flinched at first, surprised by the feeling of her lips, but then he returned her kiss with passion.

"Stay with me," she said, standing back and grabbing his hand.

"Are we near anyone?" he asked helplessly. "Do I need to make an attempt at defending myself right this moment?"

She didn't reply, watching and motioning to Taverin.

"Rein?" he asked.

"Yes," she replied quietly.

"Yes what? There are people around?"

"Just Taverin out here. But we're going inside."

He didn't try to greet Taverin. "Can you please make sure you acknowledge me when I talk? I can't exactly know otherwise."

She pulled his arm to run into the ballroom, but he was heavy.

"Lord," he muttered, finally following her with speed enough. "Tell me when you're going to do these things! You'll need to learn; I could be blind for up to ten bloody years!"

She spun around, stopping suddenly. "What?"

She saw him sigh painfully at his own words.

"Why did we stop?" he asked, trying desperately to push that aside.

"Ana is already past us," she whispered. "She's fighting...for you. For us; our council."

Ten years?

She silently fingered the ring on her left hand. She was almost officially his, and...

"Thank you for the explanation," he said, grinning, but underneath the pride she could see his relief about Ana's alliance.

"We're running," she told him, and he followed without delay.

But the sight of the ballroom hit her as hard as a fist.

Bodies were lying everywhere, from both councils, and blood was spattered over all of the walls. Screams were piercing through her like knives.

She felt Traith trip over a dead body and turned when he swore and let her go. "This couldn't look good," he said. "*Sounds* horrible..."

"Get ready," was all she could say, and she pulled him into the fight.

But she felt her hand yanked from his, and she was grabbed and flung by the forearm to the stone. Traith turned in her direction when he lost her hand, but was cut off by men rushing past him.

Rein looked up and saw a mutated creature tearing toward her. She jumped up and twisted his arm.

Insight took over her vision. It was like a sixth sense that she had, now; it made her see things in a way that was quite different than actual sight. It was excruciatingly loud; but she saw something because of it that would have been nearly invisible.

He had a stake hidden under his cloak.

She shrunk back with fear at first, but suddenly her thoughts were not her own. In a moment, she realized with horror that she had sunk her teeth into his neck. Then she drained him.

Struggling to regain control, she pulled back. His body dropped to the floor, white. But she felt no guilt. She excused it as self-defense. Only in a battle like this could she ever allow herself to do something like that. But the frightening part was that she had no initial intention to.

Later. She could not waste time thinking of it now. She fought past the crowd until she saw Traith beyond a screen of people. Lorena ran past her, dodging blasts, and found a clear path to Traith. Rein cringed as the priestess called his name.

He lifted his bare arm, shining and cut, and knocked off different monstrous creatures that had jumped onto him. But to her dismay, transparency spread up his body until he was completely invisible; invisibility gave him an easier way of fighting blind. No one would see him, either. Rein had been running for him, but she lost him when he disappeared.

Then she saw a head knock itself into a nearby wall; it was Traith slamming a man against the stone. The creature had a pistol; it shot three times into nothing, into Traith, and a deep yell—Traith's voice—sounded. Blood gushed from his invisible chest in the three places the bullets had hit him. Traith grabbed the man and his gun, and shot him in the head. The creature clung to Traith's unseen shirt, ripping it, and fell to the floor.

Traith reappeared, and, trembling, he felt around where the blood was. He cringed as he dug his fingers into himself to retrieve the bullets. Rein finally got to him and touched him, but his bloody hand grabbed her arm tight in quick response. She kissed him again, and he opened his hand in shock and let her go.

"You should've said something," he said in apology, and she saw him clench his teeth in frustration. "Rein, please, work with me..."

She was unsure how to respond.

She couldn't bring herself to believe he was blind.

chapter 76

Daylight was beginning to seep through the castle windows. Rein saw a few Mardinial vampires suddenly disintegrate in the light.

She felt relieved in a sorrowful way.

"Being even slightly accustomed to light saved us, Traith," she managed to say.

She was suddenly forced forward. Somebody had tackled her to the ground. Before she had time to see who it was, her hair was grabbed from behind and her head was knocked into the stone.

"T-Traith," she stuttered.

He was calling to her, but he couldn't reach. He was assaulted by a group, and that was all she could see.

She regained her clearness of mind, and as her attacker flipped her around, she struck him. He was a werewolf. Ben. Her blow hit him in the mouth, and his teeth cut her hand. However, as he fell to the ground, Rein noticed Mistress across the blood-stained ballroom. She was pinned against the wall by Helena.

She had come back.

Rein jumped up and evaded Ben. She reached Traith, who was lifting a body off his shoulder and throwing it in a pile of others.

"You're holding up well for a blind man," she said.

"Rein?" he asked. "What—? Who hit you? Damn this!"

She smiled at him, but his face was grave. "At least you have a pile there," she said thoughtfully.

"Not much else I can do, Rein," he said. "Did you need me?"

"Helena and Mistress are fighting, and it does not appear as though Mistress is the aggressor. We need to get to Helena, and *now* might be a good time."

"What is it exactly that will kill her?"

"Her own sword."

A grin flickered about his mouth. "Ironic."

With Rein in the lead, they darted across the room toward the clashing Council Leaders. Mistress's eyes were beginning to roll back in her head; she was being choked violently.

Helena turned, sensing their approach.

"Harker?" She laughed devilishly. "Your escape method was excellent! I can imagine it is helpful having a woman who loves you enough to rescue you when you are incapable of rescuing yourself." She laughed louder.

Traith lifted his chin in defiant anger and reached out in front of him, by chance grasping the charging winged woman by the neck.

"Rein, now," he urged as he held Helena as tightly as he could before her constricting hands wrapped around his neck, too.

Rein's mind reawakened.

She concentrated intensely, and she paused time.

Everything stopped. Fights froze in mid air. The pain, however, was excruciating. She was controlling the lives of every other being in the castle along with Helena, while keeping Traith and Mistress immune to her power.

Traith yanked his neck out of Helena's hold, sighing roughly. "Mistress, I can't see, grab Helena's sword before Rein loses focus. *That* bloody thing is her weakness."

"The sword?" Mistress seemed baffled as she pulled the sword from the scabbard. It immediately burned a fiery blue, and the presence of it felt cold on Rein's face, even from a distance. But in that instant of distraction, she lost her hold and fell to the ground, nearly unconscious.

Time had begun again, and all the fighting resumed. Mistress teleported Traith over to where she was standing, handing him the flaming sword.

"Use it!" she yelled, her eyes turning yellow.

"What are you *talking about*? I can't see the bloody thing, let alone—"

A heel lashed out and whipped against Traith's face, and he grunted and fell onto the stone. It was Helena.

She kicked him again after he was down and grabbed the sword before Rein had time to gather herself and get to it first. Traith rolled over to his stomach, holding his face.

"*Where?*" he shouted, asking Mistress. "Where the hell is she?"

"Traith!" Mistress called.

Rein blinked and saw Traith fumbling in his own darkness for Helena. The winged woman turned and threw out her hand, and with that movement, Mistress was smashed backward into the stone. Rein felt herself regaining strength; she tried to scramble up and trip Helena.

But all that was heard was the evil vampire's laugh.

Rein felt a sudden pang of stinging and burning and screamed.

The sword flared within her body.

She heard Traith shouting for her in frustration and question.

Rein's scream choked; she let her stare fall down; the sword, Helena's sword, had punctured through her chest as she was leaned over.

Rein's whole body suddenly stiffened. "Traith..."

All she heard back was his calling her name desperately, and then his grunt as Helena hit him once more.

Rein could make no response, and her eyes did not blink. She felt blood rising from her stomach and out the side of her mouth. She bent over, holding her middle, and buckled to the floor. She was trying to push off the stiffening pain, but she was still lying on the ground coughing up blood and panting, struggling desperately to stand. It felt like her skin was stretched over her bones, pulling. Blood spurted through her fingers as she shakily held the wound.

Time slowed again, if only in her mind, and things were quiet in her head. Quiet for once. The peacefulness was frightening, however. It was, perhaps, that she was numb or overwhelmed with pain; it was hard to distinguish. She looked up at the red-haired woman and turned her attention to Traith, who stood up, still calling for her. The blood still cascaded like a waterfall out of her chest; it wouldn't heal on its own. The blood stopped suddenly; she knew she was being cauterized, and the blood flow ceased. She knew she could die. If it was her heart, if the sword was lodged in her heart, she knew she would die. It was close enough to a stake. She didn't know yet, however, and the sensation was terrifying...

Outside her mind, an odd whirlwind began to form around Helena. Mistress held out her red glowing orb, eyes on fire, and recited a bizarre spell. Helena froze, her hand still holding onto the sword that pierced Rein's chest. Fire still blazed out of the sword, burning Rein with an icy-heat.

Traith knelt down and spread his arms, desperately searching the ground for the body of his lover.

t raith's hands found nothing but cold stone. At a time when he needed his sight the most, he felt like an infant, touching his surroundings in vain.

And where was Helena? Was he going to get hit again?

But then he felt it; the smell was so appealing! It was blood—Rein's blood. No. That yearning in his body had to be restrained.

He wasn't going to do that to Rein again.

He cursed himself under his breath, and then flinched when a wet hand grabbed his fingers.

"*Traith*!" Mistress screamed at him, still holding Helena in a frozen state. "Seize the blade! I can't hold her for much longer! I am not as strong as your lover!"

He knew it was Rein's hand he held. The long, smooth, thinness of it, the way she held him. It led him to her chest, where he grasped the sword's handle, removing Helena's hand from it. He drew it out with a quick pull. She gasped in pain as he held the blade in his hand, and he craved to see her state.

Mistress was pleading for him to finish Helena. Still holding Rein's hand, Traith followed up Helena's arm and grabbed a hold of her hair. He drove the sword in front of him with intensity, thrusting it through her chest. Mistress let the Mardinial Leader out of her mental grasp as the sword entered. It made no difference where.

He had done it.

He had killed his immortal creator…the one who had ruined his entire life. The one who wiped his memory. The one who had lied to his own flesh and blood. The one who had first plotted and managed to kill Rein so he had to turn her, and the one had tortured so many others…

He heard a sudden screech, and he felt a hole materializing in her stomach as her flesh decomposed, growing larger and larger. He backed up. She let out another shriek, and he felt an agonizing pain overwhelm him. He felt her hand; it was clawing down him.

Then she fell.

He instinctively yanked away, and he heard her wings flapping a final time.

"Why-y...d-do you fight...a-against it?" she asked, with her last breath.

He staggered back a few steps. "Because it's the best thing I can do with what you changed me into."

She screamed deafeningly, and in an instant, her body turned to dust and vanished. Traith shook his head, feeling the grit of it on his face.

But then his moment of victory was shattered. With breathtaking force, Traith was crushed backward by an animal. It was the werewolf Ben. He must have heard his wife's scream and run to the site.

Traith smacked against the stone wall hard and grunted as he fought the beast.

"Do you enjoy killing women, Harker?" Ben swore as he fought the vampire. "First your own admirer, and now mine?"

Traith felt weaker at Ben's words; his mind began to cloud again. He knew Ben wanted him to lose strength over his words, but Traith couldn't shake the crushing reaction.

"How does she make you *feel* every time you see her? Don't you feel cursed? You ruined her life! She'll never be normal again, and you did it!"

"Stop it!" Traith was slammed into the stone again by Ben's hands.

"Such a hellish creature, you are, doing that," Ben snarled while beating him. "And before that, your parents, who raised you and fed you and housed you and loved you! And right in front of poor, poor Ana. She's scarred for eternity by that sight!"

"So am I!"

"Seems to me you have a problem with killing your loved ones! The girl out on the balcony must be next, no?"

He shook his head in fury. "No!"

"No? Am I lying about everything? Am I wrong?"

"God, stop it!" Traith's voice was trembling, and he was desperately striving to break free from the werewolf.

His body was being crushed. His strength waned as he thought about Ben's words. He knew he had to stop thinking about it. He attempted shocking Ben with energy, but it didn't seem to affect him. Every time he strained to teleport, Ben was there as well. He couldn't even attempt to use his other powers. He was being pounded, beaten, for the first time in an unarmed fight.

chapter 78

traith strained to keep a grip on Ben's nose. His own strength far surpassed the werewolf's, but he was almost completely out of fuel. He had not slept for days. He had managed to go for three days without a single vial of blood. His body was suffering in the early morning sunlight.

Ben still tore at him without any loss of energy. Traith felt his body numbing, and slowly, with every blow, every time he hit the floor, he lost more strength. Another blow from Ben's fist, and he fell nearly limp. He struggled to fight, but his body wouldn't. Ben's other hand pushed Traith's head up, lengthening his neck. He was going to tear into him. Rip him apart. Perhaps worse—make him a werewolf as well as a vampire. Or just torture him until he found a stake.

He braced himself for the incoming pain.

Ben fell onto his chest, and Traith puffed out hoarsely in pain. He hadn't been expecting that. But then there were no further hits.

Traith was limp with exhaustion and defeat. He felt and smelled blood seeping from Ben's slack body. He felt fur—Ben, with blood matting on his chest.

Then the body was lifted off of his chest. Ben was dead; he must have been. Traith covered his face and tensed, just to be sure he wouldn't be tricked. Mistress?

"What has he done to you?" a whisper spoke softly, and immediately he knew it was not Mistress who had killed Ben.

It was Ana kneeling down beside him. He tried to sit up, but she pushed him down. "No, please relax. Loosen your muscles. You won, Traith. Your council won. Everyone else has died. You killed Helena."

He let go then. He was safe from any more attacks. He had a moment to heal.

Her hands were on his face, assessing the severity of his wounds. He felt her hands trembling against his cheeks as she felt the damage. Then her warm touch disappeared, and in that moment, he quickly covered his face. It would take a few moments for him to heal himself, perhaps even a few hours. He was so weak; his face probably looked horrid. He didn't want her to see it anymore, whether it was or not.

She tore off the little remains of his shirt and overcoat, which were hanging off of him. He heard her breathing hard and quick. She was *still* breathing. Human blood still flowed in her. She was nearly human, and living warmth comforted him. He said nothing and closed his eyes, letting her patch up wounds even though they would heal on their own. His chest was left bare, and he knew that he now had severe wounds covering his entire flesh. He could feel them, and he knew Ana was staring at them. But he didn't care about her apprehension. He gritted his teeth in pain. He was so tired…

"Take your hands off your face," she said gently. "I already saw it."

"Am I…disfigured, right now?" he asked awkwardly. "Stupid question."

"No," she said, wiping the blood off of his face. "Not disfigured, just…oh, you look awful. He had no right." She began quietly crying. "He had no right to say those things to you. I *am* sorry I never listened, Traith."

He forced himself to crack a smile in response. He took her hand that was stroking his face and laid it aside gently. He sat up slowly, his right arm stiff, holding him up.

Rein.

"Where…?"

"Rein is right here. I'll lead you to her."

He felt so helpless and awkward, and he was still trying to shake the unending guilty thoughts out of his mind. He staggered up, having regained a portion of his strength. But Ana didn't take him far. She placed his hand a few feet from where he had been, on Rein's body.

Bending down, Traith felt the blood that stained the ground and, trembling, managed to find Rein's arm.

She was not conscious. He felt her chest, which was still burnt, and realized that the wound was indeed in her upper chest, possibly in her heart.

"It didn't pierce her…"

"It does appear that way, Traith."

He flinched when Mistress replied despondently from somewhere near him.

"She is still singed," he said hoarsely. "She hasn't healed...but she grabbed my hand; she wouldn't have been able to grab my hand if—"

Then there was the moan that diminished his fear.

"It is during times like these that I am glad I am already dead," Rein rasped. "That was bloody close, love, but I..." She pulled him closer. "I'm right here, Traith." Pulling his face down to hers, she sucked in the taste of his lips, kissing him passionately.

chapter 79

R ein let him sit back. She smiled, but her heart sank when she saw his face and his chest more clearly. Large, bloody gashes filled her sight. They ran up and down his body, as if he had been trampled by some sort of spiked animal. Beneath the blood that was trickling down his face, she saw his cloudy, blind eyes again, and an ill feeling sunk to the bottom of her stomach.

She was yearning to know what had happened to him.

Then she did.

Ben and what he had said…

"I'm sorry," Rein whispered, reaching out and embracing him once more, her face against his.

His response was delayed until he realized what she was doing, and he held her back.

"I'm sorry I was not next to you," she murmured shakily. "What he said…Oh, Traith, I'm sorry I couldn't have been there to help you with Ben. What he said—"

"Sorry?" he rasped, and he appeared shocked. "Rein, I *did* do all those things, and you were almost dead. I couldn't see where Helena's sword had hit you, and I thought—"

She put her finger over his mouth and held him tighter. Mistress, standing behind him, was staring up into the dawn sky, which was becoming brighter and brighter by the minute. The sun was glaring over the horizon. Looking around the castle ballroom, her eyes glazed over at the sight of death around her.

All was silent in the hall, and Rein witnessed the hundreds of people that were dead. But she was uplifted when she saw two shadows coming forward. It was Lorena and Jacques, who had returned to his human form as the sun began to rise and the moon disappeared. With them was Taverin, still in one piece and without a scratch. From the other end came Magellan: a mage, like Lorena. No others had escaped their sleeping graves.

Taverin walked past Mistress and knelt down by Rein, embracing her in relief. Ana walked over to the others, head down.

"And what have you to say for yourself?" Mistress asked her, breaking the silence.

"What's she doing?" Traith whispered in question in Rein's ear.

"I-I mean to...compensate for the faults of my past," Ana replied quietly. "I know that you couldn't possibly have empathy enough to accept me after all that I have done, but..."

Mistress looked down at Traith, and he was quite aware she was staring at him.

"What have you, Traith?" Mistress sighed and asked kindly. "What shall I do with her? The decision is yours. She is your kin; you tell me."

"My," Taverin said. "I do believe that I missed a lot over the past couple of days, haven't I? Oh, but I killed quite a few of them, Rein! I—"

"Shh, not yet," Rein murmured. She looked around with a heavy heart. "Many of our own have died tonight, haven't they?" she asked Mistress while leaning on Traith.

"Nearly everyone."

"Are *we* really all who survived?" Lorena asked as she dusted off her dress. "Between both our council *and* the other?"

"Yes," Magellan answered her as he stared unwelcomingly at Traith's sister. "And *still* we have a traitor in our midst!"

"Stop," Lorena said, staring at Traith. "We don't need to feed the fire."

"Harker, you look awful," Jacques said.

"Thank you, I do appreciate it."

"Well, let me—"

"No," Traith answered him as he stood up. "I don't want your help."

"I'm a doctor, for Heaven's sake!"

"And I'm a vampire. I'll heal without medical attention."

"Your sight will return, Harker," Mistress joined in. "Do not worry."

"Not soon enough for me," he muttered, shaking his head a little.

"Well, how about it?" the woman asked. "What shall I do with your sister, Traith?"

After he stood, he groped around until he felt a wall. Rein almost felt as though he was too embarrassed to be near even her.

Why did he always do that?

He finally turned his head in their general direction. "Her council is gone, isn't it? And she will not get far without a shelter. Not now. We have shattered much of the world's evil, but not all of it."

"But what is left is still running rampant," Mistress said. "But singly; hopefully, under no particular leading. This is what we must do now—take care of what we can find, one by one. But I'm sure someday, as hard as it is to speak of, Helena will be replaced. By a higher power, something will be formed, and the best that we can hope for is that we can detect that formation early, and stop it before it begins." Mistress took the flaming sword from the ground and it vanished in her grasp. "And this sword is now mine for protecting."

Ana had been following Traith without him knowing. She embraced him slowly. Rein smiled to herself from next to her own sister; Traith didn't seem to know at first how to respond, but he put his arms around her and embraced her in return.

"You need to make your own life, Ana," he whispered to her. "You can't live with me."

Ana looked up from his arms, sorrow in her eyes. "Traith, please—"

"I *am* a vampire, Ana," he said hoarsely. "I *hate* it, but I am, and no matter how I try, I can never be a normal man again...never the boy you remember from when we were young. My needs now...I won't let you see."

"Very well," Mistress replied quietly.

Ana was staring in overwhelming dissatisfaction. "Traith, I don't care! I can't live any longer without you! I need to be with you!"

"For a while you can't," he replied sternly, and Rein heard the pain in his voice, as it had cracked slightly.

He wasn't concealing his emotion as well as normal. He sincerely wanted his sister to be with him again. But he was not ready. Not for Ana, and not with himself.

"I know a small town in Southern Africa that is nearly uninhabited that you may live in," Mistress said, breaking up the painful conversation. "A town you *must,* for now, live in; as an alchemist, you can make medicine for the locals. *Probation*, of a sort, and if you prove yourself enough you will be allowed to leave. In fact, you must stay until Traith desires your return. For the time being, I will allow you to consider yourself part of this council. But you must do what you can to prove your allegiance."

Rein finally pushed herself to stand, now that she was healed, and she walked over to Ana, glancing at Traith. "I'm going to have your last name," Rein said to her, smiling and feeling her ring. "I want to know you. I trust you now, Ana." As Ana gazed at her, Rein turned her stare over to Mistress. "Now if you all would be so kind as to excuse me, I have a blind man and a human sister to attend to."

Rein held out her hand for Taverin to come, and she held Traith close to her. As Ana backed from his hold slowly, Rein saw how hard she was crying. Traith sighed; he heard and felt her pain.

"Soon, Ana," he murmured.

"Please, Traith, let me come with you," she cried.

"Give me a little time, Ana," he whispered miserably. "Then you can. I've missed you so much, but I'm so... since I remembered... I can't be near you yet, I can't..."

"I did horrible things, too, Traith, to you! And—"

"Because you were scared of me."

"No, I—please!"

The next thing Rein saw was the inside of her home, and only she, Taverin, and Traith stood there.

chapter 80

t he calmness of the last month should've been unsettling. Although the All Hallows Eve Ball had been over and the Mardinial Council gone for over a month, Rein still felt as though she should prepare for some sort of disaster. Something more. Something worse than what had happened already. Just…something.

But the last month had been silent.

She was beginning to let that peace engulf her, but every time she looked at Traith, she became unsettled once more.

He still couldn't see. To her disbelief, he was now willing to let her tend to him and help him do everyday things he couldn't, like getting his clothes and occasionally leading him around when he really needed her to. He joked about it usually, but it was obvious to both he and Rein that he was tremendously aggravated by it. He only let her help because he knew that his condition wasn't permanent. Up to ten years…He would have to get used to it, if only for a few years.

But he still hadn't been the same.

He, as well as she, had been thinking about their wedding.

Rein had her arms crossed and rubbed them while she stood in the stone doorway. The wind had picked up and blown through the opening she was standing in, making her cold. It was bitter that day, cloudy and ominous—late November. She watched as Traith's white, loose shirt and contrasting dark hair blew furiously to the side.

He had silently found his way out to the courtyard and sat still on the grass, one knee up. He wasn't facing her, but the rest of the yard, which was almost unending. And just as she was going to approach him, he picked up a small stone, charged it with fiery energy, and threw it at the horizon with all of his might. It sailed farther than Rein could see. Then after a few moments, she saw a tiny spark light up, so distant that it seemed acres away.

She finally walked down the stone steps, trying to drop her heels harder than usual so he could hear her coming. His head cocked at the break of silence.

"Are you upset again?" Rein asked as she walked into the yard and sat down beside him.

He tried not to act surprised when she touched his hand. He pulled it away. "I'm fine, Rein," he murmured, showing a bit of a smile. "I just feel like I'm going mad." He puffed out a breath of air. "I can't believe I'm saying this, but I dreadfully wish I had my vampire eyesight back."

She laughed softly. There was a pause, and Rein stared at his clouded eyes. They were searching, flitting back and forth trying to focus themselves, but it was useless. He would not look at her, but she could see the aggravation in his face.

"And it's only been a bloody month," he said. "Just a month—and not seeing your face…" He gripped the grass. "For too long, I haven't seen your beautiful face."

Rein had heard him mumble about what he'd felt before, but he didn't speak too often or too much about his feelings. It was such a shame—each time he began to recover from a tragedy, he was presented with a new aggravation. But if all went as well as was planned, this would be the last one for a long time.

"Well," she said softly. "My face is right here, and so am I. Pretend your eyes are closed and—"

"I can't pretend anymore," he said back. "I can't…and I want to marry you, Rein; I want you to be mine, and I feel like I've waited far too long. I felt like I couldn't marry you when I remembered what I had done to my parents," he choked up. "As if I were going to do it to you. But now I know we should've."

"That isn't entirely true," she said, touching his face. "So much was happening. We would've been rushing it, and it shouldn't be rushed."

"But now I can't wait." His voice sounded weaker than it had been before. "I can't wait for ten years."

She felt her lip trembling as she bit it. "But you could get your sight back in as little as one."

"As little?"

"This is just awful," she said, standing. "I don't want to wait, but I want you too *see* me. My dress, and everything."

He bent forward and held his face, smothering himself. "I *want* to see you, Rein, so badly that I fear I would give up anything else." He felt for her hand but she was now standing. "Did you get up?" he asked.

That was what he couldn't stand—needing someone else to guide him in everything. But Rein was at least partly relieved because it was only something physical ailing him, and nothing more psychological. He couldn't handle anymore mental stress, and neither could she.

"Yes," she said. "It's much too chilly out here and I'm not in the mood for the cold."

At that, he stood as well, wiping himself down. "Cold-blooded, you are."

She took his hand, and with that verification of placement he took her in his arms.

"What do you want to do, Rein?" he asked sincerely. "You decide. Neither decision will be comforting, but we must make one." He took a breath. "I want to marry you, Rein." The way he spoke made her want to cry. "I'll pretend if you can."

"I want to be yours, too," she said. "And I don't want to wait *years*."

He stroked her hair as he held her, and she felt him shudder. "Me either."

chapter 81

He was standing at the front of a little church, waiting for Rein to walk down the aisle. He could hear the sound of birds outside the church; detect the faint smell of the garden that surrounded it; feel the vibrations of any subtle movements in the aisle; see only blackness.

Then he heard the piano music sound from the side of the church. They were getting married with no guests except for Taverin, whose quiet outbursts of excitement gave him a feeling of exhilaration. He realized that Rein must've been walking toward him already.

But then, suddenly, he felt like he had fallen asleep. He could almost see her, as if he were dreaming. He could see her eyes sparkling and her hair tied back loosely. Her dress had a low-cut neckline, provocatively revealing the top of her breasts. Her thin waist called for his touch, and her elaborate dress hugged her every curve all the way down to the floor, with a long train behind it, soft folds and hangings enhancing its beauty. A lace veil covered her heavenly face.

Just when she got close enough for him to take it off...he could finally see her face...

Wait—

Was it a dream?

The minimum amount of time for his sight to return was an entire year, and it had only been a little more than a month.

A chill ran down his body because he swore he could see her figure. It couldn't be a dream...

Her hand touched his. He swore he was beginning to see it...

"Traith, your eyes are setting fire again," he heard her choke.

He felt himself smiling. He saw a blur of a smile and heard her laugh, and she grabbed him before the priest had had a chance to say anything. Her cheek touched his, and he felt tears on her skin.

He could see his wedding.

epilogue

It snowed that night, but he'd kept on walking. His half-gloved hands were gripped as tightly as they could be around the front of his long coat. He couldn't feel his fingers anymore; the wind was so bitter cold that all his extremities were completely numb. His steps were heavy in the snow, and although he had boots on, snow still managed to get down into them, freezing his feet even more. He heard a wolf's cry echo in the vast Romanian wilderness; *I, too, am mourning the loss of the leafy tree canopies that would give full cover from the icy rain and snow that now falls from the clouded January sky*, he thought, as if that were what the wolf cried for. The wildlife that lurked in the large forest seemed to be growing restless underneath the bareness of the icy trees. Restless, yes... hopefully not hungry.

He never really knew where he'd hidden away. Somewhere to get away from the death...really, suicide of his lover. The witnessing of it— seeing her thrust herself upon that piece of wooden rail—was torturous.

But he felt his heart begin to pound hard when thinking of it. It was the first time in his life he'd ever felt his heart beat.

He knew he had to be close, but if he wasn't, he knew he would die within hours. He was so cold; he knew frostbite had taken at least two of his fingers by then. He must hurry...

He tried to look ahead, but the mix of the ice and snow driving hard into his face made it painful to stare out. His long, dark hair was being driven back fiercely. He'd walked this far to find Traith. *Walked...*

Just as he fell deeper into the snow, he could see a dark, massive building yards ahead, beyond the trees and violent weather.

His icy lips curled slowly into a tiny smile.

Harker Manor. It stood large and wide, dark and foreboding. He knew Traith probably sat within the castle, reading or training.

He'd lived there with Traith once.

And he'd finally found it again.

acknowledgements

The first people I have to thank, and must mention, are my parents. Not only have they been my financial support, considering I'm too young to really put out money for promoting and publishing, but they've also always been my biggest fans, ever since I even began writing when I was old enough to pick up a pencil. I love them both more than words can say, and am completely grateful.

I also want to thank my grandparents, who were also a huge help financially and a great support.

Thanks to Sue Alcorn, who helped me get my foot into both the literary *publication* world and the literary *psychological* world, by giving constructive criticism and pointers, and teaching me things I would never have known otherwise.

Finally, I want to thank my closest, dearest friends, who cared about my writing even before it was put in print.

Thanks! My dream has come true because of you all.

Breinigsville, PA USA
07 December 2010

250817BV00001B/73/P